Acclaim

"There is something so sweet and poignant about V. Romas Burton's writing. *Justified* is a beautiful story of bravery, faith, and the bonds that so richly bind us to others along our journeys."
—CASEY L. BOND, bestselling author of *Where Oceans Burn*

"Picking up after the shocking events at the end of *Fortified*, *Justified* is a soulful, classic fantasy that delivers the unashamed biblical themes that I've come to expect from a V. Romas Burton book. While the overarching plot continues with beloved characters, this story also introduces new characters in a meaningful romance that will find a place in your heart. Once again I was left thrilled by the twist at the end and cannot wait to get my hands on the next book!"
—BRITTANY EDEN, bestselling and award-winning author of *Wishes* and *Hearts*

"A stunning sequel to *Fortified*!"
—AJ SKELLY, bestselling author of The Wolves of Rock Falls series and Magik Prep Academy series

"*Justified* is a story of finding light and love amidst tragedy and trauma. Anyone who has ever suffered can find hope in the characters of V. Romas Burton's book as they struggle to overcome past wrongs and hurts. Influenced by the Biblical story of Rahab, the themes of forgiveness and new life will resonate deeply within readers as Ben and Rae's fragile faith takes root.

A riveting tale of good vs evil, laced with a beautiful romance between two broken souls, Justified is a must-read for lovers of fantasy, heart, and adventure."
—CRYSTAL D. GRANT, bestselling author of *Shadowcast*

PRAISE FOR FORTIFIED

"*Fortified* is a riveting, beautifully-written adventure full of intrigue, betrayal, strife, and one woman with enough faith and bravery in her heart to face it all."
—CASEY L. BOND, author of *Where Oceans Burn*

"Burton's new book is filled with fast-paced action, her signature faith-based content with hard-hitting themes and characters you want to root for. The story of embracing faith and becoming confident in abilities and self is one that any young person will love. Humor, touching moments, wholesome friendships between young women of different backgrounds, political intrigue, and a burgeoning romance will keep you flipping pages and leave you impatient for the next book. Another fantastic tale, and one I'm eager to follow!"
—C. M. BANSCHBACH, award-winning author of *The Wolf Prince*

"For fans of empowered heroines, soulful themes, and gorgeous worldbuilding reminiscent of CJ Redwine, Morgan Busse, and Mary Weber, *Fortified* is the kind of pure romantic fantasy that will leave you swooning. Get ready to meet Devora, a young woman with powers the kingdom hates in a fight for her life, and the secretive hero we've all been waiting for, Captain Blake, who helps her survive and is the most appealing sort of strong, silent, military version of Mr. Darcy type. Political intrigue, unexpected friendships, and the ending—my heart! Read and see for yourself!"

—BRITTANY EDEN, author of the *Heartbooks* series

"The depth of this story just left me breathless. Action, romance, intrigue, and characters who linger long after the story is finished! I can't wait for the next installment in *The Legacy Chapters*!"

— AJ SKELLY, bestselling author of The Wolves of Rock Falls series and Magik Prep Academy series

"*Fortified* is an exciting tale of redemption, empathy, doubt and faith. The fast-paced fights and intriguing twists had my head spinning by the end. I'm left waiting on the edge of my seat for the next installment in this new series."

—TABITHA CAPLINGER, author of *The Wolf Queen* and The Chronicle of the Three series

"What a journey! *Fortified* kept me enthralled from the first page with its rich story world and intriguing twists and turns. Walking alongside Devora as she develops deep relationships, grows in strength and integrity, and triumphs over increasingly difficult circumstances was both emotional and so rewarding. Action, romance, humor, mystery--this book had everything I look for in a fabulous read and more! When can I snag Book Two??"

—LAURIE LUCKING, award-winning author of *Common*

"*Fortified* is a well-balanced, character driven story that will hit you in your sweet spot so you won't put it down! Prepare for unexpected twists, well-delivered humor, and an ingenious sub-thread that makes the story come together in the final moments of the climax. Burton's story is perfect for fans of CJ Redwine who are looking for clean YA fantasy with a meaningful message and deep character growth."

—LAURA ZIMMERMAN, award-winning author of *Keen*

"Romas Burton has a way of luring you into the world with enchanting prose and heart-pounding scenarios. *Fortified* kept me flipping pages to find out every one of the characters' secrets. It is a must read for fantasy fans who love a visceral experience with twists and turns around every corner."
—CANDICE PEDRAZA YAMNITZ, author of *Unbetrothed*

"With dazzling world building, strong female characters, epic battles, and all the swoon you could want... *Fortified* is the fantasy you need in your life right now!"
—Alison Morquecho, The Bookish Camper, Influencer and Book Reviewer

"A truly enthralling tale. Full of heart pounding moments, intriguing characters, and swords! I am eagerly (and impatiently) awaiting the next book."
—Aly Shaver, The Little Librarian, Influencer and Book Reviewer

JUSTIFIED

Other Books by V. Romas Burton

Heartmaker Trilogy
Heartmender
Heartbreaker
Heartrender

The Legacy Chapters
Fortified
Justified

THE LEGACY CHAPTERS
JUSTIFIED
Quill & Flame
PUBLISHING HOUSE
V. ROMAS BURTON

Quill & Flame
PUBLISHING HOUSE

Justified

Copyright ©2024 by V. Romas Burton

Published by Quill & Flame Publishing House, an imprint of Book Bash Media, LLC.

www.quillandflame.com

This is a work of fiction. Names, characters, and incidents are products of the author's imagination or are used ficticiously. Any similarity to actual people, living or dead, organizations, business establishments, and/or events is purely coincidental.

Cover design by Emilie Haney, www.EAHCreative.com

To anyone who has been told your past mistakes define you,
they don't.

Chapter One

Papi always said, "If the sun is shining, I will still have hope." But the day Papi was taken, the sky filled with smoke and ash. The sun no longer shone, and Rae lost all hope.

Since that day, Rae never saw the raw beauty of the sun's light again. Soon after King Atol ordered Yekel to be destroyed, Kadeshian troops easily marched through the citadel's broken walls and invaded. A thick veil of gray obscured Rae's vision of the sun as enemy soldiers led her to the Temple of Pahga. She didn't know then that it would be two years until she would rip the gray mesh off her face and replace it with a crimson scarf. One symbolized bondage, the other power.

Breathe, Rae told herself as she blinked through the scarlet mesh concealing her identity. Now wasn't the time to dredge up the past. Not when standing in the Fighter's Ring. She needed to focus.

"Come on, Burtow!" Jasper, the Keeper of the Coins, screamed. Spittle ran down his scraggly black beard as he waved his abacus in the air. The metal beads chinked with each jerky movement. "He's only a small lad."

Rae couldn't help but smirk. Her ruse of dressing like a man fooled every brute in the Dark Market. Some of the other men wore full face coverings like hers, but none chose a color as bold as red. Still, none of them knew who she was. Unfortunately, she remembered many of them.

"I bet my whole month's wages on you, Burtow," another man by the name of Kindling, shouted from outside the Fighter's Ring.

Idiots, Rae thought, readying her stance.

Burtow, a tall, brutish man with a mane of wheat-colored hair barked out a laugh. In a blink, he barreled toward her.

Rae released another cleansing breath.

First, thrust bladed palm into throat.

Burtow stopped in his tracks as Rae's palm, angled like a blade, pounded into his throat. He choked, then stumbled back a few paces.

Smack temples to disorient.

The crowd silenced as Rae's palms vibrated against Burtow's sweaty temples. The man grunted and tried to push her away but failed.

And for the finale, my specialty.

Taking a shallow breath, Rae spun around and buried her foot in Burtow's soft gut. As he bent forward, she thrust her palm into his chest and sent him flying onto his backside. Once he landed, she yanked the crimson cord from her waist and wrapped it around Burtow's thick neck. She had never killed anyone during these fights, and she never intended to. The cord was all for show, just another part of her act.

"That won't be necessary," Jasper growled, hatred gleaming in his beady black eyes. He hit a miniature gong with a mallet, indicating the end of the match.

Rae dropped Burtow's head from her grasp, allowing it to thud onto the dirt ground. She flung the cord back around her waist and faced Jasper, her leather-gloved palm stretched out.

Jasper gritted his crooked teeth before tallying the winnings on his abacus. Rae knew she was still an underdog in the Fighter's Ring, but over the past few months she had slowly climbed the ladder in the Dark Market's underground street fights, one match at a time.

The metal beads clashed against one another as Jasper cursed under his breath. He hated that this fighter, whom he didn't know, earned so much coin. This made Rae's unblemished record of victories all the more satisfying. Jasper deposited her winnings into a leather sack and dropped it into her palm.

Rae bounced the pouch in her hand. The weight was acceptable. Hopefully, it would be enough to pay for the freedom of another enslaved woman.

"Once again, the winner of our opening fight is the Crimson Cord," Jasper announced to the crowd.

A few men grinned, knowing their risk of betting on a rookie had paid off. But most scowled at her. They didn't like the mysterious man who appeared out of nowhere and took their coin.

They've taken so much more from me. Rae gripped the sack. She bowed to Jasper and exited the secret location without another word.

Rae kept her gloved fingers clasped tightly around the leather sack as she crept into the alleyway. It was well past midnight and thieves were notorious in the Dark Market, especially at this hour. Though her disguise convinced the gamblers she was a small man, she couldn't take any chances with one of the gangs.

Lifting to her toes, Rae sprinted through the narrow streets, making sure to double back and retrace her steps, just in case anyone tried following her. She wouldn't give the Street Rats or the Falcons the chance to take her hard-earned money. Not when every coin mattered so much.

After a few more cycles, Rae was convinced she was alone and dashed toward the outer wall of Yekel. The alleyways fanned out into a larger road where the rubble of houses stood just before the stone entrance. Rae clenched her teeth, remembering the grand homes her friends and neighbors once had before King Atol set their land ablaze. What kind of king would harm his own people?

Rae shook her head, wanting to rip off the crimson scarf tied around her face. After breathing in the smoke, *menta*, and sweat of the Dark Market, she would welcome a breath of clean air. But it would be unwise until she was alone. Her reputation had already been tarnished once. She wouldn't allow it to happen again.

A series of footsteps came from the left, so Rae slid into the nearest alleyway. She could defend herself easily, but tonight she wasn't in the mood. It had been four years, to the day, since Papi had been taken by King Atol's men. Four years since she helped Nadia and the other girls flee. Four years since she gave herself to General Yada to save the others and he punished her for her actions.

An involuntary shudder raced across Rae's skin as a squad of Kadeshian soldiers marched by. She cursed, thinking she'd barred herself from feeling fear.

I'll always be with you, the Beast of Fear whispered.

Rae held her breath until the bronze armor of the soldiers was out of sight. With all her senses on alert, Rae made sure to keep her gaze forward and ears open for anything suspicious. As she rounded the next corner, the Temple of Pahga came into view. Stark white marble columns gleamed in the moonlight. Rae shuddered at the sight of the temple's entrance with its intricate white archways and evil hidden behind them. She would never step foot in it again.

Squaring her shoulders, Rae jogged down the narrow dirt road until she eventually arrived at a small, makeshift village resting inside the outer wall. Peace eased her thundering heart as she gazed upon the homes of the only survivors of King Atol's raid and Kadesh's siege of Yekel.

Only fifty homes held what was left of the original citizens of Yekel. Unfortunately, those who King Atol didn't take, General Yada enslaved to reinforce Yekel's outer wall with hand-carved bricks.

Rae ducked behind a shattered cart and whistled the secret greeting, alerting Master Monham that she was a friend, not a Kadeshian. After a few agonizing moments, the familiar shuffle of the old potter's feet came to the slatted wooden gate. The gate was a small comfort to the Yekelians; the Kadeshians could easily stomp over it and take what they wanted. But, lately, General Yada's soldiers had been occupied with another battle against Tenton and had left the small number of Yekelians alone.

"Hiding your identity again, I see," came Master Monham's throaty voice.

Rae snorted before peeling the red scarf off her face. The crisp night air twirled around her cheeks, cooling her damp skin.

"No one needs to know who I am," she clipped, handing the sack to the potter. "Or what I do." She absentmindedly ran her hand over her sheared blonde hair, thankful she'd shaved it short as soon as she was free of the Temple. Since then, she had cut the white-blonde strands every other week.

The old man sighed and stroked his thinning gray beard but closed his fingers around the sack. "You don't need to give all your earnings, Rae. We'll free the others. Somehow. Tunri will provide."

Rae snorted and pushed past Master Monham, trying to ignore how bent his shoulders had become with the hard labor General Yada required of the males. She hated the general and everything he'd done to her and her people.

"I don't need your god's help," Rae replied over her shoulder. "*I* will bleed those Kadeshian men dry of every ounce of coin they have." She stalked toward the splintered wooden door at the end of the row.

Yes, bleed them all, the Beast of Rage huffed.

"Rae, wait," Master Monham called, hobbling to catch up with her.

Rae stopped but didn't turn around. The potter was a kind man, but she didn't want anything to do with his faulty religion or absent god. She'd already been abused by one deity and wouldn't allow it to happen again.

Master Monham gently grasped her gloved palm and placed the leather sack into it. Rae spun around to protest, but the weathered man held up his gnarled hand.

"You've saved many women with your earnings. I want you to keep this to prove what Tunri can do if we only have faith."

The fury boiling in her chest dulled as she looked into the old man's green eyes. Though his body was weary and worn, his gaze was alive with defiance and hope. Something most of the Yekelians had lost years ago.

Rae nodded stiffly and tied the sack to her belt. She was too tired and sore to argue with Master Monham about his god. Maybe tomorrow, when they went to market, she would convince him to take the coin and gain freedom for another trapped woman.

"Trust Tunri," Master Monham called as Rae continued toward the crooked door of her home. "He will provide."

Rae lifted her hand in acknowledgment but kept her back facing the potter until she knew he had shuffled into his own home.

Releasing a breath, Rae reached to open her crooked door then paused. The door was already askew. Her heart jumped to her throat as she fisted the cord around her waist.

Has one of the gangs from the Dark Market found me? Has Jasper discovered who I really am?

Quickly, Rae wrapped the red mesh back around the entirety of her face and head, making sure her true identity was concealed before she crept through the door. The musky scents from the Dark Market lingered on the thin scarlet fabric. Keeping her breaths shallow, Rae silently crept along the dirt floor.

The moonlight shone upon large scuff marks in the dirt. Whoever was here wanted to be found.

A match suddenly lit up in the far corner of the room, illuminating her small, squared living area in an amber glow. Rae trained her body not to jerk at the surprise. Her enemies always enjoyed frightened prey. She wouldn't give them that satisfaction.

Yet as she faced her intruder, she couldn't stop the fear billowing in her chest.

What is he *doing here?* The Beast of Fear cried.

The soft light of a candle grew, revealing the soulless dark eyes and sleek black hair of General Yada.

Chapter Two

Rae swallowed her terror, hating that the presence of General Yada still caused her lungs to constrict with panic.

Flee or Fight? Flee or Fight? the Beast of Fear taunted.

General Yada sat poised on one of Rae's two wooden chairs. Folding one long leg over the other, he placed the flickering candle on the low rectangular table before him. A ghost of a smile lined his thin lips as he took in her street-fighting attire.

"The Temple dresses were far more flattering on you, my dear," General Yada crooned.

Rae subtly looked for something she could use as a weapon. "What do you want?"

Sighing, General Yada stood to his full height and dusted off his pristine brown military uniform. The Kadeshian crest of two interlocking circles with a sparrow in the front gleamed in the candlelight. She had seen the insignia so many times, it was burned into her memory. Rae glared at the three bronze cords around the general's shoulder, indicating his rank in Kadesh's army.

"Still hate me?" General Yada smirked, transforming his tanned angular features into something playful yet sinister.

The general used to drone on about his past love affairs and about how so many women desired him. But not Rae. She hated him. And that's why he wanted her.

"What do you want?" Rae ground out again, gripping the red cord around her waist, ready to wield it if he came closer. Thankfully, he kept his distance.

"Right down to business, as always." General Yada frowned then pulled a scroll from his belt. He tossed it to Rae who let it fall to the ground at her feet. If the general was annoyed, he didn't show it. "As you may have heard, we recently lost General Sage at the Battle of Edo. The cause of his death is unclear, but regardless, he's gone."

General Yada strode to Rae, much like he had many times in the past. But she wouldn't cower this time. She was no longer anyone's property. Lifting her chin, Rae stared into the general's emotionless dark eyes, refusing to back down.

"You don't need to hide from me."

He started to reach for the red mesh scarf still around her face when she slapped his hand away and grabbed his arm. Bending General Yada's wrist toward him, Rae locked her fingers around the pressure point at his elbow and squeezed. General Yada gasped and wrenched his arm away. With a curse, he stepped back.

"Don't touch me," Rae growled. "You no longer own me."

General Yada rubbed his arm with a scowl, but his devilish smile returned as he fixed his mussed hair. "I'm going to forgive that outburst," he replied coldly, gesturing to the scroll on the floor. "It's rumored that a Seer escaped from the Fortress, Tenton's prison. With your job in the market, I want you to find out what the other merchants and people have heard." He waved to the red scarf with a look of disgust. "You can question those brutes in the Dark Market, as well."

Rae sneered. "Why would I do anything for you?"

A genuine look of hurt crossed his face before he masked it. "Did I forget to mention my leverage?" He snapped his fingers, and two soldiers in bronze armor stepped out from the dark corners of Rae's home next to the general.

Rae couldn't stifle her gasp. *Have they been here this whole time? How could I have not noticed them?*

You're not as safe as you thought you were, the Beast of Fear whispered.

Rae's throat dried. Blindfolded and gagged, a young woman struggled against the soldiers' grasps. The Kadeshian soldiers forced the girl to her knees. Rae focused on the flailing woman, recognizing the bright yellow hair all too well.

"Nadia!" Rae cried, rushing toward her bound and gagged friend.

General Yada's soldiers immediately whipped out their knives and held them to Nadia's neck, stopping Rae in her tracks. Nadia lifted her chin, allowing Rae to see that fabric had also been stuffed in her ears. She couldn't hear any of this conversation and was unaware that Rae was even there.

Why is she back here? Everything Rae suffered was to keep Nadia and the others safe.

Everything you sacrificed was all a waste. It meant nothing. You are nothing, the Beast of Fear sang.

Nadia scrunched her nose before attempting to speak muffled words. The Kadeshian soldier on the left shoved Nadia in the shoulder.

Rae clenched her jaw, wanting to tear the soldier apart, limb from limb.

"You will do this, Rae," General Yada demanded. He ran a hand through Nadia's short hair. Rae remembered shearing Nadia's yellow hair short, four years prior. Now it was past her ears. Nadia jerked away and Rae was thankful to see her friend still held the same fire.

"Find the information I seek," the general demanded. "Or else your time in the Temple and your secret identity in the Dark Market will be revealed, *and* this one will become my new pet."

"No!" Rae cried, unable to control the outburst.

She had done everything in her power to keep the past hidden and her alter ego to the shadows. She couldn't allow General Yada to take away what little control she had. And she would never allow him to touch Nadia. Yet, Rae's thoughts succumbed to General Yada's words. Like they always had. After all this time, his spun words and threats still caged her.

The general quirked a brow but smirked, knowing he already won.

Rae thinned her lips, fisting her hands at her sides. "I'll find the information you seek . . . but I want something in return."

General Yada frowned. Rae never asked for compensation before and her heart almost burst in her chest when the general responded, "I'm listening."

Finding her courage, she replied, "If I do this for you, no harm can come to Nadia and—" Rae paused. Did she dare to ask for more?

Remember the last time you stood up to the general, the Beast of Fear reminded her. The glowing eyes of the imperial opal statue in the Temple slammed into her thoughts, and Rae shuddered. The last time she stood her ground, the punishment was severe.

Swallowing her fear, Rae continued, "And you must grant freedom to the other women—the other Priestesses, as you call them—in the Temple. And to me. You must allow us all to leave Yekel safely."

General Yada straightened his stance. Although he wasn't a large man, like some of the others Rae endured, he still stood taller than her and had wide, pointed shoulders. She had never feared any man more than she feared the general. Clasping his toned arms behind his back, Genearl Yada lifted his sharp chin.

After a few agonizing moments, he finally replied, "The Priestesses stay and so will you. But, to show my benevolence, I'll release your friend."

With a snap of General Yada's fingers, the soldiers carrying Nadia threw her to the ground and melded back into the darkness.

"You have one week, Rae. Or all your secrets will be known."

Lifting his hand, General Yada traced Rae's cheek. Despite being thankful that the scarlet mesh protected her skin from his touch, she jerked her head away from him..

A week wasn't enough time to gain information. She had to haggle for more time. "Two. Give me two weeks."

A glimmer of interest and excitement flashed in General Yada's greedy eyes. "What will you give me in return?"

Dread slithered through Rae's gut as she forced herself not to remember the general's wandering hands. She swallowed as she fisted the heavy sack of coins on her belt from her winnings in the Fighter's Ring. Untying the leather pouch, she flung it at his feet. "That should be enough."

General Yada quirked a brow at the bag. "I have no need for your tainted coin. But how about you visit me in the Temple instead."

Rae's insides twisted, her stomach threatening to lurch out of her throat. "No, never."

The general opened his mouth to respond when he paused. He titled his head to the side, as if someone were speaking in his ear.

Rae's heart almost burst through her chest when General Yada replied, "Two weeks, Rae. And don't bother trying anything sneaky. You know I have eyes everywhere." Lifting his hand, he snuffed out the candlelight, cloaking the room in darkness.

Pulse roaring, Rae scrambled to find a match and candle. She struck a match on the side of her boot. The small flame assisted her in finding the candle General Yada dropped on the table. Rae quickly lit the candle, along with the oil lamps she kept in the windows. As soon as her home brightened, she turned to find Nadia slumped on the floor. All traces of General Yada and his men were gone.

Ripping the red mesh off of her face, Rae hid it and the crimson cord in her pockets then hurried toward her friend. She stomped over the scroll the general left as she untied Nadia's blindfold and bonds. Nadia blinked wildly before scrubbing her tongue on the back of her hand, ridding her mouth of the taste of the gag.

Rae grabbed Nadia's shoulders. "Are you okay, Nadi? What are you doing back in Yekel?"

"Rae, you're alive!" Nadia cried, taking the fabric out of her ears before wrapping her arms around Rae's neck. "I was meant to sneak in undetected, and they caught me right away. This was my first mission, and I already failed."

Rae stiffened at the hug, gently pushing Nadia away. "Slow down. Of course, I'm alive. But what are you doing here? I thought I told you to never come back to Yekel."

Rae would never forget the day she smuggled Nadia and the other girls out on a cart headed toward the countryside, knowing they'd be safe if they could flee the city. For reasons unknown to Rae, Kadesh only wanted the city of Yekel and ceased their attack as soon as it was taken.

Nadia wiped the tears building in her eyes. Sand and sweat matted her light brown tunic and dark pants. Clumps of mud and leaves gathered on Nadia's boots, and a smattering of twigs stuck in her hair.

"Why did you walk through the jungle to get here?" Rae asked, her throat tight with worry. The thick tropical jungles of Grenly were filled with wild animals, hunting for their next prey. Though the jungle stretched to the edge of Yekel's rolling dirt hills, the journey was treacherous. What was Nadia doing?

"I was sent here by Warden Hazor," Nadia replied, reaching into her pocket. When she pulled her trembling fingers back out, she rotated a thin piece of charcoal between them. "He told me to go a roundabout way so I wouldn't get caught." Nadia rolled her eyes. "Look how well that worked out. This was my first mission of espionage. I told the warden I wasn't good at being quiet, but he said I was to come here anyway." Nadia bit her lip to prevent her tears from falling.

"Hey," Rae soothed, wanting to reach out toward her friend but found her hands plastered at her sides. "It'll be okay. At least, you weren't arrested."

Or worse.

Nadia shook her head, but instead of speaking, she pulled out a small notebook and began writing.

Rae's lips tipped up. "You still have that?"

Nadia kept her brows furrowed as she focused on the page. "Yes. I would never get rid of it. You made it for me, remember?" She flipped the pages of the notebook toward Rae. Countless images of inventions and quickly scratched ideas flashed before Rae's eyes.

The gifted Tinker is back! Squawked the Beast of Envy. *You have no gift. You weren't chosen.*

Rae buried the thought away. "You said Warden Hazor, as in the warden of the Fortress, sent you?"

Nadia nodded.

"Nadia, what were you doing there?"

Nadia blinked at Rae. "You haven't heard how King Atol changed the Categorizations?"

"What?" Rae gasped, sitting on one of her wooden chairs.

Nadia ran a hand through her short hair and sat in the other chair. "Those who categorized the stones for Vlacklear were sent to the Fortress to become soldiers."

"That's absurd!" Rae replied, her anger rising. "Why would he do that?"

Your sacrifice was for nothing, the Beast of Rage barked, laughing at her. *You got them out of Yekel, but the Categorization*

Call didn't give them a better life, like you thought it would. Who knows what horrors Nadia and the others suffered?

It's time for revenge.

Fury simmered in Rae's chest. When she sacrificed herself for the others, she told them to flee, knowing that when their Categorization Calls came, it would give them better futures. Futures far from General Yada and his brothel.

But instead, Nadia was sent to a prison filled with thieves and murderous men.

How did Nadia survive? Were the others sent to the Fortress, as well?

"Was it all the Categories, or just Vlacklear? Are the others okay?"

Nadia placed the charcoal behind her ear, looking more like the carefree girl Rae remembered. "As far as I know, if they didn't categorize for Vlacklear, they're still in Kopet."

Rae breathed a sigh of relief. Kopet was a village in the countryside, closer to the western region of Tenton than Yekel. The others were still safe.

She glanced over at Nadia. Nadia had matured quite a bit from her young age of twelve summers. No longer was she wiry and awkward but had grown into a young woman. And that's what scared Rae the most.

"But *you* categorized for Vlacklear?"

Nadia nodded. "I didn't even get a chance to say good-bye to the others before the guards sedated me and brought me to the Fortress."

Rae choked. "They what?"

"I found out later that other citadels had uprisings about the Categorization changes. By the time the King's Categorizer made it to Kopet, Tenton's soldiers didn't want any more trouble."

Rae seethed, hating the cursed kingdom she lived in more and more. "I'm so sorry, Nadia. But if you're getting special missions from the warden, you must have done something right."

Nadia stood from the chair and paced the room. "Not me. It was Dev. She's the best soldier in Tenton, and now she's gone, too." Nadia stopped, ran her hands through her hair again, and sucked in a few breaths, as if trying to hold back more tears. "Warden Hazor said Dev was smart and would be okay, but I don't know. I heard some rumors as I traveled from the Fortress, but they can't be true."

Rae had never seen Nadia, her little Nadi, so distraught. Nadia was always so happy and free. Because Nadia was younger, Rae always watched over her when Nadia's parents went to invent. Nadia's parents, like Papi, had been blessed by Tunri with the Tinkering gift, as well.

"I'm sorry, Nadia," Rae repeated, unsure of what else to say.

But Nadia wasn't listening. She found the scroll General Yada gave to Rae. Shock and horror covered her muddied face.

"Nadi? What is it?"

"How could this have happened?" Nadia exclaimed, her eyes scanning the scroll. "The only reason Tenton won the Battle of Edo and rescued Princess Haden is because of Devora..."

Rae frowned. "Is that your friend—"

"This can't be right . . . " Nadia flipped the crumpled parchment around to reveal a black and white sketch of a girl a few years younger than Rae. She had dark hair and big eyes. Beneath her name were the words: WANTED FOR TREASON.

Rae narrowed her eyes at the king's seal at the bottom of the page. Why would King Atol order the arrest of a war hero? Or was Nadia mistaken about the girl?

But as Rae continued reading, she paused, her heart stopping. Under the name DEVORA MEDEE was the label of SEER.

Chapter Three

Rae, Rae's House, Yekel

Rae snatched the scroll from Nadia's hand. Could the information she needed to free all the women in the Temple and escape Yekel have just fallen in her lap?

Rae spun to Nadia. "You know this girl?"

Nadia nodded fervently. "That's Dev, who I was talking about before. I tried to find her when we returned to the Fortress after the Battle of Edo, but the warden sent for me right away. He said there was an important undercover mission for me." Nadia waved her hand in the air then pouted. "I didn't even get to go to the ball in Dev's honor."

"That's probably a good thing," Rae murmured, forming a plan as she read the scroll again. "Something must have happened there for her to be a fugitive now."

Rae pursed her lips. If Nadia knew this prophet, she could lure her to Yekel. The Seer was obviously on the run and would need somewhere to hide. Once she was here, Rae could capture her and hand her over to General Yada. She wouldn't just bring him information on the Seer, she would bring him the Seer, herself. Then the general couldn't refuse to set the women in the Temple, and her, free. Nadia would be safe, the enslaved women would be free, and Rae would never set foot in Yekel again.

A pang of guilt twisted in Rae's chest, but she smothered the feeling. It was a cruel future for the Seer, but life was cruel. The women in the Temple had suffered enough under the general and Kadesh's rule. It was Rae's job to set them free.

Rolling up the scroll, Rae tucked it into her pocket. "Do you know where your friend is now?" she asked nonchalantly as she grabbed an oil lamp. She headed to the small kitchen at the back of her home.

A musty smell lingered in the place where she set the lamp on a tall, square table and prepared a platter of dried fruit and meat for Nadia and herself. She was quite famished after her fight in the Dark Market.

I need to convince Nadia to try to contact the Seer.

Rae wouldn't be able to smuggle Nadia out, but the Dark Market had ways to send messages in and out of Yekel. If Nadia invited the Seer here, Rae's plan would unfold nicely.

"The last time I saw her, she was riding her giant elk-thing back to the Fortress," Nadia called from the front room. "After that, I was sent away. We had other friends, as well. Who knows where they are now?"

Rae scrunched her brows. *A giant elk?* She'd never heard of such a creature. But, then again, she'd been locked away in the Temple of Pahga for two years, then kept a low profile the past two since then. The horrifying memories of those two years in the Temple—the things she'd seen, been subjected to—tried to squirm into her thoughts but Rae shoved them away. That was the past. She was no longer a slave.

Lifting the stone tray, Rae strode back into her main room and set the platter before Nadia. Nadia relaxed into a wooden chair as she scribbled in her notebook. Brief glimpses of the young girl Rae knew appeared as Nadia glanced up from the pages with a small grin.

"Please, eat," she offered, trying her best not to wince as Nadia looked up at her with genuine admiration in her eyes.

If she knew why you saved her from being sent to the Temple, what really happens there, she wouldn't think so highly of us, the Beast of Fear tittered.

Rae had always wanted a little sister. She remembered Mami and Papi discussing it, but after that, her memories were blurry and obscured. Rae wasn't sure why she couldn't remember, but when Nadia came into her life, Rae decided she would take her as her own sibling.

But when King Atol ordered Yekel's top Tinkers to be taken, including Rae's father and Nadia's parents, Nadia, Rae and Rae's mother were left to fend for themselves. It was only a few months later when Kadesh struck. Rae was thankful Nadia and the others were still young enough that she could disguise them as boys and send them to the outskirts of Yekel.

Rae blinked the memories of smoke and pain away and mustered up a smile. "You are welcome to stay here as long as you need."

"Thank you, Rae," Nadia sighed with relief. She plucked a dried date and popped it into her mouth.

Rae nodded and went back to the kitchen to retrieve a pitcher of water and two clay cups. When she returned, she placed them on her low rectangular table and began filling the cups.

"So, you were sent here on a covert mission?" Rae asked, trying to think of a different way to gain information about the Seer.

If General Yada knew this, why did he let Nadia go so easily? There has to be more.

"Mhmm," Nadia replied, chomping on a piece of dried meat as she took her *ligula* and a thick stick from her pocket.

With a press of the button, the knife flicked out, and Nadia began whittling the wood. Rae smiled, remembering all the fun inventions Nadia created and tested when they were young. Recalling all the suggestions Rae gave to improve the design, she couldn't believe the *ligula* still worked after all this time.

You weren't chosen, the Beast of Envy hissed. *You have no gift.*

"Warden Hazor mentioned something about infiltrating the Temple of Pahga," Nadia added. "There's a giant statue in there or something?" Nadia shrugged. "He was discreet with the details."

"What?" Rae's throat constricted as the water she was pouring spilled over the clay cup and onto the floor.

"Uh, you're still pouring." Nadia pointed to the overflowing cup.

Rae gasped and tilted the pitcher up, the floor now a mess of mud.

"Yeah, I don't really want to go back there either," Nadia said, absorbed in her whittling. "I remember it vaguely from when I'd bring a harvest sacrifice to Pahga, but my memories are a bit hazy now."

Rae spun around, placing a hand on her temple. Black dots lined her vision. Her heart pounded against her ribcage, threatening to burst. She couldn't allow Nadia to enter the Temple. She wouldn't allow her to see the horrors inside.

A memory seared into her thoughts, breaking through the boundaries she had placed. *Tall shining imperial opal. A statue. A swirling orb of light. Strings of light pulled from Rae's chest. Pain . . . so much pain. Ribbons of darkness wrapping around her soul, pinning it down, chaining her to evil.*

"Rae?" Nadia asked. "Are you all right?"

Rae blinked wildly. *Why would Warden Hazor want anyone to go inside the Temple? Is he a believer in Pahga?*

"Rae?" Nadia asked again before softly touching Rae's shoulder.

Rae whipped around, the pitcher of water flying as she tried to grab Nadia's wrist. So many times she had been tossed around with the power to do nothing. Now, when anyone approached her too quickly, Rae reacted swiftly. Thankfully Nadia was already there, blocking the attack. The clay pitcher shattered against the wall, breaking into a few large pieces as Rae panted, staring at Nadia with wide eyes.

A cold sweat dripped down Rae's neck, her chest heaving as she stared into her friend's concerned gaze.

"Rae," Nadia breathed, her chocolate eyes analyzing Rae's face. "What happened to you?"

Rae backed up and ran a hand over her sheared hair, trying to shrug off her panic.

"Nothing." She added a weak smile a bit too late. "Nothing, Nadia. Don't worry about me."

"But—"

"I don't think it's wise for you to go to the Temple." Rae strode toward the broken pieces of pottery, hating that she reacted so violently. She hadn't experienced an episode in months. Hopefully, Master Monham could craft her another pitcher.

"Since Kadesh came, a lot of things have changed. General Yada changed the rules of the Temple of Pahga. There are still sacrifices, as well as other ceremonies performed in the Temple." Rae kept her back to Nadia, not able to meet her friend's probing gaze.

A long pause stretched between them before Nadia asked, "What kind of ceremonies?"

Rae shrugged as she collected more shards of pottery. The less Nadia knew, the better. "Tomorrow is market day. I'll be selling my fabrics. Come with me and Master Monham can answer more of your questions. We can work on a plan to get you out of here. Maybe we can also find out more information about your Seer friend, too."

When Rae finally gathered enough courage, she stood and faced Nadia. The last time Rae had seen Nadia, the girl barely stood at Rae's shoulders. Now, Nadia could look Rae straight in the eye. Rae schooled her features. Lying to Nadia was the only way to save her life. If Rae told Nadia about what General

Yada had done, Nadia would want to fight the general himself. And General Yada would pounce at the opportunity to take another woman for his Temple brothel. Rae'd seen General Yada's lecherous look far too many times to trust him. He would wait the two weeks, Rae was sure of that. But it was the one moment past the two week mark that worried Rae.

"Stay the night and come with me to the market in the morning," Rae repeated. "There, we should be able to find out more information about your Seer friend and the Temple."

Rae didn't give Nadia a chance to refuse before she offered her blankets and pillows, then excused herself for the night.

As she lay on the thin cot that made her bed, Rae fixed her gaze upon the swath of fabric covering the door to her rooftop. Memories from the Temple poked and prodded her mind, but she refused to let them in. She would never go back. Nadia had to get the Seer to Yekel. Delivering the Seer to General Yada was the only hope she had of leaving this wretched place for good.

As soon as the sun rose the next morning, Rae rolled out of bed and dressed in her usual market attire: a long black skirt, billowing white shirt, tan apron, and a bright blue scarf tied around her short blonde hair. It was a modest outfit, but Rae didn't want to draw any more attention to herself than necessary. The blue scarf was bold, but she'd learned that modeling her wears increased her profits exponentially.

The scroll with the Seer's information sat on the edge of Rae's bed with General Yada's seal on it. Rae scooped it up and tucked it into her apron. It may be useful later on.

Once she collected her dyed fabrics into a wicker basket and grabbed an extra set of clothes for Nadia, Rae headed to the main living area where Nadia had spent the night.

"You look great!" Nadia grinned with a smile. It seemed a good night of sleep was enough to revive and transform Nadia back into her easy-going self. Nadia started to reach toward the scarf but pulled back. "Did you make that yourself? It's stunning."

Rae hid her grimace behind a smile, wishing she hadn't reacted so frantic when Nadia touched her shoulder last night. "Yes, I used Mami's old recipe for dying all types of fabrics. Everything sells well but my scarves are the most popular. Here—" She handed Nadia a flowing white shirt and dark skirt. "I know you hate skirts, but you'll blend in more easily if you wear it. You can change in my room if you like."

Nadia scrunched her nose at the clothes but took them albeit grudgingly. She hurried to Rae's bedroom. Within a few moments, Nadia returned, looking the picture of a lady, even with her shorter hair.

She's beautiful, and *Tunri blessed her,* the Beast of Envy whispered.

Rae rummaged through the basket and pulled out a long head scarf in a beaming canary yellow. "You can wear this so the soldiers know you're with me."

Grinning, Nadia gasped and snatched the yellow scarf out of Rae's hand. "I love this color." In one swoop, she wrapped it around her neck and head.

Silence like a thick blanket surrounded Rae and Nadia as they headed from the outer wall of Yekel to the inner city. Piles of rubble and stone stretched alongside the wide dirt road where buildings, shops, and homes used to stand. Though the destroyed structures looked to be abandoned, Rae knew they held some of the citadel's deadliest gangs. Thankfully, their members rarely came out during the daytime.

"It's gotten worse," Nadia whispered, her round eyes taking in dilapidated buildings.

Rae adjusted the basket on her hip and nodded. "Yekel is only a shadow of the great citadel it used to be."

The dirt road rose at a steady incline until they reached the gates of the inner city. People bustled within the inner wall, readying their booths for market day. After Kadesh had taken control of Yekel, General Yada allowed the Yekelians one day a week to sell their wares in order to make some kind of living. Unfortunately, most of the coin was taxed and given back to Kadesh.

Rae tightened her grip on the basket, hating that she was forced to give her hard earned coin to the terrible country. The coin bag from her street fight winnings smacked against her thigh as she stepped toward the gates. Well, at least that coin was untaxed.

"Rae," she said, holding out a square piece of parchment. Every vendor was given an identification parchment so General Yada could keep track of their earnings. When she first applied for the documentation, she made sure not to give her full name. Kadesh had already taken so much from her, they couldn't have her name, too.

The tall Kadeshian soldier on the left mechanically took the parchment. His bronze armor glimmered in the early morning sun as he marked the paper with a piece of charcoal before noticing Nadia.

"This is my apprentice," Rae added, giving the soldier a shy grin. Though she hated playing the part, she knew how to do it all too well.

"Did the general approve this?" the guard asked, shooting Nadia a look that sent chills down Rae's spine.

Rae quickly stepped to the side to block his view of Nadia and held up the still rolled scroll with the Seer's warrant on it. "Is his seal not enough? Or should I tell him that you questioned his authority?"

The soldier diverted his gaze and handed the identification parchment back to Rae, his face paling. "His seal is satisfactory. Proceed."

The soldiers opened the gates and Rae breathed a sigh of relief. At least that was easy enough. Now she just had to keep every leering soldier away from Nadia for the rest of the day.

Nadia stayed close to Rae as they wove through the bustling market. Yekelians and Kadeshians intermingled with one another, peddling goods, and haggling prices.

They continued a bit further until they reached a wooden booth with a bright orange canopy, and Rae couldn't help but smile at it. She'd worked tirelessly to earn her small space, and she was proud. Placing her basket on the long rectangular table beneath the canopy, she ushered Nadia in, hoping her vendor neighbor hadn't seen them. But as a plume of purple-colored smoke blossomed before her booth, Rae knew it was too late.

"Ah, Rae, my darling! Have you brought customers for me to enchant today?" the Wizard Wankle said as he stepped out from the cloud of violet smoke. His gaudy dark blue turban matched his shimmering cloak.

Rae coughed and waved her hand, trying to disperse the fake magician's colored cloud.

"This is my new apprentice," Rae explained, trying to block Nadia while ushering her into the booth. "I expect you to respect her as you do me." Nadia was already drawing too much attention. And that was never a good thing.

"Of course," the Wizard Wankle said, twisting the end of his pointed black mustache with his fingers. "But if she ever wants to know her future, send her my way." He reached into his cloak and threw a handful of blue powder on the ground before running back into his tent.

Nadia snorted. "Who was that?"

Rae sighed, trying to wave the blue dust away from her booth. "The Wizard Wankle. He believes he's a prophet blessed by Pahga." Rae rolled her eyes. "He's not, but he won't bother us."

Nadia poked her head out of the booth and took another look at the Wizard Wankle's midnight colored tent before twisting her head to peer down the other side of the street. "Do you have any other interesting neighbors?"

Rae shook her head as she laid out her colored scarves. "Master Monham is on the other side. He's a potter and a good friend. He should be here soon, and then your questions will be answered."

Nadia nodded then went to inspect the back of Rae's booth.

Rae tried to ignore the simmering guilt that had taken root in her heart as she swept and prepared her booth for market day. Nadia and the Seer hadn't been through the horrors Rae endured. If they had, and knew what Rae was planning, they would know her actions were justified.

Chapter Four

"I'm not sure this is a good idea," One Shot muttered, his baritone voice low.

Devora shushed him as she peered around the corner of the tawny stone surrounding the citadel of Grenly. It was well past midnight and the guards on duty were just beginning to look drowsy.

Devora glanced at her tattered purple sash. The queen's handmaidens mended it after she'd won Regulus Protecti and was named the Defender of Tenton. Devora snorted at the title and how useless it was. Defender of Tenton or not, she couldn't wear her family's sash openly now that she was wanted for treason. With a sigh, Devora wrapped it around her wrist. "My Sight is leading us here first."

Before Warden Hazor freed her from Level Five of the Fortress, he explained to Devora that only a Seer could find another Seer. She didn't believe him until she actually started *searching* for Kanna Blake, Matthias' mother.

As soon as Devora fled the Fortress with Vinn, the giant elk-like creature she'd freed from the Fortress, and One Shot, her assassin friend the warden had also freed from the Fortress, she placed all her effort into looking for Kanna first. Initially, Devora didn't know whether to search for the Seer or the princess. Both were equally important. But once she sought wisdom from Tunri, He directed her toward finding Kanna first. Once Kanna was found, Devora would then focus on finding

Princess Haden. Whenever Devora closed her eyes and thought of Kanna, a purple stream of light flooded her Sight—leading straight to Grenly.

"Plus," Devora added in a hushed tone, "You've seen the king's announcement."

One Shot grunted as he checked the arrows on his crossbow.

They had been riding for three days to get to Grenly. Poor Vinn barely had a few moments of rest before they were on his back again, racing to flee the palace soldiers tailing them until a day ago. Only a few hours after they left the Fortress, the news of her and One Shot's "treason" burned through the kingdom and northern villages. Devora thought about the wanted posters. King Atol must have used magic in order to get their faces plastered throughout all the cities in Tenton already.

The young guard pacing in front of the iron-wrought gate surrounding Grenly yawned loudly. His shining silver armor screeched as he stretched his arms above his head. It was almost time.

Devora slunk back into the shadows with One Shot, pulling her dark cloak down to cover her face. No doubt her violet Seer eyes would catch the light of the moon. Thankfully, the warden packed her and One Shot additional clothes. Devora couldn't imagine traveling in the beautiful scarlet gown she'd worn to the ball at Maldove Palace.

Devora ran her hands over her pants, remembering when Matthias gave them to her. And the look of sheer torment clouding his eyes when he betrayed her to the king. Fury coursed through her at the memory, but she still missed him. Conflicting feelings of love and hate swirled through her like oil and water, always meeting but never intertwining.

Shaking her head, Devora tried to rid her mind of Matthias. She didn't know when she'd see him again. *If* she'd ever see him again. Especially if King Atol had anything to say about it.

The young guard yawned again and scratched his chin. He was barely sixteen summers and was already stationed as Grenly's first line of defense against intruders, which made her plan all the more perfect.

"When I signal, you know what to do," she whispered to One Shot who gave a prompt nod then disappeared into the jungle trees.

Thankfully, the jungles of Grenly were thick and lush enough to hide Vinn while Devora and One Shot gathered supplies and information on Kanna's whereabouts. When Devora explained the plan to the giant elk-like creature, he wasn't upset to have some time alone.

Crouching, Devora fisted a smooth gray stone in her palm before launching it as far away from the gate as possible. It cracked against a tree adjacent to the far wall. The guard's slumped posture immediately snapped straight.

He gripped his hands around the mech still sheathed on his belt. "Who goes there?"

Devora waited a moment before flinging the next stone a smidge closer to where she was hiding in the trees.

The guard tensed, fear visibly crawling across his youthful features as he shakily unsheathed his mech.

"Show yourself!" he barked, his voice wavering. He swished the mech back and forth.

Devora clucked her tongue. *His form is terrible. Matthias would be horrified.*

The young soldier swung the mech a few more times, slicing nothing but the humid night air.

If Devora hadn't unfairly been named a fugitive and been sent running for her life, she would've felt bad for scaring the young soldier. But she *was* a fugitive *and* was running for her life, so she hurled the last stone. As soon as it smacked against the hard ground, an arrow embedded itself in the wall next to the guard's head. And that was all it took.

The guard shrieked, dropping his mech as he clamored toward the gate. "Intruders! Intruders! Open up!" He grasped the iron bars, pulling with both fists.

The clanking of chains echoed through the trees as the gate opened. Devora grinned. Fear was always the best distraction.

She waited until a squad of soldiers marched through the gates, searching the surrounding trees, before she slipped through undetected. Breathing a sigh of relief, Devora spun around to find One Shot waiting for her as planned.

"Nice shot, as always," she complimented. "Come on."

When they first arrived in Grenly, Devora searched for the familiar vine she used when meeting Tristan beyond the outer wall. But upon investigation, she discovered that all the vines and limbs hanging over the wall into Grenly had been sheared. Either it was a coincidence, or the king had been spying on her. Devora guessed it was the latter. He didn't want her to return home.

Luckily, her years of studying war and battle tactics proved an advantage in this situation. During the Battle of Mongo, a port south of Yekel, Tenton soldiers used fear to outwit the Kadeshians. Knowing the Kadeshians were a superstitious people, Tenton's soldiers placed warning sigils around the Kadeshian camp, leading them to believe they were from one of their gods.

The generals of Kadesh's army were up all night, trying to calm their skittish soldiers, who did not wish to displease the gods. And that was when Tenton struck, annihilating Kadesh and seizing the Mongo port.

Devora and One Shot slinked against the outer wall, stopping every few feet. Now that attention was on the gate, more soldiers spilled out into the main street. Devora ducked into an alleyway. Even with the slight limp from his injury in the Battle of Edo, One Shot followed close behind.

Marching steps rushed by the alleyway, and the soldiers' armor shimmered against the midnight moon.

Why are there so many soldiers here?

Devora never remembered there being so many of His Majesty's Army in Grenly. A few for security reasons, but nothing like the rows of soldiers she witnessed. Something was up and it wasn't good.

Devora closed her eyes and searched through her Sight. The stream of purple light spun and wound through the city of Grenly, stopping at the governor's mansion.

Opening her eyes, Devora stared into the dark. Papa had been the Governor of Grenly for at least twenty years. If Kanna came to the governor's home, Devora would've known about it.

So why is my Sight and Tunri leading me home?

"Almost there," she whispered to One Shot, who nodded. Though he was almost the size of a giant, Devora was thankful that he was quieter than a mouse.

Holding her breath, she raced out of the alleyway, knowing One Shot was right behind. Just ahead stood her home, the window to her room facing the outer wall, its shutters opened to let in the night breeze.

Devora slowed her steps, then chuckled to herself. *So that's why there are so many guards.*

King Atol assumed she would come here first and planned to trap her. And although he was correct in his assumptions, Devora wasn't as naive as the king perceived.

Earlier that day, Devora and One Shot overheard the soldiers outside the wall complaining about having to make sure Governor Medee's home had extra guards posted around it. Devora and One Shot eavesdropped on the guards long enough to know their shifts changed every three hours. And, if she had calculated correctly, the guard shift change would happen in three...two...one...

Devora watched her home in amazement as a slew of guards rotated from around the corner of the governor's mansion.

Thank Tunri that she and One Shot waited and observed before diving headfirst into the house.

"Now's our chance."

As the old guards marched away from the governor's mansion, they stopped before the replacement soldiers and gave their report. When the guards continued conversing with each other and weren't paying attention to their surroundings, Devora and One Shot dashed toward the house. They didn't head toward the open window, though that would make this task easier. Instead, they ran around the side of the house where the servants' door to the cellar was located.

Please let this work, Devora prayed as she clutched the cool metal handle.

Licking her lips, she pulled the handle, and the door opened.

"That was lucky," One Shot commented, frowning at the open door.

"Extremely lucky," Devora responded and disappeared into the dark cellar with One Shot two steps behind.

They quieted their steps as Devora tried to remember the cellar's layout. She hadn't been in the cool, dark basement since she was a child. When her gift was discovered and she was confined to the house, she'd played down here all the time. To her, it seemed, the servants were her only friends.

Though, as she got older, she distanced herself from them, believing she was superior. Pain twinged in Devora's chest at the memory. All the servants in her home cared for her, made her awful dung tea, and kept her secret. They could've easily reported her to the kingdom, but they didn't. And how did she repay them? By being a spoiled brat.

"Which way?" One Shot whispered, his voice cut off by a thunk and a groan.

"Are you okay?" she asked, groping the air to find her friend in the dark.

"Wish the ceiling was a bit higher," he muttered, and Devora stifled a snicker.

"Just a little further," she replied as her hands grazed the wooden shelves filled with jars of preserved fruits and vegetables from her mother's garden.

They crept along the earthen floor, their footsteps lighter than feathers until a door in the ceiling squeaked opened. Devora froze, fear consuming every fiber of her being. *Is it the king's soldiers?* If they found her and One Shot, they would be taken back to the palace...and killed.

Paralyzed, Devora didn't know what to do and froze on the spot.

Suddenly, a hand wrapped around her wrist and pulled her into one of the spaces between the shelves storing food. One Shot placed his hands on her shoulders to help Devora find her balance and then patted her head. She released her breath as they both crouched, watching a wooden ladder descend into the cellar.

A plump foot encased in a white silk slipper eased onto the ladder, the wood groaning under the weight of the round woman. A gentle candle flickered between her wrinkled fingers.

"I've got to teach the younger maids what ingredients they need," muttered the familiar voice of Madge, Devora's old nursemaid and the head servant of the Medee home. "I'm getting too old for this."

Devora started forward, but One Shot pulled her back. "Are you sure you can trust her? Your home has been taken by the king."

Pausing, Devora considered his words. King Atol *had* taken her house. She remembered Matthias saying the king promised to lift Mama's and Papa's house arrest, but considering the increased number of guards, he lied. Even with the King's deceit and Devora's previous abhorrence to the people of Grenly, she knew the people were still loyal to Papa. Plus, Madge had every opportunity—for sixteen summers—to turn Devora in to the kingdom, and she hadn't.

"Yes," Devora replied with a resolute nod. "Madge has always been loyal to my family."

A thought struck Devora. *Does King Atol know Mama's and Papa's servants kept my gift from him?* Surely he would have killed them all for treason if he had known.

But Madge was still here, alive and grumbling about her old back between the bundles of dried herbs. Maybe the king didn't know or hadn't properly weighed the servants' loyalty to Mama and Papa.

Devora swiped a strand of loose hair off her forehead. She didn't have time to think about that now. She needed to get to Mama and Papa. Tunri had been urging her to come home. There had to be something her parents knew that could help her find Kanna Blake.

"But is she loyal to *you?*" One Shot questioned, nervousness on his brow.

"We'll have to find out." Devora darted from the shelves before One Shot could stop her.

If anyone could help Devora find her parents, it would be Madge.

"How hard is it to distinguish star anise from cardamom? Honestly," Madge muttered, her weathered voice still as crackly as Devora remembered.

"Star anise is shaped like a star," Devora said, stepping before her. "Cardamom isn't. Shouldn't your maids know that, Madge?"

Madge jumped what seemed like ten feet in the air, dropping the spices on the ground. They scattered everywhere, looking like ants searching for food.

Devora immediately ran to Madge and gave her a hug. "Please don't scream," she whispered. "I only want to see Mama and Papa, and then I'll be gone."

The old woman stood stunned for a few moments before she wrapped her plump arms around Devora. "Oh, my dear child, you're still alive."

Devora melted into the embrace. It felt like it had been years since someone had held her with such care.

The embrace she shared with Matthias on the battlefield slashed through her thoughts, but she pushed it away, her heart squeezing at the memory.

Madge then released her and patted Devora's hands and arms, her voice low. "Are you hurt? I heard you were in battle and then the king arrested you! But look at you, alive and well! We all know he's hiding something. I knew he couldn't best Governor Medee's daughter." Madge smiled until her hands reached Devora's cheeks. "Your eyes," she gasped. "Quick, we must make the Subtle Tea to hide their color."

The old woman darted toward a bundle of dried herbs when Devora stopped her.

"No, Madge, I'm not hiding my eyes anymore. Tunri made me a Seer, and I'm proud to be one. He will protect me from the king, but I will no longer hide my gift."

"Oh, my girl," Madge said, tears building in the wrinkles around her eyes. "How you've grown."

"We need to find your parents," One Shot interrupted, frightening Madge so much that she shrieked.

"One Shot!" Devora hissed. He shrugged.

"What's going on down there?" A masculine voice demanded.

Madge placed a hand over her heart then glared at One Shot as she shouted up the ladder. "Nothing at all. I just saw a mouse."

After a few moments, the footsteps receded from the doorway.

"Who was that?" Devora asked, anxiety creeping up her neck.

"Most of the king's soldiers stay outside the home. Your father is still the governor and has some clout. But there is one guard who patrols the home at night. He's too serious for such a young man of eighteen summers." Madge shook her head, then pointed at One Shot. "Who is *that?*"

"This is my friend—" Devora began.

"From the Fortress?" Madge frowned, casting a skeptical glare at One Shot. "You couldn't make friends in Grenly, but you made friends in prison?"

Devora furrowed her brows. "Yes, that's right."

Madge gave One Shot another once over and huffed before facing Devora. "Sir Brannock holds the key to your parents' room. At sundown, they're locked in. He usually requests—more like demands—a cup of tea, which is what I was making when I came to the cellar."

"He locks Mama and Papa in?" Devora cried, outraged.

Madge shushed her. "The Governor and First Lady have been compliant so far, but the house arrest still stands." The old woman reached out and grasped Devora's hands. "Sir Brannock carries the key on his belt. I can make a strong tonic and put it in his evening tea. It may take some time, but he will be snoring soon, and you can steal the key."

Elation filled Devora's chest. "Thank you, Madge. Who knew you were so sneaky?"

The old woman huffed. "Don't thank me yet. I've only gotten one other person to your father successfully."

Devora blinked. "What? Who?"

"A tall man, not as tall as this fellow"—Madge swatted at One Shot—"but tall. Nice looking, also too serious for a young man. He said he had an urgent message to get to the governor. Oh, what was his name?" Madge tapped her thick finger against her small chin. "Bart, Blithe?"

Devora's heart pounded in her chest.

"Blake?" One Shot offered.

Madge snapped her fingers. "Yes! Blake! He was here not a fortnight ago."

Devora swallowed, trying to soothe the dry spot in her throat. Matthias had come here, to her home. Was he trying to help? But a fortnight ago was before the battle. Before their kiss.

Devora shook her head. She couldn't think about what Captain Blake may or may not be doing. She needed to get to Mama and Papa.

Chapter Five

Rae, The Marketplace, Yekel

"Good morning, Rae," Master Monham greeted, his face bright and jovial, like always. "Isn't it a lovely day?"

Rae snorted. How Master Monham could always be happy, she had no idea. "It's all right, I suppose."

Master Monham gripped a log of clay as he hobbled to his booth. Master Monham always worked on a piece of pottery during market time. The spinning of his potter's wheel piqued the curiosity of passersby; thus, bringing himself—and Rae—more sales. Sometimes he would form a beautiful bowl or vase. Others, he would create animals or flowers. But the people of the market knew that, if they came at just the right time, Master Monham would give his work of art away, free of charge.

Rae had watched the potter repeat this practice for two years and never understood why. He slaved over his potter's wheel all day long, creating unique, one-of-a-kind pieces. Why would he give one away without asking for anything in return?

"I see we have a guest today." Master Monham gently placed the log down, wiped the red clay off his hands with a cloth, and faced Rae and Nadia. He bowed. "I am Master Monham, the finest potter in Yekel and, dare I say, Rae's friend."

Rae's lips ticked at the corners. "How bold of you, Master Monham. Here I thought we were only acquaintances."

Master Monham stood tall, still wearing his grin as Nadia stepped forward, her hand outstretched. "I'm Nadia."

Master Monham gently shook her hand. "Are you also a friend of Rae's?"

Nadia gave a nervous chuckle as she fiddled with a stick of charcoal. "Rae and I grew up together before..." Nadia scratched her neck, diverting her gaze.

Master Monham nodded, his gray brow furrowed. "Yes, I understand."

"I'd like to know more about the Temple of Pahga and what goes on in there now. Rae said you could answer my questions," Nadia announced, and the entire market stood still.

Out in the main street of the market, Mistress Clack stopped with her tray of rolls. Master Tuck ceased his banging on the new piece of armor he was forging. Even the Wizard Wankle paused his ridiculous prophecies.

The only person unfazed by the statement was Master Monham. His green eyes stayed kind as he slowly nodded his balding head. "I will do my best to answer all of your questions. But that is something we cannot discuss here."

"Why not?" Nadia questioned, eyeing the market people who hesitantly returned to their daily work. "As far as I remember, Pahga always took part of the harvest. I used to bring the offering myself. Why is everyone acting so strange?"

"Things are not how they once were." Master Monham gestured toward an oncoming company of soldiers. Each bronze armored soldier marched perfectly in line with his neighbor. The Kadeshian crest of two interlocking golden circles with a sparrow between glistened on their chests with each step.

Rae's gut squeezed. She knew why the company was parading through the market. It was what they did the first Sancti of every month. When she was younger, she believed in the holy day of Sancti. Mami would make fresh orange blossom rolls to share with their neighbors. Papi always had a new invention to show to the kids before the prayer scrolls were read, asking Tunri to bless their food and families. But now, since the Kadesh invasion, Rae wanted nothing to do with the holy day honoring Tunri. If a God like Him allowed something so horrible to happen, why should she honor Him?

As Rae watched the gray veiled heads between the soldiers glide through the market, her rage boiled. General Yada knew Sancti was sacred to the Yekelians, so he purposefully paraded his brothel of stolen women through the market on their way back to the Temple of Pahga. It was the only time the women were allowed out of their marbled prison.

Rae gritted her teeth, trying to bury the memories. Everything in that temple was tainted with evil. To force it in the Yekelians faces was cruel and General Yada knew it.

"Make way," the soldier at the front barked, frightening a huddle of small children as they scurried around the corner. His shoulders were as wide as a doorway, his gaze hard and unwavering.

Chills coiled around Rae's spine. She busied herself with organizing her fabrics, trying to ignore the brute coming her way.

He will come for us! the Beast of Fear squawked. *We must hide!*

We can kill him, the Beast of Rage whispered. *You know we can.*

Sir Rickter haunted Rae's nightmares for months after she bought her freedom from the Temple. He always spoke cruelly to the girls he sought in the Temple and was even less kind to Rae.

When he learned Rae had left the Temple and started her own booth at the market, he purposefully sought her out and tried to force her to go with him.

"Just like old times," he'd grinned maliciously.

But Rae stood her ground, and with the eyes of the other vendors on them, Sir Rickter released her. Thankfully, her past had not been revealed, though Sir Rickter had threatened to return.

It wasn't until she, as the Crimson Cord, battled the knight in the Dark Market and left him within a breath of his life, that he left her alone.

"I hear you've been terrorizing a young woman in the market," Rae said, disguised as her alter ego, the Crimson Cord. She held her crimson cord snug around Sir Rickter's thick neck.

"What about it?" the knight wheezed, blood seeping from his bruised lips. He clawed at

the rope, unable to squeeze his fingers beneath it.

Rae tightened her grip, and Sir Rickter grunted. The crowd gathered around the Fighter's Ring silenced. Never had the Crimson Cord killed a man. But maybe he would now.

"Leave the girl be, and I will give you your life."

"Why do you care? She wouldn't pleasure me. Why are you so special?" the knight coughed.

It took every ounce of strength Rae had to not pull the red cord as tight as she could. She only tightened it enough to make Sir Rickter beg for mercy.

"Okay," he gasped. "Okay, I'll leave her be."

"Swear it," Rae demanded. "Swear it on the name of Pahga."

Sir Rickter's dark brown eyes bulged.

Being a religious man, Sir Rickter took the teachings of Pahga seriously, which was why he frequented the Temple multiple times a week. Rae knew if he swore on the name of Pahga, he wouldn't go back on his word.

"I swear it," he croaked.

"Louder," Rae growled. "I want witnesses to hear."

Sir Rickter clawed at the scarlet cord around his neck, but Rae wouldn't relent. Just like he was never merciful to her, she would never show sympathy to a monster like him.

"I swear to not bother any Yekelians in the market again," Sir Rickter cried.

Rae released her grasp on the cord, allowing the fibers to burn across Sir Rickter's throat.

He folded forward with a gasp, rubbing the spot on his neck. Spinning around, he glared at Rae before scrambling away into the awestruck crowd.

"Rae?" Nadia asked, pulling Rae from her memory. "What was that?"

The group of soldiers passed through the market without any fuss.

Rae slowly shifted her gaze to the gray-veiled heads disappearing around the corner. As the Crimson Cord, Rae vowed to never kill any of the thugs she battled in the Dark Market. But Sir Rickter was the first man in the Dark Market she wanted to kill, and she always wondered if she should have finished him off.

Folding a bright magenta scarf into a square, Rae sighed. "Those are the Temple's Priestesses. They're women who have been taken by the Kadeshian soldiers to serve Pahga in the Temple."

Nadia's face turned whiter than the clouds in the sky. "Taken? Does that mean..."

Rae couldn't meet Nadia's eyes. Those eyes so full of hope and love. Nadia had always trusted Rae. Never questioned anything she said. But she couldn't bear for Nadia to know the punishment she endured for freeing Nadia and the other young girls. Temple Priestesses used to be those who volunteered to serve Pahga; they were never forced to perform. But General Yada changed that, as well.

"With Tunri, there is always hope," Master Monham cut in, saving Rae.

Thank you, Master Monham, Rae thought as she busied herself by folding her fabrics and scarves.

Nadia studied Rae carefully before Master Monham piped in again.

"Since you're going to be dwelling with us for the time being, I would love to have some young hands help me mold my pieces."

Nadia shot one more look at Rae before shrugging and following Master Monham to his booth.

Rae turned back to her work. The morning crowd of Kadeshian merchants would arrive soon. If she played her cards right, she would be able to make enough to free another woman from the Temple's clutches.

"What's this?" Nadia asked as she pressed the pedal beneath Master Monham's pottery table. The wooden table spun faster, splattering Nadia's skirt with wet clay. Her eyes lit up. "That's brilliant." Whipping out her notebook, she scribbled a few things down.

Chuckling, Master Monham brought a three-legged stool up to the table. With a small groan, he eased himself onto it. He reached down and slapped a lumpy piece of clay on the rotating table.

"Pottery is a fine art," he began as he pushed the pedal beneath the table.

Rae couldn't help but stop and watch the glop of clay spin around and around.

"It takes patience, skill, and a careful hand to create something beautiful." He flattened his palms against the lump of clay. Within moments the clay's sides began to smooth. "Many in this world believe beauty is instant. A new scarf, a new perfume." He took his hands from the clay, now shaped into a smooth tube. "But if that beauty does not first come from within, then is it truly beautiful?"

Master Monham lifted the pottery to show Nadia. Curious, Rae leaned over to see what the inside of the clay cylinder looked like.

"It's still rough and clumpy inside," Nadia replied, poking the wet clay.

Master Monham chuckled as he placed the clay back on the table. "Outward beauty is easy, simple. But inward beauty takes time to mold. And sometimes—" Master Monham slammed his thick fingers down on the clay, flattening it.

Rae and Nadia jumped at the sudden movement.

"Why did you do that?" Nadia cried, completely focused on the flattened clay.

Master Monham smushed the clay a few more times before rolling it into a ball. "Sometimes a piece of pottery needs to be remade until its inward beauty is easily seen on the outside."

"I feel like you're trying to say more," Nadia said, quirking her lips.

Master Monham nodded. "We are the clay. Tunri is the potter. He will continue to mold and remake us until our hearts are more beautiful than our heads."

Rae frowned and turned back to her scarves. She'd heard this tale before. Master Monham used to visit her in the Temple. Not for services, but to give her and the other women a few hours of peace. He would pay for a slot for each woman and sit and talk with them. Mostly about Tunri and how He hadn't forgotten them.

Rae scoffed as she laid a lilac scarf over a turquoise one. If Tunri hadn't forgotten them, why were there still women enslaved to the Temple? Why was she still stuck in Yekel? Why was General Yada still allowed to threaten her?

Turning back to her booth, Rae focused on the few customers coming to her table.

Only evil lurked in that Temple. Rae vowed never to set foot in there again.

Rae's day at the market proved profitable. She sold more fabrics and scarves that morning than she had in a long time. Maybe it was good fortune or maybe it was the presence of Nadia modeling her scarves while laughing and working with Master Monham. Rae growled at the young soldiers who gawked at her friend. Thankfully, the Wizard Wankle scared them off by offering to tell them how they would meet their untimely ends.

"Thank you for earlier," Rae told the Wizard as she finished cleaning her booth. One of Mistress Clack's jelly rolls had been accidentally squashed right on top of Rae's white tablecloth. The stain was mostly gone after Rae's ferocious scrubbing.

General Yada allowed the Yekelians only one day a week to sell their wares and have a break from their normal labor. Naturally, the Yekelians chose Sancti for their market day. Traditionally, Sancti was meant to be a weekly day of rest, but the Yekelians couldn't afford to anger General Yada any further. The last time they pushed him, labor on the wall doubled and another Yekelian woman had been taken to the Temple.

The Wizard Wankle adjusted the yellow gem on his giant turban. "I don't like customers lurking around my tent without intending to pay," he said while stretching his vibrant cloak over his thin shoulders. But Rae knew the Wizard disliked the Kadeshians just as much as every other citizen of Yekel.

As the Wizard returned to his tent, Rae found Nadia and Master Monham had finished cleaning his booth. "You were a huge help today." The old man grinned, the corners of his eyes crinkling like spider webs. "I wish I could have such wonderful help every day."

"It was great, " Nadia said, whipping out her notebook and charcoal. "I learned so many new things. I can't wait to tell Dev." As she went to scribble in the notebook, she paused, her excitement draining as her shoulders slumped.

"I'm sure your friend is well," Master Monham said. "If she is as bright as you told me, she'll be okay."

Rae tried to subtly question some of her buyers about the escaped Seer, but no one knew anything. One girl with shining white-yellow hair and bright greens eyes held a spark of recognition at the name, but quickly denied any knowledge. There was something familiar about the girl, too, but Rae couldn't discern why. She searched her mind for a clue but came up blank. Rae stopped questioning when the girl paid handsomely for a cerulean scarf and hurried away.

After the young woman left, a group of Kadeshian's chatted amongst themselves. Once Rae heard them whisper something about a "Seer" she tried to listen in.

"I heard the king of Tenton has quite a nice sum lined up for the first person to find the escaped Seer," a thin man with a hooked nose said.

"I'll bet the king of Kadesh will pay ten times that amount then!" another man with a white turban countered with a laugh.

Fear struck Rae's heart. *What if Kadeshian soldiers—or worse, General Yada—finds the Seer first?* She needed to find the Seer before any of them so *she* could use the Seer as leverage and save the enslaved women in the Temple.

As the men moved away from her booth, Rae gathered what was left of her unsold scarves and fabrics into her wicker basket. Placing it on her hip, she moved next to Nadia. "Come on. Let's head back to my house. I'd be happy to make you some of Mami's orange blossom rolls." She turned to Master Monham. "You are welcome to join us."

The old man bowed his head in thanks as Nadia brightened. "I love those rolls! I remember smelling them when I went to your house to learn hemna before you celebrated Sancti." Nadia stopped, her brows furrowing. "Rae, do you still celebrate Sancti? Because I—"

"No," Rae replied quickly. She knew Nadia and her family used to follow Pahga before Kadesh forced their perverted version of the religion upon Yekel. Rae didn't know what Nadia believed now. But Rae certainly wouldn't be celebrating Tunri.

Nadia's mouth closed, her flattened demeanor returning.

Master Monham cleared his throat. "I celebrate Sancti. Do you wish to know more about Tunri? You are more than welcome to join me for prayer service tonight."

Rae winced as Nadia swiveled toward Master Monham. "I would love that. And could you tell me more about how the Temple has changed?"

Master Monham nodded. "Now come. Rae doesn't often offer to make those delicious rolls, and I don't want her to change her mind." He winked, making Nadia laugh.

The two took off together chatting away.

Little Nadi, taking someone from us again, the Beast of Envy tsked.

Rae straightened her shoulders. No, she was pleased Nadia and Master Monham became fast friends. Master Monham would distract Nadia while Rae found out how to get a note of inquiry out of Yekel to the girls in Kopet. Maybe they knew more about the Seer. The Seer was on the run and would have to make her motives known eventually. All Rae had to do was wait.

Chapter Six

The citrusy scent of oranges consumed Rae's small abode as she grated the rinds of the succulent fruit. As she fell into a rhythm, memories of Mami flooded her thoughts.

"Like this," Mami said, placing her rough, yet gentle hand over Rae's small one, which was clutching the metal grater. She guided Rae's hand up and down over the sharp holes. Small spirals of bright orange peel tumbled from the holes, enveloping their home in a fragrant fruity aroma.

Rae was just about to turn sixteen summers. Her Categorization Call would be a few days after the next Sancti gathering. Rae was now old enough to make her own dish for the weekly prayer service and her nerves made her fingers tremble. She'd never cooked for so many people, so Mami suggested making orange blossom rolls. Rae loved the rolls and had seen Mami make them hundreds of times. She was confident she would succeed.

But after a few failed attempts—the yeast didn't prove enough, and the orange rind was too thin as she had added too much flour—Rae decided she would rather pick some fruit for Sancti than make anything.

"Mami, I've tried a million times," Rae exaggerated. She pushed the half-grated orange away. "I just can't bake."

Mami laughed, the sound soft and warm. She swiped a tan hand across her brow, pushing her long blonde curls out of her chestnut eyes. "And you'll try a million and one more because I know you can do this."

Rae glared at the oranges. Why wouldn't they just cooperate and create the succulent rolls her mother made?

"You can't be so quick to give up, mija. *When life throws everything it has at you, are you just going to run away?"*

Rae blinked at her mom. The conversation had suddenly turned serious. Mami was referencing the recent news. As one of Yekel's top Tinkers, Papi had been taken to Maldove Palace. He'd been gone for weeks without a word. Yekel was barely surviving after King Atol ordered it to be set on fire. And now Kadesh had broken through the southern end of the Edo desert, only a two days' journey from Yekel. The citizens knew they were defenseless, and the king, so far, offered no aid.

Mami smashed the orange against the grater until it was nothing but pulp. "You must be strong, mija. *You cannot allow yourself to fall into despair. Remember what Papi said, 'As long as the sun is still shining—"*

"'I will have hope,'" Rae finished quietly. She crossed her arms over her chest. "I'm sorry, Mami. I pray every night that Papi is okay."

Mami rushed to Rae and scooped her into a hug. Sweet orange pulp squished against Rae's arms, but she didn't care. They both knew Kadesh was coming and they had nowhere to hide.

"Ouch!" Rae gasped, throwing down the grater.

Blood beaded around the sheared piece of skin on her knuckle before dripping down her finger. Rae immediately stuck her finger into her mouth as she rummaged around the kitchen for a clean rag. A small pulse throbbed from the tip before she secured the rag tightly around her injury.

Kadesh had come less than a week after that memory. Rae never got a chance to Categorize. She was never given a chance to leave this cursed city. And it was the last Sancti she spent with her mother. Rae wished she could've perfected the orange blossom rolls by then. Instead, since buying her freedom from the Temple, Rae worked tirelessly to get the recipe right, recalling every step and ingredient from memory.

She branched out to making other types of breads and pastries, but the orange blossom rolls were her pride and joy.

Rae quickly got back to work, knowing Master Monham and Nadia were waiting in the other room. Master Monham no doubt was telling Nadia every little detail of what happened once Kadesh had taken over the city.

Mami had been in the first wave of women taken to the Temple of Pahga. When Rae was taken a month later, she asked about Mami. Some of the women remembered her. Others just looked at her with dead eyes, saying if her mother wasn't physically dead, she wouldn't be the same if Rae found her. Rae tried searching the Temple when she could, but she couldn't find a trace of her mother. Mami was gone. Tears became Rae's only food, day and night.

Rae smashed her palms into the dough, beating it with more intensity than needed. She hated General Yada and Kadesh. She hated King Atol and his greed for Tinkers. She hated the solider who'd come and taken her father from their home.

Rae paused. She hadn't thought about that soldier in a long time, but she would never forget his face. His cold, unfeeling gray eyes. If she ever saw him again, she would make him pay.

Revenge is sweet, the Beast of Rage growled. *It will be ours soon.*

A bluster of laughter floated from the other room.

Guess they're not talking about the demise of Yekel, Rae thought as she set the dough aside to rise.

While they waited for the rolls, Rae arranged a platter of cured meats, cheeses, and dried fruit. Mami would have scolded her from the grave if Rae wasn't hospitable to her guests. Leveling the tray on her hip, Rae grabbed the new pitcher Master Monham had graciously given her and joined the others.

"After that she slapped me clear across the face!" Master Monham said, causing Nadia to erupt into a fit of giggles.

Rae couldn't help but smile. Her small home had never held so much laughter, so much life.

"And she still married you?" Nadia asked.

Master Monham scratched his balding head with a nod. "I don't know what she saw in me."

"Aw," Nadia said, placing a hand over her heart. "What a great story."

Master Monham's smile fell ever so slightly. "It is. We would've been together forty summers this past season."

Rae carefully placed the tray and pitcher on the table and gently laid a hand on Master Monham's shoulder.

Mistress Monham was already ill when Kadesh attacked. The Kadeshians didn't see any use for a fragile old woman. She and the other "useless" members of Yekel were killed on sight.

"I'm so sorry," Nadia whispered.

Rae gently squeezed his shoulder. "She is at peace."

Master Monham placed his hand over Rae's. Deep set wrinkles creased his suntanned skin. "Thank Tunri, she is."

Rae dropped her hand. *How could he still thank Tunri when his wife, his only love, was killed right in front of him?*

Rae kept her mouth shut. She and Master Monham had engaged in this argument many times over the past two years. It always ended with Rae being furious and frustrated and Master Monham telling her to trust and have faith. After one particularly nasty argument, Rae didn't speak to the potter for weeks. It wasn't until she saw a dove made from clay sitting on her booth at the market that she knew Master Monham was only trying to help her cope with her own anger.

I will never leave, the Beast of Rage commented. *I'm the reason you've survived for so long.*

Rae sat between Nadia and Master Monham and poured water into three clay cups. They sat on the floor around the table, as there were only two chairs and three people.

Believing in Tunri didn't quench her anger. The only thing that satiated her fury was beating those who took advantage of her again and again.

Beat them until they're gone, the Beast of Rage snarled.

Taking a deep breath, Rae steadied the fury rolling in her chest. Just hearing about Mistress Monham set her blood boiling. Rae passed the cups around and took a drink, cooling her anger. Luckily, there was another brawl in the Dark Market tonight. She stretched her fingers, ready to release her pain on another victim.

Yes, the Beast of Rage seethed.

Master Monham took a sip of tea and picked up where he left off explaining the events of the Kadeshian invasion. Nadia had been present for the beginning of it. But after Rae sent her to the countryside, where the Kadeshians didn't venture, Nadia wasn't sure what happened.

Master Monham explained how Kadesh took Yekel swiftly then ordered all men to work on rebuilding the citadel's walls—which Kadesh had destroyed—while the women were forced to bring water and replacement tools to those working or to be taken to the Temple.

As he was speaking, Master Monham paused. Rae knew he was waiting to see if she would speak up and explain what had happened to her. But when Rae opened her mouth to recall the horrors she'd endured, her tongue turned to stone. Her heart pounded against her ribs, as if it would explode out of her chest. Nadia stared at her with keen eyes exposing Rae's omissions.

Say nothing, say nothing, squawked the Beast of Fear. *Nadia will turn on you if she knows.*

Little Nadi would never understand, the Best of Envy added. *Life has always been so easy for her.*

Clearing her throat, Rae stood. "I need to finish the rolls," she declared and headed to the kitchen. After a moment, Master Monham continued answering Nadia's questions about Kadesh and General Yada.

Rae took a deep breath, calming her pulse. She smashed down the pain, the hurt, the loneliness, the jealousy, and the fear, leaving only her rage as fuel. They didn't need to know her pain. They didn't need to know her panic and terror. They would only judge her.

Rolling the orange blossom dough out on her wooden board, Rae separated it into palm-sized spheres then placed them in her kiln. She knew what people said about the women in the Temple. Whether they were taken against their will or went willingly, it didn't matter.

Although General Yada referred to them as Temple Priestesses, *Trixie Girls* was the favorite label of the Kadeshian men and soldiers. Unfortunately, some Yekelian men used the term as well. It was derived from the Kadesh term *retrix*, or harlot.

Rae furiously stoked the fire, its heat blazing across her cheeks and shaven head. The Temple required all its females to grow their hair long. General Yada said Pahga, the Queen of Heaven, wanted her followers to be satisfied with the Temple Priestesses, so they must never cut their hair. The moment Rae was free, she sheared every follicle of hair off her head and burned them.

Rae stepped away from the fire, not realizing tears were rolling down her cheeks. She quickly swiped them away.

You must be strong, mija.

"I will be, Mami," Rae whispered, thinking of all the coin she would make at tonight's brawl. With it, she would be close to freeing another trapped woman.

Burying the pain deep in her heart, Rae took the rolls out of the oven. For two years, all those men abused her. They were beasts, monsters. And she couldn't do anything about it then.

But now, with her new freedom, she was a *Trixie Girl* no longer. As the Crimson Cord, she would be the monster. And she would make them pay.

Chapter Seven

Excusing herself for a moment, Rae rushed to her room and gathered her fighting clothes along with her crimson cord and face scarf. It was well past sundown, and she needed to make her way to the Dark Market. Her nerves were itching to release her pent-up fury.

Voices drifted from the living room carrying Master Monham and Nadia's endless conversation. Rae was a patient woman, but her patience was starting to wear thin. *How long are they going to talk?* Returning, she plated the last orange blossom rolls and brought them over to her guests.

We need to beat something! the Beast of Rage cried.

Rae gripped the tray tighter before she set it down in front of Nadia and Master Monham. She needed the pair to finish their jovial conversations and soon.

Despite Rae's distress, there were some highlights to the evening. The duo raved over her delicious orange blossom rolls. Rae almost blushed at all the praise. For a brief moment, she envisioned a life where she could bake what she wanted all the time, not just when she scrounged up enough coin for the ingredients.

Rae sighed. That life would never happen. She was lucky enough to have the materials to dye and sell fabrics. Some of the Yekelians scraped just enough to find food for their families. Rae pushed her dreams aside. Right now, she needed to focus on getting information about the Seer and freeing the women from the Temple.

As the conversation droned, Rae's leg wouldn't stop bouncing and her fingers kept tapping on her knee. Jasper and the other fighters were probably wondering where the Crimson Cord was.

Biting her lip, Rae squeezed the bag in her lap holding her fighting attire. She worked hard to build up her name and fearsome reputation. She had never missed a fight. And she wouldn't start now.

She bolted to her feet, causing Master Monham and Nadia to pause their chatter about the mechanics of a more sophisticated pulley system in a nearby well. While Rae wished she could engage in the conversation, like she used to discuss tinkering with Nadia, she had more pressing matters to attend to. Besides, inventions were not her thing. Papi had the gift and so did Nadia. But Tunri decided not to bless Rae with the tinkering gift.

Papi always liked Little Nadi better, the Beast of Envy crooned. *He would light up when she came over to invent with him. He never cared for us like that.*

"I believe I left some material in the market," Rae explained, smoothing her features. Sometimes it scared her how easily she could lie now. "Please stay as long as you like before you head to the Sancti gathering," she added to Master Monham, who gave her a knowing look. Rae brushed it off and focused on Nadia. "There is extra fruit and meat in the kitchen. Help yourself to anything you like."

Before they could stop her, Rae dashed out the door. Typically, she slipped out from her room, where the hidden door in the ceiling concealed her exit. But leaving outright instead of sneaking around seemed like a better option tonight.

The cool evening air embraced her, and she let out a sigh. Finally, she was free. She was ready to break into a sprint when the door behind her creaked open.

"What's going on, Rae?" Nadia called from behind.

Rae spun around to find Nadia's harden gaze and defensive stance, almost as if she were ready to fight. Rae couldn't help but smirk, knowing *she* was the one who'd taught Nadia every hemna technique.

Well, not every *technique.* Rae kept a few secret moves to herself.

Rae schooled her features in an impassive mask. "I told you I left some fabric at the market."

"Don't treat me like a child," Nadia bit back, and Rae raised her brows. Sighing, Nadia ran a hand through her short hair. "I know everything isn't fine. I know you sacrificed yourself. And from what I've heard from Dev and the other Tenton soldiers, the Kadeshian generals are not kind."

Rae's throat constricted, her soul wanting to confide in someone, but she kept her lips tight.

"Please," Nadia pleaded. "Tell me what I need to know then we can both leave this place for good. You can join me back in Juro. The Fortress isn't the best, but I'm sure you could sell your scarves in the capital."

Rae bit her lip, her frosty walls thawing slightly. "We'll be lucky if I can get *you* out."

Nadia waited, watching Rae, knowing there was more.

Rae hesitated as she grasped the sack in her palm. She could trust Nadia, right? And Master Monham already knew about her alter ego and her time at the Temple.

If you tell her, she'll tell everyone your secrets, the Beast of Fear whispered. *We can't trust her.*

We can't trust Little Nadi, the Beast of Envy added.

Leave to fight. Now! the Beast of Rage roared.

Pushing a gust of air from her mouth, Rae rubbed the back of her neck. "Sorry Nadi, I really have to go."

"Well, I'm coming with you," Nadia huffed, stomping next to Rae.

"No," Rae barked, flinging her hand up. "You can't come. The market at night is not a place for..." Rae started to say a child, but after giving Nadia a once over she realized Nadia wasn't a child any longer. She'd grown up, and Rae had missed it. "It's better if I go alone. There are gangs and other troublesome people who lurk in the market at night. I wouldn't want you to get hurt."

Rae could see Nadia calculating how she could convince Rae to let her come. She recognized the rebellious flair in her friend's posture.

Swallowing, Rae allowed another half-truth to slide from her lips. "I was also going to try to find out information on your Seer friend." She clutched the pack over her shoulder, digging her nails into her palms. "I overheard some of the merchants gossiping about an escaped prisoner from the Fortress. I told them I would meet them tonight for information." Rae held back her wince. She lied easily in the Temple. She lied easily in the Dark Market. She even lied easily at the daytime market. But lying to Nadia pinched her chest.

It's not a complete lie, the Beast of Fear whispered.

It was true. After she made enough coin in the Fighter's Ring, Rae planned on fighting for information about the Seer and then feeding it back to Yada. Guilt twinged her chest again, but Rae ignored it. Having a conscience wouldn't save the women from the Temple.

"Rae, thank you!" Nadia exclaimed, wrapping her arms around Rae in a hug. "I knew I could count on you."

Rae involuntarily stiffened at the touch before giving Nadia a quick pat on the shoulder and scooting out of the embrace.

"Yes, I was waiting until I learned something to tell you," she mumbled, continuing the lie.

Tightening her hands around the sack, Rae peered up at the moon. She had already wasted enough time. Spinning around, she started toward the market.

"I'll be back in the early morning. Enjoy Sancti with Master Monham. And Nadia,"— Rae peered over her shoulder—"I'll know if you try to follow me. Remember who taught you everything you know."

Nadia pursed her lips but stayed planted in the threshold of Rae's door.

Breaking into a sprint, Rae rushed to the market gate which had less guards at night than during the day, making it easier to sneak into the city. She glanced over her shoulder to find Nadia still standing there, watching. Rae lifted her hand, and Nadia returned the gesture before filing back into the house.

Relieved, Rae ducked into an alleyway and changed into her fighting gear: black leggings with a matching black tunic and her braided scarlet cord, snug around her waist. She wrapped a thick swath of fabric tight around her chest, flattening her curvaceous form. With other squares of fabric, Rae stuffed her sleeves, giving the impression of a thin, but toned male physique. Rae lifted the red mesh from her sack and wrapped it around her face, her alter ego rising from the depths of her rage.

Time to fight. Time for blood, the Beast of Rage chanted.

Rae rounded a few more corners before she arrived at the secret entrance of the Dark Market. Each night the entrance changed. Throughout the city, hidden clues were scattered, explaining where the next location would be. But only those who had been to the Dark Market before would know how to find them.

Rae rapped her signature knock and waited. After a pause, the splintered brown door creaked open. A man with an eye patch and three missing teeth peeked out.

"Name?" he grunted.

Rae stood there. After her fight with Sir Rickter, she made sure never to speak much, fearful someone would recognize her voice.

The man stepped out further. "I said, what's yer—" Upon seeing Rae he stopped. His crusty demeanor immediately transformed into one of adoration. "Oh, Master Cord, welcome welcome!" He ushered Rae in, bowing.

Rae had practiced her "man" walk for days until she got it right. Stalking slowly, she strode past the doorkeeper.

"The gangs have been anxious for your arrival, especially Booker Row of the Street Rats. It seems the fights aren't as exciting without you," the doorkeeper blabbed on.

Though the doorkeeper had never visited *her* in the Temple, Rae wasn't sure if he'd seen any of the others. She didn't trust any of the snakes in this den.

"Right this way, Master Cord," he continued, marching ahead of her into the dark musty tunnel.

As they continued farther into the corridor, the familiar scents of sweat, ale, and *menta* plumed around her. Rae hated all of the smells but most of all *menta*. It was a local plant in Yekel that, when burned, gave its inhalers "visions." Rae remembered when the Wizard Wankle claimed he would soon come into a great fortune and could finally leave Yekel after sniffing a barrel of the stuff. That was a year ago, and the Wizard was still at the market every Sancti.

But more than that, General Yada would burn it when one of the Temple Priestesses had disobeyed. The fumes would consume her senses before the general left her at the mercy of the imperial opal statue of Pahga.

Rae snuffed out the memory before her panic could set in. She'd only been through the experience once. But once was enough. She'd learned quickly to obey the general's orders without question. Though she hated her life in the Temple, she still wanted to live.

The tunnel jutted right then left before stairs appeared. The doorkeeper continued to ramble about some new gambler who just arrived from Juro, the capital city of Tenton. Rae kept her stoic stance and ignored the man as her mind prepared for her first fight.

In order to get the most coin, she should fight a merchant or a knight. But to glean information, she would have to fight a Street Rat, a member of Yekel's most notorious gang. The doorkeeper said Booker Row, the new leader of the Street Rats, was asking for her. They were the eyes and ears of the city, and nothing happened without their knowledge.

Rae inwardly groaned. Though she hadn't lost a match yet, she hated fighting the Street Rats. They always smuggled knives or some other contraption into the fight. Jasper would have to stop the brawl, pat them down, and then restart the match from the beginning. It was tedious and annoying because it happened every single fight when a Street Rat was involved.

Once Rae and the doorkeeper climbed another set of stairs, they finally arrived at the Dark Market. It wasn't like the regular market on Sancti. There were no colorful booths or children giggling as they ran through the tables. Instead, everything was cold, dark, and quiet. Rae stepped inside the entrance of the Dark Market—The Whispering Hall. Transactions shuffled beneath tables and across whispered lips as illegal goods passed hands. Any deal on parchment was then put to flame or eaten by the distributor, leaving no trail.

Rae kept her face forward as she stalked through the dense crowd. The only loud noise came from the room at the far end of the spacious hall: the Fighter's Ring. Her second home.

"Make way, you plebs," the doorkeeper snarled, shoving a short man with a long brown beard out of the way.

The short man whirled around, ready to attack, but stopped when he saw Rae. His thin lips broke into a grin. "The Crimson Cord is here!" he shouted in a high nasally voice.

Those around cheered and Rae almost blushed at the response. But as she recognized the faces of her past visitors, the feeling shriveled.

Remember why you're here, Rae. Coin and information.

Infusing every cell in her body with fury, Rae found Jasper, the Keeper of the Coins. The beady-eyed man didn't spare her a glance, but Rae could tell he was excited by how fast he was swishing the beads on his abacus.

"You're late."

Rae narrowed her gaze at the abacus. She knew the Keeper of the Coins wasn't completely honest about how much coin he gave to the winners. But since she'd almost killed Sir Rickter, her winnings had always been correct.

Rae lifted her chin at Jasper, and he finally looked at her. "Who would you like to fight? Everyone is eager for a show after this mess is done." He flicked his spindly fingers at the two men fighting in the center of the room.

Rae analyzed the fight. Their stances were wrong, their posture was horrible, and Rae wasn't even sure why a man with a wooden leg was fighting in the first place.

Shaking her head, Rae focused on the room.

Coin first or information? Coin or information?

Does it matter? the Beast of Rage roared. *We need to fight!*

Her eyes locked onto a man with a hood over his head. In the dimness of the room she couldn't make out any of his features. She watched him for a moment before he lifted a gloved hand. Between his leather clad fingers was a rolled-up piece of parchment. On it held King Atol's seal. If anyone could give her more information about the Seer, it would be that man.

Rae's heart beat in her chest. She needed that parchment.

She nodded her head toward the cloaked figure.

Jasper peered over. "Ah yes, I was curious to see if you would notice our newest gambler. He's all the way from Juro. Calls himself the Winner." Jasper cackled to himself. "We'll see if that's true."

Jasper waved over his minions to send word to the Winner that the Crimson Cord wanted to challenge. Gamblers usually didn't brawl themselves but had a fighter enter the ring for them.

As Jasper took care of the details, Rae stepped into the fighting ring. It was dusty and cracked, but the makeshift square brought her more peace than any prayers or temple had. Pounding out her rage and fury was freeing.

"Attention!" Jasper's crackly voice rang out as he stepped onto the Fighter's Ring. "Tonight, we have a special treat!"

The crowd immediately fell silent, anticipation rising as the men clung to their coin purses.

"Not only has the Crimson Cord delighted us with his presence"—the crowd interrupted with a loud cheer—"But," Jasper continued, holding his abacus high. "We have a new competitor."

Rae paused. The glint of greed and excitement in Jasper's eye sent anxiety rushing through her veins. The last new competitor was her, and that was over a year ago. Who could it be?

Jasper licked his yellow teeth and grinned. "Gamblers and gangs, I present to you, the Goliath!"

For the first time since her season in the Temple, fear iced Rae's veins. Out of the crowd stomped the tallest man she had ever seen.

Chapter Eight

Devora, Governor's Mansion, Grenly

Sir Brannock's snores filled the familiar white stone corridor as Madge, Devora, and One Shot glided across the plush, purple carpet. The knight dozed off exactly ten minutes from when Madge gave him the strong tea, which made Devora wonder if King Atol was sending soldiers to guard her home just for show. If a real threat came to Grenly, she didn't trust Sir Brannock to defend himself, much less her parents.

Devora held her breath as she tiptoed past the burly guard. With his thick brown beard and furrowed brow, he looked much older than his eighteen summers. The knight was probably thankful for the easy assignment of walking around their mansion rather than fighting Kadesh.

Holding her breath, Devora carefully plucked the key ring from his belt. Sir Brannock released a guttural snore, and Devora almost dropped the iron ring. Thankfully, she held onto it and hurried away from the sleeping knight.

Once they snuck past Sir Brannock, Madge lit a candle and motioned them to follow her down the rest of the corridor. The thick rug absorbed their footsteps, allowing the trio to stride easily without making a sound.

After rounding the corner, Madge opened her palm, and Devora gave her the key.

"I can't believe Mama and Papa get locked away each night," Devora whispered. "Like prisoners."

Madge placed the key in the lock and smirked. "Oh no, my dear, your parents stay put because they want to. They can leave anytime they wish."

Devora furrowed her brow at the odd comment before Madge swung the door in. "I'll keep watch out here," the maid offered. "Good luck."

Confused, Devora stepped in her parents' bedroom. It was just as grand as she remembered. Though none of the gilded sconces lining the walls were lit, Devora had memorized the features of the room long ago. Thin muslin drapes hung from the open windows, fluttering as a cool evening breeze rushed in. A roaring fire crackled to her left and Devora paused.

Why would the fireplace be lit?

She strode toward the hearth. Grenly was hot and humid the majority of the year. There was hardly ever a need for a fire's warmth. Even when the temperature did cool, it hardly called for a fire of this size.

Devora studied the open window and the smoke puffing up the chimney. Upon further inspection, she discovered a sheet of iron resting above the fire. Using the wooden handle attached to the sheet, Devora pushed the piece in, causing the smoke to be blocked from the chimney. The smoke immediately billowed into the room, then made its way toward the open window. Devora grinned and pulled the metal sheet back out, impressed.

"A way to communicate using the smoke," One Shot said, studying the fire as he leaned on his good leg. "No wonder you're so smart."

Devora couldn't help but chuckle. Of course, Mama and Papa wouldn't sit idly by while King Atol tried to arrest her. Using smoke signals was an effective way to communicate with the outside world. Devora remembered reading about the secret communication in her father's textbook from Vlacklear, *Speaking When You Can't: General Teague's Guide to Espionage and Communication.*

But who are they trying to talk to? Devora wondered. *And where are they?*

She took a step forward and her foot pressed on something beneath the purple and gold rug. A crack snapped from the closet. Before Devora could blink, a rope wrapped around her ankle and pulled her feet first into the air.

Squealing, she fumbled at the rope, trying to break free.

"Good catch, darling," Mama said, her voice coming from the corner of the room.

"Thank you, my dear," Papa replied, his voice coming from the opposite direction.

Devora twisted her body, trying to pin their location. "Mama, Papa, it's me. It's Devora."

"Hold still," One Shot said as he wrapped an arm around her shoulders and easily untied her foot from the trap.

Devora's feet slammed onto the ground as her back fell into One Shot's arm. She glanced up at the tall man. Dark shadows rimmed his charcoal eyes. Devora had thought that freedom would ease One Shot's mind. But when she engaged her soulsight, his soul looked wearier than before. Blue clouds of sorrow spiraled from his soul. Only a single spot of yellow—a spot of hope—remained. And if that wasn't enough, Devora noticed how his injured leg from the Battle of Edo kept bothering him. He tried to hide it, but she knew it pained him.

One Shot helped her stand, then took a step back, absent-mindedly brushing the spot where Devora could see his soul. She remembered One Shot said that he could feel it when Devora had accidentally looked inside his soul before.

"Hands where we can see them, please," Mama demanded in her elegant voice.

Devora frowned. *Do they not recognize their own daughter?* Devora suddenly remembered Madge telling her, "Good luck." What did the maid know that she didn't explain earlier?

A prick poked Devora in the back. She immediately spun around, while launching away from the knife.

"For Tunri's sake, Mama, it's me," Devora growled.

A moment passed before the strike of a match sounded and a candle lit. As soon as the warm glow of the lantern danced across Devora's face her parents gasped.

Devora stood stunned at the sight of them. Gone were her parents' fine silks and robes. Both wore brown leather leggings, white tunics, and brown boots. Papa had grown so thin since she'd last seen him in the Fortress. Mama had no paint on her face at all. But what shocked Devora the most was her mother's short hair. Glance Medee always prided herself in having long, shining ebony hair.

"Devora?" Mama whispered, taking a tiny step forward. "Is it really you?"

Devora furrowed her brow. "Who else would it be?"

She started toward her when Papa held out his arm. "Careful, Glance. It may be another one of his tricks."

Devora glanced at One Shot and he shrugged but kept his crossbow taught. She faced her parents. *What has King Atol done to them?*

"When I was seven summers I had my first prophetic vision. I went screaming in the streets about a viper coming to attack Lower Grenly," Devora said, figuring she needed to give them evidence that she was truly herself.

Papa lowered his guard, his eyes immediately filling with tears. "Devora," he sniffed. "You're alive."

Devora fisted her hands on her hips. "Of course. I told you I would become the best soldier in Tenton, and I did."

Her father burst into laughter and rushed toward her, her mother not far behind. Tears flowed down Devora's cheeks at the embrace. She missed them so.

"Oh, my little dove," Mama cried. "I'm so proud of you. I've kept up with everything you've done. You were so brave."

Devora wiped her eyes on her sleeve. "Thank you, Mama." She pulled back to look at her parents. Though they were different, they were still the family she loved. "We don't have much time. King Atol probably already knows I'm here, but Tunri guided me back to you."

Mama cupped Devora's cheek, peering into her violet eyes. "Yes, I see you've finally embraced who you are. Please forgive us for making you hide all those years."

Devora placed her hand over her mother's. "You were trying to protect me. No apologies needed."

"Devora," Papa said, transforming back into the strong governor Devora knew him to be. "We've been communicating with our allies and heard of your escape. However, the king sent two of his spies earlier this week, disguised to appear like you." He crunched his hand into a fist. "Thankfully, they were disposed of before they found out who our allies were, but King Atol is cunning." Papa smirked. "I'm glad your mother's design for the trap worked."

Devora gasped. "Mama, *you* made that?"

Mama dusted off her shoulders. "I attended Vlacklear Academy too. Thank you very much. In fact, I excelled in creating traps."

Devora couldn't help but laugh, so thankful her parents were alive.

"Before we continue," Mama said, she gestured to One Shot, who had taken to standing awkwardly by the wall with his crossbow. "Who is this?"

"This is One Shot," Devora explained, striding next to her friend. "He's a comrade I made in the Fortress."

Mama's brows rose up her forehead, her eyes twinkling. "Ah, I see."

Devora scrubbed a hand over her face. "No, Mama, not like that. Really just a friend." Even after everything that happened, Mama was still trying to marry her off.

"A pleasure to meet you both," One Shot said, bowing deeply. "Madam Medee, though I owe my freedom to your daughter, I assure you she and I are only friends, nothing more."

"Very good, son," Cusha Medee said, reaching up to clap One Shot on the shoulder. He quickly slung his arm around One Shot's neck and pulled him close. "Is there anyone else I need to know about? Any prisoners who fancied my daughter?"

"Papa!" Devora groaned and gave One Shot a warning look.

The tall man cleared his throat, a playful glint twinkling in his eye. "No, sir, no *prisoners*."

Devora narrowed her gaze, thankful One Shot kept his mouth shut. She didn't have the time or energy to dredge up her emotions for Matthias. She then remembered what Madge said, the captain had visited her parents.

"Mama, Papa," Devora exclaimed. "Madge said Matt—er—Captain Blake came here less than a fortnight ago."

Anticipation squirmed through her veins as her parents shared a look.

"Yes," Mama said, striding to her wooden oak desk. She pulled out a piece of parchment wrapped in a black ribbon. Tied in the ribbon was a dried purple rose. "He didn't say much but said to give this to you when you came. We didn't know what he meant, but after everything he's done for your father and I, we trust him." Mama held out the paper and flower to Devora.

"Though, I'm worried as to how he knew you'd be coming," Papa confessed, taking Mama's hand in his own. "Captain Blake is an incredible soldier, but he may be in over his head with the king."

Devora fingered the flower. Avoiding its thorns, she plucked it from the ribbon and brought it to her nose. It smelled lovely, just like her favorite rose soap Papa bought her. And the color was stunning, almost the exact shade of violet as her eyes. Why would he send her a purple rose? Was there hope for their relationship after his betrayal? Did she desire reconciliation?

Placing the flower on a nearby table, Devora began to untie the black ribbon when she remembered the imperial opal ring Papa had sent. "Papa, did you send me an imperial opal ring?"

Guilt strewed over the Governor's features. "As much as it pains me to say, yes I did."

"But why? Captain Blake said it would kill me. Why would you send me something like that?"

"We've always known imperial opal would harm you," Mama interceded. "It was one of the first things recommended when we found out about your gift. But we refused. Even a short exposure could kill you."

"King Atol knows the strength of imperial opal," Papa growled. "When I was being less than cooperative in his dungeons, he forced me to write you that note." Papa balled his thick hand into a fist and slammed it into the wall. Devora jumped. "He said if I didn't comply, he would see to it that your mother was killed and Grenly set aflame."

Devora shook her head, unable to believe the lengths King Atol would go to for control over her father.

"I prayed to Tunri that someone would intercept the parcel and tell you what it really was." Papa kept his eyes glued on his fist.

"Thankfully, someone did," Devora replied, looking down at the scroll from Matthias.

Papa asked her more questions, but his words turned to mumbles as Devora untied the black ribbon.

Why is my heart beating so fast? It's not like this is a confession of love or anything, right?

Yet as her eyes scanned the note, her heart plummeted. Columns and rows filled with symbols stared back at her. She immediately recognized the puzzle. It was one Tenton used when trying to send a message without the information falling into the wrong hands. Another strategy described in General Teague's book. A Counter Code, it was called. The decoder had to count the number of symbols and match them to letters to find the source that held the rest of the message. It could be a scroll, a prayer, a book, anything. Once the correct source was located, each symbol represented a number. Using the source, that number would guide you to the correct word, eventually writing out the message. She studied about them a week before her Categorization Call.

Devora scanned the note again. It was a tedious but effective way of communicating.

"What does it say?" One Shot asked, peering over her shoulder. "A code?"

"What kind of code?" Papa's eyes lit with excitement.

"A Counter Code," Devora said, already having counted the symbols to find the source.

Sixteen symbols. The sixteenth letter in the Tentonian alphabet was *preco*. It was also a reference to prayer or prayer scrolls. Every noble family in Tenton owned the standard Tentonian prayer scroll. Even if they didn't follow Tunri's teachings, having the scrolls showed the noble family's reverence and respect to Tunri. And Matthias knew this.

Devora's head shot up. "I need the prayer scrolls."

Mama hurried to her desk again and pulled out their family scrolls. Devora winced at the sight of them, remembering how she so carelessly tossed them aside.

Thank you for forgiving my ignorance, she thought to Tunri.

Mama, Papa, and One Shot carefully laid the scroll out on the floor, using clay bowls and cups to press the corners flat. The elegant, lined ink of prayers to Tunri shined against the fire's light.

Devora crouched next to the prayers and laid Matthias' note next to it. Before she could say anything, Papa placed an inked quill in her hand.

"Thank you," she said and got to work.

An hour passed before Devora finally finished the code. Ink smeared across her thumb and pointer finger, but she had done it.

Leave it to Matthias to send the most complex Counter Code I've ever seen, she thought as she rubbed her sore neck.

Taking the parchment in her hands, she read:

Devora,

I will spend eternity trying to earn your forgiveness.

Below are coordinates where a trusted ally will meet you to find further information about the princess' whereabouts. The ally also has vested interest in searching for my mother.

The ally will have a means of communicating with me. When you meet them, send word.

A drip of ink splattered on the symbols above, as if Matthias had hesitated when writing the conclusion. Devora could imagine him leaning over the parchment, brows furrowed, eyes stormy. Her stomach filled with butterflies just thinking about it.

This rose reminded me of you. Not a day passes that you do not cross my mind. I pray when we meet again, you will forgive me.

Tears collected in the corners of her eyes as she tried to read the coordinates. She made out a few numbers, but her emotions got the better of her and the tears took over.

"Devora!" Mama gasped, coming beside her. "What is it?"

Before Devora could protest, Mama took the note and read. "Oh," she said softly. "I see." Giving Devora back the note, she lifted her chin. "Do not waste tears on the past, my dove. Save them for the joys of the future." Mama planted a kiss on Devora's head and stood.

"Cusha, ring for Madge. Devora and her friend need supplies and nourishment for the next few days."

"Where are we going?" One Shot asked, slinging his crossbow across his back.

Devora dried her tears and stood. She looked at the note again. She thought her future with Matthias was over. But maybe, after a long explanation, there was still hope.

Pointing to the coordinates Devora turned to One Shot and said, "We're going to Yekel."

Chapter Nine

Not good, Rae thought as the tall, thin man strode into the Fighter's Ring. She backed up into the corner of the square.

This guy has to be at least half-giant, he's huge!

Very few giants frequented Yekel now. Since Kadesh offered the giant men and women jewels to fight for them, most had left Tenton. Rae had seen the giants before but never dealt with them personally as they passed through Yekel toward Kadesh. Master Monham and the Wizard Wankle said most of them were kind enough. Although she heard some stories of giants trashing a vendor's booth if they were cheated, a response Rae could understand.

"Fighters, ready!" Jasper yelled, spittle flying from his mouth. "Go!"

Rae usually launched into the fight, already having her technique figured out. But that was because she knew all the fighters in the Dark Market. During the day, when she brought water and supplies to the Yekelian workers, she studied the men. Memorized how they walked and moved and made special note of weaknesses like a former injury. She used those observations to her advantage in the Fighter's Ring.

But this man, the Goliath, she knew nothing about.

Her breaths were hot as she quickly analyzed him through the red mesh.

Unnaturally tall. Try to stay low.

Thin limbs. Easily sprained.

Thick black hair, kind eyes. Nice to look at.
What?

Rae mentally slapped herself. *Focus, Rae. Men are beasts, monsters. This one is no different.*

"Get on with it, Cord!" a brute yelled from the crowd.

Fight, fight! the Beast of Rage added.

He was right. Rae was stalling, and they all knew it. She was surprised to note that the Goliath hadn't made a move either. He simply stood there, watching her. For a moment, Rae thought he'd seen through her disguise. But then he blinked and started walking around the square toward her.

Rae sprang into action, her mind reeling as she darted away.

First, swing legs out from beneath him.
Then, pin him down by any means necessary.
Last, subdue with cord.

Rae's muscles pumped with adrenaline as she raced toward the Goliath. Not only did she want to fight, but she wanted to know more about the Goliath's sponsor, the Winner. Something told her the Winner knew about the Seer. When Rae beat the Goliath, she would find out all she needed to save the women in the Temple.

As soon as Rae closed in on the Goliath, she swung her leg out. Just when her foot was about to contact his, he jumped back. Rae's leg kept going and she flailed to the side. Thankfully, she caught herself and sprang back up.

Analyzing him again, she rethought her plan.

First, jump onto his back.
Then, pull him to the ground.
Last, subdue with cord.

Licking her lips, Rae started toward the Goliath again. But as she jumped, he swiftly dodged out of the way.

Frustration and fury hammered her chest. *How does he know all my moves? And why isn't he attacking?*

Rae was so lost in her rage she hadn't noticed the silence. The crowd usually yelled and cheered during the brawls. But the only thing she could hear was Jasper's abacus beads clinking back and forth.

Rae growled, hating the Goliath more and more, even though he hadn't laid a hand on her. *Am I not good enough for him? He doesn't want to waste his time on someone like me?*

What bothered her the most was that his features never wavered. Most of her opponents growled or spit at her when they fought. But the Goliath remained stoic as he dodged each attack. It made Rae furious.

Beat him! the Beast of Rage roared.

Seething, Rae rushed forward without a plan. She knew it wouldn't end well, but she didn't want to think anymore. She wanted to fight. She *needed* to fight.

The fight was over before it even began. With one movement, the Goliath kicked her feet from beneath her, as if flicking away a pesky fly. The air rushed from Rae's lungs as she landed flat on her back, staring at the ceiling through her red mesh.

Get up.

GET UP!

Everything she'd worked for would be gone. She had to move. But her limbs refused.

Before she could force herself to rise, a large black boot gently laid on her stomach. The Goliath peered down at her, his eyes still kind, his features shifting into a look of remorse.

"Sorry," he muttered, his voice deep and rough.

Rae almost thought he meant it.

The crowd stayed quiet, not knowing how to react. Rae closed her eyes, wishing the Goliath would crush her with his big foot. After crawling her way to the top, she was defeated so easily. Was she really that poor a fighter? Or were her previous opponents all so weak?

You've never been good enough, the Beast of Envy piped in.

Jasper said the Winner came from Juro. Maybe the Goliath was from there, too. Were the fighters in the north tougher than the south?

We'll always be too weak, the Beast of Fear sobbed.

Rae's thoughts spiraled until Jasper declared the Goliath the victor. The crowd cheered, but not as loudly as they usually did. Maybe they disliked the new fighter as much as Rae did.

Once the foot lifted off her chest, the Goliath offered her his hand. Offended, Rae slapped it out of the way and stood on her own. She didn't need his pity.

With her fighting spirit crushed, Rae turned to leave when Jasper intercepted her.

"The Winner has requested your presence." He rattled the beads on his abacus back and forth as he took a few more bags of coin. "And here." The Keeper of the Coins handed her a bag filled with heavy gold coins.

Rae looked at the bag then up at Jasper. "What's this?" she asked in the deepest voice she could manage.

Jasper flicked his hand. "The Goliath doesn't want the winnings. He said to give them to you."

Rae clenched the pouch in her gloved hand. "You can tell him to shove his winnings—"

Jasper clucked his tongue and waved his finger at her. "I didn't know the Crimson Cord had such a temper." Rae swallowed her words. Jasper smirked. "I suggest you see the Winner. There are many of high nobility in Juro who choose fighters as their personal knights. Maybe this is your way out."

Rae caught the sadness in Jasper's voice. Like the rest of the Yekelians, he was doing what he knew in order to survive. If any of them could flee, they would. There were only two ways out of Yekel: paying an unattainable sum of coin, or death.

A spark of hope ignited in Rae's chest as she bowed to Jasper and headed to find the Winner. She kept the coins, knowing she could use them to buy one more woman's freedom.

The Winner had rented a room in the back of the Dark Market. It was dim like the rest of the market and filled with *menta* smoke. Rae resisted the urge to cough.

When the smoke subsided enough, she saw the Goliath standing next to a seated pair behind a rectangular table. The Goliath's long arms were crossed over his chest, and the kind eyes from before were gone, replaced with a cold stare.

Did I imagine the remorse in his tone? she thought. But shoved it away.

Revenge! the Beast of Rage begged, but Rae buried the thought. For now. She needed to gamble correctly if she wanted to save the temple women and flee Yekel.

"Ah, the Crimson Cord," the Winner said, not bothering to rise. "I've been watching you for some time."

A dark hood, pulled low over his face, obscured any defining features. Now that she was closer, Rae noticed that the figure next to him was a woman. But instead of a dark hood, the woman wore a familiar veil of dark mesh over her head. Rae's heart constricted.

A Temple Priestess? Here?

General Yada never let the women leave the Temple unless escorted by his minions. Rae's eyes darted around. Although the general knew about the Dark Market, he never came, and as long as the Dark Market gave him a percentage of their earnings, he let them be.

Looking closer, Rae discovered that the woman's veil wasn't gray like the Temple Priestesses, but black. The woman was still stiff as stone. Rae recognized that stance. Was she being forced to be here?

Rae despised the Winner and the Goliath more than before. "What do you want?" she growled through the red mesh covering her face.

The eyes of the Goliath burned into her, almost as if he could see through her disguise.

The Winner gave a sultry chuckle, one Rae had heard from men like him many times. She hated it.

"Just to talk, my friend." The Winner snapped his fingers, and the Goliath pulled a wooden chair before his boss. "Please, have a seat."

Rae plopped down. She crossed her arms over her chest, mimicking the Goliath as she glared at the Winner.

"A little birdie told me you have the information I need," the Winner crooned as he snapped at the Goliath again.

For the first time, the tall man growled at the Winner. Something passed between them that Rae couldn't distinguish. The woman gave a small cough, and the Goliath poured the Winner and Rae a drink.

Rae quirked a brow at the strange interaction but decided to take the bait. "What information?"

The Winner pushed forward the rolled piece of parchment from earlier across the table. Tenting his fingertips on his lips, he leaned forward. The dim light of the room displayed thick lips curling into a sly smile. "I'm looking for a certain person, someone who has been hidden for a long time."

Rae rolled her eyes at the cryptic talk. She was already irritated and didn't want to stay here longer than needed. "Look, I don't have the time or patience for this nonsense. Without a name, I can't help you."

The Goliath smirked at her response, and she could've sworn the woman behind the veil laughed.

The Winner drew back, offended. "It's on the parchment."

Snatching the paper up, Rae made a show of unrolling it begrudgingly. The dark ink came into view, and Rae's hands froze. Her mind immediately soared back to her time at the Temple. Kanna Blake. The only woman in the Temple who didn't receive visitors. The only woman in the Temple who was called a criminal and treated like one. But Rae never knew why.

Kanna had always been kind. Rae blinked and before she could stop it, a memory from the Temple squirmed into her thoughts.

One month had passed in the Temple and Rae had already lost her will to live. She was a new addition to General Yada's brothel, and the Temple visitors took notice.

Rae tried to hide, tried to flee, but was never successful. She eventually submitted, feeling her soul crumble away with each visitor that stalked through her door.

After her last appointment, she fled from her room, trying to find an escape. But all she found was a stairwell leading to a dead end. Rae crouched into a ball and cried. Never had she thought that saving Nadia and the others would lead to this. If she had known, she would've fled with them.

The pain was too much, and her heart couldn't bear it. She found a sharp rock on the ground and sliced into her skin. A dribble of blood oozed out of her arm. It was the first time Rae had felt something other than numbness in weeks. As she raised the stone to make another cut a voice spoke from beside her.

"What's the matter?" a soft female voice asked.

Rae jumped into the air, trying to suppress her scream. The sharp rock clattered to the ground as Rae scurried from the voice.

"It's all right," the voice soothed. A thin hand stretched out from iron bars lining the wall.

Rae narrowed her gaze. It was dark at the end of the hall, but her eyes adjusted enough to see a figure seated behind the cell bars.

"Who are you?" Rae asked. "Are you a Temple Priestess?"

The women sighed. "I'd say more of a prisoner, but I think in either position I would feel trapped."

Rae blinked, unsure how to respond.

"How's your wrist?"

Rae peered down at her hand. The cut she made wasn't too deep, and the wound was already starting to clot. She squeezed her fingers around it.

"I'll live, unfortunately."

"I hope so," the woman confessed. "Your life is far too valuable to throw away."

Rae grunted. This woman was probably crazy from being locked up down here so long. "Sure it is."

Rae could almost hear the smile in the woman's voice as she added, "The actions of others do not define who you are. Only you decide who you want to be."

Rae resurfaced from the memory. Kanna had helped her in her darkest time, and Rae would never forget it. After that night, Rae tried to visit Kanna whenever she could. Rae told her all about Mami and Papi, and Kanna told stories of her husband and two boys. Rae owed Kanna her very life, for it was Kanna who helped Rae buy her freedom from the Temple.

But Rae had been gone from the Temple for two years. Kanna told her to leave and never look back. Who knew if she was still there? Rae glanced up from the parchment, realizing she hadn't spoken in a few moments.

"I may have heard of her," she said. Folding the parchment, Rae slid it back to the Winner who handed it to the Goliath. The Goliath placed the parchment in a lantern hanging on the wall.

Rae watched the paper burn until it was nothing but ash.

Rae leaned back in her chair. She owed Kanna tremendously. She wasn't about to hand her over to the arrogant brutes in front of her.

"What payment do you require?" the Winner asked nonchalantly.

Rae studied the three. She should have asked for more coin, but the Goliath's winnings were enough for her to free another woman and purchase more supplies for her shop. No, what she really wanted was another fight.

Fight and win! the Beast of Rage resurfaced with a bark.

Extending her hand, Rae pointed at the Goliath. "I want to fight him. For real this time. No dodges, no deflects, a real fight. If he wins, I'll tell you what you want to know about Kanna Blake. But if I win, you tell me who you three really are."

The Winner and the woman shared a look before glancing at the Goliath. He never broke his gaze from Rae as he stepped forward.

Bowing his head, he answered. "I accept."

Chapter Ten

Devora, Outskirts of Yekel

After a tear-filled and lengthy farewell, Mama and Papa snuck Devora and One Shot out of the governor's mansion without being noticed by King Atol's numerous guards. Waiting in the thick brush of Grenly's jungles was Vinn. He had been successful in keeping himself hidden while One Shot and Devora were away. Devora wasn't sure whether the giant magical creature had the power to turn himself invisible or if he was just that good at hiding.

The elk-like creature nuzzled into Devora's hand before she and One Shot climbed on his back. When Devora first entered the Fortress, Vinn spoke to her telepathically. Devora still wasn't sure how or why she could communicate with the animal. But instead of trying to figure it out, she placed her hand on the silky white hair covering Vinn's neck and told him the coordinates from Matthias' code.

Vinn, thankfully having a keen sense of direction, snorted and started south. Daybreak was in a few hours, and they had to get as far away from Grenly as possible before sunrise.

Devora clamped her fingers around Vinn's shining white fur and leaned forward. The purple sash around her wrist gleamed against the bright moon. One Shot, seated behind her, did the same. They rode in silence, not wanting to alert anyone or anything to their presence as they barreled through the jungle.

Thick, emerald leaves, bigger than Devora's head, slapped against her and One Shot's sides as Vinn galloped.

Vinn's gait was long and fierce, and it took every ounce of strength Devora had to not fall off. She glanced over her shoulder. Thankfully, One Shot was still back there. Although with his unnaturally white knuckles fisted around Vinn's hair and his eyes squeezed tight, Devora wasn't sure how much more riding One Shot could take. He said he was fine, but his reaction to Vinn darting between the tall palm trees said otherwise. And Devora was still concerned about his leg. It had only been a week or two since the Battle of Edo when his leg had been impaled with a massive shard of glass created by Kadesh's giants. Though his skin had mended, Devora knew the injury was deep.

An hour later, they were far enough from Grenly. Giant palm trees surrounded them as Vinn slowed to a pleasant trot. They still had an hour or so before sunrise, so they kept moving. As fugitives traveling on an enormous white creature, it was difficult to remain unseen during the day. So, the group decided to move during the night and rest during the day.

One Shot breathed a sigh of relief at the change of pace.

Devora turned to check on him. "How are you faring?"

"I've been better," he replied stoically, his eyes now open and his grip looser.

Devora laughed, enjoying his blatant honesty. "Let's travel until sunrise and then we'll find somewhere to rest. Sound good?"

One Shot nodded. "You're in charge."

Devora pursed her lips. She didn't want to be in charge of this venture at all, but here she was. Tunri had set her on this path, and she was just trying to make the right decisions.

"You can be in charge, if you'd like," she offered. She'd been quick to accept Warden Hazor's quest in finding Princess Haden and Kanna Blake, but One Shot never said anything regarding the matter.

"I'm good," he replied in his deep voice. "You're better at making quick decisions than I am."

Devora wasn't sure how to respond, so she kept silent.

Vinn sniffed the air every few meters, trying to decide which direction to take. After a moment, he chose an opening to his left and continued east.

Taking a few steps, Vinn paused, his ears twitching. Devora slowed her breathing as an eerie aura crept over her skin.

Has King Atol found us?

She'd never heard of the king keeping soldiers in Grenly's thick jungle, but after everything she'd experienced in the past few weeks, she wouldn't put it past him.

Just then a streak of orange and black zinged through the air barreling into Vinn's front legs. The giant elk stumbled then reared back on its hind legs as Devora and One Shot held on for dear life.

An orange and black striped tiger circled around them, baring its long, white teeth.

Devora held her breath, remembering the iron-armored beasts from the Battle of Edo. They were far bigger than the tiger before her, but that didn't mean she was happy to see the growling feline.

The tiger leapt again, this time clamping its jaws around Vinn's hind leg. Vinn roared and bucked, sending Devora and One Shot flying off his back. Devora smacked into the trunk of a tall tree, causing several papayas to scatter around her from the impact. One Shot, a few meters away, was already on his feet. Leaning on his good leg, he had his crossbow resting on his shoulder as he positioned a shot.

The tiger kept its jaws clamped around Vinn's legs. Vinn tried to shake it off, stomp on it, anything, but the feline wouldn't relent.

"One Shot, shoot! Now!" Devora cried as blood squirted from Vinn's leg.

With a grunt, One Shot unleashed a series of arrows into the tiger's hide. The feline roared before thumping to the ground, dead.

Devora sprang up and hurried toward the animal whose jaws had thankfully released Vinn's leg. With One Shot's help, they were able to drag the tiger away from Vinn. The giant white creature moaned. Blood marred his perfectly white hair. He lowered his head and licked the seeping wound.

Devora placed a hand on Vinn's nose as he cleaned his leg. "We need to find a stream to clean the wound and rest. It wouldn't be wise to continue with him injured like this."

"Agreed." One Shot nodded, his dark eyes scanning the jungle. He hadn't lowered his crossbow just yet.

The sun peeked above the horizon. Thankfully, Grenly's jungles extended almost to the border of Yekel. With Yekel being another day away, the trees would be an excellent place to hide, and they offered an added benefit of shelter from the burning sun.

Vinn's ears twitched as he scanned the jungle. He then limped forward toward a small creek before hobbling in a circle, clearing a spot for them to rest. Once satisfied, the giant elk crouched to the ground.

Devora and One Shot followed. In a matter of moments, they cleaned and bandaged Vinn's wound.

With a bow of his head, Vinn carefully stood to his full height and slowly limped to the stream, lapping up a well-deserved drink.

One Shot and Devora set out a few bags of dried fruit, a loaf of bread, a jug of water, a hunk of cheese, and some cured meats that Mama and Papa provided. Although the jungle was moist and cool, wafts of heat swirled by, reminding Devora how they never needed a fire for warmth in Grenly.

Vinn returned and lay behind Devora.

Time to rest? The elk asked in his soft voice.

Devora patted him on the side. *Yes, thank you, my friend.*

Vinn lowered his head to the ground and promptly closed his eyes.

Leaning against Vinn's soft hair, Devora also felt the pull of sleep tugging at her. But what One Shot said before the tiger attacked still bothered her.

She cleared her throat. "Why are you helping me?"

Devora remembered asking Matthias the same question only weeks ago when he agreed to help her train for the Regulus Protecti tournament. Devora's heart surged, and her hand went to the pocket of the pants he had given her. Pulling out a piece of tan fabric, she unfolded it to reveal the purple petals of the rose he'd given her. Though they were crumpled and wrinkled, they still smelled like bliss. Where was Matthias now?

One Shot paused, his fingers pinching a chunk of cheese. As he set the piece down, he blinked at her, confused. Devora placed the petals back in her pocket and engaged her soulsight. His soul was still more blue than yellow, and it concerned her.

"Why wouldn't I?" He placed his hand over his chest where the light of his soul shone. "I know when you're doing that."

Devora released her soulsight, heat tinging her cheeks as she focused on tearing off a piece of bread.

"I know you were falsely accused," she started. "But that doesn't mean you have to help me look for Princess Haden or Kanna."

Devora popped the piece of bread in her mouth, anxiously awaiting his reply.

One Shot slowly ran a hand through his shaggy black hair. Matted with sweat from the heat, it clung to his forehead and covered his eyes.

"You used your pardon to save me, and you befriended me when no one would look my way," his bass tone rumbled. "The only other person to do that was Matthias. But I guess he had to."

Devora's gaze shot up at the mention of the captain. "Why did he have to be your friend?"

One Shot placed the cheese in his mouth and chewed for an agonizingly long time. Devora fiddled with a bag of dates, stirring them with her finger as she waited.

"When he first entered the Fortress, Matthias was my cellmate," One Shot replied. "Given my reputation, I wonder if the Warden wanted to see if Matthias would cower away or try to fight me. But he didn't do either." A ghost of a smile lined One Shot's thin lips. "Instead, he became my friend."

Devora's heart warmed, remembering how Matthias had convinced One Shot to join them at the Battle of Edo. That was why One Shot agreed so readily.

"The first few months Matthias was there, he was rarely allowed to leave the cell, and neither was I. So, he taught me the fighting techniques he'd learned at Vlacklear, and I told him of my crossbow and recipes—"

"Whoa, wait," Devora held up her hands. "Recipes? You cook?"

One Shot quirked his brow. "I bake."

A laugh burbled in her throat, but she kept it down. "And shoot scarily accurate arrows into people's hearts?"

Upon seeing the giddiness trying to escape from Devora, One Shot's tone flattened. "I don't see why I can't do both."

Unable to hold it in any longer, Devora burst into a fit of laughter. Tears streamed down her cheeks until One Shot sent her a deadly glare.

Wiping her eyes with her fingers, she smiled. "I'm sorry, One Shot. I just wasn't expecting that."

"Who do you think made that cocoa cake you enjoyed?"

Devora gasped, remembering the cocoa cake Matthias brought her after the first round of Regulus Protecti. "That was you? It was amazing! How did you get the ingredients and the blue paper in the Fortress?"

The cake had been so beautifully made and wrapped, Devora assumed Matthias purchased it from a patisserie in Juro.

One Shot shrugged, still offended by her laughter. "I used to have kitchen duty before Nadia."

The mood immediately dampened into despair as soon as One Shot mentioned their friend. Warden Hazor told Devora not to worry about Nadia, Reese, Hestia, Ida, or Sir Jacques. But she did. Over the course of a few weeks, they'd become her family. She hoped she could trust Warden Hazor to bring them all back, wherever they were, unharmed.

"I'm sure they're okay," One Shot offered. Wincing, he moved his left leg before biting into a piece of bread. "I'm sure Matthias is, too."

Devora pinched her lips shut, not wanting to talk about the captain to his former cellmate. She was still furious at Matthias for how he betrayed her at the ball *after* kissing her on the battlefield. Though she worried about him, she wanted to slap him on his perfectly chiseled jaw.

When she didn't respond, One Shot merely shrugged and lay down to sleep.

Devora studied the crumpled leaves Vinn flattened to make their resting space. Closing her eyes, she focused on Kanna. The violet light led her thoughts through the jungle toward Yekel. Just like it had when she first deciphered Matthias' code. While she was thankful for the captain's help in guiding her next steps, he also sent her an impossibly difficult code to solve.

But I did solve it, she mused to herself.

She prayed that the 'source' waiting for them in Yekel was a reliable one.

Devora awoke in her vision, scrambling for bearings. The enclosed space surrounding her was dank and musty, like the lower levels of the Fortress. But this wasn't the Fortress.

Whispers danced around her ears. Figures cloaked in robes, concealing their identities, passed by her. Devora searched the room. This was a place where secrets were revealed and buried.

The clinking of coins chimed ahead, and she followed the sound. Cloaked figures exchanged bags of coins and hushed words. But she continued on to where a warm light beamed.

Shouts and curses chased out the whispers as Devora entered a square room crammed with bodies. In the center was another square made of sticks and rope. Only when two men entered the marked off square, did Devora realize it was a fighting ring.

She focused on the fight, recognizing One Shot as one of the participants. The other was a smaller man clothed in all black with red mesh over his face. A matching red cord wrapped around his waist.

Devora studied the man. Something about him was different.

But she didn't have time to think about it because the fight began. One Shot dodged the other man's attacks easily and was victorious.

The vision shifted and spiraled into a large marble building. It was cold like the previous room of whispers, but there was something else here. Something dark. Something evil.

An eerie sensation rippled across Devora's thoughts as she continued across the creamy white stone. No one was around. Lining the stone walls were a series of black doors, each one adorned with a symbol carved in gold and scrawled in Kadesh's tongue.

The vision spun her around to face a statue in the center. Molded from imperial opal stood the likeness of a woman draped in swaths of fabric. But something wasn't right. This woman had two giant horns curling from the top of her head. Her shining straight hair swung down to her waist as her hands outstretched to the vacant room.

The statue was disturbing enough, but what rattled Devora most was the place where the horned woman's heart should be. An orb, filled with dark light spun of its own will in the statue's chest.

The evil of the statue's presence weighed on Devora's mind. She tried to flee, but the eyes of the statue glowed, almost putting her into a trance. Black spirals of smoke leeched from the cavity in the statue's chest. Devora was confused until she engaged her soulsight and saw her own soul being pulled into the statue.

Pain ripped through her core as Devora struggled, fighting against the possessed statue. Then suddenly the vision went black.

Devora's head slammed on the jungle floor as the giant elk shrugged off sleep and rose from behind her.

Groaning, she rubbed the back of her head noticing her ebony hair was frizzier than it had been in the north.

Humidity is the worst.

She undid her plait and redid it before filling their water jug in the creek, doing her best to keep the purple sash around her wrist dry. Her vision of the fight and the statue stealing her soul troubled her.

Where was the fighting ring? And why was One Shot fighting?

A chill ran down her spine. She didn't want to know where the statue was, but she had a feeling she would find out soon.

With a peek at the sun, Devora calculated it was an hour before dusk. They'd had to wait for the cover of nightfall to travel for most of their journey. But since the jungle trees covered Vinn entirely, Devora decided it was time to continue.

When she walked back to their small camp, One Shot was already up and had gathered all their things in preparation for their departure.

"With the covering of the jungle, I figured you'd want to move quickly," he said.

Devora nodded. "Thank you, yes."

After Vinn drank more water, he returned and lowered himself to the ground. Devora checked his wound and was surprised to find it almost healed.

"It seems you have more than one power," she said to the creature as she rubbed his nose. Vinn flapped his lips and nuzzled her hand, making Devora laugh. "Are you sure you can continue? One Shot and I could walk."

Vinn snorted. *He cannot walk well, and I am healed.*

Devora nodded and climbed up on Vinn's back with One Shot following her. In a matter of moments, they were off. Galloping at full speed, Vinn darted between the tall jungle trees. Devora could feel the excitement pouring off the giant elk. She remembered the chains wrapped around Vinn's neck and limbs—how his ribs had stuck out of his sides. Devora rubbed the animal's neck. How long had it been since Vinn was free to run wherever he pleased?

She still couldn't understand why Warden Hazor had treated Vinn so horribly. Now that she knew the warden a bit better, he didn't seem as terrible as when she first arrived at the Fortress. If it weren't for him, Devora and Matthias would have probably been hanged by now.

It was almost midnight when they reached Matthias' coordinates. Devora breathed a sigh of relief, thanking Tunri for the cover of nightfall. As soon as they reached the outskirts of Yekel, it was as if every scrap of foliage died. There wasn't a tree or bush as far as the eye could see.

The barren landscape was similar to Juro. But while Juro was frigid, Yekel was hot and dry like a desert.

"Vinn should probably stay in the jungle," One Shot advised, his calm gaze analyzing the land before them.

"I agree." Devora patted Vinn's neck, relaying the plan to him. The creature did not like leaving Devora alone, but she assured him they would be safe and would return as soon as possible.

Snorting, Vinn reluctantly lowered to the ground. *Be safe*, he whispered in Devora's mind.

You too, Devora replied and watched as the giant creature melted back into the thick jungle.

"The cover of night should help us get to the city," Devora said to One Shot. "But let's do our best to not be seen."

One Shot nodded and kept the arrows in his crossbow poised, ready for anything.

As the two crossed the thick sand, Devora held her breath, praying no one would see them. They strode along for what seemed like years when a city with a half-destroyed wall came into view. Tall, unwavering stone jutted from the barren landscape. Devora assumed the broken stone was where Kadesh invaded years ago. *Why isn't it already repaired?*

Guards patrolled the damaged section of the wall. She and One Shot immediately darted in the opposite direction. In a few more steps they would be where the code led. Matthias' source had to be around here somewhere.

They finally reached the exact coordinates along the outer wall of Yekel.

A door the exact shade of the stone blended into the wall. With the darkness of night, it was nearly impossible to see. If Devora hadn't searched her thoughts and seen the purple Seer light piercing through the wall, she would never have thought to check the stone for a door.

"Should we knock?" One Shot asked with raised brows.

Devora took a breath and nodded, doing her best to trust the word of the man who'd broken her heart.

One Shot knocked three solid times and waited, his hand steady on his crossbow.

The door creaked open, revealing a figure in a black cloak. Devora took a hesitant step back. One Shot raised his weapon.

The figure stepped out from the doorway and pushed back its hood.

Devora's jaw dropped, unable to comprehend what was happening and who stood before her.

"My dearest honeybee," Tristan crooned. "Did you miss me?"

Chapter Eleven

Rae, Fighter's Ring, Dark Market

Rae shoved through the crowd of men, the evil in the Dark Market weighing heavily upon her shoulders. She'd fought hundreds of men in the last year. So why did the fight with Goliath feel unfair?

Rae banished the thought. Life wasn't fair. She accepted that fact a long time ago. When she suggested a rematch to the Winner, she half expected him to laugh in her face. Any sponsor would have outright refused, especially after their fighter beat the top fighter in the ring.

But Rae knew the Winner and his crew weren't an average gang visiting the Dark Market. How did they know about Kanna? There was something off about them. Something—Rae thought—that would lead her to more information about the Seer.

Rae barreled up to Jasper who sat at a rickety table in the back corner of the squared room. Stacks of gold coins spread around him as he counted the evening's fights on his abacus. The Keeper of the Coins didn't look up as he said, "There will be no additional winnings for the same contenders to fight."

Rae stared at the man, realizing that, for the first time since entering the Fighter's Ring, she wasn't fighting for coin. This time, she was fighting for her pride.

It had taken her months to build up her name. She wasn't going to let some mysterious giant-like man ruin it.

"No coin is necessary," she grumbled, trying to keep her voice low. "Just the ring."

Scribbling on a piece of parchment with a large, white feather quill, Jasper flicked his wrist at her. "Very well. Once the last fight finishes, the ring is yours."

Anticipation and excitement coursed through Rae's limbs. She quickly bowed and turned to tell the Goliath.

"Tell me, Cord," Jasper called out to her. Rae stopped and glanced over her shoulder. "Why fight again? Why not just take his winnings and do what you wish?"

Rae stared at her black leather gloves. Even though the Temple destroyed her, even though she'd sank to the depths of the Dark Market with the worst criminals in Yekel, there was still a spark of morality in her heart. Tunri turned a blind eye as she was abused by the Temple and she hated Him, Pahga, and all other gods for it. But if she didn't win the coin to free the Temple women fairly, then she didn't win it at all.

"To prove my worth," she muttered, then stalked away.

The Fighter's Ring cleared out as soon as the last fight ended. Judging by the dreary look of the men's stature, it was a few hours until sunrise. Rae knew she would be exhausted when helping distribute water and supplies to the workers tomorrow, but she had to do this. She needed to know all her sacrifices, all her lies, all her schemes, were justified.

As soon as the last fighters and gamblers left, Rae entered the ring. She walked around the square, remembering her first fight two years ago.

Freedom never felt so good. Unfortunately, freedom came with a high price. Two weeks passed since Rae had scrounged enough coin to buy her freedom from the Temple. She knew General Yada would make the price to leave incredibly high. He wanted to break her, kill her hopes—all so that she would give up and stay there forever. But there was something the general didn't know about Rae. She never gave up.

It was only a few days after she left the Temple that she caught wind of the fights in the Dark Market. Though she wasn't a Street Rat or a Falcon, Rae learned hemna and other fighting techniques from Papi before he was taken to work for the king. It had been a while since she fought, but after she saw the amount of coin she could win, Rae was determined to enter the Fighter's Ring.

In two weeks' time she'd created a name, a disguise, and sold enough scarves to pay the entrance fee. She didn't have a sponsor or gang to pay her way, so she had to do it herself. And if she won, she could start to save the other women from the terror of the Temple.

Nerves bounced in every fiber of her being as she located the secret entrance. The cool night wind kissed her freshly shaven head, shaking her already trembling knees. She needed to put on the last piece of her disguise. Having already strapped down her chest and donned wider pants to cover her hips, the last thing she needed to do was cover her face.

Hesitant, she held up the crimson fabric. Other men in the market donned the full-face coverings, and Rae thought it would be the perfect way to hide her identity. However, the Temple always forced them to wear veils while outside, and Rae hated the covering. But she was also relieved that when she was free, no one would know who she was and what she'd endured. Unless they visited her— and such things weren't discussed outside of the Temple walls—Rae could have a fresh start without the taint of her past.

While covering her face made it difficult to breathe, Rae didn't want any of the men in the Dark Market to know who she really was. That way, when she bled them dry of coin and beat them senseless, they would have no one to blame but themselves.

Gathering her courage, Rae tied the red mesh around her face and head then knocked on the door.

The next hour went by in a blur. The doorkeeper, amused by her appearance, allowed her in and swept her through the Dark Market. The silence and eerie atmosphere raised the hairs on her neck. It was too quiet, too cold. As they kept walking, the doorkeeper led her to the makeshift arena, the Fighter's Ring, where it was anything but cold and quiet.

Rae coughed at the acrid burnt stench of the menta *smoke filling the air. The doorkeeper laughed and gave her back a good pat, saying the smell produced winners. Rae fought to keep herself from falling over with the blow.*

Eventually, they found Jasper, the Keeper of the Coins. The scrawny man stroked his spindly beard, studying Rae's outfit with a quirked brow. It seemed no one else had as vibrant a color on as she did.

"Very well," Jasper said after some quick calculations on his abacus. "You can fight Grogus in the next round. But first—" he held out his hand, and Rae placed in it the brown leather sack filled with the last coins she had.

Rae had stopped believing in the power of prayer when no one came to save her from the Temple. But, in that small moment where she gave up her last savings, she prayed that some god, any god, would multiply her coin so she could free the others.

Jasper wrapped his long fingers around the sack, eyeing it like a delectable treat.

"Good luck, Cord," Jasper chuckled and shuffled away with the doorkeeper.

Unease crept up Rae's spine at Jasper's tone, but she brushed it off and headed toward the ring.

The last round ended and members of the Falcons, one of the local gangs, kicked dirt over the drops of blood on the earthen ground. Rae swallowed the fear building in her throat, regretting her decision.

Stupid. What a stupid decision, Rae. You haven't fought in years. You're weak and untrained. You're going to get killed and not help anyone.

As anxiety oozed from her pores, Rae felt a small warmth swirl in her chest. It was something she hadn't felt since Papi was taken. Rae concentrated on the sensation.

Hope.

Something inside of her heart fed her hope, encouraging her that she would succeed.

With her newfound hope, Rae entered the ring. Not long after, Grogus entered. Rae screwed her lips in a disgusted frown beneath the red mesh. Not only did Grogus have three chins and too many rolls to count, he smelled like cow dung baked in the sun.

No wonder Jasper laughed, *Rae thought as she analyzed the rotund man.* Grogus could easily sit on me and win.

Thankfully, Rae knew hemna *and within fifteen seconds of analysis, she was ready to fight.*

"Begin!" Jasper shouted.

Rae's eyes darted around. The crowd seemed uninterested in the fight. Men were chatting with one another about bets they wanted to take later in the night.

Good, *Rae thought. She wanted them to be unsuspecting of what she was about to do.*

Grogus lumbered toward her, walking as if he were in slow motion.

Taking a breath, Rae launched herself at Grogus.

First, hit pressure points on shoulders, waist, and thighs.

Blading her hands, Rae jabbed at Grogus as hard as she could. There were so many layers of flab, she needed to use heavy force to reach the pressure points under the surface of it all.

Grogus flailed, losing the feeling in his limbs, and Rae smiled.

Next, plant foot in gut to leave unbalanced.

Rae dug her heel into his stomach. A sizeable gust of air, smelling of fish and ale, rushed from Grogus' lips. The large man toppled backward before falling.

Last, the finale.

Rushing behind him, Rae untied the bright crimson cord from her waist and looped it around Grogus' thick neck. His lazy eyes bulged as he clawed and scraped at the cord.

Rae tightened the cord just a smidge. Not enough to suffocate Grogus, but enough to allow those watching to know she was serious.

The crowd, to her satisfaction, stared, awestruck. Every eye that ignored her before was now glued on the fight. Of course, it'd taken her less than thirty seconds to subdue the blubbering beast flailing below her.

"Yield," a deep voice from the crowd said.

It was then Rae noticed that Jasper had come to the edge of the arena. His abacus clicked and clanked as men redid their bets. Greed glinted in Jasper's eyes as he took the coins and grinned at Rae.

"Master Cord," Jasper announced. "The Falcons yield the fight. You are the winner."

Rae released the cord from Grogus' neck. The man sputtered and spit all over the floor. As soon as he came to, he tried to rush Rae when her back was turned. Luckily, after being trapped in the Temple, Rae was always aware of her surroundings. She quickly spun around and kicked Grogus in the face. Blood squirted from his nose. Clutching his broken nose and muttering curses, Grogus fled the ring.

Rae faced Jasper, his face paled upon seeing Rae's reaction. But he recovered quickly.

"Your winnings, Master Cord." He handed Rae a black leather sack three times the size of the one she gave him earlier.

Giddiness bubbled in her chest. She could free at least one woman with that much coin, maybe two. And possibly purchase some new supplies for her scarves too.

Rae reached for the bag, but Jasper pulled back slightly. "Although," he started. "You can bet your winnings and fight again to receive even more."

The Beast of Fear slammed into her head, telling her she must be happy with what she earned. She wouldn't get lucky again.

But the Beast of Rage whispered, "Why not?"

Grinning beneath her mesh, Rae nodded and received an equally wide grin from Jasper.

"Excellent choice, Master Cord. If you'll follow me."

Rae studied the haphazard ring as she brushed away the memory. After that first fight, Jasper paired her up with harder opponents. The gangs heard of this new, mysterious fighter and wanted to see how he would fare in a real fight.

But just like with Grogus, Rae defeated them all.

Rae ran her fingers along the thick black cords forming the ring. The fraying edges spiraled out of control. If she stayed on this path, would she spiral out of control, too?

At the sound of a throat clearing, Rae turned around and saw that the Goliath had entered the ring. The Winner and his woman were just outside the cords. Though they kept their coverings on, Rae noted the Winner's tapping fingers and the woman clasping and unclasping her hands. They were anxious.

Good, Rae thought, just as she had during her first fight. She didn't want their pity or anyone else's. She would beat the Goliath and rightfully earn his winnings.

Crouching low, Rae analyzed the tall man again.

Tall, thin limbs.

Large feet, thin hands.

Narrow shoulders, long legs.

It was then that Rae noticed something she hadn't before. The Goliath favored one leg over the other. It was slight and to an untrained eye would be nearly impossible to detect. Rae fought the grin wanting to plaster itself across her lips. She had found the Goliath's weakness.

Yet as her gaze traveled to his face and she looked into his kind eyes, her stomach made the same flip-flop motion as it had before. Brushing the feeling aside, Rae turned away, pretending to focus on securing her boot.

Rae stood. "Ready when you are."

The Goliath nodded, then shifted his stance.

Surprised, Rae recognized the defensive stance. It was one of the four stances used in hemna. Though she hated to admit it, she was impressed and now even more curious about the tall man.

Rae didn't waste any time. She launched herself forward, planning to go for his right arm and then his weak left leg. If she could dislocate his shoulder, he would be helpless, and she could easily knock his leg out from beneath him.

But as she reached to twist his arm around his back, a force like none she had felt before thrust her away. Landing on her backside, Rae gasped for breath, staring at the Goliath.

How did he learn that *move?*

From an early age, Papi taught Rae the strategy of hemna: using your opponent's strength against them. There were many different kicks and punches in her lessons, all of which were easy for Rae to duplicate. But it wasn't until she was older that Papi taught her a more sophisticated style of hemna. One that allowed the fighter to barely touch his opponent, but still emanate a considerable amount of power. Only a handful of soldiers who fought in the beginning of the Tenton-Kadesh war knew these moves and Papi was one of them.

Rae hopped up and brushed the dust off her pants. The Goliath stayed in his defensive stance, his dark eyes watching and waiting for her next move.

He may think he was being clever, that she wouldn't know the hidden styles of hemna. But she did. And now he'd opened the doorway so she could use them as well.

Fight! the Beast of Rage egged her on, and Rae didn't need much prompting.

Bending her knees, Rae dashed toward the Goliath. She acted as if she were going toward his arm again, but at the last moment, she crouched down and swung her leg out, connecting with his feet.

The Goliath reacted faster than Rae suspected. He jumped to the side and her leg missed both of his feet. Though he tried to hide it, Rae noticed his wince when he landed too hard on his left leg.

Growling, Rae didn't give him a chance to recover as she came at him again. But with every blow she tried to make, he deflected or dodged it entirely. It wasn't until Rae almost trapped him in the ring's corner that she realized he hadn't attacked her outright.

He pities us, the Beast of Envy sighed.

The thought sent Rae's rage through the roof. She didn't need anyone's pity.

Forgetting all civility, Rae balled her hands into fists and punched the Goliath in the chin. The tall man's eyes went wide at the impact of her swing.

"Fight back!" she growled and punched him again.

But the Goliath didn't fight back. Instead, when she went for her third swing, he grabbed her fist. His fingers were so long they encased her whole hand entirely. With one arm, he stopped her entire attack. For the first time in a long time, Rae knew fear.

"I don't wish to harm anyone," he replied calmly, his dark hair falling between his eyes. "I only agreed because you seemed to need a fight."

Panting, Rae wrenched her hand out of Goliath's grasp. "I don't need your pity. If you're not going to fight, then get out of the ring."

A spark of challenge ignited in the Goliath's eyes. He glanced over to the Winner and his woman. Rae could see from the corner of her eye that the woman gave a nod.

She's the one in charge?

"Very well," the Goliath replied, and before Rae had a chance to react, he thrust his palm into her stomach, launching her across the ring.

Rae's arms dangled in the ropes around the fighting ring. The Goliath's force was unlike anything she'd experienced, and she found herself almost giddy to have a worthy opponent.

Untangling herself, Rae came up with a new tactic to defeat the Goliath. Since he knew hidden hemna, she knew exactly how to defeat him.

First, distract with gut kick.

Rae quickened her steps, circling around the Goliath until she found an opening. Jumping up, she extended her boot into the Goliath's toned stomach.

Next, swipe feet from beneath him, starting with weak leg.

Rae had to work fast. While the Goliath was suffering the impact from her blow, she crouched down and kicked his left leg out from beneath him. With a grunt, he grabbed his thigh, falling to his knees.

Last, the Crimson Cord specialty.

He was fast, but not fast enough. Before he could stand, Rae rushed behind him with her cord. She readily wrapped it around his neck, and he froze. Slowly, he placed both hands in the air in surrender.

Kill him! the Beast of Rage demanded, but Rae ignored the demand.

She kept the cord loose. Rae usually would tighten it for dramatic flair. But seeing the Goliath's instant submission twisted something in her chest. Maybe he wasn't like the Street Rats or the others she'd fought.

Panting, Rae released her cord from the Goliath's neck. It'd been a while since she worked so hard for a win. It was refreshing to have a challenge. Then Rae did something before she could stop herself.

With her face still covered in mesh, she extended her hand to the Goliath.

The tall man glanced up at her. Sweat slicked his pale forehead, dripping down his temples. His dark eyes stared up at her, as if seeing into her very soul. Rae wanted to retract her hand, but her muscles wouldn't listen.

The Goliath cautiously laid his large hand in her petite one and stood. Rae followed his ascent, her neck craning as he stretched to his full height.

"You sure you're not a giant?" she asked before she could stop herself.

What's the matter with you? she scolded herself.

The Goliath smirked and butterflies took flight in her stomach. "Pretty sure."

"All right, all right, enough of this," the Winner groaned, waving his hands in the air. "You won fair and square, Crimson Cord."

He took a look around. The Fighter's Ring was empty save for the four of them.

The Winner started to take off his hood. Anticipation hummed between Rae's ears. Who could the mystery gambler be? Was it a Kadeshian general? Someone from King Atol's council?

But as the Winner took off his hood, Rae frowned. A man with sun kissed skin and a chiseled chin grinned at her. Though he had a nice smile and lush chestnut locks, he was too short to be Rae's type.

"Who are you?"

The man deflated, then puffed his chest out. "How can you not know who *I* am?"

Rae shrugged. "I have no idea who you are."

The Goliath broke out into a deep laugh, startling Rae.

"I'll have you know I single-handedly took down—"

"I think that's enough." The woman next to the unknown man stepped up. "We don't need everyone knowing your past." She turned her veiled face toward Rae. "Congratulations. I haven't seen such hemna techniques. As my comrade stated, you won, and we will tell you who we are."

The woman pulled at the edge of her veil and the Goliath stopped laughing. "I don't know—"

"It's fine," the woman replied. "She can be trusted. For now."

The black veil crumpled in her hand, and Rae gasped. Standing before her, was none other than the Seer.

Chapter Twelve

Rae, Fighter's Ring, Yekel

Rae couldn't believe her luck. The Seer that General Yada hunted stood before her. She quickly tried to devise a plan to capture the Seer and take her to the general, but her mind went blank. After entertaining Nadia and Master Monham and her two intense fights, Rae's mind and body were exhausted.

Her eyes darted to the Winner. Though he was handsome, she knew his kind. Selfish and greedy; the kind of man who would do anything to squirm out of a tough situation. But why was he with the Seer?

Rae focused on the Goliath. Drops of sweat still lined his forehead from their fight. When he adjusted his posture, he tried to hide the pain in his leg. A surge of regret spiked Rae's heart. His eyes locked on to her, watching her with an intense gaze. Rae's stomach squeezed, and she assumed the response was because she had only a few orange blossom rolls for dinner and was hungry.

Clearing her throat, Rae asked in her deep voice, "Why do you need to know about Kanna?"

The Winner opened his mouth to speak, but the Seer stepped forward. "She is the mother of ...a friend of mine. He's been searching for her for many years." She paused as if deciding how much she should share.

Guilt twisted Rae's heart. Another mother taken and lost to the Temple. Kanna had spoken about her two sons. From what she told Rae, one was incredibly intelligent while the other, though somewhat of a troublemaker, had a good heart. For the first time, Rae didn't want to hand over the Seer but to try and help.

If we trust her, she will betray us, the Beast of Fear countered. *Turn her in, now.*

The images of the other women still left in the Temple filed through Rae's mind. She couldn't sacrifice all the lives of those women for the Seer, a fugitive. How could Rae know if the Seer was innocent? What if she really *had* kidnapped Princess Haden and this was all a ruse?

Fight and defeat her, like you did with the Goliath, the Beast of Rage cackled.

Rae shoved the thoughts away. Her gut instinct was that the Seer spoke the truth, but she had to continue with her plan to help the Temple women and flee from Yekel.

Guilt pricked her chest again. She supposed she could share some information with the trio to lessen her guilt.

Remembering that she stood before them as the Crimson Cord, Rae tweaked what she knew to fit her disguise. "There were whispers of a woman name Kanna Blake being held in a cell beneath the Temple. No one knew much about her, and only a few were allowed to see her: General Yada, the new ruler of Yekel, an elderly woman who supplied salves and health treatments, and sometimes another Temple Priestess."

That's enough information, she thought and clamped her lips shut before her conscience encouraged her to share more.

"We'll never get an audience with the general," the Winner groaned, raking his hands through his thick waves.

Rae scoffed and pointed to the Seer. "She's a fugitive. I don't think going to an egotistical officer from Kadesh would be a wise choice."

"So, you're from Tenton then?" the Goliath asked quickly.

Rae bit her lip, cursing to herself. He'd been quietly studying her this whole time. She'd given too much information away.

"Help us," the Seer pleaded, her violet eyes bright and striking in the lantern light of the Fighter's Ring.

Rae wanted to refuse. She tried to muster the anger and fury she held when she first came to fight tonight. But there was nothing to grasp. Sighing, Rae stroked her mesh covered chin; a gesture she hoped looked masculine.

"I'll tell you more at the next fight." Without giving them a chance to respond, she started toward the exit.

"Thank you, Crimson Cord," the Seer called out.

Heart pounding, Rae took hurried steps away from the trio. She rushed through the front of the Dark Market where the Whispering Hall stood. Only a few cloaked figures remained, murmuring secrets to one another. Uneasiness coiled up Rae's back and down her arms. She took large, hurried steps until she reached the doorkeeper.

"I pray it was another successful evening, Master Cord." He bowed and opened the door.

The moment Rae left the Dark Market, she sprinted as fast as she could.

Zigzagging through the stone alleyways, Rae retraced her steps several times. She knew the Seer or the Goliath may try to follow her to gain more information or to find out who she was. And she couldn't let that happen.

After reassuring herself for the twentieth time that no one tailed her, Rae headed home. A single candle glowed in the front window, and Rae feared that someone had broken in. But then she remembered Nadia.

Rae took a deep breath to steady her thumping heart. She couldn't allow herself to be paranoid. She had to keep her head. The only way to get close enough to the Seer and get her to General Yada was to gain her trust.

With one last look around, Rae stepped into her home to finally rest for the night.

The next brawl wasn't until four days later. Rumor had it that Jasper had taken ill. Usually fights took place every night. And though Rae didn't always participate in the nightly fights, having four days to rest was a treat.

Rae skipped as she passed out supplies and water to the men breaking stone for bricks.

"What's got you in such a good mood, Rae?" Old Charlie asked. He covered his blue eyes with his gnarled hand to watch her against the burning sun.

Old Charlie was about the same age as Master Monham but acted as if he were thirty years younger. He always pulled pranks on the younger men or cracked a joke when the Kadeshian soldiers weren't paying attention. Rae enjoyed when she could work alongside Old Charlie's group. Life seemed less dim when he was around.

"Oh nothing," Rae straightened. She handed Old Charlie a chisel so he could carve his round stone into a rectangular brick.

Old Charlie wiped the sweat from his wrinkled brow, then ruffled his white hair. "It's a fella, isn't it?"

Rae scoffed, making a face of disgust. "Absolutely not. Men are—"

"Gross, horrid pigs," Old Charlie finished for her. He took the chisel and flipped it in his hand before chuckling. "I know, Rae, I know."

Rae softened her hard demeanor. "There are just none left like you, Charlie."

Old Charlie laughed heartily, causing the Kadeshian soldier nearby to turn their way. Rae held her breath. She hated gaining the attention of the soldiers. They didn't care if you were tall, short, thick, thin, had long hair or had it shaved. As long as you were a woman, they would torment you.

Luckily, the soldier turned back to the other guard and continued talking.

"I know there's someone for everyone, Rae, even you."

Rae's heart warmed at the sentiment, but she knew Old Charlie was only trying to be kind. Even if she wanted a relationship, no man would desire her after finding out about her past. It was bad enough she suffered through the Temple, but she'd broken and bruised so many others, any man would see her as a beast and a monster.

"Thank you, Charlie," she replied. "But I'm happy being alone."

Old Charlie nodded, not pressing the subject any further.

They worked the rest of the day with light conversation about the weather and the upcoming market day at the end of the week. Before long, it was time to go home.

"I'm back," Rae called as she entered her small abode.

Nadia kept to the house most days, trying to figure out a plan to get in the Temple then flee Yekel. Master Monham supplied some information about the Temple, but not enough for Nadia to enter and exit safely. General Yada banned Master Monham's visits to the Temple once he discovered he used his time teaching the women about Tunri.

Though Nadia hadn't compiled a full plan yet, Rae was impressed with her espionage and ability to gather intel.

You could help her, a soft voice she didn't recognize encouraged.

Rae frowned. After she'd convinced Nadia she was going to find information about the Seer, Rae never expected to run into the Seer herself. That was four days ago. Rae told Nadia that some men thought they heard the Seer may be heading to Yekel but they weren't sure. That small amount of information was enough to keep Nadia hopeful and she'd been planning ever since.

Rae, however, had been wracked with guilt. She already lied to Nadia on multiple occasions. Sooner or later, it was going to catch up with her.

"Hi, Rae," Nadia greeted, waving from where she sat on the woven rug in the small living area.

Pieces of parchment filled with sketches of the city spread around her in a semicircle. Nadia held a piece of charcoal in her hand as she added details to the one closest to her.

"Making a map?" Rae asked, setting her sack down before joining Nadia on the floor.

Nadia nodded. "Yes, I figured if I got a better grasp of the entire city, I could try to find a way in the Temple without getting caught. Then I could learn more about that giant statue the warden was talking about."

Rae studied the drawings, taking in every detail. Nadia's precision was remarkable. The position of the Wizard Wankle's tent, right down to how many steps led up to the Temple doors. Everything was exact.

"This is incredible," Rae breathed, wishing she had something like this when she left the Temple.

The twists and turns of the citadel always confused her greatly. It was only when Rae started finding the different entrances of the Dark Market that she really gained a sense of where everything was.

"Really?" Nadia gazed at her with wide eyes, full of admiration and trust.

Guilt gnawed at Rae's thoughts, but she buried it and stood. "Really."

"You think it'll help me get into the Temple?" Nadia focused back on her sketch of the governor's mansion.

The former governor of Yekel, Governor Trela, led the citadel until General Yada freed him of his position by hanging him on the gallows after Kadesh's invasion. Now the governor's mansion was the private residence of General Yada.

Rae held back a shudder. "I don't think it's wise for you to go to the Temple."

She hung her sack on a hook by the door. Getting Nadia into the Temple wasn't the hard part. It was getting out. Alive. The only reason she was free was because she paid an exorbitant amount to General Yada for her freedom. It had taken her months to earn so much coin. Thankfully, her visitors deemed her worthy to receive all sorts of lavish gifts she could pawn.

"I need to get information about the Temple back to Warden Hazor," Nadia explained. "I don't know how, but it will help Dev."

Rae nodded, understanding the urgency. She had been counting the days. There were only nine left until her deal with General Yada expired.

How are you going to convince the Seer to trust you? the Beast of Fear cawed. *Will you hand her over to General Yada, knowing what he'll do? You don't have much time.*

Rae shook her head. She would figure out something soon. "I'm going to prepare my supplies for market in a few days. Are you coming with me?"

Nadia shook her head, and Rae was surprised to discover the disappointment that swirled in her heart. "After talking to Master Monham, I decided it was best to keep a low profile. Market day has a lot of Kadeshian soldiers, and if I want to be a proper soldier of the Fortress,"—Nadia gave a mock salute—"then I need to remain as hidden as possible."

Rae nodded, agreeing with the logic. It was why she'd hidden herself as the Crimson Cord. But another question came to mind.

"How can you gain more information for your map without being seen?"

Just then, a light knock tapped on Rae's door. Nadia sprang up from her position on the floor. She opened the door a hair, just enough for Rae to see a women with a jade head covering standing outside. The scarf wrapped around the woman's silky, chestnut hair, and covered her nose and mouth, leaving only her umber eyes in view. Rae immediately recognized the scarf as one a Yekelian woman purchased from her a few market days ago.

The woman handed Nadia a stack of parchments. Nadia took them and handed the women three gold coins. Joy filled the woman's face, and she bowed low before scurrying away.

Nadia closed the door quickly and studied the sketches.

Rae took a step closer to peek over her shoulder. Dark lines crisscrossed on the page to create different avenues and alleyways of the citadel. While they weren't as detailed as Nadia's, they were still exquisite.

Nadia flipped the parchment over and read the descriptions and distances of landmarks on the map.

Rae raised a brow. "Is it wise to trust someone in an overthrown city?"

Nadia glanced up. "She was recommended by Master Monham. So far she's done excellent work and hasn't been discovered." Nadia tapped her chin. "At least, not that I know of."

Rae blinked, still trying to picture her Little Nadi, who laughed and smiled more than she talked, as a serious adult. "That's good."

"Mhmm," Nadia replied, studying the parchments. She flopped back on the floor and began duplicating the sketches on blank pieces of parchment. Rae noticed that Nadia had two copies of every page of her map. She probably wanted a spare in case she lost one.

With Nadia consumed in her work, Rae slid back to the kitchen. Though she was thankful for some time alone, Rae couldn't help but feel the tug of loneliness. She was always okay with being by herself. But lately, with Nadia staying with her and Master Monham visiting, Rae enjoyed having her home filled with others.

After Rae washed up and ate dinner—she also set out some food for Nadia, who was too engaged in her work to notice—she slipped off to bed, wondering if she would always feel this alone.

Chapter Thirteen

Rae, Marketplace, Yekel

It was market day again. One week had gone by and Rae was no closer to handing the Seer over to General Yada than before. She felt the noose of time tightening around her throat as each day ticked by. Yet, after hearing so many stories about the Seer from Nadia, Rae wasn't sure if she wanted to hand the girl over. Now wasn't the right time to grow a conscience.

Rae anticipated seeing the Winner, the Seer, and the Goliath, but they were nowhere to be found once Jasper had opened the fighting ring again. Rae was surprised at the disappointment she felt when the Goliath wasn't there. However, like all her other unexplained feelings, she locked it away.

But last night, Jasper had a note for her.

"From the only fighter to beat you," he said with a wry grin.

Rae snatched the note with a scowl but didn't read it until she was alone.

Forgive our absence, the elegant message read. *We intend to meet with you again tomorrow night.*

Relief relaxed Rae's tense muscles. But what followed was confusion. Why did she care if the odd trio were okay? But at the thought of seeing the Goliath again, her heart raced. Frustrated, Rae crumpled the note and stuck it in her pocket.

Shaking her head from the memory of last night, Rae gathered her market supplies and snuck out of the house before Nadia woke. Because Nadia loved her orange blossom rolls so much,

Rae made more and left them out for her to enjoy. It only slightly eased Rae's loneliness and guilt.

Nadia worked tirelessly to complete her mission. Rae could've helped more. But after she told Nadia there were rumors the Seer was heading to Yekel, Nadia didn't ask for Rae's help again, so Rae didn't offer.

Rae adjusted the sack on her shoulder as she moved her basket of scarves to her hip. *Why would she ask? I've been closed off and dismissive toward any question.*

We don't need to share anything with Little Nadi, the Beast of Envy hissed.

The morning sun creased over the horizon, painting the sky in light blue and orange. Enjoying the peaceful stillness the early morning brought, Rae slowed her steps. Mornings were always her favorite time of day. Only the breeze accompanied her as she produced her documentation card for the guard.

The burly guard snatched the card. "Where's the other girl?"

Rae figured he would ask and already had her lie ready. "The general didn't see her fit to be my apprentice after all." She waved her hand in the air. "I'm not one to question his judgment."

The guard gave her a skeptical look but let her pass.

Sometimes it worried her how easily she could lie. A few years back, her pulse would've raced, and her palms would be clammy as she spoke the falsehood. But her heart and hands were unaffected as she headed toward her booth.

Rae tried not to think of how far she'd fallen. Not just on the social ladder, but the spiritual one. What was the state of her heart? Her soul?

The hairs rose on the back of her neck as she remembered when General Yada forced her in front of the imperial opal statue of Pahga. The memory of streams of light yanked from her chest, from her very soul, and reeling into the statue; being replaced with something dark and sinister.

Is that why I keep hearing voices in my head?

Rae lifted the basket and placed it on the table in front of her booth, pushing the memory away. If she dwelled on it too much, she would dig herself deeper and deeper into a pit of depression and self-loathing. She'd already experienced that once and never wanted to do it again.

The Wizard Wankle popped up by her side in a plume of blue smoke. "Where is your lovely assistant today?"

Rae coughed, using her hands to fan the smoke away from her booth. "She's occupied elsewhere."

The Wizard's thick brows creased as he frowned. "Pity. The lovely blonde had an exciting aura around her."

Of course, she did, Rae thought before she could stop herself.

Nadia was different. She always had been. When Tunri bestowed the gift of tinkering upon the people of Yekel, Nadia was one of the ones blessed. She was only three summers when she created her first invention: a mini catapult that launched seeds in the air for the birds. Though young herself—only seven summers—Rae remembered the jealousy she felt. Papi had the gift, and adored Nadia for also being a Tinker. But Tunri passed over Rae. Just like He always had.

Suddenly, an insane idea soared into Rae's thoughts. If the Wizard caught on to Nadia's aura, maybe he *actually was* a prophet. Rae always thought the man was a joke. But maybe he wasn't. If he could see the future, maybe he could give Rae guidance on how to save the Temple women and gain her freedom without handing over the Seer.

As he turned to leave, Rae caught the bell sleeve of the Wizard's robe. He peered down at her with a look of surprise as he held his giant turban in place.

"Are you really a prophet?" she whispered.

The Wizard donned his market day persona once more. "But of course, my dear! I wouldn't lie!"

Rae gave him a flat look, knowing that every self-proclaimed prophet was a glorified fortune teller. Except for the Seer. Her bright violet eyes burned straight through Rae. No, Rae's gut knew the Seer was a real prophet.

Rae licked her lips. She'd evaded the Wizard's invitations to read her future for years. But now, for some reason, anxiety consumed her thoughts about the future, and they wouldn't back down.

"Can you tell me my future?" The market wouldn't open for another hour, so they both had some free time.

The Wizard placed his thin hands over hers and bowed. "It would be my honor. Please." He gestured to his peaked tent.

Trepidation scattered along her nerves, but Rae stepped inside.

The light of the sun immediately vanished as the Wizard followed her in, shutting the tent behind him. Small holes in the top of the tent's canvas allowed slender beams of light to shine through, emulating stars.

The inside of the tent was the shade of midnight. Streams of light fell from the ceiling, bouncing against a shining orb placed in the center of a circular oak table. Rae's brows lifted at the fine quality of wood, not knowing how the Wizard procured such a beautiful piece.

With his robes billowing like water, the Wizard Wankle shuffled around the small space. Finally, he sat in a grandiose red velvet chair behind the fine table.

"Please." He gestured to an identical red velvet seat across from him.

Rae hesitated, then sat down. Her muscles immediately relaxed into the soft plush. She wondered how the Wizard Wankle was able to have such finery when she never saw anyone enter his tent.

Rae scanned the room again, not liking the darkness crawling around her.

Flee, flee while you can! The Beast of Fear squawked.

"Let me see your hands." The Wizard held out his own thin ones. Obnoxious gold rings and baubles decorated his lanky, tan fingers.

Rae automatically balled her hands into fists, then forced herself to lift her right arm to the table.

The Wizard took her hand more gently than she anticipated. Lines of worry creased his dark eyes as he studied her palm.

What is he seeing?

After what seemed like an eternity, Rae asked, "What is it?"

The Wizard said nothing. He took her other hand and the worry lines deepened. "I cannot see where the path you're on will lead."

Rae resisted the urge to roll her eyes. *Of course.* This was all a ruse like she knew it would be.

But then the Wizard continued. "We will need more power if you want to know your future."

Before she could respond, the Wizard produced a delicately carved clay pipe. Rae instantly recognized Master Monham's signature dove engraved on the side of the piece of pottery. A familiar acrid smell consumed the tent and Rae knew the contents of the pipe were not as beautiful as its exterior.

Leaning back into the chair, she crossed her arms over her chest. "I'm not taking *menta*."

The Wizard Wankle nodded. "I wholeheartedly understand. Alas—" he gave a small shrug— "to amplify your aura, you need a catalyst."

He will know your past, he will know your pain, he will know your shame! The Beast of Fear cried. *Run! Flee!*

Rae ignored the voice, curiosity tugging her toward the pipe. She'd heard *menta* had given individuals visions. Could it be true? She only experienced its side effects once and hadn't received any visions.

Rae chewed the inside of her cheek. But if she didn't see her future now, she would always wonder, "What if?"

"Okay," she agreed, leaving the Beast of Fear screaming in her mind.

The Wizard Wankle snapped his fingers and produced a flame at their tips. Rae jerked back, startled at the sudden surge of power radiating from the Wizard. He lit the pipe and handed it to her.

"Once you breathe in the *menta*, place your hands on the orb. I will then be able to see your future."

Rae's fingers trembled as she took the pipe. The dove Master Monham carved stared up at her with innocent eyes, urging her to run away. But Rae had already committed. With her heart thrumming, she placed the pipe to her lips and took a breath.

The taste of dirt and leaves filled her mouth as she inhaled the *menta*. But before Rae could spew it from her lungs, a haziness blanketed her senses. Her limbs went limp. She could barely keep her head up when the Wizard placed her hands on the glowing glass orb.

A bright light shot into Rae's mind's eye. She jerked back, trying to free herself from the orb, but her hands welded to it. It was as if a powerful force held her there as it probed into her thoughts. One by one, memories that Rae kept locked away were revealed.

Her first night in the Temple. Her first visitor. The pain she felt. The tears she wept. The injuries she inflicted on herself. Faces of the friends she'd made. Faces of the friends she'd lost. And finally, the real truth as to why she refused to speak about the horrors of the Temple. The large statue of Pahga, carved from imperial opal. Rae had seen too many lives lost to the goddess. The pain was too much to bear.

Rae blinked. Hot, wet tears streamed down her cheeks as she peered into the glowing sphere. Her mind cleared enough to realize this wasn't her future, but her past. Then the orb spun revealing the face of the Goliath. He wasn't standing in the Fighter's Ring where she met him. He was somewhere unknown to Rae.

Rae frowned. *What is he doing in my future?*

Another image swept by, and Rae sucked in a breath. It was the Seer, struggling in the hands of General Yada. But as she looked closer, she wasn't sure it was General Yada. Another Kadeshian general, perhaps?

Although she had yet to hand the woman over, regret stabbed Rae in the chest.

But before she could dwell on it, the orb hissed and screamed, showing Rae's face once more before turning black. Regaining power over her limbs, Rae wrenched her hands to her chest. Heat radiated from her fingers.

The Wizard Wankle quickly tossed a thick cloth over the orb. Judging by the look of horror on his face, he hadn't known about Rae's past.

"Rae," he whispered, tears glistening in his dark eyes. "I didn't realize."

Rae's defensive walls immediately shot up. She roughly scrubbed the tears from her cheeks and stood.

"Thank you, Wizard." She bowed. "What payment do you require?"

He shook his head, his loose turban now askew from the gesture.

Rae's throat tightened. "And for your silence?"

The Wizard held his hand up, a gesture of peace. "I will tell no one, you have my word."

"Your word isn't enough for me," she retorted, stepping forward. "Swear it. Swear it on the false god you serve. You will say nothing of my past or of who I know."

Rae knew the Wizard had seen the Seer. He could easily squeal on her, and General Yada would arrest her for aiding a fugitive.

The Wizard Wankle retreated from Rae and shrank back into his ornate chair. With fearful eyes, he crossed his fingers over his heart and kissed them. "I swear to tell no one of what I've seen today."

Believing him, Rae curled her fingers and nodded before hurrying out of the tent.

The mid-morning sun blinded Rae and she stumbled back, placing her hand over her eyes. The images of her past still floated in her subconscious, waiting to torment her when she was alone.

Bury the pain, bury the pain, the Beast of Fear whispered.

She shoved her fears away, trying to keep them in the dark.

Shielding her eyes, Rae hurried back to her booth. The market was busier than it had ever been. New merchants and traders from Kadesh arrived and were trying to stake their claim in the Yekelian territory.

Rae hurried to her booth, stumbling as the effects of the *menta* wore off. She was a fool to have looked into the future. Why did she think she would be able to save the Seer *and* the Temple women? Her future showed the Seer in the hands of a Kadeshian general. Rae would sacrifice the Seer. One life was worth all the others.

The image of the Seer struggling against who she thought was General Yada soured Rae's thoughts as she quickly set out her colored fabrics.

Was that future really set in stone?

As she hung her freshly dyed scarves, she peeked over at the Wizard's tent. He hadn't emerged yet. He usually stood outside, attempting to lure travelers into his space, but he was nowhere to be seen.

"Rae," Master Monham called.

Shocked by his voice, she spun around, not realizing the potter had been there the whole time. Taking a breath, she slowed her pulse. "Master Monham, you scared me."

The old man eyed her. "Not much scares you, Rae." He gestured at the Wizard Wankle's tent. "Why were you in there?"

Rae stiffened. Master Monham hadn't yet arrived at the market when she first entered the Wizard's tent. It seemed like she was only in there for a few minutes.

How long was I actually in there?

"I had a few questions for the Wizard." She shrugged, trying to brush it off as nothing.

But she knew Master Monham could see right through her. Yet, instead of chastising her, he merely said, "I'm always here for you, Rae. Any time. For anything. Please remember that."

Master Monham's words warmed her heart. "Thank you."

Their conversation quickly ended when a flurry of travelers swarmed their booths. The merchants' wives and children all wanted a piece of pottery or a new scarf. In the bustle, the Wizard exited his tent, donning his usual alluring persona.

A taller woman with beautifully dark skin came up to Rae's booth. Her eyes gleamed with delight at the colorful fabrics.

"See, Jarrick? *This* is the teal I want." The woman swatted her hand toward a man covered with countless swaths and bundles of fabric and jewels from the other booths at the market.

But though he seemed to be only a pack mule for the lady's shopping, he gave her a warm smile and replied, "Of course, my love. It is a stunning color on you."

The woman preened as she held up the teal scarf. "I'll take everything you have in this color."

Rae jerked back in surprise. "Everything?"

"Yes, yes," the woman said, already tying the teal scarf around her head.

Baffled, Rae collected every scrap of teal fabric for the woman. The couple paid her handsomely before continuing on their way.

Rae stared, awestruck at the bag of coin left on her table. She didn't notice another figure had come into her booth.

"Hey, you."

Rae snapped out of her daze, turning to the man who called out. Irritation was plain on her face at his lack of basic manners. "May I help you?"

Annoyance laced her words as she recognized the solider who watched over her and Old Charlie yesterday. Now that he was closer, Rae noticed his dark skin, leathered and stretched by too many hours in the sun. His brown eyes were young, but devious as he openly assessed her assets. Rae resisted the urge to spit in his face as he licked his lips and grinned, showcasing a chipped front tooth.

"Yea, you can help me. How about we take a walk?"

Rae subtly glanced to her right, wondering if she could catch Master Monham's attention. But a gaggle of women were fighting to purchase his last set of dove engraved plates.

"I apologize, but I can't leave my booth," she replied with the most civility she could muster. "If you're not going to purchase something, I must ask you to move on."

Fury at her refusal lit the guard's eyes. "You will come with me or else."

Rae noted how he was in commoner's clothes, not his bronze military armor. He was off duty and was trying to fill up his idle time. Rae curled her lip. If this urchin faced her in the Fighter's Ring, she would've already broken both his ankles.

"Or else what?" she growled, crossing her arms over her chest.

She knew there were too many witnesses. He couldn't force her to leave. And if he tried, Rae knew how to make a scene.

A sly grin crossed the man's thick lips, sending a cold shudder down Rae's spine. "Or else Old Charlie may not make it through his next workload."

Fear pierced Rae's heart. She wouldn't let anything happen to Old Charlie. But before she could even refuse, the guard's hand clamped hard around her wrist. "Now, move! I know your kind."

His words stung more than Rae thought they would as she gasped and struggled. But the guard wouldn't relent. "Let me go!"

He pulled tighter and harder, knocking over parts of her display, but no one helped. If they saw, they looked away. Like they always had.

Rae's mind flew through possibilities, her blood rushing between her ears. She had to wait to attack until no one was nearby.

But as she started to form a plan, a tall shadow loomed over them.

"I believe the lady asked you to let her go."

Rae glanced up. Her heart unexpectedly fluttered as she gazed upon the face of the Goliath.

Chapter Fourteen

Rae, Market, Yekel

The kind gaze she'd witnessed in the Fighter's Ring had been replaced with two dark eyes consumed with rage.

The guard glanced up at the Goliath, squinting into the sun. "You can have a turn after."

Before Rae could react to the comment, the Goliath wrenched the man's hand from her wrist and twisted it behind his back. The man squealed like a mouse in the paw of a lion.

The Goliath leaned down toward the scrambling guard. "Don't make me break your arm."

The threat sent chills over Rae's skin, and she hated to admit she enjoyed someone defending her for once.

The guard sputtered something about reporting the Goliath to General Yada and the next thing Rae heard was a pop and a shrill scream.

The Goliath threw the guard to the ground.

"I'll report this!" the guard yelled, drawing the eyes of the crowd. He clutched his shoulder where his arm hung unnaturally low.

The Goliath didn't spare him another glance as he faced Rae, the flame in his gaze vanquished. "Are you all right, miss?"

Rae stood at a loss for words, and she quickly remembered the Goliath had never seen her face before. A wave of heat flooded her cheeks as she fumbled for something to say.

"Ah, yes." She dipped her head, keenly aware of her shaved hair. She quickly placed her cerulean scarf over her head.

"Thank you so much for intervening. Not many are willing to go against General Yada's soldiers."

The Goliath's sharp jaw clenched at her statement, so she added, "Can I offer you something from my booth to show my gratitude?"

She gestured toward her toppled over table where all the fabrics had fallen into the bustling street. Rae winced, taking in the sorry display.

What are you doing? He's the enemy, the Beast of Rage roared.

That's why I want to know him, she justified as she tried not to notice the lean muscle of the Goliath's long arms.

Hurrying toward the fallen fabrics, Rae gathered some up, trying to wipe off the dust and grim. As she went to grab a lilac-colored square, thin, pale fingers clenched it at the same time. She peered over to see the Goliath with a handful of her other fabrics.

"Thank you," she said quietly, taking the bundle from him.

Why is he being kind? He didn't even know who she was. And if he did, he would surely treat her like the guard had. Or reject her immediately.

"I don't believe I'm in need of any head scarves today." The Goliath gently pushed one of the dangling scarves out of his face. When he locked eyes on Rae, he smirked. Rae's heart leapt, and she coughed to cover her surprise.

"Are you sure?" she asked, deciding to enjoy this small moment. "You would look handsome in my signature Lovely Lilac." She held up the dark periwinkle square in her hands, evoking a wider grin from the Goliath. "No? How about Emerging Emerald? Merry Marigold?" Rae held up the scarves, and the Goliath laughed deeply. Her stomach fluttered at the sound.

She shouldn't—couldn't—flirt with the enemy. Or *any* man. The Goliath was the same as all the others. And if he found out she was the Crimson Cord, who knew what he would do.

"They are very well made." He fingered the Merry Marigold. "Do you like this one?"

The clementine fabric shimmered in the sun, reminding her of the ripe oranges she and Mami used for their orange blossom rolls. Every fabric told a different story Rae held close to her heart.

At the thought of her mother, a knot formed in Rae's throat. She swallowed it down and nodded. "Yes, that's one of my favorites."

The Goliath untied the scarf. It was so delicate compared to his large, rough hands.

"It reminds me of oranges," he murmured, plucking two black scarves from an adjacent stack.

Rae perked up. "Oranges?" She watched him lay the black scarves and the bright orange one over his arm.

"Mhmm," he replied.

Rae eyed the other scarves, remembering the Seer wore a black one over her head. *Are they for her? Why would he be buying her scarves?*

Why do you care? the Beast of Envy cooed.

Rae went back to organizing her scarves. *I don't care*, she told herself as she watched the Goliath out of the corner of her eye.

He kept his head down as he dug through his pocket then placed a handful of silver coins on the table. They clinked and rolled about. "I thought I smelled oranges the other day. It reminded me of home."

Rae's heart stopped. *The other day?* Her mind quickly remembered she made the orange blossom rolls right before she fought him in the Dark Market. Fear prickled her skin. *He couldn't have figured me out.*

He has, he has! the Beast of Fear cried.

While the Goliath counted the coins, Rae subtly sniffed herself.

Do I smell like oranges today? No other scent beside her herbal soap came from her.

Who knew the Goliath had such a keen sense of smell?

The tall man pushed too many coins toward Rae, and her eyes widened.

"I can't accept this. The scarves aren't worth half of this." She shoved the coins back.

The Goliath stopped the money from rolling off the table with his large hands. "I don't care for all the coins jingling in my pocket." He gently moved the pile forward again.

Rae hated that his gentle stubbornness was working on her. She should just take the coins and use them to further her efforts to free the women from the Temple. But she also knew that if she stopped now, the Goliath, and this small happy moment, would vanish.

Straightening, she placed her hands on her hips, doing her best to make herself as tall as possible. Her head still only reached the Goliath's chest. Peering up at him, she said, "Sir, I do not cheat my customers." She playfully wagged a finger at him. "I expect you to pay the correct amount."

Amusement flittered across the Goliath's gaze as he sighed, "I apologize, miss." With a bow, he scooped the additional coins up and placed them back in his pocket.

As he started to leave, Rae's heart lurched out, wanting to hold on to this moment, wanting to hold on to...him.

"Uh, " she started then clamped her mouth shut. *What am I doing? I can never have a normal life. I don't deserve a normal, happy life.*

The Goliath faced her expectantly. He shoved the two black scarves in his pocket and tied the marigold scarf around his neck. Like a comet shooting across the night sky, the scarf contrasted his dark tunic and pants.

"Thank you, again," she managed to say. "For earlier."

The Goliath watched her with a studious gaze, then bowed. "I hope we meet again soon."

He turned and leisurely strode toward Master Monham's booth, which had calmed down since the flurry of woman left.

Rae attended to the other customers but kept one eye on the Goliath and Master Monham.

What are they saying?

She strained to hear, but the loud, nasally man in front of her kept commenting to his wife on which colors she should choose. Rae swallowed her irritation, knowing she needed the extra coin.

With a smile, she forced her attention away from the Goliath and focused on her customers.

At the end of the day, Rae was gathering what was left of her fabrics and readying to head home when Master Monham stopped at her table.

"Care to walk an old man home?" He grinned, offering her his clay-stained arm.

Rae snorted but smiled. "Only if you carry my basket."

"Of course." He went to take it from her, but Rae stopped him.

"I'm joking, Master Monham. Let me carry your things." And before he could stop her, she placed his bag of tools and sack filled with lumps of clay into her basket.

"Thank you, Rae."

She nodded and started through the city with Master Monham hobbling beside her. She glanced at the Wizard Wankle's tent as they passed. The Wizard never walked home with them and was always the first at his tent on market days. Rae realized she actually didn't know that much about him. Where did he sleep? Did he work at the outer wall like the rest of them?

The bits of her future the Wizard showed her flashed through her mind's eye, and Rae shook it away. She wasn't even sure if what she saw was *her* future. She had a moment of weakness and became unguarded with the Wizard. She needed to stay in control and not let her emotions guide her decisions. Hopefully, the Wizard was a man of his word and would keep his mouth shut.

"So," Master Monham started casually. "Care to share why you were with the Wizard this morning?"

Rae slid her eyes to the old man, realizing he had an ulterior motive for walking home with her. "I told you, I had a question for him."

"Ah, yes, you've never said more than a few words to the Wizard in the two years you've known him, and now you want to have a lengthy conversation with for him." He stroked his chin as they slowly strode past the Temple. "Interesting."

Rae kept her gaze forward, refusing to set her eyes on the tall marble columns that caged her not long enough ago.

"Something of importance?" Master Monham probed. "Something of love?"

Rae spun toward him with a scoff. "Why would I ask the Wizard about love? He's strange, and that turban he wears is absurd. No woman would ever like such a ridiculous thing."

Master Monham laughed heartily, and Rae realized he was trying to bait her. It worked.

She sighed, knowing he wasn't going to let it go. "I needed some...information about how to approach a situation."

Master Monham stayed silent as they exited the city, the outer wall where they lived coming into view. Finally, he asked, "Did you get the answer you wanted?"

Rae furrowed her brow, wondering why he didn't ask what the information was. She shook her head. "I'm not sure. I'm confused about a lot of things right now."

The Goliath's face flashed in her thoughts, and she forced it away. She couldn't fantasize about happily ever afters. Happily ever afters didn't exist. Especially for someone like her.

"Rae." Master Monham stopped just before the rickety fence surrounding their homes. "I've known you for a while now. Something is eating at you from the inside. You can confide in me." The old man placed a withered hand over his heart, and Rae knew it was the truth.

Master Monham had proven again and again that she could trust him. The person she couldn't trust was herself. If she let her guard down, everything would spill out. The hurt, the rage, the pain, the shame. No, she couldn't allow anyone to see it. Rae glanced at her forearm to the scar she'd made when she cut herself with the stones.

The actions of others do not define who you are. Only you decide who you want to be, Kanna had told her.

Rae never harmed herself again after meeting Kanna. Though she wanted to, she sought Kanna's soft encouraging words instead of a sharp rock to numb her pain.

Rae shifted her basket to her other hip. She didn't want to be this way, holding everything inside, keeping things from her friends. But she had to hold it together. Just a little longer. Just long enough to see all the women in the Temple freed and safe.

Then she would somehow find Master Monham and tell him everything.

"Thank you," she replied softly. "I will. But just not yet. I'm not—" she paused, then sighed. "I'm not ready."

The old man's eyes softened. "Of course. I'm here whenever you are."

Rae handed Master Monham his supplies and started for her home.

"Why don't you and Nadia have dinner with me tonight?" he called out.

Rae smiled at the offer, her heart warming.

The old man grinned. "I have a delicious meal prepared. I also have some friends I want you to meet." He rubbed his neck then continued, "And I would like to see Nadia again. I've noticed her *talent* and would love to ask her some questions about one of my tools."

Everyone wants to see Little Nadi and her Tinkering gift, the Beast of Envy sighed.

Jealousy warmed Rae's chest, but she forced a smile. "Of course, I'll make sure to tell her."

As Rae took another step toward her home, she realized she had to brawl in the Dark Market tonight. Slipping out of Master Monham's house unnoticed would be difficult.

Hastily, she spun around and shouted, "Bring your dinner to my house instead, and I'll help you prepare it."

"See you soon," he answered in agreement and hobbled to his home.

Rae raced to her house and burst through the front door, knowing she needed to pack her fighting outfit, so it was prepped and ready for a quick exit.

A flurry of papers scattered around her as she stepped inside, drifting to the ground below.

"Whoa!" Nadia cried, her hands in the air. Her eyes widened into a smile as she caught sight of Rae. "Hey Rae, welcome home."

A blush crept up Rae's neck as Nadia attempted to reorganize her papers. "Sorry," Rae said, reaching down to stack the parchments.

From the looks of it, Nadia had completed her map. Rae did her best to position the pages so they fit together like a puzzle. Once she placed the last one, she looked down at the final page in her hand. It wasn't a drawing like the others, but a code.

Symbols inside of boxes stacked on one another. Rae had never seen anything so unusual.

Why does Nadia have this?

"Is that the final piece?" Nadia asked.

Rae shook her head, focusing her thoughts. She handed the paper to Nadia, who clung to it like her life depended on it. "I'm not sure what it is."

Nadia snatched the parchment out of Rae's hand, folded it, and placed it in her pocket.

Rae cleared her throat. "Master Monham wanted to treat us to dinner tonight. He's also bringing his friends, so I offered my place since it's bigger than his."

Nadia's face lit up in a wide grin. "This is perfect. I have a few questions for him about the outer wall that I wanted to ask before the prayer service tonight." She glanced around at the pieces of parchment filled with drawings and notes still scattered around the room. Slapping her hands together, she tried to brush away the charcoal caking her palms. "I need to clean this place up."

In a matter of moments, Nadia had cleared Rae's main living space.

"Nicely done," Rae complemented, shifting the basket in her hands. It was the perfect distraction to ready her bag for the

Dark Market. "Let me put my supplies away before they get here."

Nadia nodded in acknowledgment, and Rae slipped into her room. After placing her basket on the bed, she quickly grabbed her sack and stuffed her black leathers, red mesh, and crimson cord into it. Heart racing, Rae glanced out the window. The sun sat flush on the horizon, so she had time. She just had to wait for the opportune moment.

A knock sounded at her door, and Rae hurried out of her room. In a few strides, she was at the door. Nadia sat candidly on the rug, having pushed the two chairs against the wall. Rae noticed that Nadia had even brought out cups and the pitcher of water.

She smiled. Nadia always picked up on subtle details that mattered.

A knock sounded again, and Rae turned the knob. "I was in the back—" she stopped, her jaw dropping to her feet.

"Rae," Master Monham grinned holding a platter of meat. "Thank you again for offering your home for dinner." The old man squeezed by Rae, not caring that she was stunned. "Oh, and these are my new friends I met at the market."

Rae stared, her mind going to mush. In front of her home stood the Winner, the Seer, and the Goliath.

Chapter Fifteen

Rae closed her parted lips at the sight of the trio. The Goliath still wore the marigold scarf around his neck as he and the other two waited for her to invite them in. Her gaze darted to the Seer, wearing the black veil over her face, probably to cover her bright eyes.

Rae remembered the two black scarves that the Goliath bought earlier. *Do they have the kind of relationship where he buys her gifts?* Rae's former visitors in the Temple brought her gifts. It was how she was able to buy her freedom. But a small part of her prayed the Goliath and the Seer were no more than friends.

Rae faced the Winner, realizing he had forgone his disguise entirely. Almost as if he *wanted* to be noticed.

He caught Rae assessing him and bowed deeply. "Our gracious host. Thank you for allowing us into your humble abode." Before she could react, he grabbed her hand and kissed it.

Rae simultaneously wrenched it away and shoved him hard. The Winner stumbled back into the Goliath's lean muscled chest.

Rae winced at her strength and quick reflexes. "Ah, sorry." She cupped her hands in front of her, trying to come up with a good lie, but the sight of the Goliath sent her thoughts in a tizzy.

"That's okay," the Seer responded, tilting her head to the side as she adjusted the strap of her bag. "He deserves it. May we come in?"

Heat crept across Rae's cheeks as she realized she was blocking the doorway. "Yes, of course."

She couldn't see the Seer's face but could sense a smile coming from the woman as she passed by Rae. The Winner stomped in after, grumbling under his breath about a lack of hospitality.

"Don't mind him," the Goliath said. "He doesn't understand personal space."

Rae had already forgotten the rich warmth of his baritone voice. The sound calmed her jittering nerves. Swallowing at the dry patch in her throat, she craned her neck toward the Goliath. A sweet scent of pastry and sugar wafted from his clothes. It was then Rae noticed the cloth-covered plate in his hands.

"Master Monham said we would be dining with others, so I made orange scones." He lifted the corner of the cloth. A swirl of citrusy delight wrapped Rae in a warm hug as her mouth began to water.

"You made these?"

The Goliath nodded, tucking the cloth back into place. "I told you oranges reminded me of home." He tugged at his clementine-colored scarf as if unsure what to say next.

Rae forced a smile. She shouldn't allow the door of her heart to open. But seeing this giant man with a bright orange scarf and a plate of scones had unlocked something inside of her.

Right when she was about to invite him in, a scream rattled the house. The Goliath shifted from shy baker to defender in a matter of seconds. Dropping the plate, he reached behind his back and flung forward a crossbow. Shock stunned Rae still as he gently—but hurriedly—moved her aside and barreled into the home.

"It's you!" Nadia screamed again and it took Rae a moment to realize it was a scream of joy.

Rae dashed into her home to find the Seer unveiled and Nadia hugging her tightly. Pricks of envy probed Rae's thoughts, but she ignored them.

Everyone always wants Little Nadi, the Beast of Envy whispered.

"We were trying to be inconspicuous," the Winner commented dryly. As he sat down in one of the two chairs, he laid his right ankle over his left knee. He then glanced at the low table in the center of the room. "Ah, refreshments! I do despise the heat." Pouring himself a cup of water, the Winner daintily sipped from one of the clay cups.

The Seer sighed. "It was a bit difficult at times."

"You try hiding the 'not giant' in a crowd," the Winner snorted. He gestured to the Goliath, now standing in the corner of the room.

Nadia peered from around Devora and waved. "Hey, One Shot!"

"Hi, Nadia," he replied with a polite nod.

One Shot? Rae studied the quiet man who stayed plastered to the wall. *What a strange name.*

"Is everyone okay?" Rae finally said, making her presence known.

"Rae!" Nadia hurried toward her. She grabbed Rae's wrist and tugged her toward the Seer. "You need to meet Devora. She's the one I've been telling you about."

Nadia's fingers burned around Rae's skin, but she endured it. She couldn't make another scene. The Seer turned her bright violet eyes on Rae and smiled. "Thank you for having us. Master Monham said you were a trusted ally."

Guilt twisted like a knife in Rae's heart, so she only nodded. The Seer studied Rae, almost as if she could see right through her. Warmth tickled above Rae's chest, but in a blink it was gone, and the Seer went back to examining the code Rae found earlier.

How did Master Monham know the Seer? Has he known where she was all this time?

"I would trust Rae with my life," Master Monham announced from the kitchen.

Shame fell over Rae like a blanket. But, as always, she buried it deep and played the part. "How do you all know each other?"

She glanced over at the Goliath who still stood in the corner, arms folded over his chest, cross bow resting against his long shin.

"It's actually a funny story," the Winner started. "You see, Devora and I were once engaged and she dumped me for my—" An arrow shot through the room, landing centimeters from the Winner's temple. He instantly froze, his eyes widening bigger than the moon in the sky as he stared at the arrow lodged in the wall behind him.

"Let's not burden our guests with a long and complicated story, okay Tristan?" The Seer said sweetly. But by her clenched jaw, Rae knew there was bad blood between them.

But what impressed her even more was the swiftness and accuracy of the Goliath's aim.

How had he learned to shoot like that?

"Whoa!" Nadia said, whipping out her notebook and charcoal. She scribbled a few lines mumbling to herself then snapped the book shut. "My design is still working flawlessly, I see." She sauntered up to the Goliath and began asking him questions.

Of course, it was her design. Sparks of envy escaped Rae's emotional hold.

One Shot probably likes her, too, the Beast of Envy added.

Rae bit the inside of her cheek. She had to contain her emotions. She had to stay in control. Taking a breath, Rae excused herself to the kitchen, where Master Monham prepared dinner.

"It smells wonderful in here," Rae commented, needing a break from all the strangers in her home.

Rae wasn't sure where Master Monham had found all the food, but it looked delicious.

A platter of braised meat, dripping with thick gravy lay in front of Master Monham. "Just a thank you for entertaining an old man so frequently," he replied, smiling as he ripped up pieces of parsley he had brought fresh from the plant in his kitchen window. With a steady hand, he scattered them along the top of the meat.

Next to the platter sat a pile of flat bread, fresh and warm. Figs, dates, and apricots piled high on a third plate and that was when Rae remembered the Goliath's scones.

"Oh no," she cried and darted out of the kitchen.

She flew out the front door to where the shattered plate and beautiful scones lay in the dirt. One by one, she picked each up, dusted them off, and placed them in her long skirt.

Footsteps came from behind, and Rae stilled.

"I'm sorry about your wall," the Goliath offered, crouching next to her. "I can patch that hole up if you like."

Rae's heart unintentionally thawed. "I think I'll keep the arrow there. I may use it to hang my scarves."

The Goliath smirked as he picked up the pieces of the clay plate.

"Sorry about your scones," she said. "They still look amazing."

"Thank you. I like them with sugar or cream rather than dirt."

Rae laughed unexpectedly, then stopped. She couldn't remember the last time she'd genuinely laughed. Not a forced laugh. Not a strained laugh. A real laugh.

She glanced at the Goliath from the corner of her eye. Something about this giant, gentle man put her at ease.

"What's your name?" she asked as they stood. She followed him with her eyes as he stood to his full height, still not believing how quickly he had moved earlier.

The Goliath gazed down at her, a storm of turmoil swirling in his dark eyes. He lowered his shoulders. "Ben."

Rae cocked her head to the side. That wasn't the name Nadia said before. Maybe One Shot was an alias, like Crimson Cord was for her.

So why did he share his real name with me?

She adjusted her hold on her skirt with one hand to keep the orange scones inside and reached the other toward him. Rae didn't enjoy physical contact, but she noticed the Goliath had been careful to only touch her when necessary. She appreciated that kindness.

"Well, Ben," she started. "I'm Rae. It's nice to put a name with a face."

He looked at her outstretched hand, then back at her, as if asking for permission. The small gesture set Rae's heart squeezing as she extended her palm a bit more. Hesitantly, the Goliath wrapped his large hand around her smaller one and shook it.

"It's nice to meet you, Rae."

They stood there, holding one another's hands until Nadia yelled, "Rae! It's time for dinner!"

They both flinched, and the spell was broken. Begrudgingly, Rae slid her hand back around the fabric of her skirt, holding the delectable treats.

"I'll find a new plate for your scones," she muttered, adverting her gaze as she hurried into the house.

Dinner was delicious, and Rae wished she could've enjoyed it. But Ben's presence overwhelmed her. *What do I care if he's looking at me? Why do I want to know how he came to bake and wield a cross bow? Why am I thinking of him?*

Her teeth chomped into a bit of beef that melted in her mouth, but her thoughts were elsewhere. She hadn't forgotten that she was meant to meet the Goliath, the Seer, and the Winner later tonight, too, as per the message they left with Jasper. Not as Rae, but as the Crimson Cord. How strange life was that all three of them sat in the presence of the Crimson Cord without realizing.

Rae swallowed then reached for a piece of flat bread. The conversation chittered around her, but she wasn't listening. She still needed to get to the brawl in time. Although she'd fought the Goliath again and won, her undefeated title was tainted. She had to get back to the top of the Fighter's Ring as soon as possible.

Rae started to devise a plan when something Master Monham said caught her attention.

"Yes, I sent word to the captain about the timeline through one of our trusted couriers. I'm not sure if it's enough time, but we'll have to make it work."

Rae chewed the bread, thankful she'd chosen something soft that wouldn't impair her listening.

"When he's decided something, he usually doesn't change his mind," Devora admitted. Rae noted the sadness in her tone when she spoke of this captain. Was he someone special?

"I just received a letter from him a few days before you got here," Nadia added, scooping up a piece of meat with her flatbread. "I'm glad you got here when you did because I couldn't figure out that code." Nadia popped the bread and meat into her mouth. "Good old Captain Blake, still making life hard for us," Nadia laughed, nudging Devora in the ribs.

Devora offered a deflated chuckle.

"Who's Captain Blake?" Rae asked, deciding to enter the conversation. They were planning something in *her house*, after all, she should know what it was about.

"Captain Blake is our commander," Nadia replied, munching on a fig. "He and Warden Hazor are the ones who sent me to Yekel."

"Why?" Rae asked. The room quieted, so Rae clarified. "Why *exactly* did your commander send you to Yekel, Nadia?"

She knew Nadia wanted to get into the Temple, and the warden wanted to know something about the statue of Pahga. But Nadia never explained why the mission was so pressing.

A few glances that spoke a hundred words passed between Master Monham, Nadia, Devora, and Ben. The Winner, Tristan, seemed to be on the outside of the intel like Rae.

Finally, Devora nodded, and Master Monham cleared his throat.

"I've been working undercover with Captain Blake since Kadesh invaded," the old man started.

Rae's brows lifted, realizing he was living a double life, just like her.

Maybe that's why he always understood.

"Through a network of undercover couriers, we've been able to communicate and devise a plan. Now that the king is occupied with finding his daughter and the Hidden Prophet—" he motioned to Devora—"the captain wishes to free Yekel from Kadesh's hold."

Rae choked. *Free Yekel from Kadesh? Was that possible?* Her mind became a tornado of questions and impossibilities. *What would General Yada do? Should I warn the group about the controlling general?*

Don't worry about anyone else, the Beast of Fear encouraged. *Only worry about yourself.*

Turmoil clouded Rae's spirit and she gritted her teeth, not knowing which path was right anymore. When she looked up, Devora watched her with the same studious gaze as before.

"Rae, are you all right?" Devora asked, her violet eyes flashing with concern.

"I'm okay," Rae said, gulping down her water. *Why am I so thirsty?* She balled her hands into fists. *Why are my hands so clammy?*

Devora nodded and continued. "Before we can execute Captain Blake's plan, I need to speak with the Crimson Cord."

Master Monham sputtered in his drink, coughing heavily. Nadia smacked him a few times on the back, and he wheezed.

"Thank you," he coughed again, gently patting Nadia's hand. "I'm okay. Just drank too quickly." He gave Rae a quick glance. "Why do you need to speak to the Crimson Cord?"

"Do you know the Cord?" Tristan asked, his brow quirked. "He was quite difficult to get information out of."

Rae did her best not to smile. Another look from Master Monham made it easier to keep her lips flat.

"I don't know him personally," Master Monham lied, and Rae was so thankful. "I just know of his stories. Undefeated champion of the Dark Market. The whispers say he even uses his coin to free those forced into working as slaves."

"What a chivalrous knight." Tristan rolled his eyes.

Rae forced herself to look at her food and not shoot a dirty glare at the Winner. *What's his issue with me?* But it wasn't her. It was the Crimson Cord Tristan didn't like, and Rae wanted to know why.

"We should actually be going," Tristan said, standing. "The Cord said he'd speak with us at the next brawl. Unfortunately, we were delayed." He shot a pointed look at Devora who ignored him as she sipped water from her cup. "Hopefully, he got our note."

"Yes," Devora admitted. "We should be going." She placed her hand on Master Monham's shoulder. "Thank you for this delicious meal. We are in your debt."

He patted her hand like he had with Nadia. "Nonsense. I'm always there to help others, especially followers of Tunri. Maybe you can observe Sancti with us next week."

"I'd like that."

Devora smiled and stood, along with Ben, who'd been questionably silent throughout the dinner. Although Rae did note a few times when she caught him watching her.

"Thank you for your hospitality, Rae," Devora said, holding her black veil. "And thank you for housing Nadia. She always spoke highly of you when we were at the Fortress. I'm glad we were able to meet."

Shame, regret, and a fury of other emotions burbled in Rae's chest. "Of course," she forced out. "I'll always take care of Nadia and her friends." She meant it.

Devora said she would contact them soon when she had further information and asked if they could meet here again. Rae silently agreed, not knowing how else to respond.

Devora and Tristan exited her home, leaving Ben, who lingered by the door. He glanced at Rae, tugged on the orange scarf with a small grin and headed into the night.

Nadia looked at Rae and Master Monham before she suddenly bolted toward the door. "If they're going to the Dark Market, I want to go to." She waved at Rae. "Don't worry about me this time, Rae, no one will bother me when I'm with One Shot." And before Rae could even blink, Nadia was gone.

Rae's chest squeezed. If she hurried she could stop Nadia, but what could she say? She knew her lies would catch up with her and now they had. Soon, Nadia would know Rae's secret.

The voices of the Whispering Hall bounced around Rae as she stalked through the room. Her secret would be out as soon as Nadia saw her fight.

Not if we fight her first! the Beast of Rage piped in.

Rae ignored the voice, her mind too occupied on how to keep Nadia quiet about her identity when a hand whipped out and grabbed Rae's wrist.

Rae immediately broke the contact and grabbed her assaulter's forearm.

"My, you are quick," an old hag cackled.

Rae dropped the old woman's hand in surprise. *What's an old woman doing here?*

Rae never engaged with any of the people roaming the Whispering Hall, but she'd heard stories. Tales of secrets being sold for coin and information shared for blackmail. The murmurs and secrets of the Whispering Hall were too eerie for Rae's comfort.

A black cloak enveloped the aged woman's frame as she hunched over a wobbly cane. Though the room was dark, the hag's pale, blotched skin shone in the small droplets of moonlight escaping the shuttered windows. Wisps of stringy white hair crawled from beneath the hood of the cloak, sticking to the hag's wrinkled skin.

Rae peered through her red mesh, trying to place the old hag's face. But she'd never seen her before.

The hag coughed, leaning over her crooked wooden cane. Rae wanted to help her, but she wasn't Rae here. She was the Crimson Cord and had a reputation to uphold.

"What do you want?" Rae asked in her deep voice.

"What do we all want?" the hag replied quickly, her black eyes glistening with delight. Rae stood silent until the hag answered, "Information."

Tilting her head to the side, Rae refused to speak again.

The hag cackled. "I know you wish to free the women bound to the Temple."

Rae's ears perked and the old hag noticed her more attentive stance. The hag grinned, showcasing her slanted yellow teeth.

"I can give you what you want. You only need to answer one question."

Rae narrowed her gaze. This seemed too easy, but she was curious. "How?"

"How?" the hag asked innocently.

"How can you free the priestesses from the Temple?"

Rae planned and saved for years and only managed to free a handful of women. It wasn't enough to just pay for their freedom, Rae wanted them to have a stable foundation when they restarted their lives in Yekel. She would see the freed women from time to time in the market on Sancti. Of course, they didn't know *she* was the one who freed them. The money was always given to General Yada by Master Monham or Old Charlie, who made sure the general fairly released the women.

But for this old woman to claim she could free the Temple Priestesses was too good to be true.

The hag opened her withered palm. Upon it sat an iron skeleton key. Rae stifled her gasp, recognizing the key General Yada used to lock up the Temple. The one he used to lock Kanna in her cell. The one he used to lock her and all the others in their rooms so they could only leave when he allowed. The one he wore around his neck at all times so no one could take it from him.

Rae's pulse thundered. If she had the key, she could sneak in and out of the Temple swiftly and quietly. She wouldn't have to hand over the Seer. She wouldn't have to deal with General Yada. The women, and Rae's conscious, would be free.

All questions of how the old hag obtained the key flew from Rae's mind.

Keeping her eyes glued on the key, she asked, "What's your question?"

The old crone smiled wickedly and as soon as Rae answered, she knew she made a grave mistake.

Chapter Sixteen

Devora, Dark Market, Yekel

Devora engaged her soulsight one last time before exiting Rae's home. The souls of Devora's companions lit up as she surveyed the room. Like daffodils in bloom, Nadia's soul was still a cheery yellow. Master Monham's presence shined bright as well but held a milkier glow. Devora faced Tristan next. A grayish-yellow, like clouds covering the summer sun, tinted his soul. A tinge of blue poked through. The swirl of conflicting colors in Tristan's soul worried Devora, but she hadn't the time to think about it now.

Devora checked One Shot's soul and was surprised. It was usually pale blue and sulky. But something had changed. Now the swirl rotated easily, perking up like a freshly watered lily. It was still blue, but Devora swore she saw a flicker of yellow.

She noticed One Shot's changed demeanor since he returned from the market earlier that day. Most of the time he scouted around the wall, checking for danger. If he wasn't doing that, he was usually cleaning his cross bow. One Shot never talked much, but when he did, it was in as few words as possible.

But since this morning, the tall man had been chatting about a lot of things. How nice the sunrise was in Yekel, how he wished he would've visited before he was sent to the Fortress. Devora then noticed the bright tangerine scarf around his neck. But when she asked about it, he sewed his lips shut and didn't speak again until they met up with Master Monham that evening. And Devora just figured out why.

Devora rotated toward Rae. She caught Rae and One Shot stealing glimpses of each other all through dinner. It wasn't until she remembered what Master Monham said about Rae selling fabrics and scarves in the market that Devora pieced everything together.

So, that's where One Shot got the scarves. Devora smiled to herself. She was surprised when One Shot brought her two more black scarves to use to conceal her identity. It seemed he enjoyed shopping at the market.

Engaging her soulsight once more, Devora assessed Rae's soul. But what showed on the woman's chest was something Devora had never seen. Rae's soul was midnight blue wrapped in black threads resembling chains. Devora didn't want to seem obvious as she studied Rae's soul, but an unnatural aura pulsed from the woman, almost as if her soul were crying out in pain.

What happened to Rae for her soul to be in such a state?

But Devora knew she'd stared for too long because Rae was staring back at her with a suspicious gaze.

"Thank you again for having us," Devora quickly said, blinking away her soulsight. Grabbing the black veil, Devora rose, knowing she'd need her disguise again in the Dark Market. "Could we meet here again?"

Rae adverted her gaze and nodded. Devora watched her again, trying to figure out how this woman and the woman Nadia had spoken so highly about were the same. From Nadia's descriptions, Rae was fierce and strong, a powerful force to be reckoned with. But this Rae was as skittish as a mouse. Devora was still surprised at the way Rae reacted to Tristan when they first arrived.

Devora and Tristan started toward the door, leaving One Shot behind as he reluctantly made his way toward the exit.

Oh, there's definitely something there, Devora thought as she ushered Tristan out the door. A few moments later, One Shot appeared, his shoulders slightly drooped.

Once the door shut, Tristan glared at One Shot, "Why did you shoot at me?"

One Shot kept his eyes trained forward, one hand holding his crossbow, the other entwined in the scarf. "If I shot *at* you, you'd be dead. I missed on purpose."

Devora shuddered at the chill in One Shot's voice. He was obviously displeased they had to leave Rae's home so suddenly.

"Tristan, you agreed not to mention anything of the past. *That* was the pact we made when we decided to work with you," she replied coolly. "One Shot was holding you to your word."

Tristan scoffed. "Well, if he does it again—"

"You'll what?" One Shot asked, towering over Tristan. Tristan shrank back, his head only coming to One Shot's chest. "You're nothing but a coward. Don't make idle threats."

Devora furrowed her brow at One Shot's outburst. Sure, Tristan was annoying, but they needed him to get into the Dark Market. That's why Matthias sent them to him.

Tristan knew the ins and outs of the Dark Market because it was his former gambling hub. Devora was initially frightened, remembering that Matthias told her Tristan killed one of the gang leaders when he couldn't pay off his debts. So, the three of them were extra careful to stay disguised in the Dark Market, praying no one would recognize Tristan. And so far, much to Tristan's dismay, no one had.

But, until they received the Crimson Cord's information about Kanna, Devora and One Shot needed Tristan to play his part in the Dark Market. That meant trying to keep their relationship civil.

Devora placed her hand in her pocket, feeling the drying purple rose petals. There were many times she wished Matthias were here to call the shots. He always knew what to do. And though she trusted her abilities and her knowledge, it would be nice to have someone else to rely on for all the decisions. She'd grown used to Matthias' valuable opinion and perspective.

"Let's just calm down," Devora offered, pushing the two men apart. "Tristan, you agreed to help us find further information on Kanna. She is your mother, too, after all. Once that's finish, I'll send word to Matthias, and he'll clear your debts. Until then, you're stuck with us. I suggest we all try to get along."

Tristan snorted, crossed his arms over his chest, and stomped ahead of them.

Devora shook her head, unable to believe she had ever wanted to marry him. Rubbing her eyes, she turned to One Shot. "Care to tell me what that was about?"

His stance relaxed as they strode in step with one another. "He talks too much."

Devora couldn't help but laugh. "And you don't talk nearly enough. Tell me about Rae."

One Shot's step hesitated just a moment, and if Devora hadn't spent so much time with him, she wouldn't have noticed.

"I met her at the market earlier today."

"And?"

One Shot glanced down at her, rubbing the back of his neck. "A guard was trying to force himself on her, so I took care of it."

Devora stopped, horror cinching her throat. "You didn't kill him, did you?" The last thing they needed was to be arrested for murder.

One Shot sighed. "I didn't have to, thankfully."

"Oh good," Devora breathed. "So, you like her?"

One Shot stared at the subtle stars appearing in the midnight sky. "She reminds me of Mara, but different." He shook his head. "It's hard to explain."

Devora remembered the first time she touched One Shot's soul. After a group of men attacked his younger sister, he shot—and killed—all four of them in one shot. Her heart softened, knowing One Shot's desire to avenge those who had been treated unjustly. Especially women who had been taken advantage of.

"There's something...I'm not sure," One Shot continued, shaking his head. "I would like to get to know her better." Then he laughed. "I know I don't deserve it though."

Devora twisted her long braid around her palm. "Why would you say that? You've done nothing wrong."

One Shot stopped and peered down at Devora. "What I can do with a crossbow is unnatural. I don't know how it's done, but it's not right. I'm not right. I can kill in the blink of an eye." He glanced down at his hands. "I'm a monster. I don't deserve to be happy. I deserve to be locked up back in the Fortress. I can't hurt anyone there."

"One Shot." Devora reached out, trying to console him, but he was already out of reach.

Where is this coming from? Devora thought as she watched the tall man stalk toward the new entrance to the Dark Market. Tristan had located it earlier that day and told them of its whereabouts in case they all got separated.

One Shot was kind and gentle, always trusting her plans and protecting her. He wasn't a monster. He had told her before he wasn't sorry for killing the men who attacked his sister and Devora understood. Was he feeling regret and torment now?

Already a few meters ahead, One Shot stopped and slunk into the nearest shadow, raising his crossbow. The hairs on the back of Devora's neck rose as she followed his line of sight. Standing in front of the entrance to the Dark Market was a group of men, ready and waiting for them.

Devora followed One Shot's lead and leaned into the closest shadow cast by a small cart.

Did they find out who I am? Are they working for King Atol?

It wasn't until then she noticed that Tristan and the group of men were talking. By the sword and clubs, the men were pulling out from behind their backs, the conversation wasn't going well.

Holding her breath, Devora darted to a turned over wooden cart, trying to figure out who the men were and what they wanted.

"Well, will you look here, boys," a tall, brutish man with squared shoulders and a nose that looked like it'd been broken too many times said. "The rat is back."

Devora gripped the side of a dilapidated cart as the men closed in on Tristan. This had to be the gang Tristan formerly gambled with. The gang whose leader he killed when he couldn't pay his debts.

Fear tightened around Devora's neck like a noose. She'd assumed the gang would find Tristan with all his blabbing, but she didn't think it would be this soon.

"It's nice to see you again, too, Booker," Tristan replied, feigning boredom. "After that mess with Kade I didn't have a chance to say good-bye."

Before Devora could blink, Booker whipped out two daggers and pointed them at Tristan. One laid against his throat, the other his heart.

"Keep your lying mouth shut, rat," Booker seethed. "You should be begging for mercy for what you did to Kade."

Tristan shrugged and checked his nails, still looking bored.

Devora had to admit, she was impressed with Tristan's acting skills.

Tristan pushed the blade away from his throat. "Kade threatened me first, *Bookie*. It was all self-defense."

Booker snarled at the nickname, spittle flying from his mouth as he reared back ready to stab Tristan in the heart.

Devora darted forward but paused. *Should I help?*

Tristan was her only way into the Dark Market. But she couldn't take on so many members of a gang by herself.

Before she could decide, an arrow whizzed from the shadows and pierced Booker in the shoulder. The gang leader roared, stumbling back a few steps. His hand clamped over the wound as blood seeped between his thick fingers.

Thank you, One Shot, Devora thought.

The gang members held their weapons high, searching around the front of the secret entrance. But when One Shot wanted to stay hidden, no one could find him.

Another arrow soared through the air, pinning a gang member in the thigh. He howled and the others quickly covered his mouth.

"Ah, yes," Tristan said, a new arrogance coating his words. "You wouldn't want the Falcons to know I was here. When they heard I killed Kade, they wanted to recruit me on the spot."

"Grab him!" Booker yelled, trying to pry the arrow from his shoulder.

Tristan easily dodged the first two gang members, but another four grabbed him and pinned him to the ground.

Devora started forward to help when a hand yanked her back. Her Fortress training took over and she spun around and jabbed her palm into her attacker's stomach. Only it wasn't an enemy, but One Shot. He wheezed once, trying to stay quiet.

Devora gasped. "I'm so sorry. Are you okay?"

"Fine," he coughed. "Look." He pointed to where Tristan was still being held.

Devora spun toward the scene, her braid flinging over her shoulder. Tristan was still on the ground but each of the gang members were now lying around him.

"Wh—" Devora started when out of the shadows came a familiar blonde head. Devora breathed a sigh of relief as she started toward Tristan.

"Dev! Dev!" Nadia's voice rang through the night. She waved her arms in the air. Devora quickly donned her black veil, just in case someone had heard Nadia.

"Nadia, what are you doing here?"

Nadia gestured toward Tristan. "Saving his sorry hide."

"I'll have you know I had everything completely under control." Tristan strained under the weight of the brutes lying atop him. "Did you have to knock them out so they fell *on* me?"

Nadia shrugged. "You should be thankful I even helped at all." She turned to Devora, excitement lighting her gaze. "I want to see the Crimson Cord. Please, please, please?" She cupped her hands under her chin and made her eyes impossibly big.

"I don't—"

"I want to see what his fighting style is like," Nadia cut in. "I brought my own disguise!"

Nadia unfurled one of Rae's bright yellow scarves and wrapped it around her head and face, leaving only her eyes showing.

"I think we want to blend in," Devora chuckled as she tugged gently on the bright material. Nadia would certainly draw every suspicious eye in the Dark Market.

"Oh please, Dev," Nadia begged, pressing her palms together as if she were praying. "I've been cooped up in Rae's house making maps and charts for Captain Blake. I want to go somewhere." Nadia stuck out her lower lip in pout.

"She should come," One Shot said, coming behind Devora. He tugged on the bright orange scarf still around his neck. "It'll be good to have extra eyes."

"I knew you really didn't hate me," Tristan wheezed to One Shot from beneath the pile of men. "You protected me."

His features stoic, One Shot took a step forward and sat on the back of one of the men squashing Tristan.

Tristan's eyes bulged. "Okay, okay. You still hate me."

A smirk lined One Shot's lips as he stood. With his boot, One Shot kicked the brute off of Tristan, allowing him to shimmy out of the pile. Tristan dusted off his pants and grinned, as if nothing had happened.

Shaking her head, Devora sighed. "Fine." Nadia's face lifted like a cloud. "But you can't wear something so bright."

Devora pulled the extra black scarf from her bag. Tristan said the Dark Market was, well, dark, so she was thankful when One Shot bought her the additional colored fabrics at the market. "Here." She handed the black scarf to Nadia, who wrapped it around her head as she had before.

Devora adjusted her own black veil. "Let's go."

The four of them hurried toward the entrance of the Dark Market, taking care to leave the unconscious bodies of the gang members untouched.

Tristian wrapped his dark cloak around his shoulder. "You know, keeping track of one woman is enough. Who knows what will happen with two?"

Nadia darted forward and jabbed three points in Tristan's arm.

"Ah, what are you doing?" he cried as his left arm went limp. "My arm! I can't move it!"

Nadia clucked her tongue. "I can see why Dev dumped you."

Devora and One Shot simultaneously laughed.

Tristan growled as he knocked a special cadence on the door with his right arm, shooting a glare at Nadia. The doorkeeper, an elderly man with sagging skin and sunken eyes, opened the door a crack.

"Name?" asked the crusty voice.

"The Winner, here to see the Crimson Cord."

The doorkeeper assessed Tristan. "You got that giant with you?" One Shot stepped into view, and the doorkeeper smiled. "It'll be a good fight tonight. Master Cord was in a foul mood when he came in."

The Crimson Cord is already here? Have we missed our chance? Devora needed that information on Kanna. And anything else the Crimson Cord knew about Yekel. And possibly Princess Haden, too.

Devora itched to say something. It had been difficult to keep quiet while in the Dark Market, but she succeeded. She would just have to bite her tongue. Literally.

The taste of iron swirled in her mouth as she watched Tristan banter with the doorkeeper. Tristan was annoying and petty, but he knew the rules of the Dark Market. If women were brought, they were to keep their mouths closed. Devora hated the rule, but she had to trust Tristan.

She looped her arm through Nadia's, attempting to tell her friend to stay quiet. Thankfully, Nadia patted Devora's hand in understanding.

"Come, Master Cord awaits." The doorkeeper opened the entrance, and Tristan slipped in.

One Shot bent almost in half to fit through the small space, and Devora and Nadia followed.

They hurried through a series of staircases and hallways until they strode through the Whispering Hall. Uneasiness danced across Devora's nerves, just as it had the last time. The hushed tones of secrets and deals flittered around the room.

Tristan warned them about the Whispering Hall and how to not make eye contact with anyone. Any slight inclination toward someone could have you agreeing to a deal you didn't want to make.

Devora did her best to keep her eyes and ears forward. But out of the corner of her eye, the hag who had given her the imperial opal tincture at the Fortress hobbled by. Devora spun her head, heart racing.

Why is the hag here?

Pulse pounding, Devora searched among the cloaked figures in the Whispering Hall. But

when she looked again, the hag was gone.

"Dev, what did you see?" Nadia whispered.

Devora clutched the purple sash still wrapped around her wrist and shook her head.

They soon reached the Fighter's Ring. Judging by the shouts and hollers, an intense fight was taking place. As best as he could with one arm, Tristan muscled his way to the front, One

Shot a step behind him. The men surrounding the brawl were screaming and cheering and Devora was brought back to Regulus Protecti, when the crowd only wanted to see more blood.

She and Nadia slipped through a space and made their way to the front. Nadia's form stiffened and Devora gave an audible gasp. Before them stood the Crimson Cord, his hands covered in blood.

Chapter Seventeen

"It can't be," Nadia whispered, as the Crimson Cord shook his head. She leaned forward slightly, trying to get a better look at the fight.

"Nadia, what's the matter?" Devora asked, keeping her gaze focused on the Fighter's Ring.

Thankfully, the bleeding man before the Crimson Cord wasn't dead, but something still seemed off about the way he swayed back and forth.

"Check the Crimson Cord's soul," Nadia said through ground teeth.

"What? Why?"

Devora eyed Nadia through her black veil. Something was wrong with Nadia, too. Her brow was taut, her jaw clenched. Devora couldn't remember if she'd ever seen Nadia angry.

"Do it," Nadia hissed, and Devora obliged.

As soon as she engaged her soulsight, Devora knew what Nadia discovered. The chained soul Devora had seen on Rae was the same one in the Crimson Cord's chest. Except now, the soul skittered about, panicked. Though the Crimson Cord looked calm and cool on the outside, only Devora could see how frightened he—or she—was on the inside.

Shock tingled through Devora's nerves. Rae was the Crimson Cord. Rae knew everything Devora needed to know and sat silently at dinner, saying nothing.

Devora balled her hands into a fist, trying to calm her rage. How could someone not help others when they had the means to do so?

Nadia described Rae as a benevolent woman, especially when she gave herself up to save Nadia and the others when Kadesh first attacked Yekel. Devora huffed, staring at the chained soul. The dark blue light wracked against the black chains, wanting to be free of its cage. Sympathy doused the fury in Devora's chest. She didn't know much about Rae, but she was the key to finding Kanna. There also had to be a reason Rae was dressing like a man and hiding her identity to fight in the Dark Market. Devora remembered Master Monham explaining the rumors about the Crimson Cord using his winnings to free slaves. But were the rumors true?

Devora peered over at One Shot. Did he know? Judging by his usual stoic face, he was none the wiser.

Should I tell him? Devora looked into Rae's soul one more time, but before she could decide heat bloomed between her eyes and her vision went black.

Devora stood before the imperial opal statue of the horned woman from her previous vision, and she wasn't happy about it. At least the statue wasn't sucking her soul out this time.

The spacious marble room was vacant and quiet, sending unease through Devora. Her feet padded silently across the floor as she made her way to one of the doors. A swirled Kadeshian symbol was etched across the top half of the black wood. Devora didn't know a lot of Kadeshian but she knew this symbol represented the number sixteen. The one to the right was eighteen. Doors lined the entire length of the marble room, each with a different Kadeshian number. Spinning around, Devora saw that there were numbered doors on the opposite wall as well. The one to the right was thirty-five. Next to that was twenty-six.

Confused, Devora faced the door labeled sixteen. What does this all mean? Where am I?

Placing her hand on the bronze knob, she took a breath and twisted the handle. The wooden door creaked inward, and Devora hesitantly stepped inside. Silken cloths, every color of the rainbow, draped across the walls of the room. Plush, vibrant pillows filled the floor. Two golden goblets sat upon a gilded tray, only one emptied.

Her uneasiness growing, Devora peered around. What is this place?

Shuddering sobs brought Devora's attention to a huddled figure in the corner of the room, draped in only a scarlet cloth. Long white-blonde hair splayed around the woman's bare shoulder, covering her face.

"Until next time, my dear."

A uniformed man with slick ebony hair and tan skin stroked the woman's head possessively before heading toward Devora.

Devora remembered her visions about Princess Haden and feared that this man would see her too, but the Kadeshian man simply walked through her.

Relief eased Devora's tense state before she focused back on the young woman in the corner. The woman sobbed violently, so much that she vomited all over the scarlet sheet.

Devora hurried toward her, then stopped, horrified. She recognized those caramel eyes, that small nose and those heart-shaped lips.

The woman sobbing in the corner was Rae. But not the Rae she had just met. This was Rae just when Kadesh took over Yekel. It had to be.

Anguish struck Devora's heart. She studied the young face, wishing she could help her. Although she now realized...this wasn't a vision, but a memory.

The room swirled, and Devora stood in a dungeon of some sort. Rae's long blonde hair was pulled back into a plait as she crouched in front of a cell. A bowl and spoon were in her hand. Carefully, she spooned dark broth through the bars of the cell.

Soft whispers and a few chuckles were shared between Rae and whoever was imprisoned inside. Devora tried to get a better look at the prisoner, but the sound of a door opening and shutting caused the prisoner to scurry into the dark.

Rae, however, didn't hide. Slowly, she placed the bowl down and stood tall. Time had passed since the first memory because this Rae shed not one tear. Her gaze was hard, her jaw locked as she glowered at the same uniformed Kadeshian man who was in the room before.

"Aiding the enemy again?" the man chuckled darkly. "It will cost you."

Rae lifted her chin. "You will never break me."

The man laughed, this time filled with something dark and menacing. He ran a finger across her cheek. "But it's so fun to try."

The man escorted Rae from the dungeon and up the stairs. Devora wasn't sure whether to follow or not when the memory darkened. She turned toward the prisoner in the cell and caught a glimpse of two clouded violet eyes staring back at her.

The fight was over, but somehow, Devora was still standing. Usually, when a vision, or a memory in this case, came upon her so suddenly, she passed out and fell to the ground. But Devora found herself upright, surrounded by Nadia and One Shot. Nadia held onto Devora's arm tight as One Shot stood behind her, his hands under her arms, keeping her standing.

Tristan seemed to have disappeared into the crowd, which worried Devora.

"We figured you were having a vision or something," Nadia muttered through the black fabric covering her mouth. Her eyes stayed glued on the Crimson Cord—on Rae—who was fighting the next competitor.

Devora reflected on what she'd seen in Rae's soul and shuddered. No wonder Rae's soul held so many chains. It was tormented and injured. Devora couldn't imagine what Rae had suffered. But now she wondered why Rae had hidden her pain. Did she have no one she could trust to help her through it?

"What did you see?" Nadia asked, still focused on the Crimson Cord.

Devora opened her mouth but stopped, remembering all the secrets she discovered through her soulsight. She then thought about the imperial opal poison she almost took and about the tears she wept in the Fortress after Matthias betrayed her. *Would I want someone to divulge my darkest moments to another?*

Devora shook her head. "Nothing that I can share."

Nadia whipped her head to Devora and for the first time, Devora saw a darkness lurking behind Nadia's eyes. "So, you're going to keep secrets from me too?"

Before Devora could reply, Nadia pulled away and slipped into the crowd of gambling men.

"Nadia," Devora whispered, trying to keep herself unnoticed. She tugged on One Shot's sleeve. He crouched down so she could speak in his ear above the noise. "Do you see Nadia?"

One Shot rose to his towering height, which was at least a foot above everyone else, as he peered around. When he glanced down at Devora and shook his head, her shoulders sagged. If they weren't supposed to meet with the Crimson Cord—with Rae—then Devora would go after Nadia. She had checked the purple light leading to Kanna several times earlier, and it still only led to the Dark Market. Devora needed more information about Kanna. Not just because Warden Hazor charged her with the task, but because she wanted to meet another Seer. Maybe Kanna would be able to help Devora strengthen her abilities.

And give you a way to talk to Matthias again, her heart added.

Devora turned her gaze back to the Fighter's Ring where two different men, one with dark, slick skin and the other with tanned skin, were about to duel. She hadn't given herself much time to think about Matthias. The wound was still too fresh and deep.

I will spend eternity trying to make it up to you.

Devora held the rose petals in her pocket. That's what his note said, and it still made her chest ache. She longed to see him again, but the sting of his betrayal was still too new, even though he'd explained his reasonings when he freed her. Sighing, Devora peered around the Fighter's Ring again. The crowd was beginning to thin out. Their meeting with the Crimson Cord would happen soon. Tristan suddenly appeared to her right, and Devora flinched, accidentally knocking into One Shot.

"Excited to see me?" He pulled his hood back enough so that Devora could catch his sultry grin.

"Ugh," Devora replied, adjusting the veil on her head. "No. Where were you? Do you want to be almost killed again? And put that back on." She yanked the hood down, so it shadowed his face.

Tristan enjoyed his alias, the Winner, a little too much and got *too* into character last time. Devora was worried One Shot would break him in two after Tristan had snapped at him. Luckily, One Shot's thread of patience was a lot longer than her own.

"I was just seeing if there were any profitable fights tonight," Tristan sniffed.

"Do you think that's wise?" Devora asked. "After what happened earlier?"

Tristan merely shrugged as he watched the two men brawl in the ring.

Devora chewed on her lower lip. There was something about Tristan's assistance that confused her. Matthias knew all about Tristan's lies and that he murdered a gang leader. She'd also experienced Tristan's two-faced personality firsthand a few months ago. So why did Matthias want her to trust his criminal brother? Was there really no one else that could've helped them sneak into the Dark Market?

Try as she might, Devora could not figure out the captain's plan. But she knew Tunri wanted her to trust this path, so she would.

Devora glanced at One Shot, who seemed to relax as more people left the Dark Market. He had been quiet since she mentioned Rae earlier. Devora wanted to know more about the tall man's thoughts on the woman, but she also didn't want to reveal that her vision was about Rae.

Why Rae decided to become the Crimson Cord, Devora wasn't completely sure. But it was Rae's secret to share with those she cared about, not Devora's.

As the last fight finished in a draw, the Keeper of the Coins clinked his abacus beads together and tallied up the earnings.

Devora immediately thought of Reese, always shuffling the beads on her abacus and giving probabilities. Where was she now? Where were Hestia and Ida? Were they safe? Warden Hazor said he sent Hestia, Reese, Ida, and Sir Jacques on missions away from the Fortress, but he didn't say where.

Please keep them safe, Devora prayed as the men took their winnings and vacated the ring.

Tristan collected his own winnings from the fight and tied the leather purse to his belt. Turning to her, he said, "It's time."

Devora gave a quick nod and followed him to a room adjacent to the Fighter's Ring with One Shot a few steps behind.

The room was small, much smaller than where they met the Crimson Cord last time. And it was cold. Goosebumps rose on Devora's arms as she searched the cramped space for an open window, but there was none. Two lanterns hung from opposite walls, lighting the square room in a dull orange. Other than a minute round stool in the center, the room stood bare.

"Drafty in here, isn't it?" Tristan said, dropping the deep voice he used while donning his alter ego. By his wavering tone, Devora knew he was nervous about this meeting as well.

"There are hidden exits wherever the Dark Market resides. You just need to know where to look."

Tristan, Devora, and One Shot all turned to face the Crimson Cord, who stood in the threshold of the doorway. The Cord strode in and shut the splintered wooden door, immediately crossing his arms over his chest.

Devora never considered herself to be claustrophobic. Even when she was in Level Five of the Fortress, she still felt like she had plenty of space. But hearing Tristan heavily breathing behind her and only seeing the black veil in front of her, she felt the walls closing in around her.

Breathe. You can do this, Matthias's voice coached in her head. She hated that she was imagining his voice, imagining his lips. But it did calm the frantic palpitations in her chest.

"Ah, yes," Tristan replied, lowering his voice. "You never know when the Kadeshians will want to make an arrest."

Devora quirked a brow at Tristan. She did not want to know how he knew that.

The Crimson Cord tilted his head at Tristan, then focused on Devora and One Shot. "You wanted information about Kanna, yes?"

Devora nodded, careful not to speak. Even though she knew it was Rae under the red mesh mask, she didn't want to scare her and prevent her from helping them.

"I know of a girl who used to work in the Temple," the Cord started.

Devora noted how the Cord fiddled with the crimson rope around his waist. If she hadn't known it was really Rae behind the mesh, she would have found this an odd gesture for a man. Especially after she had seen how men act while in the Fortress.

As if the Rae read Devora's thoughts, she dropped the rope and squared her shoulders.

"A *Trixie Girl*?" Tristan scoffed. "What would someone like *that* know?"

The Crimson Cord visibly winced then hardened at the implication in Tristan's voice. "If you're too high and mighty to work with someone of her former profession, then you won't be needing my help." The Cord turned to leave.

"Wait!" Devora cried before she could stop herself. She knew women weren't supposed to speak in the Dark Market, but women weren't supposed to dress up as men and fight in it either. "Please."

The Cord stopped, not turning around.

Devora licked her lips. She peered over her shoulder at One Shot, who gave her a nod of encouragement. He told her before how speaking wasn't his strong suit, so he'd trust her to do the talking.

"I don't care what her profession is. If you give me her name, I'd like to talk to her."

Devora waited, her heart pounding between her ears. She hoped—prayed—that the Crimson Cord would say the name Devora already knew.

The Crimson Cord hesitated before reaching for something around her neck. "Her name is Rae Salvar."

Chapter Eighteen

Rae's vision blurred around the edges as she stared at the blood on her gloved fingertips. She'd barely hit the man. How could she have killed him?

The middle-aged man twitched, and Rae gave an audible sigh of relief. He stood and swayed. His blue eyes glazed over as blood gushed down his nose and lips. Rae had been so distracted by the old hag before that she hadn't noticed the man's drugged state.

The skeleton key sat cold against her chest as she tried to reevaluate her plan. The crowd's murmurs were louder than her thundering heart. She knew what they were saying. She knew that her loss to the Goliath blemished her perfect record. Now that she'd drawn so much blood so easily from the drugged man, the gamblers in the Fighter's Ring would take their coin elsewhere. Bloody noses and busted lips were fine in the Fighter's Ring. But no one wanted to be known as a killer.

What will we do now? the Beast of Fear chittered.

But the man wasn't dead, he was still standing. Barely standing, but standing, nonetheless.

My punch wasn't that hard, Rae thought. Something strange was happening.

Punch him harder! the Beast of Rage encouraged.

Rae paced away from the man. If she could subdue him quickly and cleanly, she may save her reputation.

Sucking in a cleansing breath, Rae planned:

First, jab stomach.

Before she could think further, Rae rushed toward the man. The crowd started to thin and that wasn't a good thing. Even though she gained the skeleton key to the Temple, she didn't completely trust the old woman who'd approached her in the Whispering Hall.

Rae still wanted to have her fallback plan of making enough coin to buy each of the women's freedom. And she needed gamblers to watch her fights to earn it.

Reaching back, she bladed her fingertips and forced them into the drugged man's stomach. Groaning, he flopped forward.

Relief flooded her being as the men stayed around the ring and continued to gamble. She needed that coin now more than ever. The skeleton key flopped against her chest again. Once Rae freed the women from the Temple, she would need to find housing and food for all of them and that required coin.

Next, bring knee into stomach.

Rae grabbed the man's shoulders and kneed him right in the center of his gut.

Cheers built from the crowd, encouraging Rae to finish the man off, and Rae found herself reveling in their praise.

Last, finish the job.

Rae licked the sweat forming on her upper lip as she untied the scarlet cord from around her waist. Pulse thrumming, she started toward the man, who lay prostrate in the ring. She gripped the crimson cord between her gloved hands, and a new feeling overcame her. All her grief, her anger, her pain rolled in her chest, spinning harder and faster. Her emotions consumed her until she felt something—or someone—overtake her. Her feet moved of their own volition, stomping toward the man.

Finish him, a clipped, feminine voice Rae had never heard before commanded in her thoughts.

Frightened, Rae tried to pull back, but her feet kept moving forward. Inwardly, she struggled and strained, yet it was no use.

The crowd roared around her. Thankfully, they remembered she had never killed her opponents. But this time was different. This time, if she couldn't stop whatever force was controlling her, this man would really die.

Rae didn't know what to do other than watch as her hands tied the rope around the unconscious man's throat.

Stop! she yelled internally. A sickening cackle responded as her hand tightened around the rope.

Rae's eyes darted all around until they landed on Nadia. Fear pierced her soul.

Stop!

She couldn't allow Nadia to see her like this.

Now that Nadia watched the Crimson Cord fight, she would know of Rae's ruse. And behind Nadia was Ben. Rae's stomach dropped.

Will she tell him my secret? What will he think of me then?

Rae pushed the thoughts aside. She didn't want or care about any man's opinion of her.

But next to Nadia stood a figure veiled in black. *The Seer!* Maybe she could help rid Rae of the dark aura controlling her.

The commanding woman's voice returned. *The Seer will never help you. Not once she finds out everything you've done, everything you are. You are filth.*

Tears pricked in Rae's eyes as the cord wrapped tighter and tighter around the man's throat. He squirmed beneath her grip, begging for air, just as Sir Brannock had all those months ago.

Kill him, kill him, kill him! the Beast of Rage encouraged, drowning out the woman's voice.

Rae's mind reeled for a solution. If she killed this man, she would be blacklisted from the Dark Market, and the gangs would come for her. Gambling and theft were acceptable in Yekel's criminal underworld. But murder? That was a line none of them would cross. Rae promised to never take another's life.

Trust Tunri, mija, Mami's voice spoke in her thoughts. It was as if sunshine banished the cold grip on her heart.

Trust Tunri, Rae, Kanna's voice said next.

Her hands continued to pull the cord tight, seemingly of their own volition. Red pinpoints freckled across the man's face. Rae had yanked too tight. He was going to die.

Still, Rae didn't want to call out to Tunri. He had never helped her before. He let King Atol take Papi. He let General Yada take Mami. He let her suffer in the Temple. He didn't care. But she couldn't be condemned and killed for murder. She had to free the women in the Temple. It was a responsibility branded on her heart. She only needed one more chance.

Please, help me, Rae whispered to a supernatural being she knew nothing about.

As if the invisible strings controlling her had been severed, the eerie presence vacated her body and Rae reclaimed control of her hands just in time. She quickly untied the rope from the man's throat.

He fell forward, coughing uncontrollably before vomiting across the ground.

Panting, Rae glanced into the crowd. The men exchanged their bets, but something was off. Their side-eyes and whispers to one another told her enough. Though her reputation as the Crimson Cord wasn't completely ruined, it had been severely tarnished.

"Our winner is the Crimson Cord!" Jasper cried.

The crowd was somewhat enthusiastic, but Rae needed a break to sort out her thoughts.

"Try not to get *too* into harming your opponent," Jasper murmured to her as she passed him. "You know those soldiers are waiting to put any one of us on trial."

Rae nodded, surprised at Jasper's small kindness. While General Yada allowed the Dark Market's existence, if anything other than gambling and fighting happened, he would send his troops in immediately to shut it down. It had only happened once before, that Rae knew of, and that was when the leader of the Street Rats had been murdered with gumberry poison.

Grabbing the water jug Jasper handed to her, Rae headed toward the exit. She needed some time before her meeting with the Seer.

A few men clapped her on the back in congratulations for winning her duel, but all Rae wanted to do was feel the cool night air. Though Rae usually loved the power she felt while wearing the red scarf, right now, it suffocated her. Just like the gray Temple veil.

She thought becoming the Crimson Cord would lead to her freedom, but it had only wrapped her in a different set of chains.

Rae pushed through the crowd, scanning for the exit when her eyes landed on *him*. Fire and wrath exploded behind her eyes as everything filed into place.

"Leaving so soon?" General Yada asked, the corner of his lips tipped up in a smirk.

Instead of his usual Kadeshian military uniform, the general wore a commoner's gray tunic and black pants. His hair was mussed and tucked into a cap most laymen in Yekel wore. But all the disguises in the world couldn't fool Rae.

Rae wanted to tear him apart limb from limb. He was the one who set her up. She didn't know how, but he had to have drugged her opponent to make her look like a monster. To make her fans second guess their support of her. To turn their praise to judgment. All because she hadn't delivered information about the Seer yet.

"Let's not make a scene, my dear," General Yada clucked as he forcefully took her arm.

She immediately wrenched it away. "Get your hands off me."

Though the crowds had dispersed, a few gamblers lingered and cast unsure glances their way.

"If you want to keep your beloved *Nadi* safe, I suggest you follow me without fuss," he whispered coldly.

Terror iced her spine as she watched General Yada turn down the nearest corridor.

Everything in her screamed to run in the other direction, but Rae knew once General Yada set his sights on someone, he would never let them go.

Rae mechanically followed the general down the hall and into a room on the far left. She stood only in the threshold, not daring to enter into a room—alone—with this man ever again.

The room was spacious and dimly lit. Lanterns hung from each wall, lighting the area enough for Rae to notice a pile of plush pillows and scarlet fabric hanging from the ceiling. She narrowed her eyes at the resemblance to her room in the Temple. He was trying to goad her.

"Care to join me?" the general said, his broad back to her. He poured dark red wine into two silver goblets, then offered her one. "Come now, Rae, you can't enjoy our favorite drink with that awful fabric across your face."

The crimson mesh *was* stifling, but she felt protected with it on. Lifting her chin, she ignored his outstretched hand.

"Start talking," Rae demanded, folding her arms across her chest, her feet planting in the doorway. "I have somewhere else I need to be."

"So, I've heard," General Yada replied, his calm demeanor shattering for a moment. He took a long sip from his goblet. "It's amazing what you Yekelians will give for the price of freedom."

Don't take the bait, she told herself. But her curiosity was too strong. "What are you talking about?"

General Yada grinned, showcasing his perfectly white teeth against his tanned skin. "A little wizard came by my quarters the other day. He told me the most wonderful story."

Dread like nails crept over her skin. *No*, she thought, *the Wizard Wankle promised he wouldn't tell.*

We knew he would betray us! The Beast of Fear cried.

General Yada already knew about her past at the Temple and that she was the Crimson Cord. But he didn't know she knew about the Seer. And the Wizard Wankle did.

"Even with your disguise I can still read your body like a book." He licked his lips, and Rae fought the urge to shudder away like she always had.

No, I'm not afraid of him. He doesn't own me. Not anymore.

Straining to keep her posture relaxed, she replied, "Care to share the details?"

A spark of excitement flashed in the general's eyes, and it was a look Rae knew all too well. "This is why I like you so much, Rae. You never give up." He took another sip from his goblet as he surveyed her physique.

Rae hated how he freely looked at her like she was a meal for him to enjoy. She hated how all men looked at her like that.

Except for one. Ben's soft dark eyes flashed in her mind before she pushed the image away. *He would never want me if he knew.*

Rae cocked her hip to the side with a sigh, trying to sound bored. "I don't have time for your petty games." Still, she locked her knees to keep them from buckling beneath her.

As she started to turn away, the general called, "Where's the Seer, Rae? The Wizard sang beautifully once I tortured him enough."

Losing all resolve, she snarled, "What did you do to him?"

General Yada examined the jewels on his goblet. "I merely summoned him for entertainment. Imagine how surprised I was to find out he knew information about the Tentonian fugitive."

Rae's chest squeezed. *Is he telling the truth? Did the Wizard sell me out? Or was he actually tortured for information?*

She could never find her way out of General Yada's webs of half-truths. When she was younger, he talked circles around her, and she believed him. But now that she was free, she didn't have to listen.

Rae turned away. "I don't have time for this."

"Three days," General Yada barked, losing his playful demeanor.

Rae's lips gaped open. "But you agreed to two weeks. I still have five days left." Rae should've known the slimy snake would tighten his grasp around her. She should've been working day and night to figure out a plan instead of daydreaming about Ben.

"You have three days to tell me where the Seer is," General Yada repeated. "Or Nadia will be mine."

Rae's shock burned to fury as she jumped forward and fisted the general's shirt in her hand. With the other, she yanked her crimson mesh to her neck. She wanted him to see the fire in her eyes and know she was his pet no longer.

"If you touch her, I will kill you, and I'll enjoy it."

His rich scent of wine and honey burrowed into her nose, and she resisted the urge to vomit. A strand of his dark hair curled across his forehead as he gave her a sultry smile.

"Threats aren't becoming of you, Rae, especially insincere ones."

Growling, Rae reared her head back and slammed it into the general's nose. Blood spurted from his nostrils. The general reared back with a cry of pain. Without another thought, Rae shoved him away and sprinted down the hall.

She needed to get as far away from the general as she could. She had to get back to Nadia and keep her safe. Now that she attacked General Yada, he would be after her and Nadia with renewed vengeance.

Pulling the mesh back over her head, Rae raced through the Dark Market. The skeleton key thumped against her chest as she ran. It didn't matter if she had enough coin, she needed to get the other priestesses out soon, but how?

She remembered her meeting with the Seer. Maybe, just maybe, they would help her find a solution. Taking a breath, Rae searched around the Dark Market. When General Yada was nowhere to be found, Rae hurried to the small room where the Seer, the Winner, and Ben were waiting.

In order to get them to help her free the women in the Temple, Rae had to get them to trust her. The only way to gain the Seer's and Ben's trust was to be honest. And that meant telling them who she really was. She couldn't remember the last time she'd given someone her last name. In the Temple, she was only a number. In the Dark Market, she was the Crimson Cord. To everyone else, she was just Rae.

But, for some reason, Rae found herself trusting this odd group of people. Not with her past, not with her secret identity, but with her name.

"Rae Salvar knows of Kanna and can get you into the Temple," Rae forced out.

The skeleton key from the hag burned into her chest. She shouldn't have paid attention to the old woman, but now that Rae had the key, she would use it.

"Why would she want to go back there?" Devora asked quietly.

Rae paused, realizing, in one sentence, she'd told all three of them of her past. Yet the only one to act negatively was that idiot, Tristan, and she already knew what type of man he was. She cautiously turned her gaze toward Ben. His long features were calm, but a certain sadness dwelled behind his dark eyes as he tugged on the end of the orange scarf still around his neck. Was his sadness for her? For what was done to her? Or at the knowledge of what she really was?

"She has her own reasons," Rae responded curtly. "I'll tell her to expect you tomorrow night at midnight." She paused, then pointed to Tristan, still dressed as the Winner. "Don't bring him."

Tristan scoffed. "I wouldn't want to be in the company—"

Before he could finish, Ben whipped out his crossbow and pointed it at him. Tristan reluctantly clamped his lips shut.

"We'll be there," Devora said firmly. "Tell her thank you."

A small tickle probed Rae's chest, right above her heart and she could've sworn the Seer was "seeing" more than she let on. But Rae only nodded and fled the room. Time was running out. She needed to get Nadia out of Yekel before General Yada came for her.

Chapter Nineteen

"Where is that sorry excuse for a bird?" Matthias muttered.

A week had already passed since he last received word from Governor Medee's smoke signal. Devora had decoded his message and was heading to Yekel.

He knew she would figure it out. They'd never spoken of the Counter Code before, but he knew that if Devora really prepared herself for Vlacklear, she could decode it with no problem.

Matthias paced in front of the open window of his new working chambers in Maldove Palace. It was strange working part-time in the Fortress and part-time in the castle. King Atol declared it was because Matthias attempted to stop the treasonous Seer from escaping and was a hero of Tenton. In reality, Matthias didn't remember much after Devora pulled away from him in Level Five, ordering him not to come near her.

He clenched his jaw, still pained by the hurt and distrust in her bright violet eyes. One day, he would tell her everything. But right now, he was still too trapped in the kingdom's clutches. If he didn't play his hand perfectly, thousands of innocents would die, and he would be to blame.

Matthias hated being under the close watch of the king and queen. They didn't give him new chambers as a reward. They were tightening the collar already secured around his throat.

Reaching up, he grabbed the imperial opal ring, hanging on a thin silver chain around his neck. It was a gift Devora received from her father when she was still at the Fortress. Governor Medee was too wise to have sent this to his daughter. As soon as Matthias saw the gift weeks ago, he knew the ring had to have come from elsewhere. But that didn't explain why the governor hadn't informed his daughter of the lethal effects of imperial opal. Did he think she would try to use it?

Matthias fisted the ring, remembering how Devora almost *did* take the imperial opal vial in the Theater. Thank Tunri he decided to train in the Theater that night. What he still couldn't figure out was how she got a hold of the rare gem in liquid form in the first place. There were only a few places in Tenton to procure imperial opal and even those places were nearly impossible to find.

The sound of furiously flapping wings broke his concentration and Matthias rushed to the open window. Though his room was ridiculously cold, he refused to close the peaked glass of the large window until he received another message. Seeing the scruffy crow fighting against the northern wind to get to him made the chill worthwhile.

Devora's and Nadia's crow from the Fortress skidded to a halt on the stone windowsill. A few black feathers floated away from the already balding bird as it hopped toward Matthias.

Ushering the bird inside, Matthias closed the window and immediately noticed there was not only one note tied to the crow's leg, but two. Anticipation lit his nerves as he gave the crow a piece of bread and untied the notes.

Has she finally responded?

But his excitement cooled to melancholy once he recognized Nadia's slanted scrawl on the first note. The second scroll was a series of maps. Pushing his emotions aside, Matthias focused on Nadia's information about the state of Yekel's outer wall. According to the notes, the Kadeshians had been forcing the Yekelians to fix the wall that was destroyed when Kadesh invaded.

Matthias furrowed his brow as he studied Nadia's drawing of the outer wall and the inner workings of the city. With the outer wall still being fortified, getting into the city would be easy. Taking control and keeping control of it would be the difficult part.

Matthias headed toward the forest green velvet chair by the fire. Now that the fierce wind had been banished, the fire roared to life. Flopping into the chair, Matthias rubbed the bridge of his nose. Was taking back Yekel a good idea?

When he'd presented the idea to King Atol, he wrapped his reasoning in the notion that Princess Haden may have been taken to Yekel in order to smuggle her to Kadesh. He didn't mention Devora by name, not wanting to add any more targets on her back. But the king's mind was set that it was Devora who had captured the princess. Matthias hated hearing the king's slander against Devora, yet Matthias kept his mouth shut during the tirades. That was how the game was played. Speak only when necessary and make his words count. That was how he'd kept Devora alive. That was how he'd kept himself alive.

Frankly, Matthias had no idea where Princess Haden had gone or why she fled after they rescued her from Kadesh at the Battle of Edo. What struck him as odd was that she recognized the imperial opal ring when he escorted her back to the palace after the battle.

"Does it work?" Princess Haden asked, gesturing to the ring. A cold, distant demeanor had overtaken the excited and cheerful girl he'd met only hours ago.

"I'm holding this for a friend," Matthias lied.

Princess Haden snorted. "Lady Medee is not just your friend, and you can't lie to someone who's been cursed by the same witch."

Taken aback, Matthias blinked at the comment. The princess was cursed, too? Strangely, he didn't know what to say.

The carriage came to a stop, and the princess stood before Matthias could utter a word.

"Don't worry, captain. Your secret is safe with me."

Matthias shut his eyes, trying to drown out the memory with his current problems, like trying to find his mother. Warden Hazor sent scouts to Yekel months ago, and they heard of a mysterious woman being held there, a woman who may have the gift of prophecy. The warden recently gave this information to Matthias without any proof. But Matthias had to take the chance. If his mother was there, he would save her.

That was why he'd done everything King Atol and Queen Leza asked, right? The king and queen gave him hope that, if he did everything they asked, his mother would be safe. But then Devora arrived and things became...complicated.

Sitting up with a curse, Matthias pulled out Nadia's note again. It was bad enough the king held his mother over him, but then he had to fall in love with a Seer. He tried to keep his distance to lessen his emotions. He tried to be cruel toward her to sway his feelings away from adoration. And that was *before* he found out about her gift. Once he discovered she was a Seer, it was as if Tunri, himself, was saying, "This is the one."

Matthias sighed. "You couldn't have made it a bit easier?" he asked the ceiling.

The crow cawed in response and fluttered over to Matthias's feet, where it began pecking at his boot.

"What do you want now?" he growled at the bird. "I already gave you payment. Let me brood in peace."

The bird continued to peck his boot. Matthias flicked his toe, but the bird was relentless.

"All right, fine. I'll get you more bread." As he stood he noticed another note tied around the crow's neck.

Very rarely did Matthias allow himself to be overcome with emotion, but when he saw the small piece of parchment, his heart skipped. He wrenched it off the bird so fast, the crow lost three more feathers.

Holding his breath, he carefully unrolled the ripped parchment. He'd never seen Devora's handwriting before, but the moment he laid eyes on the pristine cursive, he knew it was from her.

With his heart pounding, he read the note.

I have received outside information. I may have found someone who knows K. I have met your contact and another. We are scouting the city and will send more information soon.

I forgive you.

Matthias' eyes ran over the note again and again. He appreciated how Devora was able to say everything and nothing all in a few lines. Outside information meant she received a vision from Tunri. K was obviously Kanna, his mother. Relief washed through him when he read that she met "another" meaning Master Monham. Matthias had met him before, when King Atol ordered all the Tinkers of Yekel to be taken. Master Monham's friend was one of the few people Matthias had been able to save from the raid. And his contact had to mean she'd met up with Tristan, as well.

His gaze snagged on the next phrase: *We are scouting the city and will send more information soon.* What did that mean? Was she going alone? Or with this person who knew his mother? Where was One Shot?

Matthias prayed One Shot would go with her and not his useless brother. He trusted One Shot with his life. But not Tristan. When Matthias first contacted Tristan about assisting Devora, he almost regretted it. But he knew that if anyone could get them into Yekel's evil depths to find the city's secrets, it was his criminal brother. He only hoped Tristan would keep his word this time.

The crow cawed loudly.

"Hush!" Matthias commanded, then realized he was speaking to a bird. The crow blinked at him expectantly. "Right, your additional payment."

The crow fluffed his scruffy feathers.

Shaking his head, Matthias strode toward his plate of poultry, potatoes, and bread. It was a bland meal, but it warmed his cold bones and filled his belly. He ripped off another hunk of bread and tossed it to the crow. The bird happily pecked at the piece, leaving Matthias to read over the note again.

I forgive you.

Three little words. That was all it took to bring tears to his eyes. When he agreed to turn Devora over to the king, he had no idea how the woman would affect him. By the time he realized the depths of his feelings, it was too late. The plan was already in place, giving him no choice but to watch it unfold.

In the ballroom, when Devora looked at him to plead her case, his heart broke. When she asked him how long he'd been planning to betray her, he wanted to throw himself off a cliff. But it wasn't until he saw the trust flee her eyes that his tears came.

It had been years since he allowed himself to cry. As Warden Hazor's right hand, he couldn't show weakness. It was trivial most of the time. Dealing with criminals in the Fortress never rocked his emotions.

But Devora shattered the stone wall around his heart with one pained look.

And now she was doing it again with three simple words.

I forgive you.

He ran a hand through his chestnut hair. How could she forgive him? He couldn't forgive himself for what he'd done. He *wouldn't* forgive himself. Not until he made it right, and she and her family were safe. But still, she forgave him.

Matthias sniffed and quickly wiped his eyes on his woolen sleeve as a droplet fell on the parchment. The moment the teardrop seeped into the page, the faintest lines of text appeared. Matthias jumped up so quickly, the crow squawked with fright, fluttering to the other side of the room. Knocking over his quills, Matthias grabbed the pitcher of water next to his meal. He dipped his fingers in the cool liquid and carefully dotted the area next to his tear stain. In two strides, he stood before the fire, willing the drops to dry faster. The next moments were as long as years until, finally, more text appeared.

"That's my girl," he whispered with a smile as he waited for Devora's secret message.

Five days after the next full moon.

Matthias paused, read the hidden text again. The moon was full for the first time that month last night, that meant he only had four days left. He rushed to his desk. In one fluid motion he grabbed a quill, dipped it in ink and scribbled a note to Warden Hazor. It was time for battle.

Chapter Twenty

Rae, Dark Market, Yekel

After her meeting with the Seer, the Winner, and Ben, Rae sprinted out of the Dark Market. She was still shaky from when she'd headbutted General Yada. Though she had never struck him before, she'd wanted to many times. Fear stopped her every time. She was both terrified and elated that she actually defended herself against him.

Rae knew there would be consequences. There was always a consequence when she stepped out of line. But she wouldn't allow Nadia to bear it.

Forcing her legs to run as fast as they could, Rae raced home. A small candle sat in the window, and she prayed that Nadia was there.

Slowing her steps, Rae approached her home. She didn't take off her mask, just in case General Yada's men were there. With a steady breath, she pushed open the door. Save for the dimly lit candle, night coated every crevice. It was difficult to imagine her modest living space filled with so many people just a few hours ago.

Rae crept over the threshold and closed the door. She grabbed a candle and started toward the kitchen. If Nadia wasn't in her living area, then she had to be in the kitchen or the bedroom.

A creak squeaked from behind Rae's bedroom door. Rae's ears perked at the sound, and she swiveled to change directions. Breathing through the red mesh, she opened the bedroom door.

Nadia sat crossed legged on her bed, playing with the small catapult she'd made many years ago.

Rae peeled the red mesh off her face with a sigh of relief. The cool air dried the sweat dripping down her temples.

"Why didn't you tell me?" Nadia asked coldly, her charcoal-covered fingertips pressing down the lever of the catapult.

Rae had rehearsed this conversation many times in her mind. In her scenarios, she was always calm, cool, and collected as she explained to Nadia what happened at the Temple and how Rae earned her freedom from General Yada. But now that she was experiencing this moment for real, words escaped her. What could she say? Nadia would never understand.

Rae walked forward and sat on the thin mattress. "It's not the most pleasant thing to talk about." She fiddled with the red mesh between her fingers.

Nadia snapped the lever back and the catapult, unloaded, sprung forward. "But lying to me is okay?"

Rae dragged her gloved hands over her shaved head. She really didn't want to discuss this. "Nadia, please, you wouldn't understand."

"Because I'm younger than you? Because you've got it all figured out?" Nadia snapped.

Rae spun her head toward Nadia, surprised at the outburst. There was a fire in Nadia's eyes that Rae had never seen. Nadia was always happy-go-lucky. She always let everything roll off her back and always stayed consumed with her inventions. She never had a care in the world, something that Rae always envied.

Everyone always liked Nadia better than you, the Beast of Envy whispered.

Rae smashed down the beast as she stood and yanked off her gloves. "You being younger than me has nothing to do with this." Her back faced Nadia as she dropped the gloves on a small table across the room. "And as for having everything figured out, you can be sure I don't."

She hated to admit the weakness, but she was so tired of trying to figure her way out of difficult situations. For once, she wanted to be Nadia and have everyone tell her that she was destined for a great future.

"You've been so cold to me ever since I came back here. You have no idea what I've been through." Nadia shot the accusation at Rae's back, but that was all it took to unleash the beasts Rae had been trying so hard to confine.

Rae wheeled around so fast, she almost lost her balance. "What *you've* been through? What have you *ever* been through? Our whole life, people have worshipped the ground you walk on because you have the same gift as Papi. No one even cared whether I succeeded or failed at anything because 'Little Nadi' was going to be the next top Tinker of Yekel."

Rae's words were venomous, spewing from the snake of jealousy that had coiled around her heart for years.

Nadia froze, her face white as if it had been struck. But Rae couldn't stop. Once she let the envious beast take over, she lost control.

"And what about me? Always helping Mami in the kitchen. Always preparing everything for Sancti, and Tunri blesses *you*." Rae paced with wide strides around the room, throwing her arms in the air. "And to make it even worse, I sacrificed myself, my everything, to save you and the others. General Yada made me his personal mistress as punishment for sneaking you all away." Tears pricked the corners of Rae's eyes, and soon they were rolling down her cheeks. "I tried to do something that would help everyone, and I regret it every single day."

The Beast of Envy evaporated into sorrow as Rae wrapped her arms around herself, the truth of her heart finally laid bare. If she'd known she would become a priestess—a slave—to the Temple, if she'd known General Yada would have taken her as his mistress, she would've never given herself to save Nadia and the other girls. Her soul was selfish and ugly, and she hated it.

Rae sank to her knees and sobbed uncontrollably, hating herself more and more for spiraling out of control at Nadia. She knew it wasn't Nadia's fault King Atol took Papi away. It wasn't Nadia's fault Kadesh invaded Yekel. But the anger leaked out of Rae's carefully constructed harbor like tsunami.

After a moment or two, a hand gently laid on Rae's back, and she stiffened.

"That's why you don't want to be hugged anymore," Nadia whispered, retracting her

hand.

Rae sniffed but didn't reply.

The silence stretched between them as Nadia sat next to Rae and let her cry. It was the best thing Nadia could've done. Rae didn't want any words of encouragement. She didn't need any chastisement or advice. She only wanted to know that, despite her flaws, her choices, and her past, someone still cared.

"I'm so sorry, Rae," Nadia whispered as the break of dawn creaked light through the window.

Rae lifted her swollen eyes. Nadia looked so much older than she had a few years ago. She was right; Rae didn't know what happened to her at the Fortress. Her childhood friend had been sent to prison and had come out stronger. While Rae was nothing but a broken vessel.

"No, Nadia," Rae croaked. "Nothing that happened was your fault." Nadia gave a small nod, but Rae knew she'd damaged their once solid relationship. "I'm sorry."

Nadia nodded again but stayed silent. "Here." She handed Rae a piece of cloth. Your eyes always swell like grapefruits when you cry."

Rae choked back a laugh and took the cloth. How could Nadia still speak with her after what Rae had just said?

Rae was about to apologize again when a knock sounded at her door.

Nadia's gaze swiveled toward the entrance. "I'll go get that."

"Nadia, wait," Rae started, but she was already out the door.

Murmurs floated from the front door. Rae strained her ears but couldn't recognize who was speaking. The wooden door creaked shut. Wiping her eyes, Rae stood. Now that she confessed her true feelings, she felt lighter. It was almost as if a bondage, a chain, holding her down had been broken.

Feeling more confident, Rae went to find Nadia. If anyone deserved to hear the whole story of what happened to Rae, it was her.

But when Rae rounded the corner, it wasn't Nadia who was in the living area, but Master Monham.

"Where's Nadia?" Rae asked, her voice still rough from crying.

Master Monham sat on the floor in front of the table. One of Rae's clay cups sat in front of him. He glanced at her with a sympathetic smile. "She said she needed some fresh air. Don't worry," he added at Rae's panicked expression. "She's right outside the door."

Rae sucked back her tears, trying to hide her disappointment. She would have to find another time to apologize to Nadia properly.

Rae wiped her hands along her leather slacks. Panic rose in her when she realized she was still in her Crimson Cord attire. Master Monham already knew her secret, but it still made Rae nervous to wear the disguise during the day.

"I need to change—" she started before Master Monham waved her to go.

Rae hurried back to her room. She pulled out a white blouse and chestnut-colored skirt. Throwing the disguise in the corner of her room, Rae covered it with a swath of fabric.

She wasn't sure if she wanted to return to the Dark Market. After the creepy old woman, the rigged fight, and General Yada, her escape to the Fighter's Ring was tainted. If she stayed low, everyone would forget all about the Crimson Cord.

But is that what I want?

Rae shook her head, the skeleton key around her neck swinging. She told the Seer to trust Rae to help her get into the Temple. But did Rae trust herself?

Slipping the key over her head, Rae strode to her bed and hid the key beneath it. She told the Seer she would help, and she would. Now that she had the key to open the Temple doors, she wouldn't have to bend to General Yada's will to try to save the other women. But the hag's question still puzzled her: *Were you at the Temple two years ago?*

Rae said she had been because she wanted the key. But now that she thought about it, it had been two years since she *left* the Temple.

Scrubbing her hands in her wash basin, Rae decided to ignore the creepy old hag for now. She wiped her hands and headed to the kitchen where she made a plate of a few leftover orange blossom rolls.

"I thought you may want some breakfast," she said, setting the plate before Master Monham.

The old man had pulled out a scroll and was reading it closely. He glanced up at Rae and smiled. "You know I can't pass up one of your rolls." He reached for the plump roll closest to him and took a bite.

Curious, Rae peered over at the parchment to find a prayer scroll. And, for once, she wasn't appalled by the text. "Needing guidance?" she asked, seating herself across from him.

She also took a roll, peeled off a section, and popped it into her mouth.

"I always need guidance, Rae. But sometimes Tunri speaks softly, and I have to listen closely."

"Hmm," Rae replied, studying the flakes of orange zest in the roll. "Have you ever felt Tunri's presence?"

Master Monham laid down the scroll, focusing on her. "Why do you ask?"

Rae reflected on the cold aura that possessed her during the fight. A chill went through her. There was only one other time she experienced the same feeling, and she never wanted to endure that again.

"Something...odd happened last night. I'm not sure how to explain it. But I couldn't control my movements."

Master Monham's eyes went wide. "Did you take anything when you visited the Wizard?"

Rae furrowed her brows. "Why would that matter?"

Master Monham took a breath and shook his head. "If you ingested anything the Wizard gave you during his fortune readings, other forces may have been able to enter your consciousness. Evil forces."

"What?" Rae squeaked. "Are they in there now?" Goosebumps rose over her flesh, and Rae clawed at her skin before a memory she had been trying to keep hidden away slammed into her mind.

She had visited Kanna one too many times and General Yada had enough.

"You will pay for your disobedience," he commanded coolly. His long fingers dug into her bicep as he dragged her up the stairs, away from Kanna.

Rae remembered not being afraid as her flesh scraped and tore against the hard stone steps. She knew no fear when General Yada threw her on the cold marble ground. But when she looked up into the glowing eyes of the statue of Pahga, fear dribbled into her soul.

"Pahga, take from this foolish girl all that makes her defy me," General Yada called up to the statue as he lit a match and burned a branch of menta. *"Mold her into what I desire."*

The eyes of the statue glowed brighter as General Yada stepped away, leaving Rae defenseless in the putrid menta *smoke.*

A spiral of dark light shot out of the swirling black orb on Pahga's chest, piercing Rae through the heart.

Rae doubled over, crying out in pain. Searing heat burned her chest, as if her soul was being ripped apart. The dark light tugged and pulled, chaining Rae's soul. She cried and screamed, trying to get away. But the force of the statue held her in place.

"Goddess, please! Spare her life!" General Yada finally said when Rae thought she was going to die. He stood between Rae and the statue, holding his hands up and bowing his head. "She will be better now. Thank you, Pahga."

And then, it was over. The dark light receded, taking yellow bits of light out of Rae's soul, claiming them as its own.

"I think they were already in there," Rae whispered, coming out of the memory.

The *menta* the Wizard Wankle gave her must have, somehow, amplified the Beasts' power, giving Pahga the power to control her during the brawl. A shiver ran down Rae's spine. She would never have *menta* again.

Master Monham placed his weathered hand over hers. "Rae, are you okay?"

She shook her head, finally realizing when the beasts had entered her soul. Fear, Envy, and Anger replaced the Hope, Love, and Confidence she used to have.

"No," Rae replied, knowing that speaking with Nadia, sharing about her past and her hurts vanquished the Beast of Envy. "No, but I will be."

Master Monham frowned. "The Wizard is actually why I came to see you this morning." The potter hesitated. "He's gone."

"Yes, I heard," Rae muttered, remembering how General Yada said the Wizard Wankle gave him information for his freedom.

Master Monham gently took her hands in his. "No, Rae. His body was found outside the outer wall this morning. He was killed with a crimson cord around his neck."

Chapter Twenty-One

Rae, Rae's House, Yekel

"What?" Rae gasped, choking on her words.

General Yada had twisted his words again. He told her a half-truth, leading her to believe the Wizard Wankle was free. But, in reality, the general killed the Wizard and framed Rae. She knew she would pay for the headbutt.

"The Kadeshian soldiers are already swarming the area, trying to find the murderer." Master Monham squeezed Rae's hand. "You need to stay safe. If the general knows..."

"He already knows," Rae replied, her eyes downcast.

"But he needs proof that you are the Crimson Cord," Master Monham replied quickly. "Kadeshian troops, as barbaric as they may seem, still have to follow their own laws. If the general has no proof, you can't be sentenced."

Rae thought about the crumpled Crimson Cord disguise in the corner of her room. She would have to destroy it somehow.

"I'll take care of it."

Suddenly, the door burst open. Rae jumped up, ready to defend Master Monham.

"Did you do it?" Nadia gasped, sweat glistening across her forehead.

Rae relaxed her stance. "Did I do what?"

"Did you kill that wizard?"

"Of course not!" Rae almost shouted. "How could you think that?"

Nadia breathed a sigh of relief. "Good. There are Kadeshian soldiers everywhere. I thought it best for me to lay low for now."

"Good idea, Nadia," Master Monham agreed.

Rae thought she would feel the twinge of jealousy at Nadia getting praise, but nothing happened. The Beast of Envy was really gone.

"Rae, I suggest you stay indoors at night, as well." Master Monham gave her a knowing look. "I will research more on what we spoke about, as well."

The old man grabbed the extra orange blossom roll and stood. "One for the road," he winked and headed out the door.

"What was he talking about?" Nadia asked.

Rae knew Nadia was testing her. Nadia wanted to know if Rae would trust her, or if their bond was still broken.

Rae's thoughts swirled with all the information stuffed into her head. Her alter ego was framed for murder, she had two more evil beasts inside of her, and she still had to come up with a plan to help the Seer and Ben.

"Let's sit down." Rae motioned to the spot across from her.

Nadia quirked a brow but listened. She brought out a piece of charcoal from her pocket and twirled it between her fingers.

"I want to start at the beginning," Rae said quietly. "I've never told anyone this out loud. Master Monham is the only one who knows some of what happened. But no one knows everything."

The charcoal continued to spin in Nadia's fingers, but she kept her eyes glued on Rae's.

Rae took a deep breath and explained what happened after she strapped Nadia and the other young girls to her parent's horses and carts and sent them as far away from the city as possible. Rae recounted how she told General Yada that the girls had fled, but she was willing to take their place.

It was at this point that Rae got choked up.

"Rae, you don't have to..." Nadia started, but Rae cut her off.

"No, I need someone to know. If something were to happen to me, I want at least one person to remember why I did what I did."

Nadia's fingers stopped twirling. "What do you mean? What's going to happen?"

Rae ignored the question. She knew General Yada didn't really want Nadia. He only ever wanted one person: her.

"A gray veil was put over my head, and I was led to the Temple," Rae continued.

She kept her gaze focused on her short nails, not wanting to see Nadia's face as she explained what happened in the Temple and how abused the women were. She heard Nadia gasp a few times, but Rae ignored them and continued.

"I know of the woman, Kanna, that your friends seek. I told them, as the Crimson Cord, to come find me and that I would help them get into the Temple to look for her."

"Rae, why would you ever want to go back there?" Nadia asked. Rae glanced up to see tears welling in her friend's eyes. "You don't have to, Rae. Devora is smart. She can find another way in."

Warmth spread across Rae's chest. Standing, she walked over to Nadia, crouched down, and enveloped her in a hug. Rae hadn't wanted a hug in years but feeling her friend's soft touch made her remember all the strength a touch could give.

Rae pulled back and wiped Nadia's tears. "Thank you, Nadi. But this is something I need to do."

Nadia nodded in understanding. She then asked a few more questions about the Temple, some of which Rae couldn't answer since she was confined to her room most of the time. The conversation then drifted to Nadia's time at the Fortress. Rae heard everything about the giant and Devora's Seeing power. How the Seer had won a contest that named her the Defender of Tenton. The Battle of Edo and Princess Haden. The broody

Captain Blake and how he betrayed Devora (but still secretly loved her, or so Nadia thought).

Rae was speechless at all the amazing things Nadia accomplished. No jealousy rose up to nip at her friend, but only pride. She was proud of how Nadia had taken her hardships and turned them into something good. Rae hoped she could do the same.

"And then One Shot took the cross bow that I made and shot it so accurately that it hit four soldiers at once!" Nadia exclaimed, flailing her arms in the air. She pulled out her notebook and showed Rae the original design. "I wasn't sure if it would work, but he has an amazing ability."

"One Shot?" Rae asked, pretending to not remember the gentle giant.

"Yeah." Nadia flipped through the pages of her notebook. "You know, super tall, super quiet, and usually stands in a corner or the shadows."

He does stay in the background a lot, Rae thought.

"Is that his real name?"

Nadia tapped her charcoal on the table, leaving specs of black dust. "I've actually never thought about it. That's what everyone else calls him, so I just assumed." Nadia shrugged. "If he wanted us to know his real name, he would've told us."

Rae nodded, trying to keep her face stoic. But inside a small flower of hope bloomed, knowing that Ben shared his real name with her.

"What?" Nadia asked, and Rae glanced up at her.

"What?" Rae repeated, hoping her cheeks weren't as red as they felt.

Nadia studied Rae's face then gasped, throwing her hands in the air. "You like him!"

"No!" Rae replied, shaking her head hard. "No, never. I don't want anything to do with any man ever again."

Nadia lowered her hands, a somber look overcoming her features. "I understand." She tapped her fingers on the table. "He really is a nice guy though."

"Ugh," Rae groaned, but smirked.

Nadia soon changed the subject to thoughts of designing Rae a new mask that let her breath more easily than the red mesh and Rae almost felt like life was normal again.

Rae and Nadia talked well into the afternoon, rekindling their relationship. It wasn't until that evening that Rae realized she hadn't slept in over a day. Tomorrow she would be back at the outer wall for work. She needed to rest. Thankfully, she would be with Old Charlie. She didn't want to think what would happen if the soldier who harassed her at the market was guarding them again.

Dragging herself to her bedroom, Rae pulled back the thinning blanket and slipped into her bed. Nadia decided to sleep in the same room but refused to take the bed. She said she would take the bed once Rae left for work and sleep all day.

As Rae pulled her old woven blanket over her, she realized her heart didn't feel as heavy as it had most nights. Her fears were still with her but sharing her story with someone she loved and trusted had helped immensely.

For the first time in a long time, Rae felt at peace.

Dawn approached too soon the next morning causing Rae to wish she'd gone to sleep earlier. Groaning, she rolled out of bed, barely missing Nadia's sprawled out form on the floor.

Eyes bleary, Rae slumped toward her pitcher and wash basin. After pouring water into the bowl, she dipped her hands in and splashed a handful of water on her face. The chilled liquid was shocking against her skin, waking her senses abruptly. Shivering, she grabbed a towel and rubbed it over her face. As she patted her forehead with the towel, Rae felt the beginning of her hair growth. She usually shaved her head every other week. It felt cleansing, like she was ridding herself of her past terrors.

But as she rubbed the fuzzy white-blonde hairs, Rae realized she didn't want to shave her head again. She'd started it as an act of rebellion against General Yada who loved her long, blonde hair the most. But now, she didn't feel its burden anymore.

Slipping out of her night clothes, Rae donned her worker's uniform: a white shirt and floor length tan skirt. The men who worked at the wall wore the same, except with pants. Rae missed wearing pants during the day. Her Crimson Cord clothes were so much more freeing.

The thought brought her back to the conversation she had with Master Monham yesterday. Even though she and Nadia had strengthened their relationship, General Yada framed her alias and would try to expose her secret and arrest her. Rae needed to be careful. One slip-up and everything she worked for would be gone. If she wasn't so emotionally exhausted yesterday, she would've destroyed it sooner. And now she didn't have enough time to burn the garments properly. Rae promised herself to destroy her Crimson Cord disguise after work then pushed the thought from her mind.

Striding to her dresser, Rae opened it and rifled through the colorful scarves. For work, she usually chose to wear bland colors like cream or beige. Because of Kadeshian soldiers, like the one from the market, it was best to not stand out at all.

But today Rae felt different. Her hand landed on a scarf the color of orange marmalade, and she thought of Ben. The scarf was a shade darker than his, but she liked the boldness of it.

Smiling, Rae wrapped the scarf around her neck and over her head. When she turned to exit her room, Nadia had already crawled into the bed and was snoring like Master Monham after a large dinner.

Rae held back a laugh, soaking in the joy that Nadia brought back into her life.

Once she packed her lunch, Rae slung her skein of water and sack of food over her shoulder and crept out the door. The sun hung just above the horizon, blanketing the land in a warm yellow glow. She snuggled into the scarf, pleased that its shade matched the dawn of a new day.

Men and women from the other houses strode alongside her. No one spoke as they trudged toward their slave labor. General Yada promised once the outer wall was complete, the Yekelians would be free to find employment wherever they wanted. But every time one section had been built up, another seemed to come tumbling down. Rae knew the general had something to do with the ever-crumbling outer wall but she could never figure out how he was involved.

Mistress Yena and her daughter, Dinah, strode arm-in-arm alongside Rae. They held the same job as Rae: bringing water to the male workers when they were thirsty and replacing their tools when needed.

Dinah was a year older than Rae and hobbled when she walked. Though Rae didn't wish further harm upon the woman, she knew that her limp saved her from being taken to the Temple. General Yada only wanted the best and most beautiful to serve Pahga.

"Good morning, Mistress Yena. Good morning, Dinah," Rae said softly.

Shock covered the two women's faces as they registered her greeting. Rae never spoke to the other women. She never spoke to the other workers. Rae never spoke to anyone other than Master Monham and Old Charlie.

Rae pursed her lips. *They probably think I'm rude and self-centered.*

"Good morning, Rae," Dinah replied hesitantly.

When Rae looked up, the girl gave a small smile. A thick brown scarf covered her dark blonde hair, accentuating the sprinkling of freckles across her nose.

Mistress Yena nodded in recognition but stayed silent.

They gathered around the daily captain supervising the wall's repairs. General Yada rotated his troops so frequently, none of the Yekelians cared to learn their names.

"Because of the recent murder of Antonio Wankle, each group of workers will be watched over by two soldiers instead of one," the middle-aged captain announced. His tired eyes and graying beard told Rae he wanted to be anywhere but at the outer wall with them.

Silence weighed over the crowd, having already been beaten into submission years ago. Whatever the general decided, they had no choice but to agree. The native Yekelians were no longer living but just trying to survive each day, one moment at a time.

The captain called out the day's assignments. Mistress Yena and Dinah were assigned with Master Monham and two other older Yekelian men. Dinah gave a quick wave to Rae as she hobbled to pick up the jug of water for the workers.

Surprised at the kind gesture, Rae lifted her hand.

The captain called up two more soldiers then her name. Rae relaxed when she didn't see the solider who assaulted her before. She expected to hear the captain call Old Charlie's name, but instead, he rattled off the names of two of Charlie's comrades and a man named William Shot.

Rae hoped Old Charlie was okay as she stood on her tip toes, trying to catch a glance at the new name. But she didn't need to crane her neck. There, standing a full head above the rest of the crowd was none other than Ben.

Chapter Twenty-Two

"Are you sure this is a good idea?" Ben asked, keeping a steady eye on the bustling street as he tugged on his orange scarf.

"Why wouldn't it be?" Devora replied with the same confidence she always held. "Just stand there for a moment longer. I need to finish writing your name."

Ben pressed his lips together but did as he was told. It's not that he didn't want to learn more about Rae. But impersonating a Yekelian so he could work alongside her? He wasn't sure that was the best way to gain her trust.

The steady scratch of a quill ran along the stolen piece of parchment. While he and Devora were surveying the Temple surroundings, Devora had stealthily lifted the scroll from a soldier heading toward the outer wall. She quickly instructed Ben to create a distraction, then dashed into the nearest alleyway.

As if an answer to prayer, a merchant with a cart of chickens rolled by the alleyway. Ben made sure not to carry his crossbow with him during the day, but luckily, his aim was still on point. Crouching down, he grabbed a stone and slung it beneath one of the wooden wheels. Just as he planned, the stone lodged itself in a weak point, fracturing the wood.

The wheel cracked in half, and the chicken crates soared through the streets. Ben planned to stop the cart, assuming the soldier would help the merchant move it. But what he hadn't accounted for was the cacophony of chickens that busted out of their cages. Feathers flew everywhere as the frantic hens fled from their wire prisons. The merchant cursed loudly, gesturing at the guard to help him round up the chickens. Apparently, they were for an upcoming harvest festival to honor the goddess, Pahga.

Ben tried to keep a straight face as a chicken pecked the Kadeshian soldier's shin, then fled between his legs.

He heard about the goddess Pahga before but only in passing. Now that they were trying to enter a temple dedicated to her, Ben wanted to know more about what he'd gotten himself into.

"There," Devora said, coming up beside him. She blew on the fresh ink, willing it to dry. Once it had set, she carefully rolled it back up. "Now where is that...?" She stopped, turning toward the clucking. "That's a lot of chickens."

"I created a distraction, like you asked," he replied with a smirk.

Devora laughed. "All we need to do now is place this back in the soldier's bag. But, seeing as he's still herding chickens, it won't be too hard to convince him he dropped it."

Before Ben could stop her, Devora hurried into the fray of feathers, elegantly dodging the frantic chickens. In one swoop, she bent down, gently placed her hands around a chicken's waist and hoisted it into her arms like she was cradling a baby. The chicken stopped clucking and nestled happily against Devora's chest.

"Excuse me, sir?" Devora asked, gaining the guard's attention. The soldier, who looked to be the same age as Devora, spun around. Feathers stuck out all from his mussed black hair. "I believe you dropped this." She handed the guard the scroll.

He stared at it with wide eyes. "Thank you. I would've been flogged if I lost this again."

Devora gave him a slight bow before handing him the chicken and strutting back to Ben.

"See? Easy."

Ben shook his head, impressed. "The Defender of Tenton, a Seer, and a chicken herder. You're a lady of many talents."

"Oh yes," she agreed with a firm nod. "Now, come on, let's get you to the outer wall."

They continued through the market, strewn with chicken feathers. Luckily, the merchant had collected all his chickens and was given a spare wheel by another merchant passing by.

Ben watched the trade off, wondering how big the festival for Pahga was and why they hadn't heard anything about it.

"I know you're not comfortable with this," Devora said as she looped her arm through his. Though, because of their vast height difference, it appeared as if he were dragging her along rather than escorting her through the market. "But I can't remove this veil unless I want to be arrested. And I would rather not return to the Fortress as a prisoner."

Ben snorted. "Warden Hazor would scold you for getting captured so quickly."

"He would," Devora chuckled. "But, really, One Shot. I can't trust Tristan like I can trust you. The Crimson Cord should have told Rae we're coming to meet her. I just wanted you to get to know her a little more before we ask for her help."

Ben guided them around a man holding a tray of freshly baked bread. Enjoying the crisp, doughy scent, he said, "I understand, but you know I'm not the best at making friends."

Devora peered up at him through her veil. "I'm your friend."

"Yes, probably the only one I have."

"That's not true." She shook her head. "Nadia and Matthias are your close friends, too."

Ben lifted his brows. "I'm not sure the captain would consider me a 'close' friend."

Devora waved her hand in the air, a motion Ben had learned meant she was done with the topic.

Soon, they reached the outer wall. A crowd of Yekelians in matching uniforms huddled together before two lines of bronze armored Kadeshians. Ben glanced down at his black tunic, matching black slacks and the bright orange scarf he'd purchased from Rae. If his height didn't make him stand out, his clothes certainly would.

Tugging on the scarf, Ben made sure it was secured around his neck. Mara loved the color orange. She would make tiny orange lilies out of sugar to decorate various desserts at the bakery. Ben wondered if she still baked, or even wanted anything to do with their father's shop.

"Your pseudonym is William Shot. You're taking the place of the man Rae usually works with at the wall," Devora whispered up to him.

He quirked a brow. "William Shot? Really? And how do you know all this?"

Devora shrugged. "Master Monham helped me set this up, of course."

Ben knew she was grinning beneath the veil, pleased that her plan worked. He sighed and joined the crowd, praying he wouldn't get caught.

Ben stuck out like Vinn, their giant white elk, in the desert, as he approached the group. The Yekelians nearest to him gawked at his height and shuffled away. Despite what people thought, he wasn't full giant. He wasn't even half giant. Some distant relative on his mother's side had fancied a giant, and now he was suffering the effects of that choice. He didn't know much about Ma, but Pa and Mara were normal sized. Imagine their surprise when Ben started to grow and didn't stop until he was almost the size of a tree.

"I don't remember any giants among the Yekelians," a stout Kadeshian soldier with a thick black mustache said.

Ben gave him a sidelong glance. "I'm not a giant," he deadpanned. How many times would he have to clarify?

Irritation rippled over the mustached soldier's face. He opened his mouth to reprimand Ben when the soldier from the market appeared. Shoulders heaving, the young soldier frantically combed the chicken feathers from his hair and handed the scroll to the mustached guard.

"Forgive me, sir," the young soldier breathed. "There was an incident in the market."

Ben stood as still as stone, hoping the soldier from the market didn't recognize him. It wasn't until the mustached soldier began reprimanding the young soldier on punctuality that he relaxed. A few insults later, the two soldiers made their way to the front of the crowd, forgetting all about him.

Ben exhaled slowly before he went to find Rae, which wasn't that difficult. When he locked his eyes on the bright marmalade scarf wrapped around her head, his heart flipped. He took another look, just to be sure it was really her. The same wide, caramel eyes. The same straight nose. The only difference was that her usually straight lips were curved into a soft smile.

Ben's heart thudded again, and he looked away. A smile became her.

As the mustached soldier started calling off names, Ben thought back to what the Crimson Cord had said. Rae used to work in the Temple. Tristan seemed to have known all about that, but it took Ben a little longer to figure out women who worked in the Temple were not seen favorably.

When he heard of Rae's past, he instantly thought of Mara. Because of his carelessness, his sister's reputation had been tainted forever. Thankfully, Jonathon, his friend who married Mara, hadn't cared about that, and loved her enough to help her heal her wounds.

But Ben's wounds still bled. His guilt still consumed him. Devora knew it, too. He could sense when she was checking on his soul. He always wanted to ask what it looked like but decided he didn't want to know. If his soul looked anything close to how he felt, it was an ugly, miserable thing.

"Rae and Hagga, you will be working with Maurice, Roberto, and William Shot." The mustached soldier paused for a moment, as if realizing the final name didn't match. But he soon cleared his throat and continued.

Ben waited for the group of Yekelians to call him out, to scream that he was a fraud. But they said nothing. Their blank faces stared into space as they waited for their assignments.

Ben furrowed his brow, recognizing the defeated look on the faces around him. He witnessed it daily while in the Fortress. He witnessed it in himself. It wasn't until Matthias became his cellmate that life at the Fortress became more tolerable.

Matthias had been furious when he was put in the same cell as Ben. But it wasn't the fury of the men usually sentenced to the lower levels of the Fortress. It was cold and calculating. It was then that Ben hoped to be on Matthias' side, rather than against him.

The crowd shuffled toward a cart of tools, and Ben did his best to blend in. Which, as always, was difficult.

Thankfully, no one even batted an eye toward him as he grabbed a chisel and mallet. He never worked with these tools before but assumed the Yekelians were carving bricks out of stone for the outer wall.

Just as he turned around, a flash of orange swept under him, and he was soon tugged away from the cart and crowd of people. Once at the wall, Rae spun around.

"What are you doing here?" she demanded, her brow cross, her lips pinched. She didn't seem angry but concerned.

Ben decided the best answer to this question would be an honest one. "I came to see you."

He hadn't realized the effect of his honesty until Rae blinked at him, lips parted in shock.

"But why?" she asked, fumbling with the fringes of her orange scarf.

"You two! Stop dawdling and get to work!" a stout soldier called.

Rae snapped straight and grabbed Ben's wrist. "Come on. I'll do my best to cover for you."

Pulses of heat swirled from Rae's touch on his arm. He never thought anyone, much less a beautiful woman, would want to be near him. No one ever wanted to be with someone his size.

Giant.

Monster.

Ben shook the names from his head and tried not to step in front of Rae as she scurried to the wall. When he'd killed those men, he figured his solitary future was set. He would be alone forever.

But as Rae began explaining to him what he was supposed to do, a twinge of hope pinched his heart. Maybe that future wasn't so concrete.

"Do you understand?" Rae asked, her brows raised. She waited for a moment. When Ben didn't respond, her features flattened. "Were you listening to what I said?"

Ben scratched his neck. He had spent enough time with Devora to know when to be honest and when to stretch the truth a bit. "Yes?"

Rae scrubbed a hand over her face. "Men," she groaned. She took the chisel and mallet from his hand. "Pay attention this time."

Ben nodded firmly and focused only on Rae's hands as she demonstrated how to chisel away the stone.

"You got it?"

Ben's gaze flicked up to hers. The morning sun was already beating down on the two of them, and Rae's skin and eyes sparkled in the light.

"Yeah," he said, taking the tools and looking away. He was here to learn more about Rae. So far he had only stared at her and daydreamed. "Thank you for your help."

"Of course," she replied, her tone softening. "Just chip away at the stone, and the soldiers will leave you alone." She surveyed the area around them. "I need to refill my jug and get some more tools. I'll be back in a little while."

Ben found himself at a loss for words and merely nodded as she hurried away. For the next hour, he chiseled away at the gray stone, trying to figure out what to say once Rae returned. He told Devora he wasn't good with words. Tristan was annoying but smooth with women. Matthias was cold and commanding, and apparently Devora liked that. But him?

Ben learned at an early age to keep his mouth shut. After all, what could he say? All the taunts and insults were true. He was huge. He looked like a giant. Everyone hated giants. And after he was sentenced for murder, people had even more evidence that he was a monster.

Ben grunted and shifted the chisel to a different place on the stone. A minuscule stream of pebbles tumbled from the corner. It was better to just listen and let Rae talk. He was good at listening.

"Care for a drink?" Rae's familiar voice asked.

Ben peered over his shoulder. He hadn't realized he'd been crouching in the same position for over an hour. Turning around, he eased himself onto the ground and stretched out his long legs.

"That would be nice, thank you."

He watched Rae analyze how far out his legs reached. He expected her to run away from him. Instead, she poured water into a clay cup and handed it to him.

"Do you have to get special shoes?"

Ben sputtered into the cup and started coughing. A few of the other workers glanced their way, but the Kadeshian soldiers kept their backs turned and continued their conversation.

"I'm sorry," Rae rushed. "I was curious. I've made special sized scarves for people before, so I didn't know if you did the same thing with your boots."

She bit her bottom lip, and Ben was fairly confident it wasn't the heat of the sun that made her cheeks pink. He wiped his mouth with his sleeve and studied his black boots. They were given to him when he entered the Fortress. The Warden never chastised him for his size, just told him if he behaved he would be free in due time. And before the Battle of Edo, he only had two years left. Now, he could probably never return home.

"I'm not sure," he replied. "Pa always took care of my shoes before, and these were given to me later." He decided to leave out where he had received the boots, not knowing how Rae would react to the assassin from the Fortress.

"Oh," Rae said, taking the cup from his outstretched hand. "Do you want more water?"

Ben nodded, and she poured another cup. After he drank it swiftly, Rae took the cup, twirling it in her hands as if she wanted to say more. In the end, she left to attend to the other workers.

Ben watched her leave, silently cursing himself. The next time she came around, he would be sure to say something useful.

Chapter Twenty-Three

'*Do you need special shoes?*' *Really Rae?*

Of all the things she could've asked Ben, that was probably the worst.

She'd seen how the others cast weary glances as he stalked by. Had he always been treated like that? Like a disease? No one wanted to be within ten feet of Ben. Though she enjoyed the privacy it allowed for her to talk with him, Rae wasn't sure why people were so scared of him.

She wanted to go back and talk with Ben but found herself consumed with the other workers. Every time she tried to break away, someone needed more water. Every time she started toward Ben, someone else needed a new tool. After a few hours of tending to everyone else, it was time for her lunch break, and Rae darted away from the others before they could ask for anything else.

Pulling the sack off her shoulder, Rae searched for Ben. He always stood out, especially with that bright orange scarf. When she saw him seated in the shade of the outer wall, her stomach leapt.

Stop that, she scolded herself as she made her way toward him. *I don't want to be friends or anything more. Just acquaintances.*

Ben squinted up at her as she approached.

"I wasn't sure if you packed a lunch." She held up her sack. "I always have extra."

Mami always said it was better to have more food than less, and Rae took the lesson to heart. Not everyone in Yekel was as fortunate as her, so she made sure to secretly share her food with someone each day. And today that person was Ben.

Ben didn't say anything, and Rae feared she insulted him.

Why would he want anything from you? the Beast of Fear tsked. *He knows you're tainted.*

Rae squeezed her fingers around the sack. "I can just go—"

"No!" he said too loudly, causing the others taking their lunch to glance their way. Ben lowered his voice. "I didn't have a chance to pack anything. I would be grateful for anything you can spare."

The Beast of Fear quieted as Rae pressed her back against the wall and sat next to Ben. She made sure to keep a respectable distance, not wanting him to assume she desired anything from him.

Carefully, Rae unwrapped her sack. Inside sat two squares of flat bread she made for herself and Nadia a few days ago, a small pouch of dried figs, dates, and apricots, a hunk of cheese she bartered from Master Monham in exchange for two scarves, and the last orange blossom roll.

Rae took one of the flatbreads, a few dates and apricots and a small piece of the cheese, leaving the rest for him. Folding up the remaining contents in the bag she held it out to him. "Here."

Ben glanced at the bag. "I can't take all that."

"Take it," Rae demanded, then softened. "Please. You need to work for the rest of the day. This job is grueling."

Ben hesitated but then took the sack. Rae expected him to shove the food down his throat, like many hungry men she witnessed in the Temple, the Dark Market, and the marketplace. But he didn't.

Ben carefully held the food as if it were something precious. He picked up the flatbread and pinched it between his long fingers, examining it.

After a moment, Rae asked, "Is something wrong?" She had been making flatbread for years. Her recipe was perfect.

"Did you make this?" he asked, tearing off a small corner. Popping it into his mouth, he chewed slowly.

Rae tilted her head to the side. "Yes. It's my mother's recipe."

"It's incredible. Pa makes a similar one, but he always over-bakes it. It usually tastes more like a rock than bread. But this"—he rotated the flatbread in his hand— "is perfect."

Heat flooded Rae's cheeks. Who knew the gentle giant enjoyed baking so much? She hadn't known him long, but excitement came to his eyes when he spoke about the bread.

"I'm glad you like it," Rae said. "But if you really want a treat, try that." She pointed to the glazed orange blossom roll. "It's also my mother's recipe and my favorite thing to make."

Ben placed the flatbread down and scooped up the roll. He held it close to his eyes, taking in every detail of the pastry. Rae watched him, fascinated that someone would take such delight in her baking.

As if holding a valuable gem, Ben studied the roll before carefully pulling it apart. "It smells like home," he said softly before placing a piece in his mouth.

Rae waited, not wanting to ruin his experience before asking, "Did you grow up near here?"

Ben chewed another bite, tearing the roll into tiny pieces and trying to make it last as long as possible. "No. I grew up outside of Ballear in a village called Snoken."

"Ballear is very far from Yekel."

"It is," he agreed.

Rae noted the undertone of sadness in his voice and found herself wanting to know more.

"You said your father baked flatbread?"

"Yes, he owns the only bakery in Snoken. I learned to bake when I was only seven summers and helped out every morning before my school lessons." Ben held out half of the orange blossom roll to Rae. "Why don't you sell these in the market? They're not like anything I've ever tasted before."

Rae found herself smiling at his complement. "Finding supplies is difficult. I can barter for most items, but food is already scarce. I wouldn't be able to make enough of a profit."

Rae ran her fingers along her clementine-colored scarf. Initially, she wanted to sell baked goods in the market, but after she fled the Temple, she hardly had any coin to her name. What little she had, she spent on becoming the Crimson Cord, and those earnings were to buy the women freedom from the Temple. If it weren't for Master Monham's kindness in those early days, Rae probably would have starved.

"Your scarves are nice, too," Ben added.

Red patches formed on his neck, and it took Rae a moment to realize he was embarrassed.

Rae chuckled. "I'm just happy I have loyal customers." She motioned to the bright scarf still around his neck.

A small smile stretched across his lips, and Rae swore she saw a dimple.

Ben pulled at the corner of his scarf. "My sister loves all-things orange. She always covered all the pastries in orange shavings or orange slices. My father would be furious because getting such a fruit to Snoken was difficult."

Rae had never thought about the difficulties of obtaining citrus in the north. Because Grenly was nearby, there were usually vendors who brought fresh produce from its surrounding jungles. Rae typically bartered a few scarves and fabrics for a crate of oranges when she could.

"Well, if you ever want to enjoy any more orange blossom rolls, let me know," she said before she could stop herself.

What are you doing? The Beast of Fear returned. *He doesn't want anything to do with the likes of you.*

"I'd like that," Ben said with a soft look.

As the lunch hour concluded, Rae didn't want to go back to work. If she could have sat by the outer wall and talked with Ben all day, she would have. Besides Papi, she'd never met a man who was so kind. There was a softness to Ben that drew Rae in, and she enjoyed it.

But then she remembered how quickly he'd drawn his crossbow when a threat was near. There was another side to Ben as well, and that one, Rae wasn't sure about.

The rest of the workday was dull compared to Rae's time with Ben. She spoke with him a few more times, but they were rushed conversations consisting of 'hellos', 'thank yous' and 'good-byes.'

While tending to the other workers, Rae found herself making a mental list of all the topics she wanted to discuss with Ben. But as she handed a new chisel to Roberto, she paused her daydream to eavesdrop.

"Eh, Maurice, you hear about what happened to Wankle?"

Maurice grunted as he wiped the sweat from his wrinkled forehead. "Antonio was always an odd one, but I never wanted to see him dead."

Roberto nodded in agreement, allowing a lock of his curly dark hair to hang between his eyes. "His fortunes were strange, but he was still one of us. The guards are swarming the alleys at night, looking for the murderer."

Maurice positioned his mallet on the top of his chisel. "Do they know who did it?"

Rae leaned forward in anticipation and terror.

Roberto licked his lips, excited to share the gossip. "Someone by the name of the Crimson Cord. Apparently, he was undefeated in the Dark Market until about a week ago."

Rae stiffened at the mention of her alias but quickly busied herself by pretending to check if her water jug was full.

Maurice grunted again and chiseled away at the stone. "Crimson Cord, huh? What did he have against Wankle?"

Roberto shrugged. "Maybe he just wanted to kill. You know those types that fight in the Dark Market."

Maurice nodded again and Rae tore herself away from the conversation. Either way, she was trapped. And that's exactly what General Yada wanted. If it was discovered that she was the Crimson Cord, she would be sent to prison and hanged. None of her people would come to her aid because she fraternized in the Dark Market. But if she stayed silent, she still had to dodge the soldiers' prying. It was only a matter of time before they started threatening to use force against the Yekelians to turn in the Crimson Cord.

We should just kill the general and be done with all this, the Beast of Rage snarled. *We could finally flee Yekel.*

Rae toyed with the idea until her eyes landed on Ben. He crouched at a different section of stone, having carved out a small pile of bricks already. Rae was impressed with his efficiency and felt that same tug to talk with him.

The Beast of Rage roared at her, but she ignored it. If killing the general would solve all her problems, she would've tried that long ago. The only way she would be free of General Yada and her past was to help Ben and Devora. And that's what she intended to do.

At the end of the workday, Rae bid Roberto and Maurice farewell and prepared to head toward home. It was then she noticed Ben still huddled over the stone.

Frowning, she marched up to him. "The day is done. You should go rest."

Ben peered up at her, then at the empty worksite. "I guess I got lost in my work."

Extending his arm, Ben braced himself against the outer wall and stood to his full height. Rae craned her neck to look up at him. Ben caught her staring and rubbed the back of his neck, looking away.

Biting her lip, Rae decided to be bold. "Would you like to come over for dinner?"

Ben's neck shifted from its usual pale complexion to the shade of a chili pepper. "I would like that," he mumbled.

"Follow me," Rae said and strode toward her home, wondering what new mess she was getting herself into.

Chapter Twenty-Four

Ben, Rae's House, Yekel

Ben silently walked beside Rae, trying to hide his limp and ignore the whispers of her neighbors.

"What is Rae doing with someone like *him?*"

"Where did he even come from?"

"Look how pale he is. He's obviously not from around here."

Ben released a breath, trying to control the fury in his heart. He shouldn't have come with Rae. He would blemish her reputation.

As they approached her rickety door, Ben muttered, "I don't want to cause you any trouble."

Rae spun around. She tilted her chin, a fire in her eyes. "Don't listen to what they have to say. Those gossips aren't friends of mine."

Ben was surprised she had heard her neighbors' slander and still wanted him to come with her. "I don't want anyone to think less of you because of me."

Rae's eyes widened in surprise before a deep sorrow covered them. "Don't worry, they won't think less of me because of you." She smiled and opened the door. "Come on. No gossips or harsh words are allowed in here."

Warmth spread through Ben's chest as he ducked his head to fit through Rae's door. The space was cozy and welcoming, just as it had been the other night when he came with Master Monham, Devora, and Tristan. Ben thought it was only him and Rae when Nadia popped out from the hallway.

"Rae! You're back!" She lifted her arms until she saw Ben. Lowering her hands to her hips, a sly grin crept across her face. "And you brought a friend."

"Hello, Nadia," he said, feeling the heat burn his neck.

"One Shot," Nadia replied, still grinning.

"Be—er—One Shot is going to have dinner with us," Rae said smoothly.

Ben wondered if Rae realized no one else knew his name. It was the last part of himself that still reminded him of who he really was. If he gave his name away, too, it would be tainted like the rest of his reputation. So, when the prisoners at the Fortress came up with the nickname One Shot, he went with it.

"Great," Nadia said enthusiastically. "Except, Devora wanted me to further explain the city and the pathways to the Temple. Plus, Tristan is driving her nuts. So, I'm going to sneak over to Master Monham's where she is. Have fun!"

Before either Ben or Rae could respond, Nadia sprinted out the door. But Ben swore Nadia gave Rae a wink before she left. The sound of the wooden door closing echoed through the home, filling the air with awkward tension.

"So," Rae said, taking off her orange scarf. "I thought I could show you how to make the flatbread and the orange blossom rolls, if you'd like."

Ben watched her place the scarf on the arrow he'd shot through the wall the other night. He'd never seen a woman with such short hair, but it didn't bother him in the slightest.

Noticing his gaze, Rae commented, "Ah, my long hair would get in the way a lot." She sheepishly rubbed the small blonde hairs on her head.

"I like it," Ben replied quickly, and Rae smiled. He liked that, too. "I haven't baked bread in a long time. I'm not sure if I remember enough to be helpful."

Rae flicked her wrist. "You'll do fine."

She motioned for him to take a seat at her kitchen table. The ceiling was too low for Ben to fully stand, but he would be more comfortable sitting. Rae pulled out various clay jars of differing sizes. Each held the dry ingredients necessary for the flatbread.

Ben thought of Pa's recipe as he watched Rae pour a generous amount of flour onto her wooden table, then sprinkle it with a heavy pinch of salt.

"The recipe is probably the same," she commented as she reached around him to grab a porcelain bottle with a narrow spout. Rae tilted the bottle, unleashing a steady stream of green oil. "But the difference is how you bake it."

She stirred the mixture with one hand while adding small drizzles of water from a jug with her other hand. In a matter of moments, a smooth ball of dough formed.

Rae then fisted her floured hands on her hips. "Hey, so far, I've done all the work. Papi always said, 'If you don't work, you don't eat.'"

Ben grinned, recalling Pa saying the same thing. "That's a good standard to live by."

Folding up his sleeves, Ben prepared himself to flatten out the dough. Yet, as his hands hovered over the smooth ball, they refused to move.

"Is something wrong?" Rae asked, her voice laced with concern.

"The last time I baked bread, something horrible happened," he replied, keeping his gaze focused on the dough.

"Oh," Rae said, and Ben could hear the disappointment in her voice.

But then she did something unexpected. She gently placed her hand on top of his and moved it over the ball of dough. Soft, fluffy dough pressed into his rough palms, bringing Ben back to the day he made honey buns.

He was supposed to take the honey buns to Master Garner's house. Pa asked him to do it, knowing he would have to walk through the corrupt parts of town to get there. No one bothered Ben when he was making deliveries. But, for some reason, he didn't want to make the delivery that day. Maybe he'd been too tired from waking up early to start the fire in the kiln. Maybe he was tired of hearing the whispers every time he thumped by a group of people.

So, against his better judgment, he sent Mara to Master Garner's house. It was a decision he regretted every day.

"Ben, Ben." Rae shook his arm.

Ben squeezed his eyes shut, trying to forget the memory. His selfishness had harmed his sister and, ultimately, his family. The villagers already liked to gossip about him because he was large, but once he murdered those men, it only added fuel to the fire.

"I think the flatbread is flat enough," Rae commented, releasing her grip on his bicep. The flour from her hand left a perfect handprint on his black shirt.

Ben glanced down at the parchment-thin dough. He jerked his hands back, not realizing he'd forced his emotions into his kneading. Rips and tears scattered over the dough, where he worked it too forcefully. He'd ruined it.

Ben turned away, angry that he'd destroyed something again.

"Hey," Rae said softly. "It's okay." When he didn't respond, Rae stomped in front of him and lifted his chin with two fingers. "This is just like when Master Monham messes up one of his pieces of pottery. The piece isn't ruined. It just needs to be remade."

She carefully scraped up the dough with a blunt knife and reworked it. In a matter of moments, the same smooth ball of dough was formed. Rae carefully flattened it with the palms of her hands and set it in the small kiln in the corner of her kitchen.

Dusting her hands off, she pulled out more jars and filled a tray with fruits, salted meats, and a small bit of cheese. She placed the tray on the table and sat across from him.

Silently, Rae picked up a piece of meat and nibbled on it. Ben watched her, noticing the streak of flour on her cheek.

"I'm not sure what happened in the past," Rae started slowly, examining the meat between her fingers. "But I recently learned that talking about it helps."

Ben stared, amazed at the woman in front of him. *She* wanted to hear about *his* life? But why? "I'm not very good with words," he muttered, rolling a small orange along the table.

"Neither am I."

Ben began peeling the orange. The only person who knew the full story of what happened with Mara was Devora and that was only because of her soulsight. Matthias knew some and the others in the Fortress made up their own stories about him.

Sighing, Ben started from the beginning.

Rae listened intently, never interrupting. Ben noticed her nodding every once in a while, but when he explained what happened to Mara, a deep sorrow filled her caramel eyes. Ben stopped before he explained what had become of the four men.

Rae waited a moment, then cautiously asked. "Were those men sent to jail?"

Ben kept his gaze on the citrus in his hands, the scent of oranges filling the kitchen. "No."

He could feel Rae's eyes scanning him. He couldn't bear to see the horror on her face as he'd seen with so many others. She would think the same as everyone else did. He was a murderer and a monster.

Clarity crossed her features. "I see," she finally said. "And that's why you were sent to the Fortress?"

Ben nodded, still unwilling to look at her.

Rae released a small sigh. "I know the pain your sister experienced. It's not an easy thing to live with. Have you been able to see if she's well since your time at the Fortress?"

He nodded again. "Last I heard, she married a good friend of mine. He's a kind man and will protect her."

It was then that Ben looked up to see a pained smile on Rae's lips.

"That's great," she choked. "I'm glad she can heal from the pain."

Worry weighed Ben's chest. Had he said something wrong? Was she trying to hide her fear of him? He wanted to ask her, but she jumped up.

"I forgot about the bread!"

Rae rushed to the kiln where a plume of smoke had just begun to form. Waving her hand, Rae coughed as she pulled out the dark piece of bread. She glared at it hard and then, once again, surprised Ben by starting to laugh.

She held the charcoaled bread out to him. "See, Ben? *That's* a ruined piece of flatbread."

Thankfully, Rae had some extra crackers in her cupboard. Ben tried to stay away from discussing their pasts. From what the Crimson Cord said, Rae used to work in the Temple. And though he wanted to know more, judging by the pain on her face earlier, it seemed best he kept his questions to himself.

Instead, they discussed what they had in common, which was Nadia. Rae told Ben all about Nadia's gift for tinkering and even showed him her first mini catapult.

"So, can everyone from Yekel invent whatever they want?"

"No," Rae replied, her shoulders drooping. "Tunri only chooses a few to bless with his gift. The rest of us are ordinary."

Ben furrowed his brow. Years ago, he read reports from the palace, which always made it seem that everyone in Yekel could make all sorts of things. It was how King Atol justified his actions for capturing the best Tinkers then setting the city on fire. Ben remembered reading about it just before the incident with Mara occurred.

"I would hardly call making delicious pastries ordinary," he replied with a smile. "And lovely scarves." He gestured to his own scarf around his neck.

Rae chuckled as she rubbed her arms. "I wouldn't call those gifts. They're just things I learned how to do." She gazed off into the corner. "I don't think Tunri wants to bless me with a gift."

"Why not?"

Rae darted her eyes to him, biting her lower lip. "My past isn't the cleanest."

Pain squeezed Ben's chest at the torment lurking on Rae's face. What happened to her in the Temple? He could feel his vengeance building, just like it had when Mara was attacked. He balled his hand into a fist, trying to control the desire to harm whoever hurt Rae.

"But it doesn't matter," Rae said, swatting her hand, as if pushing away the past. "I've made do. Even if I've ruined whatever Tunri wanted me to do, I doubt He'd want to bless me with a gift now."

Ben cocked his head, confused as to how Rae could see herself in such a negative way. To him, she was sunlight, radiant and bright. She chose to be kind to him when she could've run, like everyone else.

He eyed her hands lying on the table, one placed over the other. He tried to keep his distance, not wanting her to feel threatened by him. But, for a small moment, he found his courage. Reaching out, he slowly laid his large hand over hers. When by some miracle, she didn't flinch or pull away, he held it.

"Whatever happened in the past, you're not ruined, Rae. You just need to be remade."

Tears trickled down Rae's cheeks, and Ben panicked that he had said the wrong thing. But when she laced her small fingers through his, he realized, for once, he had said something right.

Chapter Twenty-Five

Devora watched One Shot limp into the monochromatic crowd of Yekelians. His height was enough to make him stand out and adding in the black clothes and bright orange scarf, he might as well have screamed, "I'm a spy for Tenton!"

But, surprisingly, no one called him out. A few Yekelian workers glanced at his length and whispered to their neighbors. But other than the hushed words, everything went smoothly. Once Devora saw that One Shot found Rae—or rather Rae found One Shot—she was satisfied and continued to scope out the city.

Although Tristan was making her crazy with his constant whining about the heat, she offered for him to tag along with her and One Shot today. But, to her surprise, he said he had other business to attend to in the marketplace.

"Nothing suspicious, I promise," Tristan said, drawing an 'X' over his heart with his finger. But it was the devious twinkle in his eye that worried Devora.

As she prayed Tristan wouldn't cause their cover to be blown, Devora studied the bustling marketplace around her. Despite Yekel being a seized city, everything seemed quite normal. There were bakers, blacksmiths, all the same people found in Grenly.

So why did Kadesh capture Yekel and stop there? Devora wondered. *Why not continue into the rest of Tenton?*

Tenton: A Condensed History claimed King Atol stopped Kadesh from seizing more of Tenton by killing their main general. But Devora learned from Master Monham that Yekel was still governed by a Kadeshian general, General Yada. And though the Yekelians were permitted to trade and sell their wares at the marketplace on the day they observed as Sancti, during the workweek, they were forced into slave labor.

Devora straightened the dark veil on her head, making sure her face was completely covered. What she was told about Yekel and what she saw with her own eyes were two entirely different things that didn't add up. Flicking her ebony braid behind her back, Devora continued through the busy street. She didn't have enough information yet. But soon, she would.

Peering through the forms hurrying through the marketplace, Devora quickly merged into the flow. Most women wore scarves as head coverings in Yekel, so it was easy to blend in. She could see why Rae had made a business of selling her brightly covered fabrics; the city streets were highlighted with bright pinks, greens, and teals. Devora wondered if Rae had made them all.

As she followed the train of people running their morning errands, Devora reflected on Rae's memories. Rae had every reason not to trust her or her group. Not only were Devora and One Shot fugitives of the law, but Rae had been horrifically abused. If that had happened to her, Devora wasn't sure if she'd ever want to be around people again.

The narrow streets soon opened into a central plaza where a large statue of a woman with curved horns stood in the middle. At first, Devora thought it was the same statue from her vision. But upon closer inspection, she realized this statue was made of bronze, not imperial opal.

A crowd of Kadeshians, whom Devora assumed occupied former Yekelian homes, flitted around the plaza, busying themselves with various tasks. One plump woman sat upon a stone bench and braided flowers into a strand. A thin, balding man swept the brick beneath the statue while a young boy, no more than eight summers, stood on a wooden ladder to polish the bronze horns on the woman.

A cool aura pressed in Devora's mind, confirming what she already wondered. Something was about to happen in Yekel, and she needed to find out what.

"Excuse me?" she asked sweetly of the plump woman on the bench. Devora covered her purple sash around her wrist with her hand. Though the woman was Kadeshian and meant to be Devora's enemy, she appeared to be anything but ruthless. Her cheeks were round, and her smile warm as she glanced up at Devora.

"Yes, dear? Are you here for the festival?"

"I'm actually just passing through," Devora lied smoothly. "What's this festival about?"

The woman paused her braiding, looking up at Devora with excitement twinkling in her eyes. "Oh, it's quite a wonderful time. We're giving thanks to our goddess, the Queen of Heaven, Pahga, for a bountiful harvest. Come and sit."

The plump woman patted the space next to her on the bench while chatting about how wonderful Pahga was. Apparently, the Kadeshians who came to Yekel were flourishing. Crops were growing, businesses were thriving, and all was well.

Hearing how amazing Pahga was from the plump woman, Devora couldn't help but wonder how this goddess could be the same one Nadia cursed every so often.

Devora nodded politely but kept her gaze focused on the building behind the bronze statue. Up on a hill, overshadowing the lower part of Yekel stood a marble building with large gray columns. Devora engaged her soulsight and searched for Kanna. The streak of purple light led straight up the Temple's steps. Devora pressed her lips together. She had to get into the Temple and soon.

But before she could disengage her Sight, warmth cracked behind her eyes and another vision began. As the vision unfolded, Devora prayed the kind, plump woman wouldn't notice anything strange happening. She had been sensing her control of her gift getting stronger, but she still needed One Shot's and Nadia's assistance when her vision came at the Fighter's Ring. Hopefully, she was still seated upright on the bench, pretending to listen.

"This isn't the best time for a vision," she said to Tunri. But the vision continued.

Glancing around, Devora noted she'd returned to the marble building and realized it was the Temple of Pahga. Now that she knew the numbers on the doors represented the ages of the women inside, she wanted nothing more than to break each door down and set the enslaved women free. That was something she intended to do once Matthias came with his forces.

But the vision rotated her away from the wooden doors and toward the imperial opal statue. The goddess, Pahga, was a beautiful woman. Tall and curvaceous in all the right places, and with long flowing hair.

Footsteps sounded behind Devora, and she spun around to see a line of people forming before the statue.

"Thank you for an abundant harvest this year, Pahga," a middle-aged man with speckled black and gray hair said. He

bent down on his hands and knees, bowing before the goddess's statue.

Devora waited for the statue to react as it had with her, but nothing happened.

The man lifted his head with tears streaming down his face, confusing Devora greatly.

"If you don't wish to bless me," he sobbed. "Please, bless my daughter."

A young girl, maybe twelve summers, took a cautious step forward. Wavy ebony hair flowed over her face as she bowed her head. It wasn't out of reverence but fear. The girl shook as her father stood and nudged her forward.

"Please, Papa, let Pahga bless me when I'm older," the girl whispered.

Frowning, the father shoved the girl forward. She cried out and stumbled before the statue.

The man raised his hands. "Pahga, I give you my daughter. Take her and use her as you will."

Devora couldn't tear her eyes away from the scene. How could he give his daughter up so easily?

The black orb on the statue's chest lit with a gray light. It swirled before a single stream of light floated from the statue, entering the girl's mouth. Devora watched, horrified, as the statue pulled the soul from the girl's body and sucked it back into the orb, leaving the girl lifeless on the ground.

But the father didn't weep, as Devora thought he might. Instead, he raised his hands in praise and said, "Thank you, Pahga!"

The father turned and exited the Temple, leaving his daughter's lifeless form behind.

Devora's stomach squeezed as she watched the scene repeat with more families. One right after the other, easily giving up their daughters' lives like they meant nothing.

Do they not understand the value of a life? Of a soul?

But when a couple approached with a newborn baby, Devora had seen enough.

"Enough, Tunri," she cried, tears forming in her eyes. "Please, I can't take anymore."

The vision dimmed as the soul left the young child, its cries silenced. But just before the vision went dark, Devora saw a face she never thought she'd see again.

Behind the statue, extracting the souls from the black orb, was the hag from the Fortress.

Gasping, Devora returned from her vision to find the plump woman still chattering. Now she was discussing the benefit of using yarrow to seal an open cut.

Hands shaking, Devora stood. "Yes, well, thank you for your time." And before the woman could utter another word, Devora hurried away.

Devora raced away from the plaza. How could the Kadeshian people celebrate in such a horrible way? She couldn't imagine Mama or Papa ever giving her away so easily. Did these people not care about their children, their legacy?

The tears she cried during her vision were still rolling down her cheeks. Luckily, the black veil shielded her face from the world. Sucking in her breath, Devora rushed back through the city. She had to find out more about the Temple, about the statue within it, and about why the hag who'd given her the vial of imperial opal was there.

The next half hour was a blur as Devora made her way from the center of the city toward the outer wall. Thankfully, the workday was at its end, and Master Monham was already home.

After checking to see if anyone was around, she quietly knocked, not wanting to bring more attention to herself than necessary.

"Yes?" Master Monham asked, opening the door a crack. As soon as he saw Devora, he smiled. "Devora, please come in. I was wondering where you had gone off to."

Devora checked a final time. Thankfully, everyone else was already in their homes, and she slipped inside.

As she took off the veil, she noted the gray dust coating Master Monham's thinning hair and fingertips. He must have just returned home.

"I'm sorry to arrive right when you've finished work," she started. "But I've been given a vision from Tunri and was wondering if you could answer some of my questions."

Master Monham's jovial demeanor turned serious as he took a damp rag and wiped his face and hands. "I'm not sure I'll be of use interpreting Tunri's prophecies, but I'll help you in any way I can."

After pouring each of them a cup of water, Master Monham gestured for Devora to take a seat. Two wooden chairs sat around a small, square table, and Devora chose the one on the left.

Master Monham eased into the other chair then took a long swig of water. "Now," he said once he finished swallowing. "Start from the beginning."

Devora began by explaining her first vision about the numbered doors in the Temple. She left out the parts about Rae but did mention the imprisoned person in what she assumed was a cell below the Temple. She then explained what she'd seen that day—the soul sacrifices. Her throat tightened as she described what she witnessed.

Master Monham's tired gaze grew wearier as Devora finished.

With a sigh, the old man rubbed his eyes. "When King Atol burned our lands and weakened our defenses, he left Yekel vulnerable to Kadesh's attack. It seemed as if Kadesh knew Yekel would be defenseless and attacked soon after the fires calmed.

"Yekel had its differences of beliefs, but a lot of us believed in Tunri. The Temple of Pahga would only require a sacrifice of the harvest, as far as I know. But after Kadesh invaded, General Yada, a devoted follower of Pahga, said a harvest sacrifice wasn't enough for the goddess. He claimed that Pahga, herself, told him she required something more. Something that would truly prove the devotion of her followers. And only those who had proven their devotion to Pahga may continue to enter the Temple."

"And by proven you mean..." Devora trailed off, not wanting to think about the enslaved women and all the soul sacrifices.

Master Monham nodded slowly. "There are other ways of showing devotion. Unfortunately, they require years of learning the ancient texts of the Pahgan beliefs. Most people would rather take the shorter route."

"But their children!" Devora exclaimed, slamming her fist on the table. "How could they give them up so easily? Without remorse? And the enslaved women? The Kadeshians are okay with that, too?"

Master Monham shook his head. "I don't know, Devora. I don't know why they allow women to be enslaved and children's lives taken. My wife and I were never blessed with a child. I always wish that instead of giving their children to their goddess, they would let another family have them. But that is not the way of the followers of Pahga."

Devora gritted her teeth as she glared at her cup of water. How could the Kadeshians be so blinded?

"Was there anything else you wanted to ask me?"

Devora glanced up, thinking about the old hag. Master Monham probably wouldn't know about her. And if he did, how could Devora ask? *Do you know if a creepy old woman is stealing the souls from the statue? If so, what's she doing with them?*

Devora rubbed her eyes with her palms before running them over her frizzy hair. "No, thank you. I think I've had all I can handle for today."

"I understand," the old man replied. "I'm going to finish washing up. Please help yourself to anything you like."

As Master Monham shuffled to the back room, Devora wondered when Tristan would be back from his "other business." After what happened with the gang the other night, Devora didn't want to let him out of her sight. But so far, he had been good on his word and kept his disguise on, so she prayed he was being honorable. For once.

Just then a knock sounded at the door. Devora jumped up. If the Kadeshians found out she, One Shot, and Tristan were staying here, she would be imprisoned immediately. Worse still, Master Monham would be punished, as well.

Three rapid knocks tapped against the door. Then three spaced out knocks. Devora recognized it as the code Tristan used to gain them access to the Dark Market.

Readying herself for defense, Devora cracked open the door.

"How long are you going to make me stand out here?" Tristan whined.

Devora breathed a sigh of relief. "Come on, hurry!" She grabbed his collar and pulled him inside, shutting the door behind him.

"My, my, honeybee, who knew you were so handsy," Tristan purred, as he unloaded various jars and sacks from his arms.

Devora rolled her eyes, then focused on the packages. "What's all this?"

Tristan untied one of the sacks and pulled out a small cream-colored cylinder. "Snacks. I told you I was going to the market." He pinched the cylinder between his fingers and took a bite. A sigh of delight escaped his lips. "I haven't had sugar cane in years."

Devora's mouth salivated as Tristan unwrapped the various sacks and opened the jars, each one containing another delicious treat. Just as she was reaching for a cocoa covered almond, she paused, remembering when Matthias had told her about Tristan stealing sugar cane when they were young.

She retracted her hand. "Did you steal this?"

Tristan bit off a hunk of sugar cane. Sweet juice rolled down his fingers. "Really?" He quirked a brow then gestured to the numerous bags and jars. "Even I couldn't steal all this."

"Hmm," Devora replied but supposed he was right. She took a handful of almonds, enjoying how bitter the cocoa tasted against the nutty almond flavor.

A few moments later, Nadia bust through the door, causing Devora and Tristan to yelp.

"Having a party without me?" Nadia laughed, snatching the sugar cane from Tristan's grasp.

"Hey!" he said, pouting. But Nadia was unfazed.

When Master Monham emerged from his room, he didn't question why there were suddenly more people in his small home. Instead, he sat with them and enjoyed some plum jam with crackers.

The four of them chatted about the day's events. Devora hadn't realized an hour passed by until another knock sounded at the door. Their conversation quieted as they waited. The same code knock Tristan gave answered, and Master Monham opened the door.

Outside stood One Shot. White streaks of flour covered his black sleeves as he bent forward to fit through the door. As soon as he was inside, he sat on the floor, knowing Master Monham's ceiling was not high enough for him.

"Where were you?" Devora questioned, taking in his flour dusted hair.

"Baking with Rae," Nadia chuckled as she took a bite of a salty cracker.

"Sure, he was," Tristan scoffed, grabbing the crackers from Nadia's hands.

"One Shot," Devora said, noticing her friend hadn't spoken. "Is everything okay?"

It was then she noticed something in his hands. Lying perfectly still, with a piece of parchment still tied around his foot was her crow from the Fortress who had been delivering messages to Matthias, Sir Blakesalot.

Chapter Twenty-Six

Who is this man, and why is he so kind? Rae thought as she watched Ben shuffle toward Master Monham's house.

She glanced at her hands, remembering his soft touch on her skin. It was so unlike the harsh, possessive, touches of other men. Ben was gentle, as if she were a porcelain cup he would break. Rae laughed. If only he knew she was the one who fought him in the Dark Market.

Closing the door, Rae shuffled back to her room. All of that felt so long ago, yet it had only been a week and a half. And now she, or the Crimson Cord, was wanted for murder, and Rae was flirting with a man she barely knew.

Groaning, she flopped down on her bed.

Rae stared at the tacked-up fabric concealing the door to her roof. Though her heart didn't feel as burdened, her beasts of fear and anger still weighed her down. But when she was with Ben, she felt lighter than air and her worries disappeared.

Sighing, Rae closed her eyes. She couldn't dream of a happily ever after. Girls like her didn't get happily ever afters. And yet, Ben's sister, Mara, had. Maybe there was hope for Rae, too.

Clinging to that fragile hope, Rae pulled her blanket up and fell asleep.

The next morning, Rae rose early to make orange blossom rolls. She knew Ben and Devora would be visiting that night and wanted to make sure she didn't burn them like she had with the flatbread. She was still embarrassed that she ruined the flatbread after boasting about her baking skills.

You're not ruined, Rae; you just need to be remade.

Ben's words repeated in her thoughts as she grated the orange peels and folded them into the dough. As the Crimson Cord, she told Ben and Devora she was a former Temple Priestess. There was a chance they didn't know what it meant, but judging by the Winner's—Tristan's—reaction, the trio was well-versed in what happened in the Temple. But Devora and Ben didn't cast looks of judgment or disgust her way. Ben even went out of his way to befriend her.

Rae glanced down at the small spheres of dough on the table, remembering how cautious and gentle Ben had been when holding her hand. She hadn't wanted to flinch away, so she didn't. Holding Ben's hand provided her with more comfort than she'd felt in a long time.

Sighing, Rae set the rolls to rise as she got ready for work. Last night, Nadia had come by after Ben left to say she would be spending the night at Master Monham's with Devora. Apparently, they had received word from their captain and needed to discuss a plan.

Rae understood Nadia was no longer a child, but after having her back in her home, the loneliness grew thicker with each silent moment that ticked by.

The pitter-patter of a rainstorm danced throughout her quiet home. Rae frowned and opened one of the shutters on her kitchen window. One of Grenly's tropical storms was heading their way, but work wouldn't be canceled. General Yada never canceled work.

Rae slammed the shutter with a little more force than necessary before placing the rolls in her kiln and returning to her room. She decided to wear a thicker teal scarf, one that was long enough to wrap around her head and shoulders to keep her somewhat dry while working in the rain. As she folded the fabric in place, she noticed the red mesh of her Crimson Cord mask, peeking out from behind the cloth in the corner.

Rae pursed her lips. She promised Master Monham she would destroy it but couldn't find the strength to do it. The Crimson Cord had granted her so much: freedom, power, authority, all things she never had while she was plain old Rae.

Pulling back the cloth, Rae folded the crumpled disguise and placed it on the trunk holding her other clothes. Gathering the large swath of fabric again, Rae folded it in half and laid it over the pile. She would destroy the disguise. Just not yet.

The sweet citrus scent of orange blossom rolls wafted from the kitchen, and Rae knew they were done. Golden-brown crust greeted her when she removed the rolls from the kiln, and Rae smiled.

Perfect.

After the burnt flatbread and Ben explaining his past, Rae never had a chance to show him her orange blossom roll recipe. Maybe tonight he would...

What are you thinking? the Beast of Fear squawked. *He may seem kind now, but he'll turn on you. You can't trust him.*

Rae shook her head. No, Ben wouldn't do that, would he? She hadn't seen one ounce of judgment in his eyes.

You'll see, the Beast warned. *You'll see.*

Shivering, Rae placed the rolls on the counter and laid a towel over them as she tried to forget the Beast's words. Ben was kind and understanding, wasn't he? Without answering herself, Rae trudged through the rain toward the worksite, praying her inner Beast was wrong.

As her boots squashed through the thick mud, she thought about Master Monham's clay and the story he told about Tunri. Could Tunri really take someone as flawed and broken as her and remake her into something new? Rae wasn't sure of anything anymore. The only thing she was certain of was freeing the women from the Temple and fleeing Yekel as soon as she could.

Thick drops of rain soaked through Rae's headscarf, leaving her chilled to the bone as she made her way to the crumbling section of the outer wall. Yekel hadn't experienced a tropical storm in ages but knowing she would be able to talk to Ben again made the dreary day less burdensome.

But when Rae arrived at the worksite and waited for the day's assignments, the tall man with the bright orange scarf was nowhere to be found. Rae's heart sagged, remembering what the Beast of Fear said.

Did I scare him off? Was he only being kind to be polite?

Her thoughts spiraled more and more as each raindrop drizzled down and the gentle giant didn't arrive. When the Kadeshian captain called out the last group without mentioning Ben's pseudonym, a lump caught in Rae's throat.

Fool! the Beast of Rage roared. *He was only using you to gain information, and you invited him into your home.*

Rae squeezed her eyes, letting the rain dribble down her face. She invited him over without thinking it through. She should've kept her distance, like she had for the past two years. Rage started to burble in her chest.

No, a new voice, one Rae hadn't heard before, said. It was calm yet commanding. Soft, but powerful. Rae couldn't place any distinction on the voice only that it...was.

Trust and see, the voice encouraged.

A lightness filled Rae's heavy soul as something new cocooned her heart. It didn't feel like jealousy, rage, or fear, but something else entirely.

Rae opened her eyes and watched the humble Yekelian people trudge over the wet, muddy ground. Her people were downtrodden and worn by the years of Kadesh's control. Rae felt that way, too. Just surviving, day-to-day. But something snapped, a chain had broken. Where there was once only fear, there was now hope.

With her newfound hope, Rae batted away the taunts and jeers of Fear and Rage and went about her workday. She still wanted to know if Ben was okay, praying he and the others hadn't been found by General Yada. But Hope reassured her that she would see them at her home that evening.

Rae slogged through the workday, keeping her mind focused on her tasks, and before she knew it, the day was done. After bidding farewell to Roberto and Maurice, she headed home.

Once she set her soaked scarf on the drying rack by the kiln, Rae found herself rushing around to tidy up her nearly spotless home. Mami always said, "A clean home is a happy home." And Rae believed it, too. She needed to do something to fight her nerves, and she'd already set out food and rearranged her pillows and two chairs a hundred times.

Just when she was about to go crazy, a soft knock sounded at the door. Rae's insides jumbled into knots as she slowly strode toward the door. Flickers of oranges and yellows from her lanterns illuminated her small home. Taking a breath, Rae opened the door.

Outside stood three figures: Ben, Devora, and Master Monham. Devora wore a black veil over her head while Ben and Master Monham were wrapped in simple cloaks.

"Please, come in," Rae said. "The Crimson Cord told me to expect you this night." She breathed a sigh of relief at how honest the lie sounded. Ben and Devora still didn't know that she was the Crimson Cord.

"Thank you," Devora replied as she stepped through the threshold.

Master Monham followed and then Ben. He paused before her, his dark eyes scanning her face. Rae wished she'd washed it after work but then vanquished the silly thought from her mind as she closed the door behind him.

"Hello again," he said softly, his voice a deep rumble.

"Hello," she managed to squeak out.

They stood there for a moment until Devora said, "Before we get started on the plan to breech the Temple, I must tell you about Nadia." She pulled the veil from her head, revealing those striking violet eyes.

Rae snapped out of her daze. "What's happened to Nadia? Is she all right?"

General Yada told you he was coming for her, the Beast of Fear cackled. *But you didn't listen.*

"She's safe, Rae," Master Monham encouraged, easing himself into one of the two chairs.

"Yes," Devora agreed. "At least for now. I've sent her to Captain Blake to deliver an important message. It seems our former method of communication was compromised." A somber look passed over the Seer's face.

The Seer let little Nadi travel alone? Anything could happen to her. Yekel is a long way from the Fortress, the Beast taunted.

Rae squeezed the fabric of her skirt in her hand, trying to reign in her fear. Devora cared for Nadia, too. She wouldn't send her on a suicide mission. "Is she alone?"

Devora shook her head. "No one will bother her, not the way she is traveling."

Suddenly, a deep voice whispered in her ear. "Devora befriended a giant white elk."

Goosebumps rose along Rae's skin at his closeness. "An elk?"

"His name is Vinn," Devora replied, giving Ben a mock scowl. "And you should do well to remember it. He carried you all across Tenton, too."

Ben smirked and bowed his head in apology. He carefully crouched through the house until he sat on the floor next to Master Monham.

"And Nadia also took Tristan with her," Devora added, an amused twinkle sparkling in her eye.

"Thank goodness," Ben mumbled, and Devora laughed.

From what Rae knew of Tristan, Nadia would probably be tempted to knock him off the elk while traveling.

Relaxing her tense stance, Rae placed refreshments on the table in the center of the room. It was a good thing Devora sent Nadia back to the north. General Yada wouldn't be able to harm her. Did the Seer somehow know that the general was after Nadia? Either way, Rae was thankful Nadia was far from Yekel.

"Will Nadia be safe since she's associated with you, and you're wanted for treason?" Rae asked, seating herself between Ben and Devora. She then realized the forwardness of her question. "Sorry."

Devora sighed. "No, it's all right. When Nadia first came to the Fortress, my other friends and I mistook her for a man. That was when she told us a little about life in Yekel. She decided to don that disguise again."

"And added a beard," Master Monham chuckled as he took a warm piece of flatbread.

The hope Rae discovered burned a little brighter, knowing her disguise for Nadia back then still worked now.

"The Crimson Cord informed me you wanted access into the Temple," Rae started. She knew they didn't have long, and she wanted to reveal her plan as quickly as possible.

Devora spread some honey on a piece of flatbread. "Yes, he told us that you would be able to help."

From the corner of her eye, Rae watched Ben take the freshly baked bread in his hands and smile. Butterflies flurried in her stomach at the gentle look.

Clearing her throat, Rae made herself focus on Devora. "Yes, I have a way to get into the Temple, but I need to know why you want to enter."

Of course, Rae already knew this. But they told her while she was the Crimson Cord. If she wanted to keep her secret identity under wraps, she'd have to keep up the lies.

"We're searching for a woman by the name of Kanna Blake. She is also a Seer, probably the only one left, other than me," Devora explained, while Master Monham and Ben silently enjoyed their food.

Rae could've sworn she saw Ben watching her a few times. But when she peered his way, he stared intently at his plate of dried figs.

Rae refocused her attention. "And you believe her to be in the Temple?"

"We hope," Devora answered honestly.

Rae drummed her fingers on her knee. It was now or never. "I was forced to work at the Temple for two years until I bought my freedom. In my darkest moments, Kanna encouraged me. In return, I visited her in her cell and brought her what little news I had of the outside world. I didn't know that she was a Seer. A strip of thick cloth always covered her eyes." Rae shook her head. "I don't know if she's still there, and I feel ashamed for not realizing there was a bigger reason why she was imprisoned."

Rae looked at her hands folded in her lap. Even with her own eyes covered, Kanna cleaned and bandaged the cuts Rae made when she wanted to end her life. Kanna had a beautiful soul, and Rae always wondered why she was imprisoned but had never asked. Knowing that she was a Seer explained a little as to why Kanna was in a cage beneath the Temple.

"I'll help you," Rae continued, reaching for the skeleton key around her neck. She had retrieved it from beneath her bed as soon as she arrived home, not wanting to lose sight of it. "But on one condition."

Devora finished her chewing then elegantly wiped her mouth. "Which is?"

Rae's hands shook. All her sacrifices, all her fights, everything was falling into place. She could justly—without guilt—free the women enslaved to the Temple.

However, as Rae opened her mouth to strike her agreement, another loud knock pounded against her door.

"By order of General Yada, you must open this door. We are here to search for the murderer of Antonio Wankle, the Crimson Cord."

Chapter Twenty-Seven

Rae, Rae's Home, Yekel

I told you, the Beast of Fear howled in Rae's thoughts as panic clawed up her throat. Her mind suddenly surged forward like she was in the Fighter's Ring, thinking of every possible solution to end it swiftly.

Rae bounced up as the banging continued.

"Open this door!" the soldier commanded.

"We must act now, Rae," Master Monham whispered.

Devora and Ben looked at her, and for the first time, Rae saw fear reflected in their eyes. Right here, right now, Rae could turn them in. And they knew it. She would be seen as a hero. It was what she originally planned to do. But she had changed.

Ben's and Devora's presence awakened hope inside Rae. Hope in freeing the other Temple Priestesses. Hope in being proud of who she was and forgetting her past. Hope for a new future. Rae swallowed her fear. She wasn't going to throw that all away.

"To the back room," Rae said, grabbing Devora and Ben's arms.

The two jumped up quickly and quietly. Once again, Ben astonished Rae with how swift he was for such a large man.

"Master Monham, answer the door. Tell them I needed to change before we enjoyed our meal."

Master Monham nodded and waited until Rae guided Ben and Devora to her bedroom. As soon as they were in, she heard Master Monham greet the soldier with his kind voice.

"Forgive us. We were just about to enjoy an evening meal when my hostess spilled jam all over herself. She is changing and will be out right away."

Thank you, Master Monham.

Facing Ben and Devora, Rae quickly explained, "I don't know how far the search will go or if they'll even come in here. But if they do—" Rae stood on her bed and pulled down the fabric she tacked across the ceiling, revealing the secret door she used to sneak out to the Dark Market. "Hide up here. If you lie flat on the roof, the darkness will cloak you." She stared at Devora and Ben, who were handling the chaos surprisingly well. "Make sure you secure the fabric back in place. If you don't they'll find you right away."

"I can do that," Ben replied. He seemed to want to say more but kept his mouth shut.

Rae nodded. "I'll stall for as long as I can."

Taking a breath, she hurried out of her room.

Keep them safe, she prayed that whatever god would listen.

Pretending to wipe her blouse clean, she shuffled into the living area. "I'm so sorry for the delay," she began. "I wasn't expecting—" her sentence stopped short.

As if he were a king in a castle, sitting in her living area was none other than General Yada.

It was as if time had reversed. Not two weeks ago General Yada sat in the same spot, threatening her to find information about the Seer. Now, he was in her home again. But instead of the smooth coolness he usually expelled, a frantic fury radiated from him. Bloodshot eyes, layered with heavy bags beneath them, glared at her. Strands of his typically slicked back hair stood from his head, greasier than usual. A thick purple bruise covered the bridge of his nose and under his eyes where she'd head-butted him. Wrinkles adorned his usually pristine Kadeshian uniform, its buttons askew.

Rae held her hands in front of her, keeping her defenses on alert. She'd never seen the general in such a state. It was as if he were a feral animal, waiting to attack. At that moment Rae remembered the key from the old hag. General Yada must have discovered it missing. That key was his power.

"General Yada," Rae said steadily, shifting her gaze to Master Monham who sat easily in his chair. He gave her a quick nod while sipping from his cup, assuring her that he wouldn't leave. "What a pleasant surprise." The words tasted like poison, but she managed to say them calmly.

Two Kadeshian soldiers stood to the left and right of the entrance to Rae's home. They kept the door open as they stared past her head, their faces hard and unwavering.

Rae licked her lips as a cool night breeze swirled through the doorway into her home. Lantern flames danced in anticipation of the general's response.

"Don't toy with me, Rae," General Yada sneered. "Where is it?"

Rae wasn't sure whether he meant her Crimson Cord disguise or the skeleton key. So, the confusion on her face was only partially fake.

She bunched her brows. "Where is what?"

General Yada growled like the Beast of Rage, but she resisted the urge to take a step back. She would not feed the Beast of Fear. She would no longer fear General Yada.

"Search everywhere," he commanded his men. The soldiers saluted and immediately tore through Rae's house. They knocked over her table, scattering the meal all over the floor. Thankfully, Master Monham inched away before the table flew.

Rae crossed her hands over her chest. "Was that really necessary? I worked hard on that meal."

As if a switch had been flipped, General Yada transformed back into his calm, cunning self. "Were you expecting others? That was quite a lot of food for a young woman and an old man."

Rae scoffed. Joining the general in banter would keep him occupied, at least until Ben and Devora could escape to the rooftop. "Where are the rules that say a woman can't eat a lot?"

General Yada chuckled, shaking his head. "Oh Rae, I've missed your fire."

Chills like pinpricks pierced into Rae's flesh. "I haven't missed yours," she retorted.

He started toward her, like a beast cornering its prey. But Rae didn't move. Surely he wouldn't try anything after she'd head-butted him before. If she showed fear now, if she showed weakness, General Yada would use it against her. Like he always had.

The soldiers almost made it to Rae's bedroom when a furious commotion sped by the opened door. Frantic voices rang through the night.

"Hanan!" General Yada shouted, pulling his possessive gaze from Rae. "Find out what's happening outside."

The large soldier barreled out the door, leaving the other to check Rae's room. General Yada stepped back from Rae. With another grin, he reached down and plucked a date from the floor.

"You can't hide them forever, Rae. You will be found out. Tell me where the Seer is."

Rae bit her tongue, refusing to give in to his demands.

Rae shrugged, keeping her face calm. "Last I heard, the Seer left Yekel. Apparently, she didn't find what she was looking for here."

For a moment, fear flashed across the general's gaze and Rae wanted to know why. But he soon covered it by popping the date into his mouth. He chewed silently, keeping his predatory stare fixed on Rae.

"All clear, sir," the other soldier coming from her bedroom said. "There's no one here."

"Sir," Hanan called through the doorway. "A fire started in the grain mill. We need more hands to put it out immediately."

General Yada narrowed his eyes as he swallowed. "Your time is almost up, Rae," he said before marching out the door.

Rae waited until the general was far away before she crumbled to the floor. Her pulse raced, pounding furiously between her ears. But she'd done it. She'd kept Ben and Devora safe.

"Are you okay?" Master Monham asked, coming to her side.

"I think so," she breathed. "Besides head-butting him in the face, that's the first time I've held my ground with him."

Master Monham chuckled. "I thought his nose looked a bit off."

Rae gave a breathy laugh and took Master Monham's offered arm. The two of them righted the table and tried to save as much of the meal as possible. Once enough time had passed to ensure General Yada and his soldiers wouldn't return, Rae went to her bedroom to check on Devora and Ben.

As she entered, she noticed the fabric hanging above her bed was secured. Relief flooded her chest. They were safe. Other than her flipped over mattress, the rest of her room seemed unharmed until she saw the trunk. Frantic, she raced toward it and ripped off the crumpled cloth. Her Crimson Cord disguise was gone.

I told you he would find it, the Beast of Fear taunted. *Now he has evidence that you killed the Wizard Wankle. You'll be executed.*

"No," Rae whispered, clawing through her room.

The soldier couldn't have found her disguise. He didn't have anything in his hands when he left.

Rae threw scarves all around her room. She crawled under her bed. She opened her trunk and dumped everything out. Where was the red mesh and cord?

Just then, a thump came from above, and Rae quickly stood on her bed. She peeled back the fabric and opened the hidden door.

Devora peeked her head over the edge, her long braid hanging over her shoulder. "Your quick thinking paid off, Rae."

Once Rae stepped off the bed, Devora flipped around, allowing her feet to dangle through the hole before she flopped down on the mattress.

Devora pursed her lips. "I hope we didn't cause too much damage with our distraction."

Two long legs slowly eased their way through the hole until they touched the ground. Ben bent the top half of his body, so he fit completely inside. "If they got to it fast enough, there should be hardly any damage," he replied.

Rae blinked. "Wait, that was you guys? How did you set the grain mill on fire from over here? It's halfway around the outer wall."

Devora grinned and gestured to Ben, who shrugged. "It wasn't too hard."

"Thank you," Rae said, not just to Ben and Devora, but to whatever god answered her prayer and kept them all safe from General Yada.

The hope in her chest glowed a bit brighter and Rae was beginning to enjoy its presence in her soul.

"I know you're probably exhausted from all this—" Devora waved her hand in the air and Rae assumed she meant the search of her house. "We can come back another time."

"No," Rae replied quickly. "No, I'm okay. Let's continue where we left off. I believe there's still some food left. And, unless General Yada's men took them, I made fresh orange blossom rolls this morning."

Devora ran her hand along her frizzy braid and smiled. "Well, I can't say no to a delicious treat. Especially since you already put so much time into it. Right, One Shot?"

Ben merely nodded.

Rae eyed him. *Why was he back to his quiet self again?*

Devora headed out to the main room where she and Master Monham discussed the poor search and seizure training of Kadesh's soldiers.

Rae and Ben stood silently in her room. Rae crossed her arms over her chest. If the tension between them was any thicker, it could be cut with a knife. But she couldn't understand why.

Did I say something wrong?

She just hid them from General Yada. She just saved their lives. Shouldn't Ben be happy?

He won't always be kind, the Beast of Fear whispered.

Destroy him now! the Beast of Rage roared.

Rae chewed her lip. "I'm glad you're okay."

Ben nodded, keeping his eyes fixed on the ground. "I'm glad you're okay, too."

Rae's heart melted.

But soon Ben lifted his gaze. Questions swirled in his dark eyes as he pulled a scarlet piece of fabric from his pocket.

"I wasn't looking for this," he confessed. "But I knew I smelled oranges in the Dark Market and at your booth." He threaded her Crimson Cord mask between his long fingers. "There was always something familiar, but I couldn't place it. Now, I know." He handed her the mask. "The rest of it is on the roof. I figured since you were wanted for murder, you'd want to hide it. I took it up there before the soldier could find it."

Rae gripped the fabric as tears pricked her eyes. "Ben, I can explain. I didn't—"

But Ben shook his head, pain lacing his features.

She had to explain. She didn't murder the Wizard. She didn't murder anyone. If only he'd listen.

But he thumped past her, his limp heavier than usual as he strode toward the main room where Devora and Master Monham chatted.

Rae gripped the fabric in her hand, feeling the Beast of Rage rear his ugly head. She gritted her teeth. Ben glanced at her one last time before he left her room, and she saw what she had feared: regret.

Chapter Twenty-Eight

Devora, Rae's House, Yekel

Devora left One Shot and Rae alone. As soon as the red mesh tumbled out from beneath the piece of cloth on the trunk, she knew One Shot would figure out Rae's secret identity. But he never asked any questions about it while they waited for the Kadeshian general and his soldiers to leave.

When the general's soldiers took longer than Devora liked, she suggested One Shot set the furthest corner of the grain mill ablaze. Nadia had left him with special tipped arrows for his cross bow that, when struck against a piece of flint, ignited.

One Shot didn't even comment on her order. Just obeyed.

Devora didn't like it. They'd grown closer since Warden Hazor broke them both out of the Fortress. She considered him a good friend now.

So when One Shot kept eerily silent, she knew the discovery of Rae's alias had hit him hard. But what Devora really wanted to know was why?

Unfortunately, One Shot's love life wasn't her business. And how could she help? Her own love life was in shambles.

Devora pulled out the dried violet rose petals. They were wrinkled and crushed but still held a faint scent. She brought them to her face as she thought about the last note she sent with Sir Blakesalot. The poor crow had given his life to ensure she and Matthias could communicate. Her heart sagged, knowing the creature died helping them. Devora didn't know who'd shot him down, but she knew their time was wearing thin. Thankfully, Matthias would be in Yekel soon.

Devora lied to Rae about Nadia returning to the Fortress. If Nadia returned there, she would be arrested for treason on the spot. No, Devora sent Nadia just east of Ballear. If she and Matthias lined up their times correctly, then he should be at least to Ballear by now. She hoped Matthias would add something more to the most recent note he sent. But it was all business regarding his departure and estimated arrival.

Sighing, Devora placed the petals back in her pocket and stepped into the main room where she found Master Monham casually sitting, as if nothing had happened. Remnants of spilled water and knocked over jars sprinkled the room. But Rae and Master Monham had tidied it up pretty quickly.

Crouching, Devora eased herself onto a purple pillow next to Master Monham. "Are you doing okay?"

Master Monham took a sip from his cup. "Sadly, I've seen far worse than what took place tonight. But I'm okay." He smiled at her. "Are you and your friend okay? I'm assuming Rae hid you well."

Devora ran her fingers over her sash around her wrist. "Yes, I'm a little shaken up. But overall fine." She glanced at the room where One Shot and Rae had yet to emerge. "Well, I'm not sure about One Shot."

"Hmm," Master Monham replied. "We shall see."

A few more moments ticked by, and One Shot finally stalked out of the room. Devora had never seen him in a foul mood, and after she saw the look on his face, she never wanted to see it again.

One Shot said nothing as he slumped next to Devora. He placed his cross bow behind him then stared at his hands in his lap.

Devora waited a moment then asked, "Is everything all right?"

One Shot gave his head the slightest shake and Devora's heart shattered. She knew One Shot could feel when she looked into his soul, but she had to know what was going on to help her friend.

Engaging her soulsight, Devora watched One Shot's soul droop and sag in defeat. The small bits of yellow she'd seen before were gone. Now it was a dark blue, almost the shade of midnight.

Fear struck Devora thoughts. She hadn't figured out everything her soulsight could do, but she did understand that the darker the soul, the more tormented a person was.

Blinking, Devora disengaged her soulsight. She wouldn't allow One Shot to fall into a pit of despair.

"Give her time, my friend." Master Monham patted Ben's shoulder. "There's something about you she likes. She will explain if given a little time."

Rae soon shuffled out of her room, doing her best to cover up the tears that were threatening to spill down her cheeks.

Devora noted that they were both equally upset. *Good, that means they both care.*

"I don't want to take too much of your time," Devora started. The sooner they figured out this plan, the sooner Devora could continue with the next part of the plan Tunri had shown her. And maybe she could help One Shot's romantic life as well.

Rae sucked back her tears, wearing the face that Devora had seen the first time they had met: guarded and hard.

"I will only help you into the Temple if you help me free the women trapped in there and take me and any others who want to flee out of Yekel," Rae said evenly.

"Done," Devora said.

Her quick response took Rae aback, shattering her hard exterior.

"What?"

Devora quirked a brow. "I don't want women to be held against their will in a sacrificial Temple. Of course, I'll help." She motioned to herself and One Shot. "We both will."

Rae's eyes darted to One Shot, who still kept his head down. "Both?"

Devora nodded. "Yes, both of us," she confirmed. "How do you plan to get us into the Temple unseen?"

Rae visibly relaxed at the mention of One Shot's assistance and joined them around the low table.

"The harvest festival starts tomorrow. The first day of the festival is filled with music, food, and wine." Rae shut her eyes and shook her head. "It's loud and chaotic, but it's the perfect distraction to sneak into the Temple."

"A good idea, Rae," Master Monham commented. "The first three days of the festival are always rambunctious."

"But won't people want to be in the Temple of Pahga during the festival to celebrate her?" Devora asked.

Rae shook her head. "According to Kadeshian law, the Temple is sacred. While she takes sacrifices and slaves, parties and dancing in Pagha's honor are not permitted in such a sacred place. The festival will mainly take place in the city plaza." Fiddling with the string around her neck, Rae added, "I actually didn't mind when the festival came around each year. It was one of the few times I could rest without being disturbed."

Devora watched Rae's gaze flick to One Shot for any kind of reaction, but he gave none.

Devora pursed her lips and elbowed him in the side. Flinching, his head shot up. For the first time since Devora had known him, One Shot glared at her. Luckily, Devora wasn't scared of glares or broody men, so she glared right back.

"Are you going to contribute to this conversation?"

The fire in his gaze dissolved. "Just tell me where to shoot. You're good at that."

Devora narrowed her eyes, ignoring the jab. "Yes, I am. You should be thankful for that, or we would've been killed long ago."

At her icy words, One Shot shrank back into himself.

"So, you'll sneak into the Temple during the festival," Master Monham said, trying to reign in the conversation and heightened emotions. "And then what?"

"Yes," Rae said. "From there, I'll work on getting the women out while you two search for Kanna. I'll show you where the stairs to the lower level are." A pained look crossed Rae's features. "Part of me hopes she isn't there and that she escaped. But the other part hopes she is, so that I *know* she'll escape."

"I understand," Devora agreed. "Where should we meet in two days?"

"The festival will begin just before dusk. I say we wait an hour in, that way the party is well underway before we meet at the outer wall where the current worksite is."

Devora pictured the half-built wall, remembering where One Shot worked. "Yes, that should do." She then grabbed her black veil and stood. "Thank you, Rae. You've been most helpful. I will be praying to Tunri for continued guidance and favor that our plan will succeed."

Rae rose and nodded. "Thank you for your help as well. Saving the women in the Temple is something I've been trying to accomplish alone for a long time."

"Too long," Master Monham added as he and One Shot got to their feet.

One Shot's neck hunched as his head brushed against Rae's low ceiling. Devora knew he was uncomfortable, but also wanted to make sure Rae and One Shot spoke before they left.

"Well, you're not alone anymore," Devora said with a smile. Reaching out, she grabbed Rae's hands and squeezed them tight. Surprisingly, Rae didn't pull away from the physical contact.

Leaning close, Devora whispered in Rae's ear. "If you talk to him, he'll understand. I didn't tell him anything."

Surprise covered Rae's face as Devora pulled back and offered her arm to Master Monham.

"Master Monham? Would you escort me back to your home?"

The old man chuckled and looped his arm through Devora's. "I would be honored, my lady."

With a knowing look, Devora placed her black veil over her head and exited the home with Master Monham.

When they were half-way to Master Monham's house, she heard One Shot and Rae talking and grinned.

"I was getting worried," Master Monham commented. "He seems gentle, but that look he gave you—" the old man blew out a breath and shook his head.

Devora laughed. "I've grown an immunity to glares from angry men. They don't frighten me much anymore."

As they entered Master Monham's home, Devora thought about all the angry glares the prisoners had given her. Even Matthias had thrown some her way.

Devora took the veil off and placed her hand on her chest. Her soul suddenly ached, thinking of Matthias. His wavy chestnut hair, strong shoulders, firm lips. Lips she wished she had spent more time kissing.

Devora folded the veil into a square and sighed. In two days, Matthias would be here. And if everything Tunri had shown her in her recent vision was correct, she wouldn't be anywhere near Yekel when Matthias arrived.

Chapter Twenty-Nine

Rae, Rae's House, Yekel

The warmth of Devora's gentle grip still lingered on Rae's hands.

You're not alone anymore.

The Beast of Fear tried to counter the statement, but the hope it brought to Rae's soul was too bright, frightening the Beast away.

Rae thought back to the sack of money Master Monham returned to her just two weeks ago, just before Nadia had come. He told her to trust Tunri. Rae thought the old man was crazy. But as she recalled the events of the past few weeks, she could see Tunri's hand in everything. With the help of Devora and Ben, the women trapped in the Temple would be finally free. And though Rae wanted to plan out exactly where all the women would go afterwards, she heard that same, strange voice from before say: *Trust.*

"Okay," Rae whispered to herself as she turned around.

Ben still stood hunched in her living space. Rae winced. It must have been painful and annoying to not fit properly anywhere.

Mustering up her confidence, she said, "I would like to explain myself."

He twisted his head to look at her. "Can we go outside?"

Nodding, Rae motioned to the open door. Ben took two steps, bent his knees then eased out of her home.

Taking a gray shawl with her, Rae followed him. The night air whispered sweet melodies of silence as they leaned against the side of her house. Rae never planned on telling so many people about her past. It was difficult with Nadia, but that had turned out okay. And, after what Devora said, Rae assumed Devora's Seeing abilities had somehow helped the prophet discern Rae's past too.

Rae tightened the shawl around her shoulders. She was thankful Devora hadn't told Ben anything. She now knew Devora respected her and thought of her as an equal, not beneath her because of what she'd done.

"So, Crimson Cord?" Ben asked, staring out into the dark night.

A soft wind whistled by in response.

Rae licked her lips, keeping her gaze focused forward. "Yes."

"Always?"

Rae furrowed her brow. "Are you asking if someone else fought you in the Fighter's Ring?" She shook her head. "It was me the entire time. Sorry about using your leg against you."

Ben placed his hand on his left thigh. "I would've done the same thing if I were you." He kicked a rock with the tip of his boot, sending it sailing toward the inner-city wall. "You fight really well. Where did you learn?"

Rae allowed herself to smile as she glanced over at him. His features were no longer hard and pained, but pensive.

"My father taught me. He said a woman should never be defenseless. He also said that, if he had a son, he would've taught him the same skills."

"Where did your father learn hemna?" Ben asked, peering down at her.

Rae held his gaze for a moment then looked away. "He fought in Tenton's army. Before the Fortress was the military academy, all men sixteen summers to fifty summers had to give two years to King Atol. If they survived battles with Kadesh, they could go home." Rae sighed. "I was only a small child when he left. But I remember Mami being so upset. She would open her bedroom window, get down on her knees, and pray to Tunri every night for Papi's safe return."

"And he returned safely?" Ben asked.

Rae's lips flattened as she nodded. "Only to be taken as a prisoner by the very nation he fought to defend."

"I'm sorry about your father," Ben whispered. "And your mother?"

Are you really going to tell him? the Beast of Fear cried, frantic. *He'll want nothing to do with us once he knows everything.*

Rae almost listened to the Beast. Almost.

Tightening her grip around her shawl. "She was taken to the Temple to serve the followers of Pahga."

Ben's eyes grew wide. It was the first sign of emotion Rae had seen of him since he discovered her secret. "What?"

"When Kadesh invaded, all women who were past fifteen summers and without any ailments or disabilities were taken."

Ben closed his eyes and leaned his head back against the wall, the fierce tightening of his fists the only indication of how furious he really was.

"And you?" he asked through clenched teeth.

Rae swallowed the lump in her throat. The Beast of Fear frantically called out to her, begging her to keep her mouth shut. But the new voice, the Voice of Hope encouraged her to trust, and all would be well.

"I was able to disguise Nadia and the other girls around our age as young boys. It may have been foolish, but it worked well enough to get them out of the city and closer to the outskirts near Grenly."

Rae never understood it, but the Kadeshian troops never ventured beyond the city of Yekel. If anyone could escape the city and make it to the country, they were free. She thought about the Wizard Wankle, about how his life was taken to make a point. No one could ever escape the city.

"I stayed behind to make sure they had all the time they needed."

Rae stared down at her scuffed-up boots. It was only the second time she'd talked about her past out loud, and she was already starting to cry.

"Rae," Ben whispered.

"I'm okay," she said quickly, wiping at the tears with the corner of her shawl. "The only other person who knows is Nadia. Master Monham would visit me and the others in the Temple to teach us about Tunri, so he already knew everything. And I think Devora saw into my thoughts or something." Rae laugh-sobbed as she tried to hide her puffy face from Ben.

"Yeah, she can do something like that," Ben replied, rubbing his neck. He blew out a breath. "You don't owe me any explanation. I understand the past being too painful to discuss."

"No," Rae answered quickly. She turned and grabbed his forearm. "You need to know I didn't kill the Wizard Wankle." Ben looked like he was about to reply, but Rae kept talking. "Many of the men who came to the Temple also brought gifts of thanks and payment. I saved these and with Kanna's help causing distractions, I was able to sneak out and barter them for coin. A year after that, I bought my own freedom."

Relaxing her grip, Rae shook her head. "When I left, I had only a few coins to my name. General Yada was furious that I'd scrounged up enough coin to buy my freedom, and he's been trying to punish me for it ever since. But by Kadeshian law, if a Temple Priestess has enough coin, she can free herself."

"So, you became the Crimson Cord to make coin and free the others?"

Rae craned her neck. Ben was staring at her not with disgust and regret, but pure adoration. Pleasant chills raced across Rae's skin.

"I used the only coin I had left to enter the Fighter's Ring." She gestured to herself. "And here I am."

Ben nodded then slowly wrapped his hand around hers. "But why crimson? Why not another color?"

Rae enjoyed the feel of his large, warm hand enveloping her own. She closed her eyes, remembering how General Yada loved her in red. Every shade, every kind of fabric, all of it red. When she was free, she thought she would hate the color. Instead, she decided to transform the color of her bondage into one of freedom. Other than a simple tan dress—which she burned—the thick red cord Rae wore around her belt was the only thing she took with her from the Temple.

Opening her eyes, Rae laced her fingers through Ben's. "Crimson is my color of strength."

Ben smiled. "I like you in any color."

Heat filled Rae's cheeks, and she looked away. "Were you angry because you thought I killed the Wizard?"

Ben sighed, stroking the back of her hand with his thumb. "I hardly think I can judge someone for that. I was upset because I thought you killed him when you could've come to me for help. I was mad because I never want you, or anyone else I care about, to bear the burden of taking a life. It's not an easy weight to carry."

Rae kept her gaze focused on his thumb creating mesmerizing circles. "Those men deserved what you did to them."

"Yes," Ben agreed. "But they should've been found guilty in all eyes first, then sentenced to death. I've been learning from Devora about the law and the ways of Tunri. It's helped me understand that more."

"Tunri is okay with murder?" Rae asked, tilting her neck to look at him.

Ben shook his head. "Tunri requires justice. Though the men who violated Mara were guilty, it shouldn't have been my hand that dealt with them." He bowed his head. "I'm still working on trying to figure it all out."

Rae chewed her bottom lip. Mami and Papi had taught her about Tunri when she was a child. But after Yekel was burned and invaded, Rae wanted nothing to do with a God who would allow such horrible things to happen. Yet, since she'd met Devora and Ben, Rae felt her soul open to learning more about Tunri.

Taking both of Ben's large hands in hers, she peered up at him. His shaggy, dark hair fell between his dark eyes, highlighting his pale skin. It was so much lighter than her sun-kissed tone, but she didn't care.

"I would like to learn more, too," she said quietly.

Ben let out a heavy breath, and Rae's pulse jolted upward.

"I would like to kiss you," he whispered.

Rae hesitated, wanting to do the same, but she knew she wasn't ready. Though she'd experienced some bouts of hope, her heart was still burdened, her soul still weary. If she were to kiss Ben, she would want to be free of her chains and ready to embrace a new future.

"I don't think I'm ready," she confessed, lowering her gaze.

Now you've done it, the Beast of Fear chittered. It had been quiet during the entire conversation up until now.

But then Rae felt Ben softly place his hand on her cheek and lift her face toward him. "You can take all the time you need. I'll always be waiting for you."

If Rae's heart could've leapt out of her chest, it would have. Every other man she'd known had forced himself on her, making the thought of love something vile and undesirable.

She feared Ben would be disgusted at her past in the Temple. She feared that he would be horrified by her fights in the Dark Market. But he'd seen past all that. He'd been able to see who she truly was underneath: a broken and beaten soul who just wanted to be loved without anything expected in return.

Another clink, like a chain being snapped, reverberated in her chest and the Beast of Fear vanished.

Tears welled in Rae's eyes again, and Ben's gaze went from adoration to panic.

"Oh no, I'm sorry. I didn't mean to upset you. I'm not good at saying the right things."

"No, no." She giggled through her tears. "You didn't do anything wrong. What you said was perfect." She squeezed his hands. "I don't think I'm ready for anything too intimate right now. But could we try a hug?"

Ben's grin reached from ear to ear. It was the first time Rae had seen him fully smile since she'd met him. "I'd like that."

Since Ben's neck was too tall and her arms too short, Rae settled on wrapping her arms around his thin waist. Her head barely came to the base of his chest. But even then she could hear the steady rhythm of his heart thumping against her ear.

Ben wrapped his long arms around her shoulders, pulling her close, but not suffocating her. He bent his head, so his cheek laid on top of her short blonde hair.

"You still smell like oranges," he mumbled.

"Is that okay?" she asked cautiously.

She could feel him smile as he replied, "I love oranges."

Chapter Thirty

Matthias, Tenton Army Camp, Ballear

Matthias placed the stone paperweight at the edge of the map of Tenton. A series of possible pathways to the southern region scattered before him. Thankfully, his battalion had marched to Ballear from Juro with little to no issues. Once they set up camp, Matthias barricaded himself in his tent. Though Devora had given him the timeframe, it was up to him to figure out the best form of attack, and soon. In just two days, Tenton's siege over Yekel would begin.

Furrowing his brow, Matthias traced his fingers over the path he decided to take. He hoped for at least five thousand soldiers, but King Atol said he would have to make do with two thousand. Matthias knew the war against Kadesh could spare the extra men, so he wasn't sure why the king was forcing him to use less. Regardless of the reason, it provided a challenge Matthias would rise against. If the king thought he couldn't take Yekel with only two thousand men, Matthias would prove him wrong.

Reaching for his quill, Matthias dipped it in the bowl of ink and made an adjustment to the route. He'd sent word to Devora, telling her of his plans, but had yet to hear back. His other spies around Tenton informed him Kadesh was still in the dark about his battalion moving south, and Matthias wanted to keep it that way.

"Captain Blake, sir," Sir Tocha called from outside Matthias' tent. "Permission to enter, sir?"

Matthias blotted the fresh ink until it dried then rolled up the map. "Permission granted."

Sir Tocha entered then placed a fist over his chest and bowed.

Matthias studied the young soldier with flaming red hair. He was barely eighteen summers. Though Matthias was only twenty summers, he'd seen enough battle and war for forty. But this was Tocha's first assignment outside of the Fortress and, so far, he'd handled everything with perfection.

"Take a seat, Tocha," Matthias said, pouring the two of them a drink. "You look exhausted."

Sir Tocha hesitated then slumped into the wooden chair in front of Matthias's makeshift desk made from two barrels and a board. The knight rubbed his heavily shadowed eyes. "I'm not used to sleeping on the ground yet, sir." The young man's cheeks turned pink with embarrassment.

Matthias chuckled and handed Tocha the steel cup. "I've slept on the ground many times, and I still prefer my bed to dirt." He took a swig, enjoying the sharp burn of the spirits down his throat. "Battle, war, it never gets easier, Tocha. We just have to pray that one day there will be peace."

Sir Tocha stared at the clear liquid inside the cup. "I know, sir. My Pa was killed in the Battle of Rendo. When I categorized to work at the Fortress, Ma was petrified the same thing would happen to me."

Matthias sat in his wooden chair. Since he took Tristan's place at the Fortress, he'd heard many of the same stories. And each one broke his heart. Because of his quick thinking on the battlefield, many men's lives were saved, and they could return home. But that wasn't the case for all of them and it weighed heavily on Matthias.

"I will do everything in my power to keep you and all the others safe," Matthias promised.

He knew it was an impossible promise, but he had to try. After King Atol forced Matthias to start spending more time at the palace, he knew his access to information would be more limited than at the Fortress. So, with Warden Hazor's permission, Matthias sent many of his trusted sources out as scouts. Most of them reported back to him in creative ways: smoke signals, codes. But when he didn't hear back from some of them, his heart gained another burden, knowing they'd most likely been killed.

Matthias swirled the spirits in his cup. At times like these, he wished he knew where Warden Hazor had sent Jacques. The warden had chosen a special assignment for Jacques before the ball, but the warden had been tight-lipped about it. Matthias just wished he could know that, if he needed to, he could reach his friend. He and Jacques had known each other for years, and Matthias considered the knight more of a brother than a friend. When Matthias first met Jacques, he was baffled at how Jacques could gain a soldier's trust after a single conversation. While Matthias had known some of the men in his battalion for years, they still only said a word or two to him. The soldiers and inmates at the Fortress respected and even liked Jacques, while they only feared Matthias.

Staring at the spirits in his glass, Matthias took another sip, the liquid burning down his throat. He wasn't Jacques, and he never would be. Though Matthias was rough around the edges, he was fiercely loyal to his men and those he considered his family. Nothing would stop him from keeping them safe.

Shaking his head, Matthias shot back the last of his drink. "I've distracted you from your purpose here," he said to Sir Tocha. "What's happened?"

Sir Tocha took the tiniest sip of the liquid and puckered his lips. Matthias struggled not to laugh. "We've captured two men trying to sneak into our encampment," Sir Tocha explained easily.

Matthias shot up, slamming his cup on his desk. "What? Why didn't you say so sooner?" He grabbed his military coat and slung it over his shoulders. "Show me."

Sir Tocha sprang up, dropping his cup on the ground. The spirits seeped into the dark ground around his dirtied boots. "Apologies, sir. This way." He saluted and hurried out of the tent.

Matthias sighed and buttoned his coat. Adjusting the captain's rank on his chest, he followed Sir Tocha through the camp of soldiers. The sun had been set for an hour, but a few souls still sat around campfires telling stories. They stiffened and saluted as he walked by. Matthias nodded in return. The only way these soldiers were able to have a few moments of peace before battle was because Matthias was constantly planning. His mind never stopped working, never rested. Sometimes it was invigorating. Other times it was maddening. Learning different hobbies helped: how to wield a new weapon, a new fighting style, a new card game. It helped fuse his restless mind into something meaningful instead of spiraling over past mistakes and regrets.

As Matthias followed Sir Tocha toward the edge of the camp he thought about his card game of Kings with Devora. It had been a while since someone beat him. Well, beat him fairly. Many of the soldiers in the Fortress claimed victory over him by cheating and were severely punished for it.

But Devora beat him fairly and he loved her all the more for it. He prayed when he arrived in Yekel, they would be reunited, and he could explain everything to her in person.

Sir Tocha stood outside a tan tent, waiting. Two Tentonian soldiers in shining silver armor flanked each side of the opening.

"We've bound them in here, sir," the soldier on the left said. A scar ran over his lip from his first battle trying to secure the eastern border.

Matthias analyzed the soldiers. They were both from Grenly. Though they weren't brothers, they had supported each other through their time working in the Fortress.

"When did you capture them, Sir Baynard?" Matthias asked.

Satisfaction rolled over him as Sir Baynard blinked in surprise. Most captains didn't care to learn their soldiers' names. Little did Matthias's men know that he made a point to learn every soldier's name that went to battle with him. If his men were willing to give their lives to protect Tenton, the least Matthias could do was to learn who they were and from where they came.

"Only a half hour ago, sir," Sir Baynard replied.

As Matthias moved toward the tent, the other knight, Sir Pent added, "Be careful of the smaller man, sir. He's quite wild."

"I'll make do, Sir Pent," Matthias said, keeping his gaze fixed on the tent.

Giving each other a sidelong glance, the two soldiers peeled back the tent flaps. Darkness inked the tent black, but Matthias could make out two figures gagged and bound to the central pole.

"Tocha, a lantern," he called.

Sir Tocha's arm extended into the tent, holding a lantern. The young man himself, however, stayed completely outside.

Reaching back, Matthias grabbed the light and shone it at the two men. The smaller man squinted while the other jerked away from the light.

A smirk ticked at the corner of Matthias's lips. "What do we have here?"

Spinning around, Matthias exited the tent and handed the lantern to Tocha. "Cover their heads and bring them to my tent immediately. Good work, gentlemen. Tell Gerard I said to give you each an extra helping of rations in the morning."

Pride radiated off the soldiers as they entered the tent and untied the prisoners.

In ten minutes' time, Matthias was back at his makeshift desk, waiting for Sir Tocha and the others to deliver the prisoners. His mind was focused and ready to deal with them as he pleased.

"Come on, you!" Sir Baynard's voice strained.

"Hold on to him tight, Pent!" Sir Tocha commanded. "He's smaller than both of us."

A yelp sounded from Sir Pent, and it took everything within Matthias to not peek out of his tent to see what was happening. Finally, the soldiers and two prisoners entered. Sir Baynard's helmet sat askew on his head as he huffed and threw the first prisoner into a chair. Sir Tocha did the same with the second prisoner, leaving Sir Pent, staring wide eyed in the corner.

Matthias held back his defeat. *If they can't handle a few scraggly prisoners, how are we going to take back a whole city?*

Tenting his fingers, Matthias placed them against his lips. That was a worry for another day. Right now, he needed to deal with the men who tried to infiltrate his camp.

"Leave us."

"But sir—" Sir Tocha was cut off by Matthias waving him away. "Of course, sir," Sir Tocha replied swiftly. With another salute, the three soldiers left.

Once he knew the men were gone, Matthias crossed his arms over his chest and leaned back into his chair. "Care to explain why you're sneaking into my camp and scaring my soldiers?"

The first prisoner broke out of his bonds and pulled the sack off his head. "It was just for a bit of fun, brother," Tristan said with a grin.

The sack mussed his hair, and a fair amount of dirt caked his cheeks, but Matthias would know that sly grin anywhere. He'd seen it too many times before something went awry.

"Hey Cap!" Nadia grinned, pulling the sack from her head. "I always keep a set of small shears in my pocket for times like these." She pulled out the miniscule clippers that were no bigger than the palm of her hand.

"You need to make me some of those," Tristan commented.

"You'll have to pay," Nadia remarked. "I don't make things for free."

"But you made One Shot and Devora a ton of things before we left," Tristan whined.

Nadia shrugged. "They're my friends."

Tristan scoffed, and feigned offense. "And I'm not? After all we've been through?"

Matthias groaned and rubbed his eyes with his fingers. "Why do you have a beard, Lapith?"

Nadia stroked the thick gray hairs coating her chin. "Isn't it nice? Master Monham let me use his beard clippings."

Matthias shook his head, unable to believe what was happening.

"Hey, it fooled your soldiers."

"Touché," Matthias replied, unable to resist a smirk. He studied the odd pair. "So, why are you really here? And please take off the beard."

"She can't," Tristan said, donning a wicked grin. "I told her not to use maisie tree sap, but she did anyway."

Nadia pinched a tuft of hair and pulled. She winced. "It's hardened now."

Matthias rubbed his forehead, his patience growing thinner by the second. "Fine. Leave the beard. What news do you bring? Is Devora okay?"

"Thanks for your concern, brother," Tristan said with a pout. "We're only family."

"Family doesn't stab each other in the back, Tristan," Matthias clipped. "Once you prove you're actually loyal, I'll start treating you like my family again."

Tristan silenced at the remark and Nadia chuckled. "I've missed your frankness, Cap. Devora is okay, but Sir Blakesalot is not." Nadia's face turned somber. "We're not sure what happened, but One Shot found him dead outside Master Mon-ham's home."

Matthias closed his eyes. He knew it was just a silly crow, but it was a silly crow who helped him communicate with those he cared about. "Was my message still attached to... Sir Blakesalot?"

Why was the deteriorating crow named after him?

Nadia bobbed her head. "Yes, which was the confusing part. Dev thinks it was a warning. That someone high up knows something is going on, but they don't know what. My bet is on the creepy general."

Matthias quirked a brow. "Creepy general?" He thought back to his research on Kadesh's invasion of Yekel. "General Yada?"

"He's oddly obsessed with Nadia's friend, Rae," Tristan piped in waving a hand. "Though I don't know why. She's rude and has no hair."

Nadia took the tiny shears and gently poked Tristan in the bicep.

"Ow! Why'd you do that?" he yelped, scrambling away from her.

"Don't talk about Rae. She kept us hidden, and she didn't have to."

"Will you two stop acting like children?" Matthias barked, slamming his fists on the wood panel that made his desk. The panel creaked under the force. His patience had reached its end. "I have two thousand men waiting for my direction. Two thousand lives in my hands, and you two can't stop bickering about nonsense."

Matthias unfurled his fists and stood, ignoring the blanched faces staring back at him. He took a breath to calm the beast writhing inside of him. This was not the time to lose control.

"Now," Matthias said, turning around. "If you're ready to tell me something important, proceed. If not, get out of my tent."

Nadia's eyes widened as she handed over a parchment tied with a piece of twine. "Devora said to give this to you. She calculated that, if you received her first note, you would be just east of Ballear. She sent us to you on Vinn because of what happened to Sir Blakesalot." Nadia tugged at the gray hair on her cheek. "I also think she saw a vision she isn't telling anyone about because she practically forced me and Tristan to leave."

"Where is Vinn now?"

"We left him inside Grenly's jungles," Tristan replied, his playful demeanor dampened. "Devora and One Shot left him there before they made it to Yekel, and it seemed to work well. It's really the only place to hide a giant white elk."

Matthias nodded as he unrolled the note.

I found her.

I'm sorry.

He scanned the note again, trying to find something more. Nadia and Tristan looked at him like he was crazy when he flicked drops of water on the parchment. But the scroll only went limp.

He let out a frustrated breath. "Do you know what she's planning?"

They shook their heads simultaneously.

"Devora and One Shot were going to meet with Rae after we left to plan something," Nadia explained. "Rae used to serve in the Temple of Pahga. Warden Hazor wanted me to find more information about the statue in there."

"The Temple of Pahga?" Matthias's mind churned quickly. He'd heard some of Kadesh's fascination with the goddess, Pahga, and the questionable practices that went along with the religion. Though he never realized it was happening in Yekel.

Matthias studied Devora's note again. It all made sense. Where else would King Atol and Queen Leza hide the Seer who prophesized their untimely deaths? No one would look for Kanna, his mother, in a besieged city.

"And Rae, your friend, she has a way in?"

Nadia shrugged. "I guess so. She was working toward freeing the women from the Temple when she said she'd help Devora and One Shot."

"I did hear a festival honoring Pahga would happen soon," Tristan said, tapping his square chin. He shrugged. "Maybe they'll use that as a distraction?"

Matthias stood quickly. Folding Devora's note, he placed it in his pocket before striding to another table pressed against the side of the tent. He grabbed a stack of parchments and laid them out across his tabletop. They were Nadia's previous drawings of the city.

Matthias pointed to the half-finished section of the outer wall. "Have they completed this section yet?"

"It was still unfinished when we left a day or so ago," Tristan replied, peering at the map.

Matthias shuffled the papers to find the one with the marble building on it. "And this is the Temple, correct?"

Nadia and Tristan nodded simultaneously.

Matthias gathered the papers, then called out, "Sir Tocha, ready the men to depart at dawn."

"Yes, sir," Sir Tocha called as his hurried footsteps crunched against the dirt.

"Cap, what is it?" Nadia asked, jumping up. "Have you figured out Devora's plan?"

His heart weighed heavy at the question. He was both elated and devastated when he read the note.

"She's found my mother, and she's going to try to rescue her alone."

Chapter Thirty-One

Rae, Rae's House, Yekel

Surprisingly, work was canceled the next day due to preparations for the festival. Rae received the news just as she was walking out her door. Bleary-eyed, she accepted the good news without question and sprinted back to her bed. The extra few hours of sleep were bliss, especially after she stayed up way too late with Ben. Even after he left, she had a difficult time getting to sleep. It felt as if the weight of the world was on her, and her mind kept generating new questions.

What if I lose the key? What if it doesn't work? What if the festival isn't as lively this year? What if Devora and Ben decide not to trust me? What if I stop trusting myself?

On and on it went. Surprisingly, Rae didn't hear the Beast of Fear asking these questions. It was just her own mind worrying, and it was refreshing. To a point.

One hour ticked by without sleep. Then a second one. That's when Rae finally heard the Voice of Hope say: *Trust.* And that was all it took to calm her frantic thoughts and whisk her to sleep.

Rae awoke around midafternoon and began her preparations for that evening. Her hair had grown fast since she decided to stop shearing it. Almost half an inch of white-blonde hair covered her head. She knew she had to blend in with the darkness. Instead of reaching for her usual red mesh, Rae tied a black scarf around her head and face, leaving only her eyes showing.

Rae slipped on the rest of her black Crimson Cord disguise, secretly happy she hadn't gotten rid of it. She'd used it for so many fights, the leather was worn and probably the most comfortable thing she owned.

The final piece of her ensemble, the crimson cord, lay on her bed, and Rae hesitated to wrap it around her waist. If anyone saw her wearing it, she would instantly be recognized and arrested. Or worse, killed on the spot. But something within her encouraged her to bring it along. After mulling the idea over, Rae decided to tie the cord around her waist but to tuck it under her tunic so it would be hidden.

After she was dressed, Rae secured the skeleton key around her neck. She then paced around her home, too nervous to do anything else while she waited for the time to pass. She prayed a few times, but it felt awkward and strange, so she just hoped whoever was listening would help her.

Finally, it was time.

Peering out her window, Rae watched the festival lanterns light up the city. Jovial music comprised of fluttering pipes and windchimes swirled through the air. The deep bass of the drums soon followed. Laughter and songs bounced on the wind, and Rae could almost see the elaborate costumes the Kadeshians wore to honor the Goddess Pahga. The festival had begun.

Dashing over the threshold of her home, Rae hurried toward the inner wall of the city. The skeleton key thumped against her chest as she pushed her legs as fast as they could go. She didn't want to be out in the open any longer than necessary. Soon enough, she saw the outlines of Devora, Master Monham, and Ben.

Slowing her pace, Rae nodded to the trio.

"Right on time," Devora said, returning Rae's nod with one of her own.

Though the fabric still covered the Seer's face, Devora had tied it around her head, similar to how Rae used to wear the red mesh in the Fighter's Ring. Devora's long ebony braid swung around her shoulder, blending into the rest of her black clothing.

Rae caught her breath then looked at Ben. As usual, he was dressed from head to toe in black. The only thing missing was the orange scarf he had bought from her.

When he noticed Rae's gaze, he quickly said, "I still have it." Passing his crossbow to the other hand, Ben pulled a corner of the bright fabric from his pocket. "It gives me luck."

Rae laughed. "How so?"

"I bought it when I first met you."

Heat rushed to Rae's cheeks, but she enjoyed the compliment.

Devora cleared her throat. "Master Monham agreed to be a lookout and to guide the women from the Temple back to your home. Once the last woman escapes the Temple, Master Monham will care for them until you return. Understand?"

Rae suddenly realized why Devora had gained the respect of the soldiers in the Fortress. Up until now, she had been the epitome of a lady: kind, gracious, and elegant. But tonight, she was a warrior, primed and ready for the battle ahead. Rae admired the fact that Devora could balance both roles so well.

"Understood," Rae replied with a nod.

"Good. Let's get going." Devora turned toward the wall and headed into the city.

Ben followed behind, keeping to the shadows. He leaned over and brushed Rae's hand as he went, sending her already jittering nerves into a frenzy.

"Tunri be with you, Rae," Master Monham said gently. Rae spun around to find the old man covered in a dark cloak.

"Thank you, Master Monham, for everything." Rae rubbed her gloved hands against each other. "And you were right. I didn't need the extra coin from fighting to free the women. Tunri provided, just like you said He would. I've decided to use the coin to help someone else."

Master Monham smiled. "He has, Rae. All will be well."

Rae chewed on her lip. "If anything happens to me…"

"Nothing will happen to you, Rae. Tunri is with you. Go." He gently shooed her toward the wall.

Rae flung her arms out and gave Master Monham a hug. The old man stood shocked, then returned the embrace. "Thank you for loving me when no one else did," she whispered before she sprinted toward the city.

Boisterous drums and trumpets blared through the city streets. Jovial dancing tunes swayed in an alluring beat. Luscious scents of roasted meat, mulled wine, and sweet cakes spiraled through the air. Rae resisted the urge to swipe some samples.

Every nook and cranny of the city plaza was congested with people, making the back alleyways clear and the easiest route to the lower level of the Temple. Rae couldn't understand why anyone wanted to be in the middle of such a loud place with so many people. It had to be because of the food.

Ben stalked ahead of them, nearly becoming a shadow himself as he kept to the dark patches of the streets. Devora and Rae waited a few streets behind. Once Ben whistled low, they rushed to his side.

"Almost there," he whispered, his eyes checking everything around them.

After traveling two more streets, they reached the Temple.

Sweat pooled at the back of Rae's neck as she stared down the building she swore she'd never enter again. She thought she would be more frightened, but ever since the Beast of Fear fled, she hadn't felt terrified. The iron door she escaped out of two years ago stared back at her, just as unwavering as when she first entered the Temple.

"Okay, Rae, it's your time to shine," Devora called over her shoulder.

She and Ben stood guard, covering Rae in case anything happened. Rae had never worked in a team before. She enjoyed not being alone.

Licking her lips, Rae pulled the skeleton key from around her neck. Instantly, Devora whipped her head around.

"Where did you get that?" she asked.

Rae paused, confused. "From the Whispering Hall in the Dark Market."

Devora leaned in closer, getting a better look at the key. "There's a dangerous aura coming from it," she muttered. "Be careful, Rae."

"I will."

Gripping the metal, Rae took a breath, and plunged the key into the iron door.

Chapter Thirty-Two

Rae, The Temple of Pahga, Yekel

When the key didn't turn easily, Rae panicked. Clenching her jaw, she shoved the iron into the lock once more. A light click echoed from the lock, and Rae's shoulders relaxed. The key turned, allowing her to push the iron door inward.

Musk, perfume, and a whole plethora of scents emanated from the lower level of the Temple. Rae held her breath, worried the smells would trigger unwanted memories.

"Follow me," she called back to Devora and Ben. "I'll show you where the stairwell to the dungeon leads."

Gathering her courage, Rae stepped over the threshold, praying she would soon be out of the Temple once and for all.

The moment Devora and Ben were inside, Ben closed the door, cloaking them in darkness. Devora struck some flint, and a few sparks flew in the shadows. In a matter of moments, a small lantern lit the stone hall. Rae studied the design of the lantern, realizing that even though it was half the size of a regular lantern, it was twice as bright.

"Did Nadi make that?"

"Yes," Devora replied. Rae could see her grin through the black mesh. "Along with a few other surprises." She patted the satchel on her side. "But I'll save those for later."

Rae turned around and led the group down the dank, narrow corridor. The lower level of the Temple wasn't constructed of fine marble like the top, but jagged, dark stone. Rae remembered sprinting down the stairs, trying to find an exit. Unfortunately, other than the front entrance and the door they just came through, there weren't any. Until she'd met Kanna.

Rae came to a section of corridors leading in different directions. She remembered the one on the left led to the stairwell spiraling up into the main area of the Temple. The corridor to the right led to the stairwell to the dungeon, and the central corridor kept going straight into the supply room.

"You'll want to go that way." Rae pointed to the far-right corridor. "You'll go straight for about thirty paces and then a spiraling stairwell will be on the left. At the bottom of the stairs there's a cell carved out of the rock. It's newer than anything else in the Temple, so I wouldn't be surprised if it were created right after Kadesh invaded." Rae tugged the black mesh off of her nose. "If Kanna is still there, please rescue her first."

Devora peeled the black mesh from her face then eyed the corridor. "She will be free."

Extending her arm, Devora handed the small lantern to Ben. "One Shot, keep Rae safe. Do not come to find me until every enslaved woman is gone from the Temple, understood?"

Ben studied Devora for a moment, and Rae caught the look. It was a look Rae had seen many times while in the Temple and the Dark Market. Devora was hiding something. But what?

"Are you sure?" he asked, taking the lantern from her hand. "Warden Hazor—"

Devora flicked her wrist. "Warden Hazor isn't here, and neither is Matthias. That puts me in charge, and I've told you the plan. Not until every woman has fled."

Ben lips thinned but nodded. "Understood."

Devora gave a satisfied nod then turned to Rae. "Your assistance has been pivotal in helping us reach our goal. Thank you for being willing to trust two strangers." Devora bowed her head.

"You've done the same for me." Rae returned the bow, shocked that Devora held her in such esteem.

"Trust Tunri, Rae," Devora said as she headed toward the dark corridor. "He's already written your happily ever after."

With two more steps, Devora disappeared down the stairwell, leaving Rae and Ben alone.

"I don't know what she's planning, but I've seen that look before," Ben commented, swinging the lantern toward Rae. "Should we go after her?"

Rae thought about it but knew not to interfere with Devora's plan. The woman seemed meticulous with details, and if she planned a way to save Kanna, regardless of where she was, Rae would leave her to it.

Rae shook her head. "No, she knows what she's doing."

"That's what scares me," Ben replied.

The two of them crept quietly toward the stairwell on the left. As her feet climbed each stone step, Rae couldn't stop the memories. How many times had she fled down the steps, seeking peace and guidance from Kanna? Some of the women were content to stay in their rooms all day and night, but not Rae. She needed to be free. And the dungeon was the closest to freedom she could get.

Once they were halfway up the stairs, Ben asked, "Are you okay? You seem incredibly calm for coming back here."

Rae's heart warmed at his concern. "That's because you can't read my thoughts and feel how jumpy my nerves are."

Ben chuckled. "I think I can help with one of those things."

She soon felt his large hand take hers and her stomach flopped. Though her fingers and palms were covered by her gloves, she still enjoyed the press of his hand against hers.

"Does that help?"

"It may have made it worse," she teased, and when he squeezed her hand, she knew he understood the joke.

As they came upon the main floor of the Temple, Rae stopped and listened. Just because the Temple was closed off during the festival in previous years didn't mean it would be this year. But after a few moments of silence, Rae concluded her assumptions were correct.

"Let's leave the lantern on the landing," she told Ben. "That way we can direct the women toward the light, and they can find their way out of the Temple."

"Good idea," Ben agreed, reaching past her to put the lantern down. The length between where Ben stood, and the top step was quite a distance. Yet he reached it with ease.

Impressed, Rae whispered. "Are you trying to show off?"

He gave a small grin. "Is it working?

She smirked. "Yes."

"Then yes."

Pulling her scarf back over her nose and mouth, Rae crept up the final stairs. Regretfully, she let go of Ben's hand, knowing she needed to be ready to defend herself if General Yada had posted any soldiers within the Temple. He never had in past years, but with declaration of a murderer on the loose, he may have added some soldiers to show muster.

Rae peeked her head around the corner of the doorway. No soldiers, no visitors. Just that horrible statue of Pahga and the rows of doors.

A spark of rage ignited in Rae's gut, surprising her. She thought the Beast of Rage was gone.

Oh, I'm still here, the Beast growled. *I'll always be here because you'll always be angry.*

Rae clenched her hands into fists and tuned the Beast of Rage out. She had to focus.

"I'll hide there."—Ben pointed to the corner beside the statue of Pahga—"It's dark and a good vantage point. That way, if we get any unwanted visitors, I can take care of them."

"Okay," Rae agreed. She hesitated then added, "Be careful."

Ben reached out and stroked her cheek. "You, too." Unlatching his crossbow from his back, he jogged to the space and melted into the shadows.

Rae sucked in a breath and headed toward the first door. She wouldn't allow herself to be overcome with emotion. Not now. She had a job to do.

Removing the skeleton key from around her neck, Rae slid it into the first door with the Kadeshian symbol for the number fifteen. Rae freed only a few women with her earnings from her fights in the Dark Market. Despite her hard work, General Yada filled the vacancies easily.

Rae glared at the symbol, hating how General Yada captured such young women, but kept her emotions in check. The Beast of Rage prowled, ready to consume her. If she gave into her rage, all of her planning and sacrifice would be for nothing.

The lock quietly clicked then eased open. Rae had never been inside the other rooms. She only met the others during their daily washings. If their treatment from their visitors wasn't bad enough, the isolation the Temple forced was maddening.

Huge palm trees, taller than Ben, lined the room. Thick, brown carpet covered the floor, emulating what Rae assumed to be the jungle ground. Pops of vibrant orange, pink, and white lilies cascaded from the ceiling, wrapping around the tree trunks. In the center lay a pile of lime and forest green pillows. Sleeping soundly between them was a young girl.

Rae stopped in her tracks, horrified. This girl wasn't Yekelian. She wasn't even from Tenton. Based on her dark skin and onyx hair, she was from Kadesh.

Tentonian women weren't enough, the Beast of Rage commented. *The general started taking his own kind.*

Rae gritted her teeth. She didn't care where the young woman was from: no one deserved to be trapped in this horrible place. Slowly, Rae approached the woman. She was still sound asleep. Rae recognized the peaceful look. Having no visitors to serve was a blessing.

Pulling the black mesh to her chin, Rae gently shook the young woman's shoulder.

The woman's long, dark lashes fluttered before she jumped awake.

"I didn't mean to sleep, Master!" she shouted, scampering away.

Trained like an animal, the Beast of Rage crooned, stoking the small spark of fury in Rae's chest. *How unfair.*

Rae tried to ignore the voice, but the Beast was right. The poor girl looked like a frightened deer.

"It's okay," Rae whispered. "I'm getting you out of here."

The young woman's big doe eyes blinked at her. "How?"

Rae extended her hand. "Trust me."

The girl hesitated, then took Rae's hand.

"Gather anything you have and quickly," Rae ordered.

The young woman was quick as a flash as she threw a few items into a sack and tied it with a string. She grabbed a dark green scarf and wrapped it around her voluminous curls and thin shoulders. Rae recognized it as one of the scarves she made.

The girl gave a small gasp. "I know you! You're Rae. You're the one who escaped and helped Trina and Lila."

The acknowledgement stroked Rae's pride, but she forced herself not to dwell on it. "Yes, and now you will too. Let's go."

Rae was careful not to touch the girl, knowing how much she'd disliked people man-handling her. But she still tried to hurry the young woman along. The girl slipped on a pair of brown boots and followed closely behind Rae.

Before they exited back into the main floor of the Temple, Rae placed her scarf back on her nose and checked the space. Still empty.

Spinning back to the girl, Rae said, "Follow the light down the stairwell. When you come to three corridors, go right. There's a door that's been unlocked. Push it open and flee from this place. Head to the unfinished section of the outer wall. There is an elderly man there. He is kind and will lead you to safety."

The young woman's eyes spun with all the information, and Rae knew she was losing time.

"What's your name?"

The girl tightened her hand around the sack. "Farrah."

"Farrah," Rae said with a smile. "You're free."

A new life sprung into Farrah's lifeless eyes. She slung her arms around Rae's neck. "Thank you."

Without another word, Farrah headed toward the stairwell.

Protect her, Rae prayed to Tunri, hoping that, for once, He would listen.

Rae opened the next door with the number seventeen on it. This woman was older and as soon as Rae pulled down her scarf, she knew exactly who Rae was.

"Are you here to free us?" she asked, already packing her things. Her curly brown hair sprung back from her face, waving in the air as she rushed around.

"Yes."

"Thank Tunri," the girl cried. "I've been praying for deliverance for so long."

Rae instructed the woman where to go and the woman repeated it back to Rae, just to make sure she understood.

"I'm not going to mess this up," she said with a firm nod. "Thank Tunri for second chances and a new life." She kissed Rae on both cheeks and darted toward the stairwell.

Rae knew the women in the next two rooms, but it was odd that they acted the same as the first two, almost as if all the priestesses had rehearsed the same speech.

Curiosity at how each of the women seemed to expect her tinged Rae's thoughts.

How could they have known I was coming?

When she unlocked the door with the number twenty-eight, a strawberry-blonde woman stood waiting.

"Praise Tunri," Rosa said, tears rolling down her face. "I didn't believe it when I saw it, but here you are."

Rae stood, confused. "Some have already fled. It's your turn, Rosa."

Rosa nodded hastily and headed toward the open door. "Yes, of course, thank you, Rae. We are forever in your debt."

Rae repeated the same instructions, and Rosa nodded fervently, not blinking as she took in every detail.

"Tunri be with you," Rosa whispered.

"Wait," Rae called out. She didn't want to keep Rosa from freedom, but she had to know. "How did you know I was coming?"

Rosa grinned. "A week ago, we all had the same dream that a figure clothed in black was coming to save us. Not all of us believed it. Most of us didn't. But a few did and thank Tunri for their faith because you have come."

A swirl of elation and confusion battered Rae's mind.

A dream? Did Tunri really use me *for something good?*

"Thank you," Rae said. "For telling me. Now go."

Rosa blew Rae a kiss then scurried toward the light.

Rae flew through the final doors, greeting each of her former acquaintances and hurrying them on their way. Each told her what Rosa said. They received a dream of her coming. As Rae heard each story, she began to realize that, though she thought Tunri had forgotten her and could never use someone like her, He'd planned on using her to free these women all along.

The thought energized Rae as she placed her key in the last door. The number was higher than the others, forty-five, and Rae thought of her own mother. Was she formerly in this room? She had never discovered what happened to her.

But as she turned the key in the lock, the chilling voice of General Yada reached her ears.

"Right on time, as always, Rae."

Chapter Thirty-Three

Devora, Temple of Pahga, Yekel

Devora hurried down the dark stone steps, following the purple light from her vision. Careful not to trip, she pulled out another small lantern from her pack. This one didn't require fire, but only the turn of a knob. Trusting Nadia, Devora did as her friend instructed. As soon as she twisted the small knob, something clicked, and a spark ignited in the lantern. The wick quickly caught and illuminated the dark space.

"Thank you, Nadia," Devora whispered as she hurried down the steps.

She didn't have much time. Rae and Ben would be occupied, but they weren't who she was worried about. She knew that as soon as Matthias read her note he would be charging toward Yekel to stop her. She expected it and hoped he would come at full speed. Yekel needed to be saved, and Matthias was the man for the job.

Yet, as much as Devora wanted to see him and face this evil together, freeing Kanna was something she had to do alone.

Once she reached the bottom step, the haphazardly cut cell stood before her. It was smaller than the cells in the Fortress. Devora extended the light. Empty, just like she knew it would be. Though the disappointment still weighed upon her soul.

Devora shone the lantern around to find no other cells, just rock.

"A cell for a single prisoner," she pondered aloud.

Warden Hazor said Kanna was imprisoned for revealing a prophecy that would be King Atol and Queen Leza's doom. But what was the prophecy?

Placing the lantern on the ground, Devora took out another tool Nadia specially created: a piece of metal with a serrated edge. Placing the tool against the rusted bars, Devora moved the metal back and forth as quickly and as quietly as she could.

The tool easily sliced through the rusting metal and in a few moments, the rods were severed. Reaching out, Devora caught the cut pieces before they clattered to the ground.

As she pried off the last iron bar, Devora stepped into the small space. Ancient symbols scrawled along the rough stone walls. Devora had studied some of the ancient text when preparing for Vlacklear. But she didn't recognize any of the markings around her.

Placing the tool back in the sack, Devora ran her fingers along one of the symbols. It was different than the others. While most were jagged lines and harsh slashes, this one was intricately carved: an arch with a vine crawling around it. As soon as she finished tracing the vine, a snap cracked between her eyes, and Devora entered a vision that wasn't her own.

A soft, soothing breeze ran across Devora's skin. Rolling hills churned beneath Devora's feet, the lush green grass spreading far beyond her gaze. A sunset painted rich purples and pinks across the evening sky. It was truly a breath-taking sight. In a flash, the rolling hills gave way to a vineyard. Hundreds of woody vines braided along one another to form a long strand. Growing every few inches were bunches of ripe, succulent, red grapes.

Devora tried to take in everything around her. The warm yet gentle air, the scent of fresh leaves, the soft dirt beneath her feet. Where was she?

Laughter echoed in the distance as a family of four came into view. The mother and father each held a son on their back as they raced through the rows of grapes. Their laughter was contagious, and Devora found herself smiling. She instantly recognized the older boy as Matthias. His gray eyes and strong chin, even as a young boy, were distinct. That meant the other was Tristan.

Matthias and Tristan's parents set them down and the four started toward a cottage at the end of the vineyard. Suddenly, the mother, Kanna, placed her hand on her head. Within a few moments, she fell prostrate into the dirt.

The vision churned, and Devora watched Kanna explaining something to King Atol and Queen Leza. Though Devora couldn't hear what Kanna said, by the looks on the king's and queen's faces, Kanna was delivering the prophecy that would lead to her imprisonment.

The room spun, and Devora was now with Kanna in the king's dungeon. Devora frowned at the filthy space. Even Level Five of the Fortress was better than this. Kanna held her face in her hands, her shoulders shuddering. Pain sliced through Devora's heart. She wished she could console Kanna, but Devora knew what she saw was in the past.

The next parts of the vision flicked by like a flame dancing in the wind. Kanna in the king's dungeon, then in a cave, then a dark, wooden room, then a dank, humid tunnel. Place after place filed before Devora's mind. These had to be all the places Kanna had been kept.

Why go through such efforts to move one woman?

Devora now realized that years had passed, and Matthias had grown older. He was bent over a map of Tenton. Black X's marked several places over the eastern and southern regions. His search for his mother had begun. Distress lined his young features, but determination clung to his gaze as he ran his fingers along the map and circled a city in the western region of Tenton.

Devora peered at the map, wondering if Matthias came close to finding his mother many times, hence her constant movement. But her unknown captors were always one step ahead.

The vision stopped at the cell under the Temple, where Devora currently stood. The scene stayed the same until darkness blurred the edges. Thinking the vision was finished, Devora readied herself to return to the present, but her mind stayed.

Confused, Devora searched around, seeing nothing but black. Then a soft voice spoke. Leaning forward, Devora recognized it as Rae's. She heard Rae and Kanna having conversation after conversation during which Rae was frequently crying and rarely, even laughing.

But why can't I see Rae?

A roughness, like hard stone, brushed across Devora's hands, and she jerked back. Rubbing her palms together, she waited, and it happened again. It was almost as if Kanna had left Devora instructions on how to follow her.

Taking a breath, Devora closed her eyes and concentrated on the feel of the invisible stone beneath her hands. There was a large bump, almost like a knob. And next to it was a tiny hole.

"My captors are scared, *Kanna's soft voice said inside Devora's mind.* They know you are coming. And I know you are, too, my fellow Seer. I have felt your presence for some time. I thank Tunri that our kind was not eradicated with the king's decree. I hope to meet you soon."

As soon as Kanna's voice ended, the vision broke apart.

Devora retracted her hand from the wall. Her heart raced inside her chest. How could Kanna have the power to leave a message within the image? Devora looked at her palm, covered in sediment from the stone. Perhaps there was more to her Seeing abilities than she knew.

Taking a few breaths, Devora reflected on what Kanna had said. She knew Devora was coming. Tunri must have sent a vision to Kanna about Devora coming to Yekel. Sliding her pack off of her shoulder, Devora recalled the vision Tunri had sent *her* about Kanna. It seemed Tunri was guiding the two Seers together.

A few days before Devora and One Shot planned to meet with Rae, Tunri granted Devora a new vision. A vision Devora chose not to share with the others. This time, it wasn't about Rae or the Temple. It was about Kanna, where she was and where she was going. In the vision, Tunri showed Devora what she needed to do and how she needed to do it. Thankfully, Nadia was still in Yekel at the time. Devora swore Nadia to secrecy as she asked for the specific tools she needed to find Kanna. She knew Nadia would soon be with Matthias, and if Matthias found out where Devora was going, he would follow.

But Tunri had a different plan for Matthias. He needed to re-capture Yekel and unite Tenton. He couldn't do that *and* search for his mother at the same time. Devora knew it had to be her who found Kanna. Like Warden Hazor told her in Level Five of the Fortress, only a Seer could find another Seer.

Devora dwelled on the happy vision of Matthias. Her heart ached for him more in the past few days than it had when he first betrayed her. Though, he did try to make it right by breaking her out of Level Five of the Fortress. Devora still wished he would've told her what was happening all along. But after speaking with Warden Hazor, she realized the web of promises and lies Matthias was entangled in was too thick for her to solve.

She chose to focus on her mission from Warden Hazor and find Kanna. After Kanna was safe, Devora would begin her search for Princess Haden.

Bending down, Devora rummaged through her pack. Nadia had thrown in a few extra inventions and tools.

"Just in case," the Tinker said.

The memory made Devora smile. She was thankful for a loyal friend like Nadia and prayed she and Tristan had made it safely to Matthias. She also hoped Matthias kept Nadia and Tristan away from Yekel. Ever since Devora had seen into Rae's soul, she had a feeling General Yada would go to any lengths to make Rae pay for leaving the Temple, including hurting Nadia. When Devora had seen Rae's relief at hearing Nadia had fled with Tristan, Devora knew she'd made the right decision.

She'd sent Tristan with Nadia because keeping him in a place filled with his old gang members and rampant gambling was not a good idea. Thankfully, his knowledge and connections in the Dark Market helped him and Nadia flee Yekel undetected.

After a few more moments of searching, Devora found the long, thin rod she was looking for. It was an inch longer than the length of her forearm and apparently could shoot a poison dart fifty yards. Devora carefully extracted the darts and put them in an empty case.

Gripping the rod in her palm, she stood and strode toward the back wall. Closing her eyes, Devora felt the cold stone, remembering the texture Kanna left in her vision. Suddenly, Devora's hand felt the knob-like stone jutting out. She opened her eyes and leaned forward. Just next to the knob was the small hole.

Keeping her hand steady, Devora lined the rod up with the hole. "Perfect," she said with a grin. It was wonderful when Tunri's plans worked out flawlessly.

Holding her breath, Devora slid the rod into the hole and pushed. A loud creaking sound came from the stone as the section with the knob swung inward. Excitement rushed through Devora's veins. Engaging her soulsight, Devora thought of Kanna, and purple light soared through the dark tunnel. Just as Tunri had shown her before.

Blinking the purple light away, Devora grabbed the lantern and held it just inside the tunnel. Like the cell, it was harshly cut, as if the digger were in a hurry. As Devora lowered the lantern closer to the ground, two sets of footprints lined the dirt ridden path. Devora wasn't an expert at tracking, but she knew enough to know that Kanna had been moved recently.

There weren't any scuffs or signs of dragging, which led Devora to believe that Kanna went willingly. However, one set of the footprints seemed hobbled, as if their owner dragged her feet.

Devora immediately thought of the old hag. At the Fortress, when the old hag tried to convince Devora to take liquid imperial opal, she leaned heavily on a cane when she walked.

Devora then remembered her vision of the old woman in the Temple of Pahga when the Kadeshians gave up the souls of their daughters. The hag had been here, too, stealing the souls out of the statue. That meant the statue had to be some kind of holding chamber.

But how could the hag siphon souls? And what was she using them for?

Devora shook her head. There were too many unknowns to answer any of those questions. But there was something suspicious about the skeleton key Rae used to open the Temple. It held the same eerie aura as the vial of imperial opal the hag gave Devora. It was too similar to be coincidental.

Touching the purple sash around her wrist, Devora prayed that Rae wouldn't regret the cost of taking the key like Devora almost had with the imperial opal tincture.

Setting the lantern on the floor of the tunnel, Devora watched the warm orange light flicker across the stone. There was no end in sight, but she figured as much. Master Monham had packed plenty of supplies, and if things did go wrong, Nadia had given Devora a pickaxe that could cut through the hardest metals. If Devora needed to make a new tunnel to get out, she would.

Hopefully, it won't come to that.

Devora pulled the pickaxe out of her bag. It was lightweight and easy to wield. She always appreciated how Nadia thought of these things.

Stepping into the tunnel, Devora swung the pickaxe at the ceiling. A chink echoed down the secret corridor. She waited a moment and swung again. When nothing happened, she swung a third time. Suddenly, the tunnel rumbled. All at once, the rocks creating the entrance way tumbled down, sealing her in.

"Forgive me, Matthias," she whispered, wishing she could send all the love in her heart to him.

Hoisting the pickaxe over her shoulder, Devora grabbed the lantern and trekked into the unknown.

Chapter Thirty-Four

Rae, Temple of Pahga, Yekel

"You've finally returned," General Yada said, taking a step toward her. "Welcome home."

"Don't come any closer," Rae warned. "I've already freed the others."

"But you haven't freed that one." General Yada gestured to the still locked door behind Rae. "She may be the most important one, too."

Don't listen to him, she told herself. *He's trying to trick you like he always has.*

General Yada interpreted her pause as his opportunity to continue. "Where did you get my key, Rae?"

Rae pursed her lips, trying to control the Beast of Rage roaring inside her.

The general let out a bone-chilling laugh that echoed through the empty Temple. "It was that hag, wasn't it? After everything I've done for her, she betrays me."

Rae's head shot up. "What?"

General Yada brushed the shoulder of his military uniform. "Who do you think started those rumors that you knew of another Seer? Who did you think told me to give you extra time to gather more information? Did you think it was providence that the fugitive from Tenton just happened to come to your door?" He chuckled, giving her the same patronizing gaze, he always had. "Oh Rae, still so naive. I orchestrated the entire thing. Did you really think I would let you go so easily?"

Backing up, Rae pressed herself against the wooden door, shaking her head. "No, that's not true."

She thought of Devora, Tristan, and Ben. How they'd come into her life so unexpectedly. How they helped her feel again. How she couldn't imagine her life without them, especially without Ben.

"You're lying."

"Am I?" General Yada asked, exploiting the crack in her mental defenses.

Could General Yada really have set this all up in order to capture Devora?

"Why do you need two Seers?" Rae asked. One thing she'd learned from her time in the Temple was that arrogant men were always ready to share how much they knew.

General Yada stalked toward Rae. "Me? I don't. It's the hag who wants them. I suppose that's why she used you to betray me." He placed his hands flat against the door on either side of Rae's head. His rich floral perfume suffocated the small space between them. "But are you going to betray me, Rae? After everything we've been through?" He stroked her cheek with the back of his hand.

Now is our time to make him pay, the Beast of Rage growled. *Remember everything he's done.*

As if a spring had finally been released, every memory from her time in the Temple flashed before her eyes. Her cries, sobs, screams, the blood from her wrists when she tried to take her own life. The leer in the eyes of General Yada and the other men. Their looks of pity, disgust, and regret when they left.

Rae suppressed the memories for so long, she'd started to forget. She wanted to forget. But the Beast of Rage wouldn't let her. Each memory fed the flames until her chest was an inferno of fury.

Slapping his hand away, Rae ducked under the general's arms, taking the key with her. "For once in your life, shut your mouth," she growled.

Intrigue and annoyance flashed through the general's eyes as he spun around. The two prowled around each other like tigers ready to devour a meal.

"You killed the Wizard Wankle for no reason. You ruined my life and countless others.'" She wished her words were actual daggers as she shot them at him. "Can't you let me be? I could finally be rid of this place, be rid of you, and you're still trying to chain me here, to manipulate me. What more do you want?"

"The moment you stepped into this Temple, I claimed you," General Yada snarled. "Do you think that any of the others were treated half as well as you? And I saved you. I stopped Pahga before she took your whole soul."

"Can you hear yourself?" she screamed. "Enslaving women for your benefit and claiming to be gracious? It was your fault Pahga even had access to my soul. You're mad."

Shaking her head, Rae stalked to the final door. If she didn't free the last woman and leave the Temple now, the Beast of Rage would take over. Not to mention, she could've sworn she heard an arrow in Ben's crossbow lock into place.

"You've lost, Yada," she said over her shoulder. "Let me and the others go in peace."

The key turned in the lock, but not before two rough hands grabbed her shoulders, throwing her to the ground. Thankfully, Rae's time in the Dark Market kept her agile. She rolled into a somersault and pounced back up, only to find General Yada there and ready to meet her attack.

He backhanded her across the face. Rae took the hit and quickly reciprocated with two jabs into his arm. The general's right arm went limp, but he wouldn't retreat so easily. He swung his left arm, trying to disorient her, but Rae ducked. The general was persistent, his eyes wide with rage as he swung at her again. She needed to think of a solution fast.

Rae jumped a few steps back, trying to find a way to evade General Yada, when an arrow shot from the corner. A small arrow, no bigger than Rae's hand pierced the general's shoulder.

He grunted and yanked the arrow from the wound. Blood seeped into his uniform, leaving a dark stain.

A crazed look crossed over General Yada's face. Now matted with sweat, his dark hair fell over his forehead. Shoulders heaving, he roared, "You are mine, and you always will be."

He barreled toward Rae until two more arrows shot from the shadows. Rae shut her eyes, thinking Ben had killed General Yada. Relief overcame her when the arrows lodged in the general's boots instead of his heart.

Ben stalked from the shadows, his giant presence looming over them. A dark look cast over his features as he leveled the crossbow at General Yada's head.

"Ben, don't," Rae said, reaching for his arm. "Don't burden your soul anymore. He's not worth it."

Ben pressed the crossbow against the general's cheek, but General Yada only laughed.

"This is what you chose over me? A giant? A monster?" he cackled, clutching his wounded shoulder. Blood seeped from his feet, pooling around his boots.

Ben gave the general a murderous glare, and Rae thought that, for a moment, he was going to pull the trigger.

"Ben," she whispered, recognizing the war raging within him. "Let's go."

Ben clenched his jaw, shoving the tip of his arrow into General Yada's jaw before finally lowering it. The general cackled again, shouting more insults at both of them. Rae truly believed the man had gone mad.

As Rae and Ben rushed toward the final cell door, the floor of the Temple began to quake.

Rae held onto Ben as he braced against the adjacent wall. "What's happening?"

"It's Matthias," Ben replied, holding her close. "He's right on time, as usual."

Before Rae had a chance to ask another question, something crashed into the side of the Temple, shaking the building. The statue of Pahga rocked back and forth, threatening to collapse.

"Free the last one," Ben said, guiding her toward the final door. "We need to get out of here."

Trying to keep her footing, Rae made it to the final door. She'd already twisted the key before General Yada attacked her. All she needed to do was give the door a push. Rae shoved the door in, but it wouldn't budge. The attack from outside must've lodged it into place.

Trying to open it, Rae threw her body against the door, but it wouldn't budge. She pounded on the door again and again, knowing she would never be able to live with herself if she didn't free every single woman from the Temple.

Then, the voice of hope spoke again, *Trust.*

It only ever said one word, but it was the one word Rae needed to hear.

Taking a breath, Rae prayed, *Help me, please.*

A new strength invigorated Rae's muscles as she rammed into the door. She expected to meet resistance when instead she flew into the room. The woman inside yelped, frightened at her entrance.

"It's okay," Rae said. "I'm here to rescue—" but she stopped.

"Mami?" she breathed, unable to believe it.

"Rae?" her mother said at the same time. "You're here?"

Rae stood awestruck, tears streaming down her cheeks, until she remembered the building crumbling around them. "Mami, we have to go."

"I can't," her mother cried, gesturing to the manacle around her ankle.

Rae's eyes went wide. What had General Yada done to her mother? She suppressed her rage and called out to Ben.

"I need your help!" Rae cried. The tall man stuck his head through the door. "Shoot there." Rae pointed at the chain holding Mami to the wall.

Ben nodded. "Don't move, ma'am."

Mami stood as still as stone as Ben lined up the shot. The sounds of buildings tumbling and people screaming echoed outside the Temple. Another crash sounded from a nearby building before something collided with the front of the Temple, rocking the entire foundation.

"Ben!" Rae cried just as he shot the arrow. It zinged though the air and severed the chain as if it were butter.

Mami rushed to Rae, gave her a kiss, and grabbed her arm. "Run, *mija!*"

As the two sprinted out of the room, Rae reached out and grabbed Ben's arm and the trio dashed toward the light in the stairwell.

"Is this how it ends?" General Yada yelled.

The trio stopped at the top of the stairs and turned. A puddle of dark blood pooled around the General's boots. His entire arm was now stained. Rae almost felt sorry for him. Almost.

"What do you want to do, Rae?" Ben asked, his features as hard as stone.

She glanced up at him. "You don't want to kill him?"

"Oh, I do," Ben replied, tapping his finger on the trigger of his crossbow. "Especially knowing what he did to you."

Rae knew Ben was fighting to find the right path just as much as she was.

Before she could say any more, a round boulder crashed through the far Temple wall. Mami held onto Rae, and Rae held onto Ben, as the entire building shook.

"We don't have much time!" Mami cried.

But the statue of Pahga made the decision for them. It swayed back and forth on its pedestal until finally crashing forward.

Screaming, General Yada flailed his good arm in the air, as if to stop the giant imperial opal statue. But he had no power as Pahga, his own goddess, crashed upon him, squashing him flat.

Mami turned away, but Rae watched it all, remembering what Master Monham had said.

Trust Tunri to provide a way.

And He had.

Ben tugged Rae's arm. "We need to go, now."

As Rae grabbed the lantern, the three of them sprinted down the steps. More boulders crashed into the Temple as they raced through the lower-level hallway. It was almost as if Tunri was keeping the building standing just for them. As soon as they exited into the open air, the entire Temple collapsed on itself.

Rae stared wide-eyed at the crumbled mound of marble and stone. Her prison, her torment, had finally been destroyed.

Smoke and flame filled the air, and Rae was brought back to the day Kadesh invaded. Ash blocked the sun, taking her hope with it. But as she gazed up at the light of a new day, she saw the sun still shone, and Rae's hope beamed brighter than it ever had.

Another boulder landed too close for comfort, breaking through her thoughts. Ben placed his hands on Rae's shoulders.

"You have to get out of here," he said, his eyes pleading. "Go to your home, get the others. I need to find Matthias."

"Wait," Rae said, latching onto his forearms. "I don't want to lose you. How will I find you again?"

Ben cupped her cheek, then reached down and gently tugged the crimson cord around her waist. "Wherever you hide, tie this on the front. I will find you. I promise."

Closing his eyes, he leaned his forehead against hers, and Rae wanted the moment to last forever. But, like every joyful moment in her life, it ended too quickly.

"Go, Rae," Ben choked, holding back his own sobs. "You're finally free."

Wiping tears from her eyes, Rae grabbed Mami's hand and fled from the burning city.

Chapter Thirty-Five

Matthias, Yekel

Matthias's battalion of men were up and ready to make their way to Yekel. The soldiers marched double-time as they journeyed south. It was hard enough moving the men, but with the added equipment and catapults, Matthias thought they would never make it in time.

The catapults were new to Matthias. He'd seen them used in warfare and had yet to be in control of them. But after seeing Nadia's drawings of the unfinished wall and structure of Yekel, he decided the contraptions would be the best choice to help them gain the offensive quickly.

Before he left Ballear, Nadia and Tristan whined, saying they wanted to come. Although Matthias knew Devora had sent them away from Yekel for a reason, he didn't want to tempt fate any more than he already had.

So he sent Nadia and Tristan to a safe house where the king's soldiers couldn't find them, and he continued to Yekel. Instead of the three days it should have taken, his battalion arrived in a day and a half. Matthias was on edge as he watched the city in the distance. He, Sir Tocha, and three other soldiers scouted the area while keeping the rest of the army hidden behind a stretch of hills.

"Seems peaceful," Sir Tocha commented, steering his horse toward Matthias.

Matthias narrowed his gaze at the city. From what Nadia recounted to him about what her friend endured, he knew there were deep evils infecting Yekel. Evils that needed to be destroyed.

"Never be fooled by appearances, Tocha," he replied. Clucking his tongue, he steered his steed back to camp.

Although worn and weary from the rushed journey, his men were still alert and ready for battle. Despite his doubts they would arrive in time, his soldiers had done it, and Matthias was impressed. They deserved a chance to rest before battle.

However, his nerves and spinning mind wouldn't allow him a moment of peace.

Where was Devora? Would the battle be a success? Or would he be responsible for the lost lives of yet more men?

Down and down his thoughts spiraled as he sat at his desk and stared at the map of Yekel before him. Frustrated, he rubbed his hand on his neck when he felt the small silver chain. Leaning back in his chair, Matthias took out the necklace with Devora's ring on it.

He pinched the ring in his fingers and brought it close to his eyes. Even with Governor Medee's wealth, he couldn't afford a ring with this much imperial opal in it. Not unless it was given to him. Devora had told Matthias that her parents tried everything to suppress her powers so she would be safe from King Atol's edict.

Placing the ring in his palm, Matthias squeezed it tightly, feeling its raw energy pulling at his veins. He investigated the origin of the ring and discovered exactly what he surmised: it had been crafted by King Atol's and Queen Leza's personal jeweler. It wasn't until Matthias met with Governor Medee in Grenly that it was safe for the governor to explain he'd been forced to write the note, to prevent the king from doing to Grenly what he did to Yekel.

The power of the imperial opal blurred his vision, and Matthias removed the chain from his neck. He couldn't wear it constantly. If he did, he would be too weak. But in moments like this, when his emotions were heightened, he needed the ring to keep his curse in check. It had been years since he transformed unwillingly. But after he'd harmed so many without knowing, he would never allow it to happen again.

Matthias secured the necklace to a loop around his belt. As long as the imperial opal was near him but not touching his skin, he was okay.

"Permission to enter, sir," Sir Tocha called.

Matthias hid the ring beneath the flap of his coat. "Permission granted."

Sir Tocha marched in, carrying a sack of candy. "I thought you would like some, sir. The men are all pleased to have something sweet before battle. Their nerves have been on edge since we arrived."

Matthias gestured for Tocha to sit, then extended his hand toward the bag. "I'm happy to hear that. They worked hard and deserved a reward. Once the battle is won, we'll bring out the wine, ale, and mead." Matthias peeled open the sack and pulled out a purple piece of candy. He immediately thought of Devora and her bright eyes. His chest ached.

"I'm sure the men will enjoy that, sir," Sir Tocha said with a grin. His face suddenly grew serious. "But, sir, how can you be so sure we'll win?"

Matthias glanced up from the oval-shaped candy. "Defeat is not an option, Tocha. The lives of our own people are on the line. It's our job to free Yekel from its enslavement and reunite Tenton."

Sir Tocha drummed his fingers against his knees, as if deciding whether to speak.

Matthias unwrapped the purple candy and popped it into his mouth. An overly sweet grape flavor coated his tongue. But the familiar taste made him yearn for home and a simpler life.

"Say what's on your mind, Tocha, before I die of old age."

Sir Tocha smirked. "I was just thinking, 'If I had half the confidence of Captain Blake, I would achieve great things.'"

The grape flavor dissolved on Matthias's tongue. "I haven't achieved as many great things as you think, Tocha."

The young soldier nodded his head. "Regardless, sir, I'm thankful to be under your command."

Matthias gave a breathy sigh. "Thank you, Sir Tocha. You're dismissed."

The soldier stood and saluted before leaving Matthias to this thoughts once more. Tocha looked at him with admiration and trust, two things that people hardly ever associated with Matthias. Cold, calculating, and brutal were usually their choice descriptions, but a few saw past that.

One Shot was the first. After Matthias made the deal to save Tristan from the Fortress, he hadn't known he would be placed in a cell with a murderer. Lucky for him, it was One Shot. The tall, quiet man helped him through one of the hardest times of his life. For that, Matthias would always be grateful.

Sir Jacques was next. Matthias met him once he'd proven himself to Warden Hazor. On a whim, Matthias entered one of Warden Hazor's spontaneous fighting tournaments and had come out the victor. And if the scars on his back were any evidence, he'd won the tournament fair and square. The prize was a job working for the warden and that was where Matthias met Jacques.

When they were first assigned to scrub the floors of the dining hall, Matthias thought Jacques was nothing but a pretty boy from a rich family. That was what the other soldiers said. But Jacques got down on all fours and scrubbed the food-stained floor just as hard as Matthias. Jacques never berated Matthias for his harsh words or stoic demeanor. Instead, he took it as a challenge to loosen Matthias up, to make him laugh, and to try to crack his hard exterior. Eventually, it worked, and Matthias found himself even enjoying scrubbing the dining hall floor, if he got to do it with Jacques.

The final person who saw more in him was Devora. Matthias's heart weighed heavily in his chest, as he remembered when she'd looked into his soul. She'd seen his very core and still cared for him. He wondered if his soul was a dismal, dying thing. It felt like that a lot since his curse. But Devora didn't say anything. He remembered her face when she'd touched his soul. It hadn't shown shock or terror, but concern. That was when he knew he was falling for her, and he had to get away from her. She'd already been dragged into enough of a mess with the king's last-minute Categorization change and the Regulus Protecti tournament. She didn't need a cursed man with a blemished past trying to win her heart.

Matthias rubbed his eyes with his palms, regretting letting his mind wander so far. He needed to do something to clear his thoughts. From the corner of the tent, he lugged out a training stick and shoved it into the ground. Practicing his hand-to-hand combat always helped dull the swirling thoughts in his mind.

Matthias removed his outer jacket, rolled up his sleeves, and pounded the stick. Over and over, his fists pummeled the wood. Each time, he felt more at ease as the sounds of his hands smacking the stick quieted his mind.

He hadn't realized how long he'd been training until Sir Tocha asked for permission to enter his tent again.

A slick sheen of sweat matted Matthias's forehead. His muscles vibrated with energy as he wiped the sweat from his face with a towel and granted Tocha permission to enter.

"Sir, the sun has just broken through the horizon."

Matthias poured himself a drink of water, threw it down his throat, then wiped his lips with his wrist. Straightening his stance, he righted his sleeves and put on his military jacket. The captain's symbol of a crown with two antlers and three rings glimmered on the right side of his chest.

"Ready my armor, Tocha. Then inform the men the battle is imminent."

"Yes, sir," the knight replied before he hurried out the tent.

Within the hour, Matthias and his men were ready for battle and began their descent on Yekel. Matthias anticipated Kadeshian troops to flood from the city and overtake the small battalion at any moment. But none came, so Tenton's troops continued on. When they were five hundred meters away, Matthias stopped the lines.

He analyzed the city, tracing every stone with his gaze. It was exactly as Nadia drew it, down to the details of the half-finished wall before him.

"Ready the catapults," he ordered, and Sir Tocha repeated the order down the line.

The giant machines creaked and groaned as the soldiers loaded them with giant stones they'd gathered from the surrounding land.

Matthias raised his arm. The catapults were aimed to shoot at the structures Nadia had mapped out along the city. The hits would cause enough destruction to ensure chaos but keep civilian casualties to a minimum. "On my signal." He waited another moment, praying that Devora and One Shot had accomplished what they needed to before he pointed his arm forward. "Release!"

The zing of the giant levers whooshed through the air as the arms of the catapults launched the boulders toward the city. Two boulders hit the outer wall, not making much of an entrance for Tenton's siege. But the next two struck the heart of the city. One slammed into a cluster of buildings while the other rammed into the side of the marble structure Matthias recognized as the Temple of Pahga from Nadia's drawings.

"Reload," Matthias ordered. He wanted to make sure the general who'd taken Yekel knew he was about to meet his end. "Release!"

The stones flew again, smashing and crashing into Yekel. Matthias hated to attack a city in his own country. But once Tenton was whole again, they would rebuild Yekel to the great city it once was.

Shouts flooded the air. Matthias gripped the hilt of his mech. There were always innocents caught in the crossfires of battle. It was a terrible thing, and he prayed that, one day, war would not be necessary. But as long as evil men roamed this world, war would never cease.

For the next round of fire, Matthias ordered the stones to be covered in pitch and set aflame. The burning rocks soared through the air, setting fire to the city.

Matthias wasn't sure where Kadesh's general or its troops were, but if they hadn't come to defend their captured city now, they'd already lost.

"Ready for charge," Matthias shouted, unsheathing his sword. The rest of his men followed suit. Pointing his sword at the broken wall, Matthias kicked the sides of his horse and yelled, "Charge!"

His soldiers joined his battle cry and descended upon the city. The colors of Tenton infiltrated every crevice of Yekel. The soldiers had been ordered not to harm any citizens unnecessarily. The Kadeshian people fled in every direction away from Tenton's soldiers, making the order easy to follow.

Matthias galloped through the city, watching the fire blaze. Flames were a harsh and deadly thing. He'd witnessed them destroy many homes and livelihoods. But after every fire there was a rebirth from the ashes and that was his intent for Yekel.

Keeping his sword held high, Matthias swerved in and out of the alleyways until he saw a familiar face waiting for him. Pulling on the reigns, Matthias stopped his horse and slid off.

"One Shot," Matthias said, more overjoyed than he'd ever show to see his tall friend. He sheathed his sword and extended his hand.

One Shot reached out and squeezed Matthias's forearm in greeting. "Matthias. Good timing."

Matthias squeezed back, then focused on the crumbled marble building behind One Shot. "Where's Devora?"

One Shot retracted his hand and ran it through his shaggy black hair. "She had her own plans."

"Did you try to stop her?" Matthias asked, his voice wavering.

"If I tried, she would've found a different way," he replied in defeat.

Matthias growled, knowing One Shot was right. Why did he have to love such a stubborn woman?

Striding past One Shot, he climbed over the pieces of rubble. Most of the Kadeshians had fled and whatever soldiers were left, should be captured. Though the city burned around him an eerie stillness lingered in the air.

Matthias closed his eyes. He blocked out the crackling flames, the shouts in the distance, the rushed footsteps, and everything else and focused on one thing: Devora. The imperial opal burned against his thigh like it always did when he used his curse with it nearby. Breathing in deeply, Matthias caught the faint scent of earth with a hint of rose.

So, she'd kept the purple rose after all. He was hoping she would just in case he needed to find her.

Matthias' eyes snapped open, his body wanting to shift, wanting to change. But he kept his grasp on it. For now.

"One Shot," he growled, then cleared his throat. "I have a new mission for you."

"Anything," One Shot replied, his crossbow ready in his grip.

Matthias stripped off his jacket with his rank and handed it to One Shot. "Take this to Tocha. Tell him to give the Yekelians a choice: they may stay here and rebuild or return to Juro, where they will be settled with new homes and a new life. As long as he wears this symbol, he has the same power I do." He undid the laces of his boots and cast them aside. "I want you to take

Nadia's friend and whoever else she deems worthy to Ballear. Once you leave Yekel, Vinn will find you and take you where you need to go."

Confused, One Shot carefully took the jacket. "What about you? Where are you going?"

"I know the monster Devora is trying to slay. It's not one she can defeat alone. I will not lose anyone else I love."

Matthias took Devora's ring from his pocket. As soon as he handed it to One Shot, he knew the beast would break free.

"Take this."

Right as the ring left his palm, his cells radiated with energy and power. Matthias had kept the beast caged long enough.

"Thank you, my friend," he said to One Shot, glancing over his shoulder. "I hope to see you again."

Arching his back, Matthias let out an ear-splitting howl. His bones elongated as thick gray hair sprouted from his body. With another howl, Captain Matthias Blake gave into his curse. Shifting into a gray wolf, he sprinted after the woman he loved.

Chapter Thirty-Six

Rae, Rae's House, Yekel

Rae grasped Mami's arm tightly. So many questions and emotions flashed through her mind but the only thing she could think was "Run!"

Smoke stole the air from Rae's lungs as she wove in and out of the alleyways. Her eyes burned, smoke blurring her vision as she darted this way and that. The festivities of the harvest festival came to an abrupt end as the Kadeshian people screamed in terror.

Rae pulled herself and Mami into an alley as a rush of Tenton's soldiers marched past. Where were Kadesh's defenses? Of course, Rae wanted Tenton to regain control of Yekel, but, for the past four years, Rae had seen Kadesh's troops swarm all over Yekel. Now that there was an actual threat, they were nowhere to be seen.

Mami coughed harshly, and Rae spun around. She placed her hand on her mother's back. "Mami, are you okay?"

"*Mija,* I am better than okay," Mami's hoarse voice replied. "My beautiful daughter is alive and has saved so many women from terrible fates."

Rae allowed them another moment of rest so she could embrace her mother. Though the smell of the strong floral perfume she'd been doused in burned Rae's eyes, she still enjoyed being in her mother's arms again after so many years.

"I missed you so much," Rae cried.

"I missed you, too," Mami replied, stroking Rae's head.

Another order from Tenton's captain bellowed through the now vacant streets. His voice was stern and commanding. Rae wondered if he was the captain Devora and Ben had spoken of before. The soldiers marched toward the city plaza without opposition.

"Can you make it to the outer wall?" Rae asked, squeezing Mami's hands.

Mami coughed again but nodded.

Taking Mami's hand, Rae guided her through several more streets before they made it out of the city. That's when Rae glanced over her shoulder. Only a few buildings were left standing, the rest in pieces.

She expected her heart to break, to feel some sort of pain at the destruction of her home. But now that the enslaved women were free and the Temple destroyed, Rae was ready to leave Yekel behind. She hoped—prayed—that what Devora said was true: Tunri had already written her happily ever after.

The rest of Tenton's soldiers swarmed the city. Their catapults sat poised on the hills overlooking the outer wall, manned by the bare minimum of troops. Rae gawked at the large machinery and wondered if they'd been made by the Tinkers that had been taken from Yekel years ago, like Papi. Had he helped design them under threat of death? Was he still working for the king? Was it possible he was still alive?

Since Rae had found Mami, she had hope that her father might be okay, too.

Huffing, Rae and Mami made it to the homes where the Yekelian people lived. Surprisingly, the strip of humble homes were unharmed, and she wondered if Tunri had something to do with it.

As soon as they made it to her home, Master Monham opened the door.

"Rae, you did it," he wrapped her up in a hug, which she graciously accepted.

Behind him, Rae saw the eyes of all the women she'd freed from the Temple. A variety of skin tones and hair colors decorated her small home, and Rae wondered when General Yada had begun to capture women from other cities in Tenton.

Weary faces shone all around, and Rae knew she needed to say something to encourage them. Yes, they'd been freed from the Temple, but what now? Their city was destroyed. Did any of them have family they could return to? How would they live?

Master Monham motioned her inside. Once she and Mami closed the door, all eyes locked onto Rae. She sucked in a breath. Rae was never one to take the lead, but she'd been so inspired by Devora's strength, she thought she should try.

Pulling the black fabric off her head and neck, she heard a few gasps at her short hair. She smiled. "A lot has happened today, but now you're free. I don't have all the answers, but I've trusted Tunri so far and I know He will continue to guide us."

The women stayed silent, making Rae nervous so she continued to speak. "Those of you who still have families here are welcome to find and reunite with them." She glanced at Master Monham, and he gave her a nod. "Master Monham will be happy to help you locate whoever you need."

A few of the beaten faces brightened and excited whispers spread around the room.

"What about the rest of us?" a soft voice asked.

Rae focused on the young Kadeshian woman, Farrah, whom she saved first. Sympathy grew in Rae's heart. This girl's own people enslaved her. Of course, she wouldn't want to go back to them. But would she want to stay in Tenton? Because of the constant war with Kadesh, many Tentonians had an ill view of Kadeshians. Some were sympathetic, but their numbers were very few.

Rae thought about herself. She was overjoyed that Mami was alive, but what would they do next? What were they to do for food? For coin? Everything had been destroyed.

Just then a knock sounded at Rae's door, and her stomach leapt.

Was it Ben? He said he would find her.

Wiping her hands on her pants, Rae opened the door. Her heart sank as she laid eyes on a Tentonian soldier with bright red hair.

"Are you Rae?" the young soldier asked, a question in his eyes.

"Yes," she responded, keeping the door open just enough that he could only see her. "What is it?" She wasn't sure of Tenton's intentions. After King Atol destroyed Yekel first, Rae would never trust the kingdom with her wellbeing again.

The soldier bowed, and Rae was taken aback. "We've been informed that you defeated General Amillo Yada. For that, Tenton is forever in your debt." Rae blinked, not knowing how to respond, so the soldier continued. "Captain Blake has ordered his troops to personally escort you and yours to Ballear."

Rae furrowed her brow. "Ballear?"

The soldier gave a small sigh. "Apologies, miss. I just follow the orders, I don't make them." He leaned forward and whispered. "A lot of times I don't understand them either."

The soldier's honesty made Rae smile. "How long until we leave?"

"The battalion leaves tomorrow at dawn. If you wish to join us, wait outside your home, and we will have horses ready for those who decide to come." The soldier bowed again and marched away.

Rae watched him march past the other Yekelian homes, wondering if Captain Blake had offered them the same thing.

Closing the door, Rae pressed her back against it. Tunri usually wasn't so fast in giving His aid, but she would take it.

The actions of others do not define who you are. Only you decide who you want to be. Kanna's words had never been truer. Tunri was giving her a second chance to be remade into who He wanted her to be.

"For those of you who do not wish to stay in Yekel, or have no other home, you are welcome to accompany me to Ballear. I don't know what waits there, but I am ready to start new."

A few of the women nodded their heads, understanding. Mami reached for Rae's hand and said, "I will go with you, *mija*. Our home is together."

Rae squeezed her mother's hand.

"I would like to join you, as well," Farrah said, pulling her green shawl around her shoulders. "There's nothing for me here."

"Then there's nothing to hold you back," Rae replied, evoking a small smile from the young woman.

Two more women decided to go with Rae. The rest still had family living in Yekel and formed a line in front of Master Monham to request his help in finding their loved ones.

By nighttime, every woman had a place to go or a plan for what would come next. Rae was astonished at how smoothly everything had gone. The women were even starting to relax and laugh a little.

Though she'd succeeded in freeing the women from the Temple, Rae's chest ached. She'd tied her red cord to her doorknob, but Ben had yet to arrive. She believed his words were true, but every moment that dragged by without him was agony.

Is he okay? Did something happen to him?

Each question led to more questions. All Rae could do to quiet her loud thoughts was pray.

Rae watched the sunrise the next morning. After yesterday's events and Ben's continued absence, she couldn't sleep. She had thought that once she'd freed the women from the Temple she would finally be at peace. But the fact that Ben had yet to come gnawed at her like a bad omen.

As she bundled up the sack containing the things most precious to her, Rae heard a soft cough as her bedroom door opened.

"Come in," Rae said, her voice scratchy.

Mami peeked her head in, then came in fully, closing the door behind her. "You didn't sleep."

The women from the Temple took up most of her living area, so Rae had opened her bedroom to Mami, Farrah and the other two women who were coming to Ballear with them. Rae thought she was quieter than a mouse as she sat up in her bed and stared out the window that morning. But apparently Mami was already awake too.

"There's just a lot happening all at once," Rae replied, tying another sack filled with her colored fabrics. Maybe women in Ballear would like vibrant fabrics. It was a good way to start making coin until she found something more permanent.

"I understand, *mija*." Mami smoothed her long blonde braid. Speckles of gray and white hair decorated the plait in a becoming pattern. "Does your unrest have anything to do with that tall young man?"

Rae's tired eyes shot to her mother. Mami hadn't even been out of the Temple for a day, and she was already figuring out Rae faster than she could figure herself.

Tired, Rae replied, "Yes. He said he would come."

Mami reached out and ran a hand over Rae's short hair. "Has he given you reason to doubt him?" Rae shook her head. "Then have faith that he will come."

Rae repeated Mami's words as she waited for Tenton's soldiers outside her door, the crisp morning air fresh on her skin.

Rae repeated the words as she untied the crimson cord from her knob and wrapped it around her wrist. She repeated them again and again as she mounted the horse given to her by a Tentonian soldier and trotted away from the only home she'd known since escaping the Temple.

Again and again, she recalled Mami's words and prayed for Ben's safety as they traveled day and night through the dirt hills of Yekel into the rolling green ones of Ballear.

A few days later, Rae, Mami, and the others arrived at a large vineyard that extended for miles. A man a little older than Mami greeted them at the wooden gate. Strings of white hair laced through his black locks. His sun-kissed skin was flawless, save for a few wrinkles around his kind gray eyes.

"From Captain Blake," the Tentonian soldier who had come to Rae's door said. He handed the man a scroll tied with a black ribbon. The rest of the battalion continued to Juro, leaving the red-haired knight as the only one to escort the group of women.

The man's gray eyes scanned the parchment before he rolled it back up. Rae recognized the eyes and wondered if this was the man that had taken Papi all those years ago. She almost lashed out before she noticed his face soften as he turned to Rae and the others.

He bowed deeply. "It seems Tenton owes you a great debt. I apologize that you cannot be more honored at this time, but that can come later. Come"—he waved them forward—"there is something my son wants me to show you."

Rae hesitated, but knew she was no longer alone. Mami and the others were with her and, as always, so was Tunri.

Stepping down from her horse, Rae handed the reigns back to the soldier, then thanked him. The others did the same before following the man into the vineyard.

Fresh, succulent grapes hung from every vine they passed. The twittering of birds danced between Rae's ears as a fresh breeze blew by. It was cooler here than in Yekel, and it was peaceful. Rae already liked it.

After walking for what seemed like ages, they came upon a large group of tents. Rae tilted her head, studying the structures. There were colors from every part of Tenton in this vineyard. There were so many dwellings, it was like a small village.

"Welcome to Totum," the man said, with a smile that creased the wrinkles around his eyes further. "A home for when you have none."

Rae stepped forward, keeping her grip firm on her sacks. "What is this place?"

"A place for those who want to live in peace and don't want to be found. Don't worry," the man said quickly. "There are rules to abide by. For one, no abuse or slavery is tolerated. There are other rules also. If any of these are broken, there is a hefty price to pay."

Rae stared in wonder at the people bustling in and out of the tents. Some were working in the vineyards, others were smashing grapes. Looking beyond the first groups of tents, Rae noticed another group of people tinkering with different forms of machinery.

Rae let out a gasp, and the man chuckled. "Ah, you found them. Not all Tinkers who were taken by the king made it to

Juro. My son did his best to save as many as he could from the king's wrath."

But before the man could continue, Rae raced through the field, her heart palpitating with hope. A second pair of footsteps followed behind, and Rae knew Mami was close by. Vines scratched at her skin, but she didn't care. She sped past the people smashing grapes, ignoring their questioning looks.

She knew she'd seen it. The familiar sandy hair. The way he swung his hammer. She wasn't mistaken. Pushing her legs as fast as she could, Rae stopped only when she saw him. His blonde hair was longer, curling around his ears, his eyes tired, but not sad. The smile lines around his lips were still there, too.

"Papi?" Rae whispered.

Papi turned around. The hammer fell from his hand, and his lips parted in disbelief before he raced toward Rae. Scooping her up in his arms like she was no more than three summers, he buried her in his chest as she cried rivers of tears. Mami soon joined their embrace, and their tears mixed together.

"I've prayed every day," Papi sobbed, kissing both of their heads. "And here you are, my family, together again."

Rae sobbed more than she ever had, not tears of sadness or pain, but of joy. Too much joy to be contained inside of her.

That evening, Captain Blake's father, Liam, set Rae and Mami up in their own tent with Papi. The three of them hugged and ate and spoke of everything that happened in the past four years. Papi cursed loudly when he heard what happened to Rae and Mami in the Temple. He said if the statue hadn't flattened General Yada, he would've taken care of it himself.

They laughed and cried some more until Mami and Papi fell asleep in each other's arms. Rae placed a blanket around them both and smiled as they curled against one another.

Her own heart sighed as she glanced at the crimson cord around her wrist. The small flame of hope still burned, so she would try. Stepping out into the cool night air, Rae tied the cord around the front post of the tent. She sent a prayer of thanks to Tunri, unable to believe He'd been able to unite her family again, then tried to sleep.

After she'd fallen into a deep sleep, footsteps shuffled outside the tent and Rae darted up, forgetting where she was. But upon seeing Mami and Papi together, she breathed a sigh of relief. It hadn't been a dream. They were really together again.

More footsteps sounded, and Rae stood fully. She didn't trust this place or anyone in it. Not yet. And no one would separate her family again.

Readying herself for defense, she launched out of the tent, barreling into a tall thin frame.

"That wasn't the greeting I expected," Ben said, holding her shoulders to steady her.

Rae glanced up, her lips parted. "You're—you're here."

He smiled down at her. "I said I would find you."

Tears pricked Rae's eyes again, and she noticed Ben's face shift from adoration to concern.

"Happy tears," she said, pressing against his chest.

As his long arms came around her and held her tight, Rae started to believe that her happily ever after had finally come.

Chapter Thirty-Seven

Unknown

"Do you have it?" the deep voice from the shadows questioned.

The old hag cradled the swirling orb beneath her arm. She'd sacrificed greatly to get to this point. Why should she hand her hard work over to a lazy, arrogant king?

"It's here," the hag responded.

"Well," the king demanded, stepping out of the shadows. "Hand it over. That was our deal."

The old woman cackled. Only fools believe in honest deals.

"Yes, yes, of course," the hag replied sweetly. But before she handed the orb of swirling souls to the king, she scraped one long fingernail over its smooth service.

An eruption of white light pooled from the sphere, illuminating every crevice of the stone room. Ear-splitting screams vibrated against the walls, sending the king to his knees, yet the hag stood firm. She'd heard many screams before, they hardly bothered her anymore.

Concealing the orb in her cloak, the old woman hobbled toward the kneeling king. With his hands cupped over his ears, his face in agony, he looked pathetic. Just as he always had.

"You've ruled Tenton for too long, Atol. It's time for your reign to come to an end."

The hag then transformed into her true form, and the king gasped.

"Please," he wailed. "I only did what I thought was best."

"It's too late," the transformed hag responded.

Holding the orb in one hand, she ran her finger along its smooth side once more. The invigorating power of innocent souls pumped into her veins. And she loved it.

Breathing in her new strength, the transformed hag lifted her young, manicured nail toward the king. "Good-bye, Atol."

The king screamed in anguish as his soul was pulled from his body. The white string of light spiraled in the air before the witch directed it into the sphere. Now that the orb had been emptied, she needed to fill it again.

Grinning, the witch turned away from the king's lifeless body, her thoughts fully focused on a young Seer eager to fall right into her trap.

Acknowledgements

When I first jumped into the publishing world, I had no idea what to expect. Never did I dream of seeing my fifth book published! There have been many learning curves (and many more to come, I'm sure!), but I thank God for each and every experience along the way.

To David, Matthew, Thomas, and Luke, thank you for always supporting my dreams. I love you all.

To my family, thank you for all your encouragement in all areas of my life.

To my college gals, thank you for always loving my stories.

To C.A.V.A., thank you for the laughs and love of Ben Barnes.

To April and Quill & Flame, thank you for your endless love of my characters and crazy plots! Not many authors can say their publisher feels like another family. I am truly blessed my books have found a home there.

To Burton's Booklovers, thank you for STILL loving and supporting my stories even when I disappear for a while because of the craziness of life.

And to my amazing readers, you are the reason I can continue to write and produce stories. Thank you for allowing me to continue to do what I love.